I0761941

Basma Abdel Aziz is an award-winning writer, sculptor, and psychiatrist, specializing in treating victims of torture. A weekly columnist for Egypt's *al-Shorouk* newspaper, she was named a *Foreign Policy* Global Thinker, and a Gottlieb Duttweiler Institute top influencer in the Arab world. A long-standing vocal critic of government oppression in Egypt, she is the winner of the Sawiris Cultural Award, the General Organization for Cultural Palaces Award, and the Ahmed Bahaa-Eddin Award. Her critically acclaimed debut novel *The Queue* won the English PEN Translation Award and has been translated into Turkish, Portuguese, Italian, and German. She lives in Cairo, Egypt.

Jonathan Wright is the translator of the winning novel in the Independent Foreign Fiction Prize and twice winner of the Saif Ghobash Banipal Prize for Arabic Literary Translation, and was formerly the Reuters bureau chief in Cairo. He has translated Alaa Al Aswany, Youssef Ziedan, Ezzedine Choukri Fishere, and Hassan Blasim. He lives in London, UK.

Here Is A Body

Basma Abdel Aziz

Translated by
Jonathan Wright

First published in 2021 by
Hoopoe
113 Sharia Kasr el Aini, Cairo, Egypt
One Rockefeller Plaza, 10th Floor, New York, NY 10020
www.hoopoefiction.com

Hoopoe is an imprint of The American University in Cairo Press
www.aucpress.com

Copyright © 2017 by Basma Abdel Aziz
First published in Arabic in 2017 as *Huna badan* by Markaz al-Mahrusa li-l-Nashr wa-l-Khadamat al-Sahafiya wa-l-Ma'lumat
Protected under the Berne Convention

English translation copyright © 2021 by Jonathan Wright

All rights reserved. No part of this publication may be reproduced, stored in a retrieval system, or transmitted in any form or by any means, electronic, mechanical, photocopying, recording, or otherwise, without the prior written permission of the publisher.

ISBN 978 1 617 970931

Library of Congress Cataloging-in-Publication Data

CIP data applied for

1 2 3 4 5 25 24 23 22 21

Designed by Adam el-Sehemy

A short dedication: To AS, and every AS
A long dedication: To that free heart, Alaa el-Dib, rest in peace

"When it was midnight we went to sleep, and then we woke up in great distress."

1

The Abduction

THEY CAME AT FOUR O'CLOCK in the morning and I was too sleepy to get out of the way in time. They trampled on the big trash bin and planted their heavy boots on the mass of bodies. My hand was crushed under someone's boot, along with Emad's arm. I gasped silently. Then someone started lifting my leg, which was stuck under Youssef's stomach, and then my body too. I clung on to Youssef's clothes, but the hand lifting me was much too strong for me. I suddenly found my head swinging through the air. I stiffened my neck to try to control it, but it was no use. I couldn't make out where the voice giving orders was coming from but it was definitely from above.

"Get up, you filthy bastard. Get up, you piece of shit. Get up, get up," it said.

As he pulled me, my head trailed through piles of trash. I started waving my arms and trying to grab hold of anything, but nothing I touched held firm. Whenever I gripped onto anything it fell apart in my hands. I picked up tissues and dirty diapers from the pile we had sifted through the previous morning, pages from school children's exercise books and the books we had arranged on the floor to sleep on top of. I got scratched by empty tin cans and found sticky substances all over my fingers. As I was dragged along the floor I grabbed bits of chicken carcasses I had seen the poultry man throw away a few hours earlier. I panicked when my body left the ground and I started writhing in the air. I automatically clenched my teeth and bit my tongue in anger. Usually when I go to sleep I try to stay half awake in order to be on guard for moments such as this, but this time I couldn't escape. I could feel the ground shaking beneath me and hear old bits of wood creaking, bones crunching, and bags rustling, but it was too late when I came to my senses. I opened my eyes only when I caught a good whiff of the rotten smell from the stuff on the wet ground, stirred up and turned over by people's feet.

I could hear Youssef and Emad's screams, stifled and hoarse, and I realized we were moving in the same direction. My head, hanging loose, banged against someone's bony knee and kept swinging back against it with every step taken by the titan carrying me, but unlike my friends I didn't utter a single sound, not even a cry to show I was there. I just tried to draw some air into my lungs so that I wouldn't die. I felt very dry inside and I wanted to throw up. Something was hitting me violently in the chest. All my weight seemed to be concentrated in my brain, which felt hot and squeezed so tight it was about to explode. My tears fell in the wrong direction, running over my forehead instead of down my nose and cheeks. I felt certain that all these things were signs that the end of the world had come, and I wished I could lose consciousness and not know what was happening until the moment of reckoning came.

It was pitch dark and the titans who were carrying us didn't seem to need any light. There were no lamps or torches or even a beam of light from a streetlamp. I heard what sounded like a hand hitting hard against something hollow, and then a short burst of cursing, which I made out to be from Emad. Then there was another bang, but no one's voice this time. Youssef didn't cry out in response to the sound and I kept silent too. I was shaking violently, in anxious anticipation for the next bang. A long time passed with no more sounds and eventually I wished they would hit Emad again so that he would make some noise to reassure me, but the blows stopped and I was left waiting in alarm. I longed for Youssef to shout out again, but he didn't. In vain I listened for the sound of my friends breathing, but I couldn't hear anything. A sudden screeching pierced my icy skin and the hand gripping my foot threw me sideways and slapped me against a wall, causing a loud booming noise, then an invisible door closed and I lost consciousness.

A rotten smell like garbage surrounded me on all sides. My mouth was pressed against a floor that was level but rough, unlike the floor I had been used to sleeping on every night. My saliva was forming a small puddle under my face. I tried to swallow it, but I couldn't close my lips. I realized I was gagged and the gag was stopping me from closing my mouth or speaking. I was almost paralyzed too: my arms and legs couldn't move and none of my muscles were receiving the signals my brain wanted to send them. Around us, it was still pitch black. I couldn't work out clearly if my eyes were open or if I had a blindfold on. I tried to open my eyes but I couldn't tell if they responded. It made no difference and the darkness didn't change. My whole body was shaking, even my imagination. It slowly dawned on me that I was in the trunk of a car and, judging by the loud noise it made, it seemed like a big one. I felt like an extension of its motor as it roared and shook. My body suddenly bounced up and down several times, then finally came to rest and settled on the floor of the trunk like a stone. My mind went blank. My ear hurt so much I thought it had been torn off when I landed.

"Wake up, you jerk," someone said. "Wake up, you donkey. Pull yourself together and be careful. There's still an hour to go before we arrive."

It was the voice of the man who had carried me. So I wasn't asleep or having a nightmare. I was in the real world and I would have to go through another hour of this torment, judging by what he said. Maybe there were other people in the vehicle, gagged like me and terrified. Youssef and Emad might be an arm's length away without me knowing. I tried to crawl on my side or on my stomach in hope of making contact with anybody, but the voice pinned me to where I was.

"Hold it, you rat. Hold it, you piece of trash. Hold it or you'll end up as minced meat under the wheels," it said.

A shiver ran down my spine. I was soaked in sweat and piss and snot and tears.

I didn't know how to pass the hour I knew was coming. Should I count the minutes off? I'm not good at counting, although I'm old enough. I may be fourteen years old or a little more. I remember the shapes of the numbers but sometimes I get them confused. If I just imagined the numbers a few times, would the hour pass and would I be free of this man who had tied me up in a tight bundle?

My counting soon began to slow down, interrupted by a frightening thought. Maybe I was going to my demise, to the place where people like me and Youssef and Emad disappear. Maybe it would be better to fall asleep here in this vehicle, bound and gagged, better than going on to the unknown place where they were taking me.

The engine stopped and the vehicle ceased to shake, but I still had severe pains in my ear and my head. I felt that my hands, which were tied up, were throbbing separately from my heart. The door opened and I could see light through the cloth that covered my eyes, so I turned my face away. The pain increased then disappeared all at once when I heard heavy footsteps nearby and smelled a familiar smell. I was lifted up into the air again but this time I remained upright, with my head at the top. The titan was holding me by the back of my collar and the seat of my pants and had moved on to a place where the air felt different. Finally I heard voices and a mixture of stifled throaty noises. I couldn't work out who was making them, but I was certain that my friends were there.

*

They threw us to the ground one after another. We curled up next to each other and didn't move. This time it was a tiled surface, hard and firm. I could hear the sound of each new body landing as they threw them on the floor. It was reassuring to know I was not alone and that there were plenty of us. Someone came around taking the blindfolds off our eyes and I saw that the titans had herded us into a large room that contained only a large table. I looked around and saw blotchy walls with the whitewash falling off. But pale lines of sky appeared between small bars at the top. They left us alone in the middle of the room, surrounded by walls at a distance. Now we could see, but our hands were still tied behind our backs, our feet were shackled, and our mouths were gagged. The only way we could communicate was by exchanging scared looks. I stared into the faces one by one. I couldn't find my two friends among the kids who were there. I would have cried if I hadn't thought of Emad making fun of me when he turned up, and he was bound to turn up. Time passed and we sat there in deep distress. We were totally powerless in a way that maybe none of us had experienced before. Some of us tried to sit up straight and others wanted to lean against the walls, but these simple actions seemed impossible at the time, though under ordinary circumstances it would never have occurred to us that we might be unable to perform them. Some of the children tried to speak, but the drawling voices, coming from gagged mouths and distorted like the meowing of cats in heat, amplified my fear and my sense of helplessness. I recognized some of the boys who were with me in the room. Most of them hung out in the same area as Youssef, Emad, and me. There were also some kids I hadn't seen before, though they looked very much like us three. There was no difference at all between the boys trapped in this room and there was nothing special about me compared to them. I didn't understand why we were all there.

Two of the titans arrived when the sun was high enough to come in through the roof openings, strong and scorching. Most of us had been wailing and howling, which made the situation worse. My tears were mixed up with the snot from my nose and I had taken to swallowing the acrid mixture so that I wouldn't look so disgusting to the others. I thought it was for the best that the titans had arrived, although the possible consequences were uncertain. It was better than waiting. As my mother always says, "Either disaster strikes or you wait for it to strike." Without glancing at each other, the two men gave us a hard look, unthinking and unquestioning, as if our presence in the room were an accepted fact and they had organized everything and knew everything, as if our fate had been decided in advance and there was nothing to discuss or negotiate. I didn't notice the bundle of newspapers that one of them was carrying until he referred to them.

"These newspapers are about you," he said sharply. "You may not have a chance to find out everything that's in them, but I'll fill you in now on what's important." He pulled out a page from a newspaper and spread it out in front of us. He put his finger on a picture of a man, surrounded by lots of words. I could see that the man in the picture was bald with glasses and shiny cheeks. I looked at the picture as the titan continued.

"This is an important man," he said. "He creates a stir wherever he goes. He's well-connected and knows important people. And he loathes you with a loathing that knows no bounds. You're insects as far as he's concerned, insects that pollute and defile the country. There isn't a pleasant place in the country that has escaped you. You smell disgusting. Vermin feed on your bodies and lay their eggs on you and inside you. This man knows that you thieve, take pills, sleep with each other in trash cans, and so on. He knows you well and everything he says about you is true. The man spoke to the ruler himself when he met him at the last celebration. He went up to him as he was cutting the ribbon, whispered in his ear, and asked for a private meeting about something important. Aware of the man's merit, the ruler didn't blow him off completely. He asked the general to stand in for him because he himself was short of time. He asked the general to meet the man as soon as possible and handle his request. And then, without hesitation, the man headed for the general's office the very next day and showed him documents about you, and then suggested an all-out hunting campaign that would put an end to your disgusting existence. The man persuaded the general that you had to be kept off the streets, so we've hunted you down as a first step."

The titan scowled and looked serious. He left the room and the other man followed him. They closed the door and we heard them putting a padlock on the chain. Our hearts skipped a beat as we tried to work out what they were going to do with us next. If they had wanted, they could have put us in jail right away or moved us to reformatories, but they hadn't done that. Maybe they were going to burn us to death, asphyxiate us with gas grenades, or hold us here until we died of hunger and thirst. The sun grew fiercer and turned the room into an oven like the one at the local bakery on the corner of our trash dump. I felt as if I were melting into the floor. On top of my snot and my tears, I now had big drops of sweat to contend with. My clothes clung to my skin, producing a burning sensation and irresistible itching.

We kept our eyes wide open, unable to relax for a single moment. We stared at each other for a while, then each of us chose a spot on which to focus, as if impervious to what was going on around us. Then we retreated into ourselves, whimpering incessantly. It was terrifying. The pangs of hunger in my stomach and brain reminded me that I was still alive and that I might soon lose even that advantage. I don't know how many hours passed until finally the door opened again. This time one of the titans came in and demanded in a loud voice that we pay attention, stop sobbing, and stop trying to take cover by the wall, which a small number of kids had done as soon as we arrived, in the belief they could keep out of harm's way that way. In reality, most of us no longer had the strength to try anything, even to cry, so we submitted completely to our fate.

"You know we've been studying your problem for years," said the man. "As soon as he took office the ruler set up a council of advisers to look into it, and this council has endeavored to work out integrated strategies and has allocated a large budget to study the problem. Remember Dr. Abdel-Samie Mukhtar, whose picture you saw yesterday? He's one of the country's greatest scholars and he's done extensive research and has numerous students. After much thought and a painstaking search for a solution, he suggested we consider you to be non-existent, that we eliminate you completely, that we remove your names from the official records, if your names are even there, and that we treat you in the same way we treat stray dogs—and the only solution for them is to kill them. There would be nothing easier than poisoning you or shooting you and having your bodies removed with the piles of garbage to be buried or burned. Dr. Mukhtar worked with us for many years and served us faithfully. He likes traditional solutions that have proved effective in practice. This proposal of his won widespread approval from the members of the council, because the country cannot afford to spend money feeding, educating, and housing you without you doing anything in return."

The man snarled and scowled as he continued: "The country is poor and many people are out of work. It cannot afford the extra costs for which you are responsible, but you do not appreciate the crisis. We have received thousands of complaints. One citizen complained that you harass his children daily on their way to school and university. Another complains that you vandalize his car. He sees your dirty fingermarks on the car windows every morning and from his balcony he has watched you jumping on it in the early hours. People are fed up with seeing you on the sidewalks, at the metro stations or bus stops, or outside the restaurants where they eat and the supermarkets where they do their shopping. What are these places to you? They can't stand the senseless, inhuman way you pester them. They are so fed up with you begging for money and food that they can't stand looking at the things they buy, because they feel you are looking at them enviously. You have started to ruin their shopping expeditions and their enjoyment of life wherever they go.

"The consultants designed a survey and the results, published on our website, showed support for the idea of exterminating you. You are of course aware that we do not take decisions without consulting citizens. We have received an endless stream of comments: a woman in one high-class neighborhood favors immediate execution and claims she will not feel safe as long as hordes of kids are roaming the streets night and day with impunity. She is threatening to abandon her house and move to another neighborhood if we don't deal with you. A doctor says you are carrying serious contagious diseases that may spread to innocent citizens. He favors getting rid of you and disinfecting the street corners where you have been congregating. He has offered to share his knowledge and help with the campaign. Sheikh Abdel-Gabbar, the prestigious sheikh of whom you must have heard, issued a fatwa some weeks ago saying that in your case the relevant principle under Islamic law is that averting harm should take precedence over serving the public interest. Do you understand what that means? Addressing the harm that you cause is more important than anything else, more important than any benefit that might be expected from you in the future. There can be no question of patiently tolerating the grave offenses that you commit. Sheikh Abdel-Gabbar was outraged at the horrific nature of your offenses: you were harassing women, terrorizing people, vandalizing public property, and inflicting harm on our close-knit society and its established traditions—our quiet, peaceful community, which has a long history and is civilized and cannot accept your vulgar and impudent behavior. What a disgrace! Anyway, people trust the sheikh and do his bidding. He doesn't make ill-informed or gratuitous rulings. He tells the truth and you have only yourselves to blame, and those who follow his rulings are blameless. The government has announced an official decision that has implications for you. Its program this year, based on the ruler's directives, is clear on two points: we need to tackle your widespread presence in the city firmly and without clemency, and we need to eradicate the endemic diseases that have been damaging people's livers. You can see that if we solve the first problem, the second will automatically diminish, because you are one of the main sources of contagion."

The titan stopped talking and started to examine our faces, which looked stunned and had turned white. We looked like we had joined the ranks of the dead before they had even carried out their death sentences on us. At that moment the man's narrow eyes could have harvested our souls just by staring at us a while. Our wide eyes bulged in anticipation of our imminent demise. They had clearly gathered us together to spare themselves the trouble of killing us in batches, which would take too long. They were going to exterminate us right here and bury our bodies in one mass grave. No one would ask after us and not a soul would ever know what had happened. Our lives, everything that had happened to us, would be forgotten. We would cease to exist. The idea frightened me more than before, and Youssef's old musings on the subject didn't help me make light of it. I wasn't frightened of death in itself. I could almost hear Youssef describing it as a long sleep, a perpetual dream. I wasn't afraid of death, but I was frightened of what would happen before I got there. It was only then that I lost my sense of hunger and thirst and no longer had any desire to piss or shit. I think I had already pissed and shat myself anyway, and I wasn't the only one. The next morning the titan pushed the door hard to open it. Some of us fainted while others shuddered in expectation of imminent death. The room smelled like a sewer. There was shit everywhere. We couldn't make jokes about it because we still had gags covering our mouths. There was a slightly playful twinkle in the titan's eyes, but I could hardly see him because my vision was clouded and he was mostly a blur. He folded his arms on his chest and started shouting roughly. He told us we had just escaped a death sentence. Escaped? Had I lost consciousness and slipped into a limbo world of pleasant dreams? Had they in fact killed us already? Would I have to start a new life alone or was I hallucinating about the prelude to my own death?

I turned my head right and left and started shaking it violently and squirming in my place. I was wide awake and around me everyone was wide awake too, though so surprised that their eyes were almost popping out of their heads. So what we had heard was real! But since we were still tied up, we had no way to express the crazy joy we felt or our feelings of deep gratitude toward the titan. We had survived, we had survived! Suddenly one boy, unable to believe the news, started jumping up and down, and the others followed him. People shouted out things I didn't understand, but they were ecstatic and wildly happy. I didn't jump up and down like them. I was so tired I couldn't move. I felt like I'd been running and jumping ever since they'd tied us up. I noticed another kid who, like me, hadn't budged. I noticed the room looked like the tray on which my mother used to spread rice to clean out bits of grit from among the grains. The other kid and I were like two grains of rice stuck to the tray among a mass of moving grains. One of the kids, overcome by the relief of surviving, crawled along the ground and rubbed his cheek against one of the titan's massive shoes. The titan looked at him for a moment, then bent down and pulled him toward him with one hand. He undid the strap on the boy's wrist and let it fall to the ground.

"Take the gag off your mouth and untie your feet, you 'body.' Use your hands. Take the gags off the others too, and none of you 'bodies' are to stand up until I tell you to."

The boy moved around from one boy to another, obediently shuffling on his knees. When my turn came and my hands were free, I grabbed the cloth that had covered my mouth. It was soaking wet. It was some minutes before we were all free, but no one dared to move. Our eyes were pinned on the titan, who put a wireless device up to his mouth, and then our necks swung round toward the door when he ordered that bottles of water be brought. We were desperate for a single drop.

"Look here, you bodies. Look at me, not at anything else, or else I'll gag you again and tie up your hands and feet. Look at me and listen carefully."

We sat up straight at the sound of his loud voice.

He stared at us pointedly for some moments and then began to explain, "We've reviewed the research that Dr. Abdel-Samie Mukhtar submitted and yesterday evening we met with the council of advisers and scholars. We found a loophole that saves you from certain death. Credit for that goes to General Ismail, the officer in charge of the camp, who decided against moving on to the next and final step before we have exhausted all possible ways of rehabilitating you. The general shared his insights with us and asked us to draft a detailed memorandum that set out what he had explained, and then to put it into effect. In short, Dr. Mukhtar had overlooked certain important aspects, which made his conclusions inaccurate and unreliable. It's true that he met some of you and asked questions and made inquiries and wrote papers that filled dozens of shelves, but he hasn't dealt with you as we have done and he didn't know you as we have known you over the past few years. On top of that, he doesn't understand the aspects that we're interested in. Although he has plenty of information, it still has a limited perspective and is confined to his area of expertise. Dr. Mukhtar ignored the distinctive features you've acquired as a result of the long time you've spent on the streets. He took no account of the natural qualities that you possess and was not aware of their value. Only we understood that. It's not the right time to explain more. Suffice it to say that you are in a better position than you or he imagined. He seems to have overreached because of the narrow scope of his theories, which made him overlook the public interest. He studied your circumstances in isolation from other problems, but he accepted the outcome when we debated your case yesterday, and today the general endorsed the decision and sent a copy of it to the ruler, and it will be broadcast on all the media. You are truly lucky. From now on you won't be sleeping in ruins. We will give you shelter in the camp and we will look after your scrawny bodies and you won't have much need for those rotten heads that you carry on your shoulders. You'll be valued and you'll be strong, smart, upright citizens as good as any others. Stand on your feet. Form a line with your colleagues and none of you try to stretch or brush the dirt off yourselves. You'll go to the cleansing unit imminently and then you'll be fed."

We reached the bathroom escorted by a titan, who stood by the open door. We went inside in groups and water came pouring out of powerful hoses. He told us to pick up the hoses and wash each other down. He said we didn't need to take off our clothes, which were so torn that they fell apart easily from the pressure of the water. We ended up almost naked, with most of us only in our underpants. Dripping wet, we followed the titan like trees with drops of rain running off them, and then he made us stand in a line. He gave us a few towels that we passed around, as well as identical clothing and rubber shoes. We took them gratefully. Our desire to acquire things had subsided. We didn't fight to get the best stuff the way we used to when desirable goods fell into our hands. We were still very tired and content with whatever we were given as long as were safe. We were all about the same size, so we were ready within minutes.

The titan led us to a place where there were rows of metal tables and handed us warm meals in cartons. It was like a miracle had taken place in front of me, right out of the blue. I had never in my life held a Kentucky Fried Chicken box that was unopened and untouched. It contained a whole chicken thigh, a bread roll that no one else had already bitten, and some French fries. I thought about Youssef and Emad and felt sad. If they had been with me, we would have made a party of it and shared the box between us. Two days had passed and I still didn't know where they were. I lost my appetite for a moment, but I soon got over it. They must have gone off in another vehicle and been dumped in another room. Maybe they were eating now, like me. The food distracted me from thinking and I started stuffing my face with the fries and chicken. I left the bread to the end. I didn't look up from the box till I had finished. I didn't know when they would bring us food again. I looked around and saw that one boy was pushing his carton away toward someone else, rejecting the food. It was the same boy who had sat still with me when the others jumped up and cheered. I regretted I had been so distracted. If I had been sitting next to him, I would have gotten more to eat.

At night I had horrible dreams. In one of them they killed three of us. I heard voices and several times I woke up shaking in my bed at the end of the dormitory. It wasn't a bed like the one in my mother's house. It didn't have any legs or planks of wood, but it was certainly different from the garbage dump and it didn't smell. There was a mattress, a pillow, and a cover for each child, and it was a private space on which the others could not encroach. We weren't in a police station and I don't think it was a prison either because there weren't any jailers. My mind was out of action all night long. Luckily I was right next to the wall, so I pressed up against it, but it was no use. If Youssef and Emad had been beside me, I probably would have slept better than I had for ages.

They counted us in the morning. We had to file out through the dormitory door one after another to the sound of the titan's booming voice. He stood outside the door holding a small piece of paper that I guessed was a list of our names: they know everything here. The dormitory emptied out completely and the titan was still by the door. Then he stepped back inside to check.

He soon returned and said, "One of you is missing. You two, count how many of you there are. . . . Or rather don't bother, because you're useless. You can't count, of course. You're still young."

We began to murmur fearfully. One of us wasn't there. How had that happened? We could only move around when the titan was there, when we were within his sight. I looked around at the boys and my heart skipped a beat when I realized who had disappeared. It was the boy who, like me, hadn't jumped up and down when we learned we weren't going to die—the same boy who had refused to eat his food the day before. Maybe he'd noticed that they hadn't locked the door on us that night or put a padlock and chain on it, as they had the previous night. He'd given us the slip and caught them unawares. Really, he hadn't needed to give us the skip. After the horrors we had been through most of us had slept like logs. I certainly hadn't seen or heard him in the nightmares that had tormented me. Even if I had heard any noise, I would have been too frightened to move. I wasn't going to risk dying now.

When it was certain that the boy was gone, we were so afraid we didn't dare speak. Spontaneously we started using sign language, waving our arms and heads behind the titan's back so that he wouldn't know we were communicating. The titan didn't throw much light on the boy's fate: he said the boy was bound to turn up, and didn't add another word. I had expected him to get angry and call the other titans to tie us up again. But none of that happened. I couldn't understand how the boy had dared to leave. Where did he think he was going? I was sure they would catch him straight away. His escape added to my anxiety. It was a strange feeling that came over me—a feeling that we were close companions. We had never exchanged a word and our eyes had met for only a fraction of a second, but we did both keep still when everyone else was jumping around to celebrate the news that we weren't going to be executed. That moment had created some bond between us, and in my mind I called him Rice Grain because of the idea I'd had at the time. He would have become my friend if there had been more time. I wondered how he would be punished if they found him.

We tucked into breakfast and all we could talk about was the boy who'd escaped. The titan didn't stop us talking, though he didn't leave the room. We started in whispers, and then the whispers grew louder as we got excited and in the end people were shouting, either attacking or defending the boy.

"The son of a bitch never thought about what he was doing. He didn't think about the fact that they saved us and they might change their minds because of him. He didn't care what might happen to us after he escaped. Anyway, he'll go back to the streets and die there."

"If that guy gets back on the streets, he'll soon get killed. People are on the lookout for us and someone might carry out the sheikh's fatwa."

"No, the boy must know a place to hide. Maybe he has a house he can go back to and lie low for a time."

"He's definitely braver than us. He's a free person who doesn't like to take orders."

"He's a traitor. He's been with us from the start and then he tricked us and ran off on his own."

"Would you have gone with him if he'd woken you up?"

The titan shouted to warn us that eating time was over. We had completely forgotten he was there.

We moved to another room where they put us in rows of wooden chairs like the ones they have in marquees for funerals or weddings. A titan called Allam stood in front of us like a statue in a public square, towering, his eyebrows knitted. His feet were slightly apart, fixed to the floor like lamp posts.

"I'm Head Allam. That's what you call me. Head is the title I prefer, because I'm the boss here and you'll obey me. All the staff in the camp are superior to you, so obey them too."

He started talking in a loud, raucous voice. He gave up using the loudspeaker and left it dangling uselessly in his hand. The loudspeaker seemed to need the titan more than the other way around. I closed in on myself and stuck to my chair while he bellowed out the rules we would have to follow from then on. I withdrew deeper into myself as he spelled out, carefully and with relish, the penalties for disobedience. I repeated to myself word for word the things I had said at breakfast about the boy who'd escaped. I hadn't said anything he could punish me for, had I? No, I had, but it was too late to do anything about it. I'm stupid and loose-tongued. Without knowing, I might have spoken in favor of what the boy had done. Had he been eavesdropping on us? Had he been watching us from the start and had he noticed that the boy and I had been too lazy to thank him properly two days earlier, and we hadn't showed how happy we were, unlike the others? He probably noted every offense and he might put me at the top of his list: the list of deviant children. They would soon get rid of me and I wouldn't be able to call on either Youssef or Emad to help me.

"None of you bodies are to sit up straight in your seats or open your traps at all. General Ismail has come from his office and will be here shortly. General Ismail is the head of the whole camp, the main head and the top leader of all the heads. The ants here can't leave their nests without his permission, and whenever one of you bodies breathes, the general knows how much air you've inhaled. You may not know it, but he's just taken on the highest office in the government for defending the whole county. Yesterday I told you what he had done for you: today he's set aside his other commitments and responsibilities and has come to address you in person to explain to you the situation you've ended up in and the future that awaits you."

This made me even more anxious and I started to shake uncontrollably. General Ismail must know about me too. In fact, he was better placed to know than anyone else. Yes, I had made a mistake and now I knew what a big mistake it was. I knew it was so big that I deserved to be punished for it. I liked what the boy had done and I'd thought of running away like him. But doesn't it count in my favor that I chose to be safe and cowered where I was? There was no way I could really have left. The general might call on me now and tell me to stand up. He might whip me with his belt or zap me with a Taser as a lesson to the other boys. I didn't really care about the boys, but I don't like anyone to punish me—in the street, at home, or anywhere. That's why I tore up my school books in my early years, because I wanted nothing to do with the school or the people there. I couldn't put up with it long enough to graduate from primary school like my brothers. I refused to stand with my face to the wall and my hands in the air. I've never hated anything as much as I hated the principal, the teachers, and the cramped classroom. They were all ridiculous. They thought they owned the children and had a proper understanding of the world, while none of them had any experience of living free like me. What a joke! Now I was back in another school, but the punishments would no doubt be more horrendous. There would be no escape from it and rebellion against it might cost me my life.

We all stood when General Ismail appeared. He made a gesture with his head and hands, and we all sat down. He wasn't how I had imagined him. He was as short as some of us children, but he was fatter of course. He had thinning hair, a broad forehead, and sleepy eyes. His cheeks were red, rounded, and chubby like those rich people's kids that drink milk in the ads. He stood with his legs together, his hands clasped over his crotch as he scanned our faces, turning his head steadily in silence. I felt compelled to stay stock-still, terrified of what was to come. I thought of passing the time in some diversion, as I usually did when I faced danger, but I couldn't find anything around to divert me except for the general, so I looked at his camouflage fatigues and lost myself in the mixture of colors.

His voice seeped into the room, soft and low. He told us we were like his children, or that we really were his children. He said it with a smile, his eyes half closed, and the lump in my throat began to go away. I waited for his voice to shake the rafters when he scolded us for what we had done in the past, but nothing like that happened. He stayed calm and I stayed on alert.

He spoke at length. He spoke about the tragedies that befall children like us, sweep them away, and destroy their futures. He told some amusing stories, though he didn't pursue any of them to the end. I identified with him and listened attentively.

"You have many problems, I know," he said, "but, as you have seen, I also know the solutions. Everything will go well, inshallah. I promise you I'll do what I can as long as you promise to help me, and I hope that the rehabilitation program that I've worked out will succeed in helping you see your country as it should be seen, and that you'll come to understand the challenges and difficulties it faces, so that you'll find out how to deal with them and overcome them."

I realized that some time had passed and so far he hadn't singled me out with a glance that would expose my secret and destroy my fragile existence. Even so, I started fidgeting in my chair, unable to stay still. I leaned back, then rested my elbows on my knees and splayed my toes inside my new shoes. Then I brought them together again suddenly as if I had been pricked by a thorn.

The general continued with a smile: "I tell you, you're *our* kids. This country's kids. You have to believe what I'm saying. I would never lie to you. I'm being honest with you, so that no one can do any harm to our country."

I was instinctively drawn to his occasional smiles—small, vague smiles that appeared mid-speech. I didn't understand what he meant by them. They puzzled and confused me so much that they added to my anxiety. Before the general spoke, I imagined myself getting up from my chair and running off, but when he started speaking I was surprised how calm he sounded, and when I got over my anxiety, his smile began to intrigue me. He was strange; he neither frightened me off nor made it possible for me to sit peacefully. Something about him unsettled me, although he showed no hatred toward us, unlike Dr. Abdel-Samie, and he wasn't brutal like Head Allam.

At the end of his speech he said he trusted us and would protect us. Then he said we would never let him down as long as we cooperated with the other heads and obeyed them, observed the rules, and followed the plan they had drawn up.

"I'll meet you often and follow your progress closely. For now, I thank you and leave you with Head Allam for a few minutes," he said.

The hall fell silent for some seconds. At the time I wondered whether we were meant to clap or keep quiet. Silence seemed more likely, but Head Allam started clapping loudly, and we started clapping even louder than him. I was amazed how big his hands were. His fingers were fat and thick, too, and his forearm was the size of my thigh or bigger.

In few words Head Allam explained the rehabilitation program. Then he turned to face the wall and briefed us on what he called the "activities schedule." He followed that up with a large map of the camp, showing the buildings we would be using. His face was expressionless when he turned to us and his voice was monotonous. He spoke in a strangely emphatic way when he pronounced the name of each place and pointed it out on the map.: "This is the training area, this is the dining hall that you've already used, those are the bathrooms, and the big hall for lectures, seminars and cultural events, and likewise the room we're in now. As for the small square you can see at the top of the map close to the camp perimeter, that's the lockup for those who disobey orders."

"No, no, don't frighten them, Head Allam," the general interjected. "Don't worry, kids, and don't take what he says seriously. Head Allam is rather strict. He likes complete obedience and commitment, but he has a big heart. Thank you very much, Head Allam. I've said enough now. I hope God grants you success and I wish you a useful stay here. You'll be a pillar of strength for the country and one of its main lines of defense."

I sat down when my turn came. They wrapped a white towel around my neck, almost strangling me, and I felt an urge to vomit. An old man with smooth hair picked up a pair of scissors and started cutting my hair without even combing it first. There was no way a comb could have untangled it anyway: even my fingers couldn't have done it. The hair fell to the floor and covered it like coarse black grass that had just sprouted. I couldn't see my face while I was having my hair cut, because I didn't have a mirror in front of me. I knew what I used to look like from my reflection in shop windows and car windows. I had often played a trick on people in cars in order to get a good look at myself. I went up to them enthusiastically, holding a dirty rag in my outstretched hand as if about to clean their windscreen. They would look in the other direction and quickly wind up the window, maybe in disgust or horror at the way I looked. Some of them pressed their phones to their ears as if they were off in another world, while some pretended to be lost in thought and that they hadn't seen me. In the meantime, I moved in and stared, not at them but at the distorted reflection of my face in the glass.

The barber soon finished my hair. My ears and the tip of my nose felt cold, like an animal that has lost its fur. I looked forward with pleasure to him applying some cologne, but he didn't and I thought I must have done something wrong. I stayed where I was, hoping he would forgive me. Surprised I was still waiting, he told me to leave. He had no reason to begrudge me the cologne. I hadn't moved when he was cutting my hair and I hadn't annoyed him in the way I used to annoy Sayed Halawa, the most popular barber near our garbage dump. Sayed's shop was well-known in the area, and we were also well-known there. I had often stopped outside the shop with Emad, staring at the customers passively having their scalps massaged. We used to stick our tongues out and play mind games with them. Sometimes we'd slip in through the door and watch them blocking their noses irritably because they expected us to stink. Once the barber shouted at us and flew into a rage when he saw us. When his shouting didn't deter us, he gave Emad some money so that we would leave his customers alone, but by doing so he created a bond with us, maybe unwittingly. We used to pass by his shop whenever we wanted some money, when the people in cars were ignoring us, for example, and we didn't have any other way to raise it. He had to pay a price to make us go away.

"Bend. Stretch. Jump. Press. Get down, boy! Get up, quickly! Your arms are like a girl's. There's no point making an effort with you. How did you sleep on the street on your own? I bet the other kids pushed you around. Push the weight forward! Push as if you were fighting off an infidel!"

Head Salem soon took us in hand. He set about dividing us into groups according to age, or rather height, fist size, and chest size. He pointed at me and I took off my undershirt. He examined my body for a moment and then consigned me to the second group, the middle-height group, not the weaklings or the big guys. Some of the children in the camp limped in one leg or had old injuries: Head Salem put those kids in a separate group and didn't look at their chests or their fists.

I ran with my group until I was out of breath. I jumped twenty times to touch the sky, as he had ordered, and then I hung onto a pole stretched between two posts. I climbed a tree and jumped to the ground from the top. I picked up one of the other boys and carried him, and then we reversed roles. We repeated the exercises, and then the first group took our place and we went to do what they had been doing. Head Salem watched over us and bellowed in a voice that almost deafened us. In his notebook he wrote down things we couldn't see. I think he was measuring our strength and sometimes he would insult one of us or throw a stone at someone if he tried to avoid doing what he'd been told to do. All that mattered to me at the end of the day was to survive and still be standing on my wobbly legs, so that he wouldn't mark me down as a failure and a weakling. At the end he made us sit on the floor and he walked around shaking his head.

"Your bodies aren't tough enough. They should be hard like real men. You're no longer children, so don't expect us to feel sorry for you. None of you will be men until you can do what you have to do without complaining."

He paused, looked around at us and then roared: "Get up, you bodies, and run some more! We'll make men of you despite yourselves, as long as I'm in charge. Run to the dining hall and don't leave anything on your plates. Anyone who stops running before they arrive won't get a meal until tomorrow. And don't imagine you're ever out of my sight, however far you go!"

I was nodding off between one mouthful and the next. I came round several times to find my head bowed so low it almost fell onto the plate. The training exhausted me and I could hardly walk to the dormitory. My whole body was in pain. The pain wouldn't go away and it didn't diminish with time. As soon as the bedding arrived, I threw myself down on it, a complete wreck. I felt bloated with all the food I had stuffed down my gullet without chewing it. My head slipped off the pillow and my eyelids drooped, but I didn't fall asleep. My mind was full of all the things that had happened since the morning. General Ismail's face constantly appeared, and the words of Head Allam and Head Salem echoed in my head like a recording.

They said we'd come to the camp to save our lives. They'd done us an invaluable favor and were going to give us an opportunity we would never have dreamed of. We'd learn new things, find out how things worked behind the scenes. People would treat us with respect. All we had to do was listen carefully, remember as much as possible, and do what was required—nothing more and nothing less.

They'd designed the program especially for us. They said it would take several months of intensive training, and we would apply what we learned carefully and faithfully. And then?

"Then we set you free, qualified for a better life." That's what they said.

"When you graduate from the camp, you'll still report to us. We won't abandon you. You'll get a regular salary and when you reach the age of majority you'll be given identity cards with an address and a profession. Most importantly, it will be a step up for you—you'll be respected in a way you never knew in your earlier life. From now on, no one will remind you that once you were street kids."

We were the children of General Ismail personally, children of the System. We would serve the country honorably and responsibly, like important, respectable people. We would defend the national interest and the security and stability of the country. There was nothing better than that. They were really interested in us, but would they give us a choice? Would it be possible to walk away and go back to the street?

I dreamed of General Ismail. He looked like my father and I had the same feelings toward him: discomfort, disgust, and an urge to disobey his orders and break the rules he laid down. In the dream I punched him on his red cheek. He soon recovered and didn't punch me back. In fact, he invited me to punch him again and, when I told him he was a stupid idiot, he drew a sword and made a cut in my neck. The blood poured out and I woke up. I could still feel the pain. I started twisting and turning in bed and I couldn't get back to sleep. I stared at the ceiling a long time in the hope that my insomnia would wear off, but it didn't. I sat up and cursed the fact that I had woken up so early when all the other children were asleep. I was tired and drained and my limbs were sore. I felt like I'd been given a nasty beating and couldn't stand up. I looked around at the faces of the sleeping children. We were still as we had been the day before—one person short. The boy, Rice Grain as I called him, hadn't come back yet.

I fell asleep again at dawn and woke up late. I struggled to my feet to get dressed and looked around to find the others leaning against the walls. None of us were in good shape. Head Allam came in hurriedly and said we would be going to the lecture hall in an hour to meet an important guest. We had to eat breakfast quickly.

The Obedience Lecture

Sheikh Abdel-Gabbar arrived, massive and impressive in a cloak and caftan. His face was round and full of health and he had a salt-and-pepper beard. General Ismail welcomed him and introduced him to us warmly and hospitably. Then they sat down next to each other on the dais. Sheikh Abdel-Gabbar cleared his throat, said a prayer, and then "Peace be upon you" at the end of the prayer, as important sheikhs do. He then launched into his sermon, his voice bellowing through the loudspeakers, as if he were preaching the sermon before Friday prayers.

"Copious praise be to God, that He has bestowed His grace and favor on you and sent you a heavenly miracle, the likes of which we have rarely seen in our time. Praise be to God that He has plucked you from darkness and saved you from the devil's snares when you were on the edge of perdition. Praise be to God that He sent you someone to guide you, to cast light into your hearts and show you the right path. He is very much like Ismail the prophet, whom God Almighty redeemed out of respect for Ismail's father Abraham—certainly not unlike him."

I turned my gaze to General Ismail and found him smiling bashfully with his eyes closed. I was reminded of my elder sister when her boyfriend came to visit us to propose, with two wedding rings.

"My children, the gates of mercy have been opened to you, so close the gates of iniquity and repent to God for the sins you have committed. God is forgiving and merciful. Don't forget that good deeds cancel out the evil deeds of the past, as long as you remain obedient. You were going through hard times, your lives were unsettled and the things you did were depraved and misguided, but today you are taking your first steps toward maturity. Now that we are here, on this distinguished occasion, I would like to remind you of the story of the prophet Abraham, when God ordered him and his son Ismail to build the Kaaba for people to face when they pray and as a place where rituals and prayers could be performed and the one God could be worshiped. I remind you of those two prophets, of the venerable Kaaba and everything that is useful to people and inspires them to be god-fearing.

"My children, Commander Ismail has built this place for you, this great camp, for you to seek God's favor here. Through serious training, through effort and sweat, and by joining the ranks of those defending our country and our religion, you can build a future that, God willing, will be promising. Through your good deeds you will secure places for yourselves in heaven and drink from its rivers. My advice to you is that you seize the opportunity, obey your leader always, remember his favors to you, and make sure you carry out orders to the letter. Meticulous work is a token of belief and obeying your master is part of obedience to God, one of the pillars of the faith. My sons, I won't detain you long today. I just wanted to introduce myself to you on my first visit. I congratulate you on your decision to attend this laudable rehabilitation course, which is endorsed by the state and sponsored by the brave and admirable leader, General Ismail. I hope to find you well on my next visit so that, God willing, we can have longer conversations and hold a series of lectures in which I can explain to you many aspects of religious law that are unclear to you, and answer your questions. Peace be upon you, and the mercy and blessings of God."

The sermon ended and Sheikh Abdel-Gabbar stood up and shook the general's hand. He turned to leave and, in the blink of an eye, he was gone. He hadn't said anything about his earlier fatwa. Had he changed his mind and forgiven us so now people wouldn't track us down in the street? Or was he testing us, waiting to see how much progress we would make and what we would be like at the end of the course? He didn't seem to be sticking to his previous attitude toward us. I didn't like to imagine he would be happy to see us killed in any case. I thought of putting my hand up and asking him what religious law had to say about the boy who had fled the camp, and whether running away meant he was an infidel. I would also have liked to ask him about the children who hadn't appeared in the camp yet. He must have known whether anyone had followed his fatwa and done them harm, or if they were still safe. I had to postpone my questions when the sheikh left, but I was determined to organize them properly in my head, because I didn't yet know what could be said and what might make the sheikh angry with me.

*

The boy who had run away didn't come back in the following days, although we were expecting him, or at least some news of him. We continued to await his reappearance impatiently. The training made us forget many things and distracted us from anything outside the camp, but it didn't prevent us from thinking about his fate. With every day that passed, the stories multiplied, each adding another detail or some figment of our febrile imaginations. When a second group arrived, it helped to spread frightening ideas among us. Alarming stories circulated and we couldn't tell which were true and which were imaginary. There were stories about plans to shove us into ovens and about ordinary people setting up ambushes in anticipation of us reappearing on the streets. There was a man who threw sulfuric acid at a boy who refused to get away from the doorway of his store. The skin on his back was burned to the bone. One woman screamed when a boy approached her: passersby gathered around and beat the boy to death. A boy's body was found in the river, and in the mortuary they discovered he was missing several organs. All these stories evolved and acquired new details. People came up with possible evidence for them. One particular piece of evidence terrified us and made us think of the danger we would face outside the camp: that some of the boys in the latest group to arrive were disappearing from time to time. In the dining room we no longer saw the lame boy or the boy whose fingers had been cut off. They never came to the training room either, and the titans didn't look for them or talk about their absence in their daily conversations. The fact that they were missing was apparently normal, unremarkable. For our part, we didn't ask ourselves where they had gone, maybe in case our fears were confirmed. We preferred to wait and keep hoping they would return, even if that was largely naive and foolish.

One nasty boy refused to let it go. One gray morning he whispered to us that all the explanations we dreamed up for the disappearances were mistaken. The children hadn't escaped. People outside the camp hadn't pounced on them or buried them alive. Proud to have information unavailable to us, he said he had been carrying some bags of trash out of Head Allam's office, next to the lecture room, when he overheard the head saying at a meeting that they planned to dump all the disabled children in the desert. He claimed he had heard this with his own ears, just one day before the children disappeared. He swore a solemn oath to that effect, mindful of the practice in our previous life outside the camp, where we held such an oath to be sacred. At the time, our throats dried up and we were terribly anxious. We weren't convinced by what he said, but his story burrowed into our brains like a maggot.

From then on we stopped talking about the children who had escaped or disappeared. We also avoided the boy who claimed to have overheard the heads. It was as if he were responsible for the missing children's fate, or at least was an accomplice in it. If he'd held his tongue he would've made it much easier for us. Was he upset because he thought we were blind and that he was the only one who could see? Or was he so frightened that his tongue got the better of him? Or did he maybe make up the story to frighten us and enjoy our confusion and our conflicting emotions? Whatever the boy's intentions, the sad truth was that we were completely dependent on the titans for our safety and well-being. So what could we make of his story? If just one of the missing children reappeared, we would have dismissed it as a lie, or maybe as a fantasy. We wouldn't have blamed him for that: we often had frightening hallucinations that we thought were real. Then the fog would clear and we would realize we had been very stupid. But the missing children were still missing, without any sign to give us hope, and deep inside I was convinced that the disabled children had disappeared for good. Maybe if Head Allam had told us he had moved them somewhere else, or that they had committed a serious offense that required expelling them from the camp, I would have relaxed, but he didn't say anything. The subject was glossed over, and we were complicit in consigning it to the deepest recesses of our minds. We swallowed it and did our best to make sure it didn't float to the surface. Silently we shared a fear that would break loose only in our subconscious. I had recurrent nightmares.

The faces of Youssef and Emad came back to me almost every night. I had a succession of dreams in which they were the only people I saw. My head was full of dark forebodings. I was haunted by suspicions that had neither beginnings nor ends. I couldn't not think about them, but I didn't know what to do. If I had asked the titans about Youssef and Emad, they would have slapped me and seen me as a wimp. Had they died along the way? I heard they had thrown some children into the river when they were moving them. They did it when the truck was halfway across the bridge that comes down near the university. The truck was overloaded, some people couldn't breathe and the situation inside was intolerable. I had also heard children from remote districts say that the titans had got rid of one or more boys before they reached the camp because there was an unexpected need for kidneys and fresh liver lobes. Youssef once told me about a movie he'd seen when he sneaked into an open-air theater, though he couldn't stay till the end. He was very sad about what he had seen. In the movie young children had been raised to obtain spare parts for adults with incurable diseases, then they killed the children one by one to keep the adults alive.

Despite the repeated gossip and rumors, which changed dozens of times a day, something inside told me that Youssef and Emad were still alive and I would see them soon. They must have had plenty of diseases, I thought, so nothing useful could be hoped for from their livers, let alone their brains, which had been frazzled by taking too many pills. And me, how long had it been since I had taken a pill? Maybe I was delirious because of the long deprivation. I kept imagining myself waking up in the big garbage dump and finding my friends and scraps of rotten chicken beside me. Then I'd shout at them, saying we should look for a new place to spend the night.

2

Arrival

When they arrived the tents had already been set up. Aida and Murad had their hands full carrying what they could in the way of suitcases and colorful plastic bags that bore the addresses of well-known shops on them. Murad was wearing a white short-sleeved shirt, dark blue trousers, and smart leather shoes. Aida had come in a linen dress embroidered in pink, a matching headscarf, and sandals with medium-height heels. She looked like they were on a family visit that wouldn't last long. The sun lingered at its zenith and the humidity made it hard to breathe. It was a merciless and unmistakable July day. They stopped a while: Aida had lowered her load onto the ground and was fumbling in her leather handbag for a small bottle of water that had been frozen when she left home. Now it had thawed and showed no sign it had ever been cold.

A small man appeared in the distance, moving toward them with rapid steps. He put his hand out to Murad with a broad smile and they embraced. He nodded at Aida, who dabbed her face, neck, and hands with the last drops in the bottle and started to look for a handkerchief to wipe away the water mixed with sweat.

"How are you, Madame Aida?" he said. "It's good to see you. My colleagues will be very happy you've come."

"May God grant you peace, Shakir," Murad replied amiably. He was relieved to have come, after deliberating about it at length.

"We've been remiss about attending since the start," he added. "We'll make up for what we've missed in the coming days, I hope."

"Are you planning to spend the night or will you leave at the end of the day?"

"We'll leave tonight, after we've broken the fast together and performed the evening prayers. You know my duties at the hospital, but I've arranged with Aida that we'll come back tomorrow afternoon and if things go well we'll spend the night here. We've brought our things and we'll leave them in the tent from today."

"Great. We're growing stronger and more determined with every colleague that joins us. Happy Ramadan! We pray these first days of the month be blessed for us all. Come, let me show you where the others are and where you can have a rest."

They went past an endless succession of tents. The whole world seemed to have turned into little caves held taut by guy ropes. Aida noticed that the tents were not arranged in any particular order, but they all had flaps hanging down to make a door that gave the inhabitants some privacy and stopped passersby from prying on them. She also noticed that there were many young people running around making a noise. There was one boy who looked like Adam, with his head shaved like his. He was holding a sword made of cardboard and slashing the air with it. He was watching them from the corner of his eye, apparently imagining that he was triumphant over an unseen enemy and hoping for some admiration.

They arrived at one of the eastern sections, where people based in the capital had assembled. Explaining the system adopted for the sit-in, Shakir said the tents were arranged geographically. Each group of provinces had its own section and its own official who arranged food, drink, and security. She looked around the place and felt fairly comfortable about it: at least it wasn't very crowded in their area. Women like her were coming and going, and they didn't seem to be frightened or anxious.

That was an important starting point, a sign that life here would be tolerable. Her busy mind picked out many details of the scene and deliberately tried to remember the most important ones. The last thing she had ever imagined was that she might one day go and protest in the street along with thousands of other people, protest about something political, but what could one do when the ruler had been abducted? What could one do when he had been removed from office and his supporters had been humiliatingly excluded from government? It had happened a few months ago, and despite all attempts, no one could find out where he was. The general had ignored pressure to reinstate him, and they no longer had any recourse other than to stage a sit-in out in public until the new regime responded. She was relieved to see there was a large shopping center and a mosque nearby, because those buildings would definitely have lavatories. She made up her mind to visit them immediately, just to be sure. She was always worried about considerations of this kind. Whenever she went somewhere new, her first question was about the lavatory and how clean and well-maintained it was and how close it would be. If she liked the bathrooms she would like the place, and if she was disgusted she would leave and never come back. She left her husband to meet his friends and acquaintances, noted the number on the tent and headed to her destination without delay.

Shakir took Murad around, receiving welcomes, exploring the place, and encouraging the people who had been encamped there for the previous two weeks. Shakir Abdel-Mutaal was an old friend of Murad's; they had known each other since their student days. When Murad was a hardworking student in the Faculty of Medicine, he had become friends with Shakir, and then Shakir had tried to bring him into the Raised Banner movement before the other groups got to him. They had argued endlessly but Shakir hadn't given up on him over the years and eventually they become close friends, even if their paths diverged. Murad continued to do well and got a job as an assistant lecturer in the university, while Shakir rose rapidly in the ranks of the Raised Banner till he acquired an important position, and their relationship remained strong.

After an hour wandering around, and with Murad exhausted and dehydrated, the two men sat down on wooden chairs that belonged to a stallholder and started to exchange news. Around them young men were picking up sacks and using whatever was at hand to cut up big plastic water containers like those used to dispense mineral water in public buildings and some wealthy households too. They split them lengthwise into two equal halves and carried them off.

Noticeably tense, Murad sighed, "The university isn't in a happy state, Shakir. The students are angry about what's happened. They're up in arms against developments but almost everyone is against them, even their old allies."

"Don't worry, Murad, we'll keep pressing."

"The young people are pressing as hard as they can in the faculties and the institutes and you are putting on pressure by being here, but the ruler has vanished into thin air. No one knows what they've done with him, or where they've taken him. It's like we're watching a film, not reality."

"Yes, the general struck his blow while no one was paying attention. We didn't expect him to detain the ruler and hide him away so easily, or hijack the ballot boxes and rig the elections. But I swear we'll hold out. We won't let them enjoy the fruits of their misdeeds."

"But we mustn't be lulled into failing to see the situation as it really is, Shakir."

"The truth is as clear as day. No one disagrees about that. The general wanted power and planned and schemed and grabbed it from us unjustly and without good reason."

"You're leaving the ordinary people out of your calculations. If they hadn't come out onto the streets against you, the general wouldn't have been able to steer events in the direction he wanted. And if those people hadn't felt the Raised Banner had let them down, they wouldn't have come out to demand that the ruler go. You have to admit that you failed to run the country properly after the first revolution."

"It wasn't just us who failed. What did you expect, Murad, when all the institutions in the state were working against us?"

"I won't mince my words. It would've been better if you hadn't put forward a candidate to stand in the elections, when things were still difficult and it was almost impossible to control the institutions you're talking about. If you'd stayed in the background you could have made major gains and you'd still be in the picture now."

Shakir stroked his light, trimmed beard and said, "It's too late to say that. Anyway, we have to resist and with patience we'll come to a satisfactory agreement. That's what always happens."

"I'm not as optimistic as you. This time the situation's different. I hope with all my heart that things are moving in the right direction. But tell me, where are our colleagues from college?"

"Some of them are in charge of the public address system on the podium we've set up and some of them are dealing with patients in the clinic. As you know, lots of people have come from the south, from the poorest and most neglected villages. Many of them have diseases and are too poor even to think of getting treated. They support us in the worst of circumstances but we're unable to reach them regularly, and the Space offers an excellent opportunity."

"Great. I can help in my specialization. If you come across anyone with an eye disease, send them to me in the tent and I'll look after the rest."

"Take a stand for once in your life, Murad. You're a role model now and you also have students here who know you and admire you. If you like, I'll assign you a corner in the medical assistance tents, so that it doesn't get chaotic. We could also set aside a room in the hospital next to the mosque, with fixed hours. Whatever suits you."

"As you wish. I'm not going to quibble with you now, not under the circumstances. I'll do my best to examine patients here, regardless of where I spend the night. Give me two days' rest and you can have me five days in the clinic, and I'll be at your service there from two to five in the afternoon."

Aida made an extensive tour of the Space. She went into the shopping center and checked out the bathrooms on all the floors, as if she were doing an official inspection, then she went to the mosque, washed for prayers to test the basins, the water pressure in the faucets, and the cleanliness and smell of the floors. She was pleased to find paper towels, which she hadn't imagined would be available, given the quantities all the visitors must be consuming. She was also pleased to find that the Space didn't have the piles of trash she had been fully prepared to criticize before the visit. She made do with a quick tour of the mosque and left a detailed reconnaissance for the coming days. Her sandals weren't suitable for walking any further, and her swollen toe was hurting so much that she couldn't concentrate. Besides, she would be coming back the next day. She easily found her tent, and Murad had gotten there first. He noticed unmistakable signs of relief on her face, and he smiled. He was familiar with her body language after many years of marriage and could read her feelings from a single glance.

"Did you meet anyone you know?" he asked.

"No. How was your trip with Shakir? Did you find your colleagues and their families?"

"Only some of them. The senior members of the Raised Banner and some of the committee officials."

"And where are the rest of them?"

"Shakir says many of them come and go. About two-thirds of the people at the sit-in are constantly on the move. There are some who come and stay for days, then they leave and are replaced by others. Some come during the day and have to leave at night. It's hard for friends to gather all at the same time. Only the top leaders never leave the place. They haven't left since the sit-in started."

Aida took their bags and started unpacking and arranging the contents.

"I don't think there are any ordinary people, Murad. I mean it's not like in the first revolution. I don't think we've won the support of any other parties. I don't know what's up with people. Wasn't the guy an elected ruler, as they wanted?"

"That's politics," Murad said dejectedly. "Alliances, scheming, endless ups and downs. In any case, nothing lasts forever and maybe things will change tomorrow."

Aida paused for thought and then decided to change the subject. "I'll call Adam at my mother's," she said. "I don't want him to spend all his time playing."

Deep inside she didn't feel that anything would change soon.

They spent a fair amount of time in the Space and Aida began to feel at home with the tent and its contents. At sunset Shakir's wife Fayza came by to welcome her and told her the iftar meals had arrived. She even gave her a choice between several dishes she was carrying. Aida saw no reason to refuse. The meals came in boxes that looked clean and carefully packed, but she didn't know whether all the food was prepared like this, or whether this was just a special welcome for them. Shakir joined Fayza and suggested they eat in their tent, which was big enough for everyone. He insisted on inviting them and Aida accepted after a little hesitation, when she saw that Murad was eager to go.

Shakir's tent had a round table of medium height and all four of them leaned over it as soon as they heard the call to prayer. Murad picked up the glass jug thirstily while Aida swallowed a piece of bread. She looked at the water and asked where it came from. Shakir's wife smiled to dispel her fears and explained how the young men had located the water pipes that ran under the Space and fitted faucets to them to provide clean drinking water.

"That's not the only source of course," she added mischievously. "Every day trucks bring hundreds of crates of mineral water, more than we need."

Murad asked about the big plastic containers he had seen the protesters cutting up.

Shakir chuckled and replied, "That's another matter, doctor." Then he leaned over and whispered in Murad's ear, "They cut them in half, fix the neck, connect them to the sewage pipes and with a little work turn them into urinals for the men. Now eat your food, brother, and don't embarrass me with such details in front of the women."

The sky turned completely dark and the protesters finished praying. Shakir stood up to escort Murad and Aida to the nearest exit point, where Murad had left his car. They walked slowly and resumed their unfinished conversation. When the edge of the Space appeared, Murad turned to Shakir and shook his head sadly. "Forgive me," he said, "I forgot to give you my condolences for the Brothers who were killed recently. Only God lives forever and hopefully this will be the last of our sorrows and misfortunes."

"They're martyrs, and they're in a better place. Some of the young men here wish they could be among the ranks of those mown down by rifles at dawn prayers. There can be no better death than that."

"Are there any other marches in the coming days?"

Shakir dismissed the idea with a laugh. "Take it easy. The last march was only a few days ago, and the ground hasn't yet soaked up the blood that was shed. You seem very enthusiastic about taking part."

"You know me," Murad replied with a smile. "I don't demonstrate and I have nothing to do with street battles. I just worry that more people will get hurt, and I want to be prepared."

"Trust in God and don't worry so much. We'll meet tomorrow, God willing, and don't forget what we agreed."

Murad and Aida didn't speak on their way home. Aida was thinking about what she would wear on her next visit and what she would pack in the way of things essential during their stay, while Murad was imagining how it would be to work in the clinics in the Space, and whether there would be enough medical supplies or the right equipment.

3

The Camp

The two heads, Salem and Allam, live in a separate building close to the main gate of the camp. They call it the Rest House. They have a whole floor each and the guards won't let anyone in for any reason whatsoever. If there's an emergency, one of us kids informs the guard, who then contacts one of the heads. I never want to be the messenger, but there are some kids who really like the idea.

In the beginning there were between thirty and forty of us 'bodies.' In the camp I've practiced counting and become more competent at it, but I stop when I get close to a hundred and I can't count any further. We've joined the rehabilitation program. Everything is done methodically and in line with the general's plan, which the heads have put into effect very meticulously and attentively. We eat, sleep, wake up, and even go to the bathroom according to a rigorous timetable. We wake up early and go to breakfast with washed, hungry faces. Then we go to the square for training with Head Salem. When we finish training, it's time for lunch, so we set off to the dining hall again and spend some time there. Then we break for half an hour and do whatever we like. We meet again in the lecture hall to listen to one of the many lessons they've arranged for us. Finally we have dinner and after that we don't have the energy to do anything else.

I've tried hard to stick to the program. Now I'm living in the camp as a body among many bodies, but I'm also one of the general's children, and all the children work hard and are committed. I've taken it seriously. In the street, my only commitment was to my friends Youssef and Emad, but they were never a burden to reckon with in the same way as now. We came together of our own free will. At first in this camp I felt alone and lost, although it was of course much smaller and more confined than the streets and the garbage dumps where I used to hang out with Youssef and Emad. In my first days in the camp I had recurrent panic attacks and would feel like I would die, but I soon toughened up and forgot what was upsetting me. I've competed with the other kids because I wanted to feel safe from the titans. Several times I've tried to win the affection of Head Salem. One day I heard him say that gallantry was part of manliness, so I went to help a boy who had dislocated his shoulder when he tripped and fell while jumping, but the titan suddenly shouted at me and called me a wimp and a spoiled brat. I backed off and left the boy on the floor. I thought that maybe I didn't know exactly what gallantry meant.

I've gradually realized I no longer know what many things mean. I've become more careful when I speak, and when Head Allam once asked me what I knew about dignity, I didn't reply. I wasn't sure what exactly dignity was and I wasn't interested. With time we've developed our own rituals, signs, and a language that only we understand. If we spoke it outside the camp, people would look at us in amazement and disdain and say we're not from this country.

Some words in the camp are strange and it took me a while to get used to them. The titans have their own language too, but did they invent it just for us? "Listen, you body," they say. "Shut up, you body." "Obey, you body." They're the heads and we're the bodies. They set the limits as soon as they brought us and imposed them when they addressed people. They became sacrosanct and it wasn't a good idea to cross them. They only rarely use common forms of address like "pasha," which is our favorite, and they don't use any other titles either: just 'head.' They're all heads, and our only option was to use the same word, at least in public. To myself I call them the titans because I've known them by that term since I lived in the garbage dump. Youssef deserves credit for that: he coined the term the first time he saw them. They were closing off some streets, setting up checkpoints, and trying to round up a group of people. Eventually they grabbed a few of them and stuffed them into a truck, despite some resistance and screaming. When they'd gone Youssef said, "No one can stand up to those titans." Emad liked the word and he added it to our private vocabulary. We three have a patent on it, for inventing it and using it. No one else uses it to describe them, inside or outside the camp.

Youssef was our leader in matters of language. He was the only one of us that could read properly and explain written things to us. He had left school in the third year of middle school and while we were looking for food or scraps of clothing in the garbage, he would be gathering books and pieces of paper. We thought he knew a way to sell them and we were surprised to find out he actually wanted to read them. He admitted to us that reading was his passion and we laughed at him for days and made jokes about it. "Shut up, Emad, Youssef's reading," or "Don't burp, Rabie, Youssef's trying to understand his book," or "Don't fart and spoil his reading session, you idiot," or "I see you wiped your ass with Youssef's pieces of paper. Please give them back to him. Some of the letters are still legible." Youssef seemed to be less ambitious than the rest of us, and kinder. After telling us he liked reading, he became even more humble, maybe because he had also been honest with himself about his own fragility. We treated him as if he were a girl, since reading is a girl thing. Emad even said he was feebler than the girls in our neighborhood, who fought each other, didn't know how to read or write, and couldn't even tell one letter or number from another.

Did Youssef choose to be the weakest of us? Not at all, but we thought he was weak-willed and weak-spirited. He didn't start fights to assert himself in the neighborhood or intimidate those encroaching on our territory. If he happened to find himself in the middle of a fight, he would withdraw rather than hit back, and he preferred coming to terms by talking rather than fighting with knives or stones. Maybe this was why he pioneered our use of the word titans as soon as he saw how strong they were. Their presence on our streets had a deep effect on him. He was very frightened of them and followed news about them in the newspapers he picked up. He kept an eye on them, but he also kept his distance and didn't try to approach them.

Life was monotonous in the camp. I made friends with one of the boys in the group to which Head Salem had assigned me. It happened without any planning during gym practice when it was his turn to carry me. When I was on his shoulders, he asked me my name. I was tongue-tied, not because I didn't want to tell him but because I had hardly said my name or heard it said since I had been in the camp, and it felt strange trying to remember it. I leaned my neck down close to his head so that he could hear my answer: "Rabie, Rabie al-Mahdi."

He looked up at me and said, "And I'm Saad. I don't know my father's name."

He and I became inseparable. We trained together. We sat on the same table at mealtimes and we walked to the dormitory exchanging news. There was plenty of Youssef about him: he was calm-natured, didn't swear much, and knew how to read. As far as I was concerned, that was enough to make friends with him.

Saad said he came from the east, and I told him I was from al-Ezba al-Mahsoura and that I knew kids from the shacks beyond the railway tracks and from the big open space, and others whose families lived on river boats. All of them had left their homes and moved into other areas. Some of them hadn't had homes in the first place. A few of us went to areas where rich people lived, where there were garbage dumps and the pickings were excellent. Most of us preferred middling areas, where people were more generous and less hostile to our presence. Some of the people there even put food and old clothes in bags and, when we were still asleep, left them for us to find in the morning.

The trust grew between Saad and me and it wasn't long before we agreed to call each other by our given names, as long as none of the other children in the group at the time were snitches. We were afraid of forgetting our real names, although we realized that names were no longer useful, since we rarely used them and the titans never uttered them. One of them would shout, "You body!" and we would all look around to see in which direction his head and eyes were pointing, or sometimes his finger, and we didn't wait to hear a name. The titan might mean one of us, or he might be addressing all of us. It made no difference. We are all "bodies" in their world, and now we are all "bodies" in the world beyond them too. We got used to being called bodies, and our real names faded away automatically. We started communicating with each other without names: "The barber's arrived . . . take your turn . . . pass me some bread from next to you . . . here you are . . . I hear you did well in yesterday's training . . . tell us what you did." That's how we started speaking among ourselves.

Saad and I tried to keep tabs on all the boys in our group and take note of every new arrival, so that no one could disappear without us knowing. Despite the titans, we also tried to remember the boys' names, so that they wouldn't be forgotten. We would recite the names to each other in secret, like some religious text.

*

The heads took turns lecturing us, either during the training sessions or in the dining hall. Head Allam spoke to us about culture and good and bad ideas. He brought up lots of things I had never heard of in my life, rather like the things that Youssef used to read to us, but more confusing and complicated. I felt very young and ignorant, and I was saddened when the head said that until they rescued us we had been living deep in the mud like worms. All my life I had imagined I knew things that ordinary people didn't understand properly. For example, I knew about the pills that the garbage collectors gathered from the dump and supplied to big dealers, who repackaged them and sold them to drugstores. I knew about the girls who shared the street with us and got pregnant and sold their children as soon as they gave birth. I also knew about organ dealers who came from time to time to buy blood and kidneys.

Emad, Youssef, and I know lots about the days of the first revolution, when the titans disappeared and big battles broke out in the main streets, around big buildings and their police trucks. We know about the fires that broke out in the ancient buildings and the treasures and important papers that caught fire there and that no one saved. We saw a fire start inside one of those places, as if some devil had lit it and disappeared. We also know what happened to the old museum. Youssef read to us about it being looted, from a newspaper he rescued from the garbage. He said a group of thieves raided the museum by night and damaged the contents. I remember well what he said about the mummy of a child pharaoh called Imhotep, who was on display among the mummies before the demonstrations. The thieves damaged the mummy and the government brought in a special team of famous scientists. They examined the mummy and managed to fix the breaks and the cracks and restore him to how he was. I was happy when I heard he was fixed. Youssef held up the newspaper and showed me a picture of the mummy laid out on an amazing bed.

The picture wasn't unfamiliar to me. It reminded me of something that happened to me and Emad. It was about two years ago, one night when we three were sitting on the sidewalk outside the museum. Two men appeared from the direction of the bus station and they seemed to be in a hurry. They were looking right and left, and then they turned toward the museum gate and disappeared into the dark. Emad nudged me and stood up, pointing to where the two men had disappeared.

"Let's go after them," he said. "We might find something useful."

Youssef objected and tried to convince Emad it was too dangerous. "We don't know them and they're not like us," he said. "They looked well-dressed. They might be museum staff. They might catch us and take us to the police station. They might even be plain-clothes policemen."

"So what? I'm going, coward," said Emad. "Stay with your magazine and I won't give you anything I get there. And you, Rabie, are you staying here too?"

I fought off my desire to stay with Youssef, in case Emad accused me of cowardice too. I stood up and joined him. It was silent. The place was frightening and almost dark and it had a slight smell of decay. We caught sight of the two men looking around with a light that one of them was holding. I think it was his mobile phone, but it was bright like a flashlight. They started picking up small things I couldn't identify and putting them in their pockets. I was reluctant to go further, but Emad didn't seem frightened of them. We moved closer until they saw us.

The short one was startled. "What are you doing here, you sons of bitches?" he shouted.

Emad swore back at him: "What's that to you, you jerk? You do your thing and we'll do ours."

"Piss off. Get out of my sight immediately, or else I'll leave a mark on your face with my switchblade."

Emad headed to the stairway, where the light was dim, and shouted out that we wouldn't be going away.

"We're not afraid," he told me. "We'll make a tour of the museum. We're just as good as them."

I felt a little braver, but I followed him slowly and warily. They were bound to be carrying a gun and they might shoot us, and no one would notice. The museum had been closed for days. The staff didn't come and go, let alone visitors. I tried to overhear the conversation between the two men as we moved away, but I couldn't catch anything at all. Actually, they didn't care whether we stayed or left. They were doing something that demanded their complete attention.

I looked around and couldn't see anything of interest. Old statues. Glass cases, some of them empty and some of them containing things that looked like spoons, but I don't know what they used them for, and some cross-shaped things. It would be best to leave, I told Emad timidly. He didn't object, though he was disappointed by the shabbiness of the museum: there was no loot, no treasures to be had. On our way out, Emad saw a corpse laid out. Its head was just a skull and the wrapped body was about our size. It was the body of a boy like us. Emad laid into it. He pulled at the shroud so violently that the body fell on the floor. The boy's skeleton came apart and the bones scattered. Emad said he had more right to the corpse's cloak, which was just tattered scraps, than a corpse that had no feelings. So he picked it up and walked on, with me behind him.

The Homeland Lecture

Head Allam said we would be really educated, outstandingly educated at the end of the rehabilitation course. He took charge of arranging the lessons and lectures we were given. He had a routine that never changed: he brought the guest who was going to speak to the hall, introduced him to us from the platform, then left the speaker and sat in the front row. No one sat next to him, and he listened to the talk without interrupting or commenting. When the lecture was over, he escorted the guest back to the door of the hall, shook hands with him and came back to us. On some occasions he asked us what we made of the lecture, and on other occasions he told us to leave without adding a single word. Most of our guests weren't heads, most of them came from outside. A fancy car would turn up and stop outside the hall. The guest would get out with the engine still running and the car would drive off like a rocket. Sooner or later the car would come back to pick up the guest and disappear from our sight in the flash of an eye.

On one occasion, on my way to the lecture hall I spotted some faces I didn't recognize; children walking side by side as if they had come from the same place. I followed them and noticed they were frightened and anxious. They didn't seem to be familiar with the layout of the place. I hung around at the door to the hall and looked at the kids going in. In an attempt to conceal my unease at the appearance of these strangers, I pretended to be a tough guy, outgoing and as enthusiastic as the boys who had more experience in the camp.

A man came into the hall wearing glasses with thin gilt rims. His face, his clothes, his shoes and fingernails all shone as if they had just been scrubbed. His eyebrows were thin and far apart. He was holding an open leather bag with a bundle of papers sticking out. As soon as his bald pate imposed itself on my consciousness, I remembered the madman who had wanted to kill us: Dr. Mukhtar. Dr. Abdel-Samie Mukhtar. The name was embedded in my brain, never to leave it and never to be erased.

Head Allam came in with him, as usual, and simply said, "Dr. Abdel-Samie Mukhtar, do you remember when we talked about him earlier? I'm sure you haven't forgotten him. He's come specially to see for himself what you've achieved and how you've managed to adapt to the camp and change into upright, well-integrated members of society."

I was stunned. The man himself had come to see us. Wasn't he afraid we might attack and kill him? Or maybe, under the protection of the titans, he wasn't afraid of anything and didn't expect to come to harm. We were all as silent as people on drugs. I was swept by a strange mix of conflicting emotions. I sat there on edge, torn between my desire to rip him to shreds and my curiosity to know what he was going to tell us, when he knew that we knew what he had almost done to us. If it wasn't for his stupid rotten ideas, we would still have been living in our garbage dumps and hiding places, with no complaints, no camps, no lectures, and no lessons. Abdel-Samie sat down robotically. He didn't greet us. He just went straight into the subject of his lecture. He didn't seem to recognize us at all, or to have done any research on us.

He started: "I intend today to talk to you about the country, because the country is everything. The country is the beginning and the end. It is the purpose that we serve and for which we make sacrifices. As the general always says, our country is the heart of the world. The general wants to produce a generation that is able to meet the requirements of society but is not a burden on it, a generation that takes the country forward and is not a wrecking ball that demolishes it. I want every one of you to become a productive individual who contributes to the progress and prestige of the country. That's the aim of us all, and for its sake we have to sacrifice whatever we possess, everything that is precious or valuable. We have to raise our country's status among nations, whatever the sacrifices."

Saad and I exchanged glances. Neither of us owned anything at all. What did this crazy guy want us to sacrifice? They had even stolen our names.

"Sacrifice in your case means toil and sweat, sacrificing that irresponsible freedom that made you like stray animals. I hear that one of you has fled the camp, ungrateful toward those who treated him so well. Certainly this is the kind of shameful behavior that betrays shallow thinking and short-sightedness, extreme stupidity in fact. Escape to where? What does he expect after his escape? And what will become of him in the years to come if he is lucky enough to survive. Someone with no purpose in life does not deserve to live. You used to live as parasites, like leeches, but now you have noble objectives and legitimate ambitions. You have advanced to a higher level and none of us would survive outside the camp. Make no mistake about it. Not a single boy will survive without a clear future or carefully planned objectives."

Abdel-Samie made a long speech, but there was nothing appealing about it. We were bored and we started to wink at each other. We mimicked the way he spoke and in the end he stood up and prepared to leave. His tone grew more and more threatening. "Don't forget, no one will give you another chance," he continued, reaching into his bag. "These papers contain some useful advice. Share them out between you and read them carefully."

He left with Head Allam and the pieces of paper were passed around. The boy sitting in front of me passed me one. I looked at it a while, but to me the letters looked like some mysterious code, so I just stuffed it into my pocket. I felt my good mood disappearing and changing into irritation. With his talk about the future and its threats, Abdel-Samie had distracted me. His speech had ruined my opportunity to join in with the laughs and jokes that filled the hall, and on top of that it had reminded me of my old friend Halim. I was shocked to realize I had forgotten about him completely and had no idea what had happened to him. He had slipped my mind amid all the turmoil we had been through.

Halim had disappeared when we were still in the street, before the titans came to get us. He had picked up his few belongings and gone off. Had he known what was going to happen? Had he been afraid to tell us? Halim had excellent intuition, but that was useless against the titans, because their intuition was superior and they had bigger brains. Even if he had known they were coming and had gone away to avoid them, he hadn't had a plan or an alternative. That idiot Abdel-Samie had hit the nail on the head: what kind of future would Halim have in life? He couldn't live on the garbage dump now that it was so dangerous, and he didn't have any other refuge. The schools wouldn't accept him and no one would adopt him of course. Halim was the youngest of us and, like Youssef, he didn't have any particular ambition he hoped to fulfill. He was too simple to have hopes and dreams. I went around asking Saad and some of the other kids who had a thorough knowledge of the places where Halim wandered and lived, but I didn't discover anything useful. I couldn't imagine where he had gone or how he had disappeared. I expected they would eventually catch him, because it was inconceivable that anyone could escape from the titans forever. There was nowhere to hide from them, not even at the bottom of the sea.

Halim defied my expectations and didn't turn up, but my nagging memory of him reminded me in turn of my mother's face. Did my mother, Firdous, know I was here? I hadn't visited her for months. She was bound to wonder where I had gone. Firdous was resourceful, yes, but she wouldn't find anyone who could tell her anything about me or where I was. We were all in the camp now. She wouldn't find anyone at the garbage dump, at the metro station, or near the tunnel. If she did perhaps come across Halim, he might have some information. He must have heard what had happened to us. I kept thinking about Halim. He might have persuaded the barber to pay him by the day for cleaning his shop or he might have found work at the tailor's. He wasn't as attached to the street as we three were. He was always of two minds about it. He came to the garbage dump and then left, staying with us for some days and then going back home, but he couldn't bear it there either. Once we visited his tin shack in the big open space near the railway line. His mother welcomed us and treated us to a delicious bowl of okra with hot peppers. The taste lingered in my mouth for ages and the sight of it haunted me for months to come. As soon as Halim saw my mother he'd tell her we'd been abducted. Had they abducted us or saved us? It didn't matter. We were here now and that was that.

Before we retired to the dormitories for the night, Head Allam mentioned the unfamiliar faces we must have noticed in the camp recently. He said new groups of boys had started to arrive from areas that were being double-checked to find the rest of us. My heart skipped a beat and I looked left and right. Some of the kids were mumbling softly and others were indifferent. A few showed signs of surprise and disbelief and I thought that, like me, they were looking for their friends among the newcomers, but none of us shared our thoughts with anyone else.

Head Allam ignored the looks on our faces and announced another piece of news that caught the attention of us all without exception. They were going to let us watch television, in order to develop and broaden our minds. At first we were quite ecstatic at the news. We stood on tiptoes as he explained that the Ministry of Social Welfare had decided to provide big-screen televisions and fancy reception equipment as its contribution to the rehabilitation program. The general had asked the minister to use his ministry's resources to make the program work as well as possible.

But my excitement was premature. It emerged that the televisions were meant for serious purposes and not just for entertainment, as I had hoped.

"You bodies won't be watching television like couch potatoes," the head growled as he prepared to leave. "You're responsible adults now and you'll have to think about what you see and work out what's good and what's bad. Listen to the news bulletin and in a while I'll start choosing important programs that are worth watching."

The plan took effect faster than we expected, and we sat with Head Allam in front of the television the following week to watch the nine o'clock news. He commented that the boy whose body they had found and whose picture was on television and on the front pages of the newspapers was the body who had left the camp soon after we arrived. We had a close look at the pictures as the newsreader read the news, but we couldn't make out anything. There was a decomposed body on the screen but the features weren't visible or the color of the clothes. The room was quiet: none of us shouted anything and there wasn't any commotion. I didn't feel as alarmed as I had been when he escaped. If I had seen the slightest sign of life in his face I might have been frightened, but he was very unlike anything living. He was more like the corpses of cats or mice that went stiff at the garbage dump. We would pick them up by their tails and throw them at each other for fun.

They put one screen in the dining hall and another in one of the lecture halls, but none in the dormitories. We took a liking to watching television every evening in the room where we had dinner, seeing the programs that Head Allam chose for us. The dining hall was more cozy and intimate. It was where we let out all the silly ideas and thoughts we'd saved up during the day, even if we often said the same things over and over. Over dinner we got things off our chests, chatted about the latest developments in the camp, and went over what we had heard in the lectures. Sometimes a small group of boys would break into a burst of extended laughter, for no apparent reason. It might have been because they wanted to challenge the strict rules and escape from the stifling atmosphere of surveillance. We set conditions for these activities: we wouldn't chat freely, laugh loudly, or push each other around unless the heads were out of the room. On rare occasions we stayed behind in the room: there would be fewer and fewer of us as time for lights-out approached, and those of us left trusted each other.

*

The training sessions continued and grew more difficult. My hands chafed and the dirty top layer of skin peeled off them; my palms were as red as ripe tomatoes. The slightest rubbing against the balls of my thumbs felt like a knife cut or a pin prick and made me start. As the resistance exercises and gymnastics continued, the redness darkened and my hands turned the same color as the raw meat they delivered to the camp kitchen every now and then, and the pain was unbearable. I noticed they were bleeding whenever I hung from the horizontal bar. Once I decided to let go of the bar before my set time was up. The titan didn't see me because he was too busy watching another boy who had lost his balance.

"You, body, you're not running after the jump," he shouted in his booming voice. "You're walking on all fours. You're a cripple. You'd be useless at anything, even cleaning up your own shit. Move your legs or you're in trouble."

Out of the corner of my eye I saw the boy trying to make more effort while he was being watched, and I realized that most of the other kids were trying to get out of the exercises. They all waited till Head Salem was distracted and then skipped a jump or a bend. But as soon as he shouted, "You, body!" they hurried to do the exercises as well as they could. However, as soon as the head wasn't shouting and a boy was sure that this time he had escaped the possibility of a scolding, he would look away so as not to attract attention, and then slack off again.

4

The Space

Things went smoothly in the Space, as Murad had arranged. He settled down to examining patients' eyes in a room that was medium-sized but so well-equipped that he was comfortable in his work. Shakir provided him with most of the equipment and supplies he might need, so he started work without delay. That said, he preferred to refer major procedures to the university hospital, where his students and assistants were based and where he continued to teach, going daily to the operating theater. Aida divided her days into three: the school, where she was taking part in preparatory meetings before the beginning of the semester; home, where she had to check up on Adam; and the Space, which she planned to explore, though it looked like that would take weeks, even with the new vigor that she felt.

Aida woke up after Murad left and stayed up late to eat the *suhour* meal before she began the next day's fasting. She was awake until the protesters gave the call for the dawn prayer. She prayed and then fell asleep. She breathed in the smell of clean fresh linen as she yawned and shook off her drowsiness. She smiled contentedly at how well she had arranged everything. She had used one clean sheet to cover the unsightly parts of the bed, which consisted of a mat and two blankets, and another to protect her from insects at night, because she couldn't stand heavy bedding in the summer. She had turned a third into a screen so that she could get changed behind it, and a fourth acted as the tent door. She had remembered to bring her own pillow, so she had everything she needed for a comfortable stay and she couldn't imagine anything better.

She lay down for some minutes, gathering her thoughts and arranging her schedule. Adam didn't need her to visit today: he had asked to spend the day with his cousins. She wouldn't go to school either; she had attended the meeting the previous day. Her morning began quietly; it wasn't packed with chores or appointments. She got up slowly, dressed languidly, and had a sense of freedom. She went out through the tent door with nothing particular in mind. She sought out the areas that were least crowded and was pleased to find for the first time an easy route to the podium, where people made speeches and announced news and the protesters gathered. The way wasn't marked of course, there were no signs on the ground or barriers, but the movement of people to and from the podium had apparently created and reinforced subtle markers.

On her way she ran into a young woman holding out a mobile phone toward an elderly man and asking him what he was doing in the Space. Aida hung around to watch what was happening, curious about the man. He didn't seem very talkative or eager to be recorded. He looked away, then turned his back on the woman and walked off without saying a word, as if irritated by her question. He soon disappeared from Aida's sight and a young man took his place. He looked like a secondary school student and, unlike the old man, his eyes sparkled with enthusiasm. He started describing his stay in the protest in great detail, explaining the demands of the Brothers and Sisters and the others who were there and calling for the return of the ruler who had been abducted. Aida followed the woman as she moved around in the crowd asking people the same questions. She finally went up to a middle-aged woman wrapped in black. Her face was plain, without make-up, and she looked severe, strong, and familiar to Aida. The woman said she came from home every day using two forms of transport, a bus and then a minibus, accompanied by three sons at various stages of schooling. Their father was dead, and the middle boy was blind and needed special attention from her. When the interviewer commented that she was surprised to find her in the protest, despite her difficult circumstances, the women replied firmly that she was in the Space like everyone else, supporting the abducted ruler and calling for his reinstatement.

Then she looked up to the sky, raised her hands and said, "O Lord, send him back safe and sound. Thwart the wiles of his enemies and grant victory to Islam and the faithful."

Aida gasped when she suddenly realized that the woman standing in front of her was her old friend Zeinab, who had studied with her for years at the College of Education. They had graduated in the same year, and then their lives had taken different paths and they lost contact. Her looks had greatly changed. She had lost her old cheerfulness and vivacity, and had acquired a severity and a gravity, but she could not forget her face. Zeinab walked off at a leisurely pace when the young woman left her. Aida hurried toward her and when they were face to face the woman looked at her expecting more questions. She soon recognized Aida and cried out in sudden joy.

"Would you believe it? Aida!" she said. "Is it really you? I never imagined we would meet after all these years."

"It's fate," Aida said with a laugh. "I saw you in the distance, Zeinab, and I couldn't believe it either."

They opened their arms and hugged warmly. They started asking each other what they had been up to in the past years, and then competed to remember funny stories from their hazy memories. Before they parted Aida described her tent to Zeinab, gave her her mobile number and made her promise to visit, accompanied by her sons, to spend a whole day with her.

After half an hour walking, her legs led her to a very noisy place. People were talking loudly, though shouting is rare during the daytime in Ramadan because it can make you even thirstier. She looked around to see what the fuss was about and noticed some pickup trucks not far off, loaded with long wooden poles and planks, and bags of sand and cement. Many coils of thick rope also caught her attention, of the kind used to tie pieces of wood together. On top of the load she noticed some young men who didn't look like building workers. They were sitting or standing as best they could among the piles of stuff and shouting at people to clear the way so that the trucks could reach their destination. Aida stepped aside, watched the trucks slowly moving, and counted them and the amounts of material they were carrying. She had the impression that a vast tower was going to be built in the Space.

Exhausted after hours of walking she retraced her steps and took refuge in the tent, awaiting Murad. But she soon felt bored, so she picked up one of the plastic seats they had rented from the tea man and decided to leave her private space and go out into public space. She sat outside and threw a passing glance at her tired feet. She was annoyed to find deep lines on the surface of her shoes and, on closer examination, patches that had lost their color and parts where the thin layer of leather had come off the surface. The shoes looked tired, though they had spent only a few days in the Space. She looked away from them and watched the people coming and going. If she heard a woman greet her, she returned the greeting. Since the start of the protest the women who had been there longest were driven by curiosity to reach out to any newcomers. She soon realized that these women, whom she had supposed to be unaware of her, did in fact remember who was living in every tent. They even gathered exhaustive information on all the neighboring families. Aida dropped some of her natural reserve toward strangers, though she didn't have any long conversations. The exchanges were brief, partly because most of the women hurried past her chair. To

Aida they looked as if they were on urgent missions. Finally Fayza turned up, like a gift from heaven. Under her arm she had a folded rug, decorated in bright colors. She was wearing a galabia that ended an inch from the ground and sandals that looked soft and comfortable but, as Aida sadly observed, allowed the dust to get to her feet.

"Peace be upon you, Aida. How are you today? I expect you're used to sleeping in the tent after all the days you've spent there," she said.

Aida returned the greeting. "All's well," she added. "I slept well yesterday, and everything's in good order thanks to you looking after us so well. We don't know how to thank you."

"Thank God Almighty. I saw you coming and going in the distance, then sitting alone on your chair, so I thought I'd drop by in case you need anything. It would also be a chance for me to give you this rug. It looks quite humble but if you try sitting on it you'll want one to take home with you. It's made of pure cotton."

Shakir's wife spread the rug out and invited Aida to sit on it cross-legged like her, and she did so. It had a pleasant coolness that was a relief from sitting in the chair, which was scorching hot from the sun, but it was hard to sit cross-legged when her skirt was tight at the heels. She had to make special precautions in case her skirt accidentally rode up her legs and revealed too much skin. Their conversation branched out into politics, gossip, and Aida's impression of the protest over the past few days. When another woman rushed past them, like the earlier women, Aida asked impatiently who they were, the women hurrying back and forth. She didn't know that some women protesters had been injured on a march in the morning.

As soon as she heard, she jumped up and offered to help, but Fayza sat her down and said, "Take it easy. That's something we've grown used to since the start. We've set up medical emergency teams. Every Sister knows exactly what she has to do. The volunteers divide the work between them, and most of them have plenty of experience and knowledge. They're nurses, doctors, and pediatricians, and the hospital opens its doors to critical cases."

"Have there been deaths? I mean, has . . . ?"

"No, thank God. The injuries weren't serious."

Aida went back to her chair, pulled her skirt down and said, "Today I saw lots of trucks carrying building materials, but I didn't know what it was for, because the tents are made of cloth and they don't need all those planks and metal bars."

"That's a stage the young people are building at the western end of the Space. Young people are impulsive these days. Since yesterday they've been rehearsing a play they want to perform in the coming months."

Aida looked relieved. "At that age our children always have different ideas from us," she said. "Take the school where I work, for example. We have lots of activities of this kind: concerts, plays, and singing, but of course under supervision so that it stays within the bounds of Islamic law."

"Shakir said they got permission from the man in charge of activities. At first he refused, but they argued with him for ages and eventually went over his head until they obtained agreement. Some of the hardliners here, in the Raised Banner but also outside it, don't like the idea, and they're right. I don't understand why the young people are wasting time and energy on these frivolous activities. Don't we have more important, more worthwhile things to do? Anyway, God guides those He wants to guide. I'll leave you now. I have to organize some things with some Sisters outside the Space."

The protesters sat and chatted at length on the ground between their tents. Most of them enjoyed the fresh air beyond the blankets and sheets that hung over the doors of the tents. They passed around boxes of dates and prepared to break their fast. Shakir, Fayza, Murad, and Aida settled down in a secluded spot with bowls of homemade food lined up close to them. Fayza took charge of the ladling and serving while Aida, who wasn't used to eating much at iftar, indulged in her favorite habit of asking questions, between mouthfuls of food, playing the role of student rather than teacher. The place still amazed her, despite all the days she had spent there: the faultless order and the strict discipline despite the vast numbers of people. Neither she nor the school management could achieve such discipline in a class of only seventy children.

What she admired most was the cleanliness, and she hoped it would continue. In the Space she didn't run into the piles of garbage that were a feature of the capital. No place in the city, rich or poor, was free from them. Even the fancy areas she knew were drowning in their own rubbish, attracting beggars and scavengers who went through the tons of refuse. More and more street children had moved in too. They had a recognized corner in every neighborhood, identifiable by the garbage dump that had recently sprung up there. When the garbage dump became a permanent feature, it meant they had colonized the place.

Aida swallowed a small piece of meat and asked, "What do they do with the rubbish? I haven't seen a single piece of paper on the ground."

Shakir took it as a compliment. He put his bread aside and started to explain: "We almost never sleep. At dawn the Brothers take turns cleaning the ground and sprinkling water to keep the dust down. The young guys compete to collect the litter into bags, and then the garbage trucks come regularly to pick it up."

Murad praised their efforts and seconded what Aida had said. It was obvious that they never relaxed, or things would have fallen apart. It was a performance that deserved admiration, and it was enough that Aida noticed it and praised it.

Shakir was doubly pleased, and Aida again expressed her surprise, "Can the garbage truck get in?" she asked. "Does the government let it in, as a favor to the protest? I mean, is the leader of the government with us? I mean, is he from the Raised Banner? Or have you made a deal with him somehow that activities in the Space will continue?"

This time Fayza took on the task of replying. She felt that the question implied an insinuation, and she embarked on a passionate defense. "Not at all, I swear," she said. "We don't know the driver and we've nothing to do with him. Would we bribe him, for example? And in Ramadan? Our rubbish is picked up during the night shift and the drivers change according to their shifts and schedules, which are prepared by their managers and have absolutely nothing to do with us. I really feel that God has set them up to work for us and made them cooperative, so that our struggle can continue, as a symbol of faith."

Aida didn't change the subject, but she wanted to hear her husband's opinion. "That's strange," she said. "What do you think, Murad? If the government wanted, the Space could be a giant rubbish dump by now, with these thousands of people here. But many days have passed and the place is still clean. It seems to be subject to some special authority!"

"The government might be worried diseases will spread and it would be difficult to control them, or the influential people who live around us are forcing them not to withdraw services from the area."

Shakir wiped his head with his hand and smiled dismissively. "I heard them say on television that there've been some cases of scabies here, and I laughed," he said. "They're the ones with scabies. But people who do their ablutions and pray, all they suffer from is high blood pressure and high blood sugar, or they have heart palpitations because of the enormous pressure they're under. I'm sure you agree with me, Murad."

"Haven't you thought they might use the drivers to gather information about the square?" asked Aida.

"Maybe, but we're not afraid of anything. Journalists come in and write about us. They even spend the night among us sometimes. Cellphones are recording and taking pictures and transmitting, and they can't be stopped. What more could the drivers add?"

The conversation continued when cups of tea and plates of *kunafa* arrived for dessert. They talked about aspects of the protest, while Aida's thoughts wandered to the image of the Space current among people outside—at school, in taxis, in the homes of certain acquaintances and relatives too. The image was a great exaggeration compared to what she could see. Anyone outside would think a second, parallel state had been set up here, with its own independent government and population. She had heard stories about an army being set up to protect the Space and goods being stockpiled in case of a long war with the government, and even crops being planted to make the Space more self-sufficient. There were stories about the murder of people the protesters saw as enemies. These stories seemed to be grossly exaggerated, but Aida's skeptical nature always made her think there was no smoke without fire. Maybe a small spark could explain a wealth of hearsay. She didn't want to get into a conversation that might put people in a bad mood when the occasion was so cheerful and pleasant. The time for that might come later. The protest would continue, and nothing on the horizon suggested that a resolution to the crisis was near.

A brown-skinned man appeared, middle-aged with a dark black mustache and thick eyelashes, almost bald. He spoke in an obviously southern accent, but he was wearing a shirt and trousers, unlike most of the protesters who had come from the countryside.

He stood halfway between Shakir's tent and Murad's tent and called, "Dr. Shakir, peace be upon you, *hajj*."

A few minutes later Shakir came out of the tent, smartened himself up and rubbed his eyes. He hadn't expected the man to come at this hour. "Welcome. You came quick, Saber. You don't seem to have much work today."

The man turned his large eyes to Murad, who strode up to find out who was calling. When Aida appeared behind Murad, the man looked down at his feet.

"For your sake, I postponed some jobs till after *suhour* and I thought I'd finish off your job first."

Shakir patted the man on the shoulder amiably. "May God reward you. We want to rig up an electrical connection from anywhere so that we can run the fan. It's hot in the tent, like sitting in an oven."

The man pointed to his right eye and then his left to tell Shakir that he was at his service. He put the toolbox he was carrying on the ground and set to work without speaking. Aida winked at Murad and he smiled back knowingly. Unlike other workmen, the man wasn't chatty. They had had headaches for the previous two months when they had the floors in their home renovated. The workmen wouldn't stop talking, given half a chance. Again and again they would talk about how clever they were, or offer suggestions and try to impose them on the client.

Aida leaned over to Murad and urged him to ask the man to set up a satellite dish and receiver. Part of her plan was to install a television in their tent. Life wouldn't be the same if they couldn't follow the news and it was difficult to go home every day to see what was happening. In fact it was impossible. She whispered to him that she wanted some news channels and wouldn't mind some old movie channels too for entertainment. Murad nodded and went up to Shakir to ask him what the electrician could handle.

As soon as he realized they were talking about him, the electrician replied without turning toward them. "I know about everything, sir, and I'm at your service," he said.

Murad explained what they wanted. Jokingly, and in anticipation of Shakir's reaction, he added: "And we don't want you to set it to the Archipelago Channel. We're tired of watching what it says about us. We'd like to hear something different. Could you handle the satellite connection if we brought the equipment?"

The man's face changed: apparently he was unhappy with the course of the conversation. He looked away and replied aloofly, "I really couldn't. It's not my line of business."

He plugged in the fan, which produced a searing blast of hot air, then he gathered up his tools, muttering away without looking at them. "What's wrong with the Archipelago Channel? It's better than the channels that have dancing and other indecencies. It's like you're not one of us, I swear to God."

Aida sat on the bed and leaned her head against the wooden pole, staring wide-eyed at her cellphone. The well-known television host Nanice al-Nahhas appeared on the screen, to present her program *Here's the Nation*. She was extremely agitated about the great scandal she had discovered: the scandal of people occupying the Space as if they were Hyksos invaders. Nanice invited viewers to watch some video clips exclusive to the program, so that they could see with their own eyes, without any mediation or guidance from her, that "the protesters were of two kinds," as she put it.

"There are wicked people, financed by the country's enemies, plotting to subvert the will of the people and restore the Raised Banner organization to power," she said. "And then there are ignorant poor people who have been tricked with money and food and who repeat like parrots that they want to restore the old ruler, unaware of the danger of doing so."

After a long introduction she said she would let the video speak for itself. As Aida prepared to watch, her head spun with many ideas about the scandal: the situation that the protesters had created definitely had various negatives, but these were side effects that were difficult to avoid. No one denied that the people living in the areas around the protest camp complained about the tents, which had become a permanent part of the scenery. They felt inconvenienced by the protesters' activities, which were unwelcome intrusions into their daily lives. It must have been very annoying: there was lots of noise, half the streets were closed, they could hardly find parking spaces, and they were forced to undergo searches whenever they came in or went out of the area. The security committees might soon assign guards to check them at their apartment doors or in the lobbies of the buildings where they lived. Everyone knew this. If Aida had lived near the Space she would have made a fuss too. She would have been irritated and angry and would have sworn at everyone, but it didn't amount to a scandal.

She thought of other things too, because they frightened her so much. They might have discovered hidden weapons, as people said, or people who had been beaten up and actually tortured. Although she was inclined to dismiss these stories, she felt compelled to think twice about the possibilities. It was true that she hadn't seen anything bad yet and the way the organization was running the protest seemed excellent to her, but the level of organization, ideal on the surface, might not reveal what was happening out of sight. It wasn't impossible that things would get out of control here and there. It was a large area and the people weren't one homogeneous block. Under these circumstances it wouldn't be easy to impose unanimous commitment to good practices.

The video began with the radiant face of a woman in her early twenties being interviewed by someone who wasn't visible in the picture. She was presumably a television reporter or part of the production team for Nanice's program. People were coming and going in the background, and there were faces Aida recognized walking briskly between the tents. The interviewer sounded distant, almost inaudible, but the sequence of confident and clear responses by the young woman made it easy to work out the questions.

"If we could be sure about our ruler's status and health, and confident that he's safe and sound, and if we didn't urgently need him among us as soon as possible, we'd tell him to stay where he is, and we'd be delighted."

"I've never seen such good behavior anywhere: no rudeness, no harassment, not a single case. Imagine, in this crowd, with people at very close quarters, the young men immediately clear a path for me or any other girl."

"Yes, the meals are free here, the refreshments, the snacks, and the fruit too. No one buys anything at all. No, I don't pay anything, and there's plenty of food—more than enough. Millions of meals come to the Space every day, God bless them. I go to the podium at noon every day, listen to the speeches, and read the Quran until iftar time, and then we eat. After that we pray together—the evening prayer, special Ramadan prayers, and night vigil prayers. We do that every day."

The video stopped and Nanice came back on screen, shouting in outrage. "Did you see that? Did you see how scandalous it is? This woman is a sample of the people in the Space. Most of them are naive and deluded. They give them food to attract them. She says there's free drinks, free fruit and meals, and in vast quantities. The woman's poor. She looks poor from her clothes. Of course there's nothing wrong with being poor, but it's wrong to exploit people's needs. And as the proverb says, "feed a man and he'll turn a blind eye." Those people you see in the picture aren't charged anything; they sleep, eat, and drink for free. Of course they won't turn down the opportunity. How can the state put up with this state of affairs? I don't see how we can stay silent and let them go on playing with people's minds. This ruler of theirs, the one who would have been a disaster if the general hadn't saved us, is he fit to govern a country as big as ours? People need to be enlightened. Look, and look again, and don't come and say we're making false allegations against them."

She waved her hand in circles and asked the director to rerun some parts of the video on free food. "Repeat it, please, repeat it so that anyone who wants can see it again," she said.

Murad came back from the special Ramadan prayers to find Aida still with her cellphone, looking angry. Before she could start complaining again about not having a large television set and how tired her eyes were from watching the tiny screen, Murad told her his news enthusiastically.

"Listen to this, I met two retired men who live in that tall building you can see there," he said. "One of them is a professor at my university. Shakir says that some of the local people come at night and spend time chatting till late. They have their *suhour* and then go home at dawn. There are more people than we expected who don't formally belong to the Raised Banner but sympathize with its position, like us."

Aida was still highly agitated and started waving her phone. "Tell that stupid woman she needs someone to explain to her that there's more to it than food and drink. There are people who find happiness in other things too—being neighbors and working together to achieve an objective that makes them feel strong and capable of changing things. Wasn't that the case during the first revolution? The simple people here are doing as best they can because they think it's the right thing to do, and if it comes to the crunch they'd be willing to give up their lives for the cause. Nanice has to admit that, even if she disagrees with them. The day before yesterday I saw with my own eyes women volunteers running to reach the casualties from the march for the return of the ousted leader. And the march started in the heat of the day when all the women were fasting! The women were attacked and beaten up and I don't think free food would be a very persuasive incentive for taking such a risk. We've been following things closely, you and me, haven't we, since the time when people first poured into the Space and started the protest? They weren't deterred by the threats or by the brutal way the police dealt with anyone who resisted. Weren't dozens of them killed in the first few days? We all knew the security agencies were working in concert again. They were back to playing the only tune they know, without a false note. It was no secret what their return meant, yet the protesters didn't run away or surrender. All for a meal and a fruit juice? They had come to defend a cause and support their leaders, and if they'd been told to go without food or drink for days, they would have done so. This television woman is stupid or she's paid by the government, but the trouble is that people outside believe it."

"What's new, Aida? The media feeds the people ready-made 'meals' and people lap it up, especially when it confirms their prejudices. But don't forget that it's frightening how they can get masses of people to behave the way they want, like machines. At this stage, the regime is using all the tools it has to break us. I only hope we can afford a confrontation, otherwise it will be a massive defeat that we wouldn't be able to sustain. Are you going home tomorrow? I need some clean clothes from there."

After about a week, Aida decided to take Adam with her to the Space. She checked the situation and was confident the place would suit him and be safe and there was no reason for him to stay any longer with his grandmother. He had shown himself willing, several times, to go and join his parents. His grandmother, for her part, could no longer put up with childish mischief and silliness at her age, though she didn't complain to Aida or Murad. It wasn't difficult for Aida to strike a deal with her son that suited them both equally. He could come with her as long as he set aside time for schoolwork and kept it up as long as he was there.

At midday Adam put on the bright and cheerful clothes he had chosen himself, as if he were going off to meet his friends. He said goodbye to his grandmother, who was torn between longing for a return to calm on the one hand, and sadness at losing the company he provided and the energy he brought to the house, on the other hand. She started to look anxious about his departure and emphasized that he and his mother should keep visiting her. She said she hoped to see them every weekend.

In the taxi that picked them up outside the big house, Aida told him again that he had to be patient and wait his turn at the checkpoints without grumbling, and that there were rules he had to follow and good manners he had to respect when among other people. He nodded in agreement with every word she said, and she smiled. She wasn't sure he had taken everything in or understood the situation, where they were going, or why she had moved there with his father.

Adam stepped forward in the line, then offered the bag to a woman in a niqab to open and look at the contents, as she had done with his mother.

The woman patted him on the head with her black gloves. "He must be your son, Sister Aida. It's amazing: he takes after you, and there's plenty of Dr. Murad in him too."

Aida was surprised that the woman knew her and her husband, since they weren't long-time residents. She thought she must be one of the patients at Murad's clinic, so she replied to the compliment in a friendly manner. "Adam's a copy of his father. He only inherited some of my traits, such as nagging. He wouldn't stop asking us to bring him to the Space, so in the end we gave in."

"God bless you, Adam. You'll be very happy here. We have games, swings, competitions, and lessons in memorizing the Quran and hadith. You'll find lots of children your age."

Adam said nothing and pulled on his mother's hand. The crowds on the edge of the Space made him feel uneasy, but the talk about great opportunities to play and have fun was enough for him to set his anxieties aside. He wasn't going to waste the remaining weeks of the holiday being bored. As soon as Aida took him past the entrance, young men came up and welcomed him with balloons, candy, and clapping. The idea was to give children a good initial impression of the place. Young members of the Raised Banner regularly adopted this method in order to draw people in, and Aida had liked it since seeing it for the first time. Adam didn't disappoint them either, or pretend to be shy. He put his hands out and took whatever gifts he could. He felt he had made the right choice: insisting on going with his parents had not been a mistake. He asked his mother to stop a moment while he put the gifts in his backpack, then he closed it tight and walked on proudly, refusing to let Aida carry it for him.

He went around with her for a while as she pointed out the Space's main landmarks. "Here's the shopping mall we visited two months ago with your aunt, and there's the big mosque, and next to it the hospital. And this, Adam, is the podium, where they broadcast songs and Quran and make speeches like the morning speech at your school. If you get lost and you can't find our tent, don't worry. Come to the podium and tell the man in charge of the loudspeaker, and he'll help you."

In the days after Adam's arrival Aida changed her habits: she had a strong sense of settling down and she no longer had to be anxious about visiting Adam. She gave up high heels and chose a pair of rubber shoes instead. She stopped wearing skirts and dresses and substituted cotton galabias that were looser and longer. In those she could move between the tents easily and take part in communal prayers from time to time. She could even sit on the rug Fayza had given her; she got used to it and didn't need a cover to hide her legs and thighs. She sat cross-legged, poring over her papers, checking the syllabus and planning lessons. When she stood up, the galabia fell down by itself, saving her the trouble of pulling it down. She kept some changes of formal clothes for going to school and back. Murad had done the same. Shirts with collars weren't comfortable in the hot weather, so he preferred simple cotton sportswear. He put aside his leather shoes and made do with light sandals. He finally got rid of the jacket and tie he continued to wear when he went to university. He left them in his car and put them on while on his way into the faculty and took them off as soon as he left.

Aida tried hard to ensure that Adam didn't feel lost in such a vast place, crowded with too many people to count. He was used to a quieter, more restricted lifestyle. His world was divided between home, school, and the boys' group he had joined under the auspices of the Raised Banner, and even that was a recent addition to his activities. Murad had relented after Aida repeatedly insisted that she wanted to develop Adam's love for Islam, in friendly surroundings that kept him away from bad company. She had also done everything possible to make sure he didn't get a bad impression of the protest, especially as there were aspects that might be hard to explain. She was frightened of finding that her sister was right. Her sister was opposed to the protest and had criticized her decision often. "What's Adam got to do with politics and government and rulers and the System?" she said. "He's too young to understand what's happening, so don't impose your opinions and preferences on him. Let him be." But Aida insisted on encouraging him to try the experience. In her defense she said he would definitely benefit from interacting with the wide cross-section of humanity that filled the Space. He would gain experiences that weren't available to many people. Besides, she didn't want him to form impressions based only on hearsay, when he could see for himself and judge. Yes, he was young but he was sensible and able to discriminate. She didn't want him to be deceived by the lies he heard. Her fears diminished and her expectations were met as time passed. Adam soon adapted to the place and made new friends there. He knew their families' tents and visited them without hesitation. He arranged to meet them and play almost every day, and his father agreed to take him to the fairground every weekend, where he and his friends would meet. Fayza was happy to look after Adam on the days Aida spent at school, and he helped her make the arrangement a success by being very adaptable.

Nothing is guaranteed of course, but Aida thought Adam was doing well and she was delighted that he had integrated without any problems into an environment completely different from the one he was used to.

A new assistant, Dr. Ibrahim, joined Murad on the recommendation of Shakir. He was a young bearded man in the prime of life, possibly in his late twenties. Superficially quiet, he rarely smiled or said much, and when he did speak, his words had a sad tinge of unknown origin, at least to his neighbors in the Space. His first meeting with Murad had been cursory; he greeted him and told him, in a sequence of short sentences, without being boastful or ingratiating, that he was still preparing for higher studies, that he had chosen to specialize in eye diseases, and that he was willing to handle some cases if there were any in the Space. That's all he said. Despite his bluntness and his social awkwardness, which was so unlike Murad, he got a job in the clinic. Murad accepted him, welcomed him without affectation, and didn't try to find out more about him immediately, preferring to test him in practice and let the long hours they were going to spend together take care of the personal relationship between them.

At first Ibrahim was responsible for deciding which patients needed simple surgical procedures. Murad asked him to put them in categories and send them to him with a summary of the case. Then he gave him more tasks: he referred some cases to Ibrahim and watched him examine the patients and prescribe medication for them. Once he was sure that Ibrahim knew the basic skills and could work alone, he left him to handle patients in the same room in parallel. After a while Ibrahim suggested installing a portable screen that would partially separate them, especially as many women refused to come in if the other patient was a man, and that was done. Ibrahim started to work like crazy, tacitly competing with Murad. He was both embarrassed and gratified by the praise he received, and this helped to make him more easy-going. Despite the progress Ibrahim had made, Murad still had more patients than him: people asked after him and sought him out by name, and wouldn't be satisfied with anyone else, not because there was anything wrong with Ibrahim but because they felt he didn't have enough experience to do quick and accurate diagnoses or know how best to treat them. Ibrahim understood that he wouldn't learn such things in lecture notes or by hiding away and reading books. He followed Murad intently, and gradually grew close to him.

5
The Training

MANY DAYS PASSED. I DON'T know how many. I started to forget the faces of Youssef and Emad, despite trying to remember. The boys that were in the camp stayed and new groups arrived, but there was no sign of Youssef or Emad. I really didn't know where they had gone. The titans had grabbed us off the ground together and carried us to the truck. The last I heard from them was when they were swearing and shouting. I didn't understand why they hadn't turned up after all this time. I hadn't shed a tear for them since the dreadful day we were abducted, and now I couldn't rule out the possibility they were dead. That idea pushed me into a deep pit whenever it crossed my mind. I couldn't believe I wouldn't see them again. For ages I had tried to be patient. I had dismissed my pessimistic thoughts and pulled myself together so that I wouldn't cry for them, because crying might be a bad omen. When I finally decided to cry, I couldn't. It was very annoying. Eventually I burst into tears after thinking about their death in a rather strange way. I don't know exactly how it happened. Maybe I was thinking about them during the training when my foot slipped and I fell. Instead of my hand catching hold of the wooden beam, my foot caught on it. I saw everything upside down and I panicked. I had seen the world upside down before and I didn't like what I saw. I saw the garbage dump and my friends and I smelled the same rotten smell. It was like I'd gone back in a time machine. I tried to shake my leg free and then, as my hopes of success waned,

I noticed water flowing down my face toward my forehead. I could cry: not in ordinary situations, but in one place and no other—when I thought I was in the garbage dump.

I bent my arms and then straightened them. I did thirty push-ups in quick succession. My performance had improved in spite of myself. On the thirty-first push-up Head Allam was nearby. We started the count again: zero, two, four. I summoned up all the strength I could muster to make him look away quickly. I went down until my nose touched the ground, then pushed myself back up in the air. While I was busy trying to impress him, I overheard Head Salim having a quiet conversation with his colleague.

"Allam, the lectures by Sheikh Abdel-Gabbar and his men work like magic on the bodies. I've noticed the amazing part they play in raising their morale. Of course they never disobey orders and in training they always do exactly what I say, but there was a massive difference between their performance before and after the sheikh's last lecture. Before the lecture they obeyed me rather halfheartedly. If I said, 'Get up, body,' they would get up. If I said, 'Lie down,' they would lie down. If I said, 'Stand up and attack,' they would stand up and attack, but after the lecture they were much more energetic and violent. It was like they were in a real battle. Sheikh Abdel-Gabbar convinced them with his measured words. A punch from one of them was like being hit by an artillery shell—quite different and unexpected. The final word will come after the program has been assessed scientifically of course, but for now we should take advantage of the influence the sheikh has over them when he quotes verses of the Quran and hadith to them. We must also give them incentives from time to time, because they lose focus as time passes and their enthusiasm wanes."

"What are you doing, stuck to the ground, you body?" he said, turning to me. "Have you fallen asleep? Or do you like the taste of dust? Have a mind to taste it again?"

I was in a really strange situation. I had been distracted when I heard them talking. I was lying on the ground and I didn't stand up at the count. I just lay on my stomach. I was told off as usual, despite my enthusiasm. I got up quickly and carried on with the exercise without speaking. I smiled slightly to myself. My hearing was still as acute as ever, even if I was no longer living on the street. My ears could pick up any whisper, the very slightest noise. People didn't envy me my hearing without reason. Thanks to that, I knew we'd often be seeing Sheikh Abdel-Gabbar.

General Ismail came to visit us one day at six o'clock in the morning, while we were doing warm-up exercises and getting ready for weapons training. We were surprised to see him, since we hadn't for a long time. We knew he had masses of things to keep him busy and awesome responsibilities up and down the country, so he didn't have many opportunities to keep up with events in the camp, or time to meet us as he had promised. The general told Head Salim to continue with the training, so all of us tried to look tough and skillful in front of him. The general watched us with a strange expansive smile. The head stopped us a few minutes later and we were dripping with sweat. We noticed the general had his arm raised to say he had seen enough from us.

We stood to attention like soldiers. The general opened his mouth and let out a long sigh. He looked around at us, one after another. Then his mouth closed, the sigh ended and he fell silent for a minute.

"I'm proud of you," he finally said. "You are truly my children, the children of the System. It's shocking to think back to the way you used to be, to think that you came from the streets, but now I can truly say that all our young people should be like you. We're now under attack abroad and at home, so don't listen to the rumors our enemies spread. Their aim is to destroy the country and undermine the System. They don't wish the state well. What is their aim? I want to hear you say what their aim is."

To our surprise we were expected to answer, so we just repeated after him, "To destroy the country."

He put his hand on my shoulder, since I was closest, and asked again, "What's their aim?"

I shouted the answer to show him how enthusiastic I was, and Saad had to hold back a laugh. I must have looked pathetic, like a kid sitting in class at school.

"Obedience is the most important thing. Children obeying their parents, of course, as the Good Lord says in His book. I know that in your childhood you didn't have anyone to look after you or sympathize with you, but that's all in the past. Have you noticed? That's for sure. Have you seen how much I care about you? I'm determined to watch over you and save you from going astray and destroying yourselves, and from evil people. You understand, of course, you understand. The people," he chuckled a few times, "they won't give you a second chance—the ones who hunted you."

"I have a heart big enough for you all," he added, his eyelids drooping a little. "All I ask from you is trust, honesty, obedience, and loyalty. Those are the most important things, and I hope you'll be able to take your country forward, to make it great again and give it the place it deserves among the nations of the world. What kind of nation?"

This time we answered without him having to repeat the question: "A great nation!"

The general and Head Salim took us out to the shooting range. We formed lines and there was a row of black guns of a kind we'd never seen before. They had long barrels so big that the bullets must have been the size of fat weasels. Head Salim ordered the kids in the front line to pick up the guns. He went around them one by one adjusting the position of the gun in their hands and on their shoulders, while the general nodded with pleasure whenever a boy stood properly with his gun, and clapped with satisfaction whenever one of us picked up the gun and held it properly in a standing position at the first attempt, without need for instructions. Head Salim looked as grumpy as ever, though he forced a small smile from time to time. They only asked us to take the ready-to-fire posture. Neither of them asked us to pull the trigger.

After that we moved to the hall, where Head Allam told us to leave the front five rows empty and remain completely silent. "General Ismail is going to make a speech, an educational lecture for an audience of heads. You're only allowed to listen. No questions of any kind, and no hands raised."

That suited me fine. I'd had enough of repeating words after him and I had no desire for more questions or answers. The general didn't change much between visits, though he didn't come often. Something about him made me feel drowsy, his voice, but he also inspired a vague fear in me. I leaned over toward Saad to whisper something, but then the heads filed in and the general mounted the platform. Craning his neck to look over the seated heads, he examined us inquisitively, as if we hadn't been there minutes earlier.

"You've been out on assignments, yes? Haven't they been out yet, Head Salim? Never mind, they'll go out soon. No hurry. Anyway, you've been here long enough to know that we follow a philosophy that's been well thought out, and that the missions you are training for and that we insist you carry out, are more important than any other task you've ever performed, or even imagined you would ever perform."

He went back to looking cheerfully at the front seats.

"Heads, good morning, I've disturbed you coming so early today. Forgive me. I'm sorry, but I wanted to address you, from here in particular: our second or first home." He chuckled again. "I'm addressing you. Yes, you are the righteous heads that our country needs. You are the pillars of the System, an inseparable part of its project. We all know that a government can be stable and sound only when those in power shoulder their responsibilities and show resolve and authority. We have succeeded so far. For sure we have succeeded. As you all know, if a ruler fails to impose his authority and cannot keep a tight grip, the state collapses. We don't care about ourselves. We only care about our country and our people. If the state goes to ruin, God forbid, the ones affected are the citizens themselves, the citizens. You have to understand that none of us are worth anything. We're not worth anything without the System! And who's going to impose strict order? We are the ones. There are people, our own people, who don't know many things, and so they need help. They need direction and guidance. There are also people who are against us. Yes, against us. But at the first sign of trouble, they're terrified, very terrified. They come to us begging for help, but what can I say? That's what they did when they were tricked by the followers of the last ruler. I won't mention his name. You know who he is. So we agreed to help. We always have to be willing. We stripped him of power by the will and command of God Almighty, without whose will and command nothing can happen. We installed another man we know well. We trust him, and the most important thing is trust. Why? Because we love this country. We love your country, the country of us all.

"Children at the back of the hall, you too must know that prestige comes from strength. You have to be strong. Strength, morals, and faith." He clenched his fist and raised it in the air. He waved the fist and said, "Those who desire evil have no morals. No morals and no conscience, no religion either, I tell you, they have no religion, and we can wipe them out and protect people from them." Saad rubbed his hands together as if killing an insect, and sneaked a malicious smile. I nudged him gently to make him stop joking and leave me alone to listen.

"I salute you for your courage, for the progress you have made, and your sacrifices. Don't let anything hold you back or prevent you from achieving our national objectives. No doubt we will take the country forward, through the will and power of God, despite the difficulties, because God is always on our side."

"Clap, Rabie. Why aren't you clapping with enthusiasm? Smile, because the general might see you with that miserable expression on your face. Clap, brother. What harm will clapping do?"

I followed the advice of Saad, who had started clapping as soon as the speech was over. I applauded too, long, sustained applause, and I was the last to stop, but my clapping was lukewarm and half-hearted. There was an invisible wall between me and the general, and I had definitely decided I preferred heads Salim and Allam, despite their roughness, although most of the kids were enthralled by the general. They talked about him when we were sitting together and made up fanciful stories about his brave deeds standing up to the country's enemies, setting an example with his bravery and by risking his life. They didn't forget his kindness, or how he had defended us against the others. For them he played the same role as the older street thugs had done, and they made him into a role model. They tired themselves out imitating him and, like kittens, lost themselves in trying to please him. Did they really like him? Some of them looked out week by week for a sign that he was coming, and if he came, they hoped that he would give them an encouraging look or a gesture of approval. They really were his kids, and when they praised his exploits in unison, I looked like an orphan. After that speech I walked away slowly with Saad.

"Tell me, Saad," I asked, "what did he mean? And what happened to the ruler and his group?"

"Didn't you know? He disappeared, like the kids who have disappeared from here."

"I know he disappeared, but where did he go?"

"I told you. He disappeared, vanished into thin air. And he was replaced by someone the general likes. But don't bring that up. It's a dangerous subject and just causes trouble. If one of the other boys hears you, you'll end up locked up in the isolation room. Or maybe you'll end up in the same place as the boys who've disappeared, and then you'll find out where they've all gone."

Saad laughed as he answered me, but I was very serious, tense too. I felt alienated whenever the general visited. I thought I might like him like the others if I could understand what he was saying.

"What did the general mean by governing and authority, by nation and order?" I asked, ignoring Saad's cheerfulness and flippancy. "I understood from what he said that they're different names for the same thing. Do they all mean our country?"

"What's all that to you? Are you going to stand for election and put up posters in the streets?"

"Enough of all that then, but tell me, what were the plans he mentioned?"

"Well, you've got the rehabilitation program that we're in, and Dr. Abdel-Samie's project too. One of them rehabilitates us, and the other exterminates us and buries us."

In high spirits, Saad kept joking and shrieking with laughter, while I kept asking questions, but without receiving a single satisfactory answer. My need for Youssef hadn't diminished; I hadn't outgrown my dependence on him. He would have explained complicated things to me in simple terms, without annoying me or making fun of me.

Another question occurred to me and I couldn't resist asking it: "Are you afraid of the general, Saad?"

"I'm afraid of him and not afraid of him at the same time. That's the truth."

Saad paused for a moment and his smile was replaced by a thoughtful frown. "I am afraid, Rabie," he finally replied. "But being afraid is all we do here. There's something about him that repels me, so I don't mind making fun of him either.

I get lost in what he says whenever he meets us, but I can't relate to him, no matter what he says. Like me, you may have noticed that what the heads say is easy to understand. They shout and give orders. They either forgive you or punish you, and you don't have to think too much. You don't have to think at all. With them, white is white and black is black. They say exactly what they want from us, with no room for guesswork, and no room for choice even. But the general's different. He doesn't say anything clear. He repeats himself and goes around in circles with no result. My head spins like yours. I try hard to follow, yet every time he meets us, it ends without me understanding the purpose."

"What's all this about strength? Who's strong and who's weak?"

"No, you're making too much of it. Don't trouble your head, Rabie. There's no point in questions and answers anyway. Nothing will change even when you understand. Your problems won't be solved, believe me. This is the only thing that's certain, not just a matter of probabilities."

I walked on in silence, but my thoughts were not silenced. I was convinced that Saad didn't like the general, and I assumed that Youssef would share my feelings about him. My questions piled up. Whenever I sought an answer to a question, it produced another question. And with every word my mind came up with, a forgotten incident flashed up, taking me back to my early years. Who could I trust now, and who trusted me? Should I trust Halim, who had left us in the garbage dump? Should I trust Firdous, my mother, although she left me to the streets? Maybe I should trust the heads because they were the strongest. Are only the strong worthy of trust, while the weak can't be trusted? I'd known a long time that the weak don't trust anyone, and they can't be trusted either. That's how things were in the streets.

Under my breath I said, "I trust Youssef and Emad, but Youssef is weak and Emad is the opposite." How could that be? Youssef dreamed of writing stories, and Emad dreamed of being a titan. I just liked their company and I didn't tell my secrets to anyone else. I continued to trust them although they were complete opposites. I never told one of them anything I'd hidden from the other. It's true.

"You're talking to yourself now," said Saad. "You'll go mad, Rabie, and our situation here doesn't allow for madness. Next time don't listen to the general. Block your ears and just listen to the heads."

I held my tongue and made sure to keep my mouth shut so that Saad wouldn't bother me and stop me daydreaming about old memories that sprang up without warning. Emad always liked to follow the titans. He dreamed of wearing a security forces uniform and helping them teach criminals a lesson, but his dream was very far-fetched, so he picked arguments with everyone he came across and got into fights. He played the hero in them, in the hope that his dreams would come true. I think they were real in some sense. He protected us and no kids dared approach us when he was around. Youssef was offended by his manner, but he managed to avoid him and his trouble making. He left him to the difficult task of defending us and the area, but kept well away from him, doing good deeds and being a daydreamer. Youssef remained an observer on the margins, maybe because he was convinced there really were other possibilities or because he despaired of convincing Emad of his ideas and winning my support—that was also a possibility. Anyway, he continued to spare us his annoying thoughts and made sure not to say anything to upset Emad. Youssef was too clever to make Emad angry, and Emad sought out other friends who would encourage him, friends who raided the nearby dumps with him, helped him in arguments, and tried to be tough like him. One day Youssef started telling us stories he had made up about us, with places, characters, battles, and heroes drawn from his fertile imagination. There was always a place in them for friendships and betrayals too. Surprisingly, Emad was crazy about them. He asked Youssef to repeat them to us day after day, without caring how he was portrayed in them, whether as good or bad. Youssef told Emad he was now like Abu Zayd al-Hilali, the ancient adventurer about whom endless tales are told. Emad was delighted, even more so when Youssef told him about Abu Zayd and his exploits and glories.

I knew about Abu Zayd when I was young. Firdous told me about him, and about a man with a fiddle who went around the country telling stories about him. She had never seen the fiddler herself, but my grandmother had told her about him and taught her some stories about him. Year after year she promised my mother she would see him. My grandmother turned gray and died. My mother grew up and left her hometown, got married, settled down in the slums and had children. She never forgot the stories and she passed them on to me, her youngest son. It felt as if she were entrusting me with an important secret, a family heirloom I should memorize and recite, maybe the only heirloom she had acquired and could pass on to me. In fact, Abu Zayd and Emad had nothing in common, except that they both appeared in stories—Abu Zayd in the backstreets and coffee shops, Emad in the garbage dumps and shantytowns.

I came around from my reverie when Saad hit me on the shoulder. "Have you woken up from your daydreams and will you eat with me? Or shall I go alone?"

"No, I'm very much awake. I'll eat with you, but I won't fill you in on any of my daydreams, even if you beg me."

"All the better. I'm hungry and I don't want to lose my appetite because of you."

We went into the hall and each of us took a box. Then we sat down with our faces turned to the television screen, which was on, unusually since it was only midday. Saad ripped off the top of his box and had a good look inside. He pointed out that the meals had gotten bigger and I agreed. I watched Head Allam walking around between the tables with his piercing eyes, like an examiner watching schoolchildren on a surprise patrol during exams. Maybe he was checking to see if the extra food was enough to fill us, or if we would leave any of it in the box, in which case he could reduce the meals to their original size. Maybe neither. Maybe he only wanted to sound out our impressions of the general's visit. Saad looked away from me to the television, so I looked up at it too. The general's face filled the screen. He looked as red as his carefully knotted red tie. Words flashed over his suit and then disappeared. I couldn't read well enough to make out a single word. Within moments the pictures started changing, against a background of powerful music that sounded like a war march. Then that stopped and a reporter appeared in the street, asking people what they thought of the new ruler's achievements. People replied in the same vein: "The general's the bravest man in the country. He put his neck on the line for us"; "The general saved the country from a terrible fate. Who knows what would have happened if the old ruler had stayed on? It would have been a disaster, but God was kind to us"; "No one loves the country as much as the general. We support him a hundred percent and we're with him whatever he decides. Hopefully we'll stand on our own two feet again and defeat that dastardly Raised Banner organization. With our lives and our blood we'll defend you, General."

The children in the hall perked up in when he mentioned "the rehabilitation program," described as one of the new ruler's greatest and most important projects. We saw a live picture of the general on the screen, with tears in his eyes, shaking his head as he spoke about the dire state the country had reached in a year of misrule by the old ruler.

He quickly dried his tears and smiled. "Don't worry. We have a packet of measures and projects that will put us back on the right track. The first, hopefully, is the Children Are the Heart of the World project. We've been planning it for months, but I wanted to make it a surprise for you. Happy? I'm sure you're happy. This project will take a huge burden off the shoulders of poor families, and of the state too. We're going to rehabilitate our homeless children and give them a sound, disciplined education."

The channel went back to shots of the reporter and the people gathered around him. It zoomed in on the face of a woman spouting prayers for the general. "May God protect you, just as you protect our children. May God be generous to you, just as you are generous to the poor."

"Is the general the new ruler?" I whispered to Saad. He said nothing.

We finished off the food in the cartons, leaving only the paper that was shiny from the fat it had absorbed. If we could have stopped the fat running out of the hamburgers and into the paper, and then drunk it ourselves, we would have done so at once. If they had given us ten cartons each we would have finished them off and drooled for more. We ate as if we were making up for what we had missed in past years, and the training, all that jumping and running, must have had a major effect on our appetites too. The television program ended and the picture of the general disappeared, but Head Allam didn't disappear. He stayed in the hall and didn't tell us to leave or turn off the television. Resignedly we stayed where we were, hoping he would ignore us for a while. He pulled out a chair and sat down. He showed signs of being preoccupied, and an uncomfortable and portentous silence fell over us. Eventually he dismissed us and we hurried to the dormitories exhausted.

I got into bed without taking my clothes off. I put my hand in my pocket to empty it out, and took out a folded piece of paper. I opened it and remembered it immediately. It was the instructions that crazy Abdel-Samie had given out to us, like the instructions you find on the back of exercise books at school.

"Are you asleep, Saad?" I said. "Can you read this piece of paper? Let's have fun with it a while. I no longer feel sleepy."

Saad sat up and took the piece of paper. He looked hard at it and then started to laugh, as cheerful as he had been earlier in the day.

"Have a listen to this: 'A proper upbringing from childhood is fundamental, especially as the country goes through such difficult times. Neglect for children and indifference to education do great harm to the individual and society. The state acts as father to the people, so its rules must be obeyed and respected. Every individual is a soldier who makes sacrifices for the sake of the country, and personal needs should not be taken into consideration, only the interests of the state and of the whole. Freedom has limits and rules, and in crises no form of freedom can be demanded, because freedom leads to chaos. The streets are a source of danger. In vulnerable societies, they must be under the complete control of the security forces. The phenomenon of homelessness must be eradicated, and the homeless moved to isolated areas so that they do not contribute to the destruction of society by spreading diseases and propagating the values of irresponsibility and degeneracy. The corrupt elements who cannot be reformed must be uprooted and eliminated at any price.' What's wrong with that? Now you know what the piece of paper says, so you can sleep with an easy mind."

"Abdel-Samie hates us, and I hate him," I said. "What does he know about being homeless and living on the street? He has his house, his car, his books, and his papers. None of us dispute his right to them, so why does he dispute our right to our way of life?"

Saad laughed again, though he lowered his voice so as not to wake up the other boys. "The man's interested in us. He's still planning our future. Sometimes he submits his plan to the ruler, and sometimes he gives it to us direct. He's like the history teacher we had in the first year of middle school. He gave us a sermon whenever possible and reminded us we were bound to be punished. Whenever we managed to find a way around his orders, we heard him threatening us. His last words were always, 'As you do, so shall you be done by.' He repeated it to us a thousand times. Do you understand it?"

"No, and I don't understand what Abdel-Samie says, but I've worked out what annoys me about him."

"Go on, say it. Today's your day. Even if you keep us up all night. I'm listening."

"You know what, Saad? I feel I'm missing many things here, and I don't know how to describe them. I have food and clothing and I don't have to rummage in trash cans. But I'm not the same as I'm used to being. In the street that so upsets Abdel-Samie I had advantages that ordinary people don't have. I lived on my own terms and I wasn't afraid of anything. Could I see that the people coming and going looked at me with disgust? I could. But also with admiration! Don't laugh. I'm sure the boys and girls whose families pulled them along by their arms crying, and denied them the pleasures of the street that we enjoyed, looked at us with envy and secretly hoped their chance would come and they could be in our place. Then they could do what they liked, beyond the control of any other human. In this camp, which Abdel-Samie praises so highly, I've lost my sense of superiority. Imagine, in the street I thought I was on top of the world. I inspired fear in many people, but now I'm the one who's afraid."

One day Head Salem ended the training early, saying there was a very important lecture that we had to attend. It must have been, or else he wouldn't have pushed us into the hall before we'd even done shooting practice and had lunch. Head Allam went on ahead, accompanied by a middle-aged man who seemed to be in a hurry.

He was about to start speaking to us before we were all there, but the head stopped him and introduced him to us. "This is Dr. Abdel-Qawi Azzam, an eminent legal scholar and a lawyer of wide repute who is assigned the most difficult cases and who has experience in international affairs. Listen carefully and we'll have another session after dinner for further clarification."

The Conspiracy Lecture

"Good morning, I'm delighted to be here among you today. I'm Dr. Abdel-Qawi Azzam, the head of the Social and Criminal Studies Center and a university professor. I was honored to be a member of the advisory council that recently studied children in your situation. Recently, by coincidence, I've also been supervising a doctoral thesis that contains a whole chapter about you. Without going into too many details, that's why I was interested in talking to you. The student who's writing the dissertation is studying the organizations and civil society groups that operate in secret and catch young people in their snares. In short, dubious organizations. They trick people they think are weak or have bad intentions. They have many methods for doing this, and they constantly exploit legal loopholes to avoid any oversight by the security agencies.

"I'll take you back a little, so that you can understand the subject and learn about all aspects of it, right from the start. Among the general's instructions, we received an order to carry out a quick survey to find out how many of you there are in the whole country, east and west. We sent requests for statistics to the entities and institutions that have dealings with you. Most of them cooperated and sent us what we needed, and even more than we needed. Even the cleaning companies that employ you illegally complied with our request. They sent lists of your names. Amazingly, some of the organizations that claim to look after you refused to provide us with information. Then, after investigations, it emerged that many of them are involved in illegal activities and have aims that are nothing to do with helping you.

"Do you know Amina Shaaban? I'm sure some of you know her. Unfortunately we discovered that her organization is an example of the ones corrupting and misleading young people. She's a cunning woman and extremely wicked. Her only concern was to poison your minds and exploit you to damage national security. This woman, and there are many others like her, owes allegiance to foreign powers conspiring against us. She receives bags of money from them. She is now being held to account for the crimes she has committed. She will get her just deserts and she won't be able to harm other children."

Amina? Of course I know Amina. I said to myself. But does he mean her, or someone else?

"You may not know it but you were on the verge of getting involved in crimes that could have put you in prison until your dying day. So I was anxious to warn you. You should also be aware that these diabolic 'rights organizations' didn't defend you when the ruler was about to approve the plan to get rid of you. In fact, they started defending people's right to a clean and healthy life at a safe distance from your filth. They benefited financially from having you with them, and at the same time they worked against you.

"You're not to blame, of course. No one showed you what's beneficial and what's harmful. That information isn't available to everyone, but you have to understand that ignorance of the law is no defense. From now on you have no excuse, so listen carefully to what I say. You're safe as long as you stay loyal to the country, keep your eyes wide open for any tricks, and are wise to foreign conspiracies that hide behind façades that look sincere and honorable to those who do not know."

I hoped we would see Amina in the camp. She'd definitely come up with new ideas for how we could avoid all the orders and the training and the lectures they forced us to hear. Amina always knew how to get things done. Youssef was the first to meet her, at the big gray bins. As usual he was looking for books and pieces of paper. Maybe she had been watching him for a while and knew what he was after, because she waved some books and pens at him from a distance. Youssef reacted immediately and walked toward her. She offered him the things she was holding and asked him his name and where he lived. When he was evasive she shrugged her shoulders and left. She made another visit about a week later but found me instead of Youssef. I recognized her from his description and from the books she was holding. I waved to her and shouted that Youssef hadn't come today. I offered to take the books and give them to him.

"I'm Amina, and who are you?" she said.

"I'm Rabie and I don't have a home."

She laughed, said she would come back another time and asked me to pass the books safely on to Youssef. She only learned his name from me. From a bag on her back she took out a sealed carton of fruit juice and threw it to me. I caught it and stepped back next to the bin. I pulled the straw off the carton and stuck it in the small hole covered in silver foil. I wrapped my lips around the straw and started to suck up the sweetness, without stopping until the cartoon made a slurping noise. I threw it away and looked for Amina, but she had disappeared.

Amina often visited us after that. She started talking to us about the importance of education, qualifications, and university. She listened patiently to what was on our minds. She wasn't snobbish and she didn't tell us off or treat us with contempt. She brought story books and crayons and drawing books and sometimes she brought us blankets in the cold, and woolen socks and gloves, and she didn't ask for anything. I introduced her to our group. I spoke to her about Emad and she saw Halim with us several times. Halim and Youssef were the ones closest to her and they appreciated her gifts. She included them in sessions where she read to Halim and asked him to say back to her what she had read. Or she would listen to Youssef reading and trying to act out what he read. Emad and I didn't need exercise books or pens. Emad went off to look for someone who could supply him with a gun. It was his treasured wish to own a gun, which would give him the upper hand if he ever came into conflict with the other kids. I happily started hanging out with Amina. I liked talking with her, I was relaxed about her and her interest in us, but I didn't do the things that would have made her happy. I didn't draw or learn anything, and I showed no interest in reading.

When we became friends, I told Amina about the big fancy cars that had started visiting us every now and then. Men and women got out of them and wrote down our names and ages and the addresses of those of us who had homes. They gave us salty crackers and sometimes triangular wedges of processed cheese. They asked us lots of detailed questions, most of which we didn't answer, and then they would offer to take us off with them. I asked her if she worked with the people in the cars, and she denied it. She advised me to run away as soon as the cars appeared and not to give any information about myself or my friends to people I didn't know. Amina left in a hurry that day and the atmosphere was tense later when streams of cars came to the dump.

Head Salem doubled the amount of time set aside for shooting practice, since we were still novices. He taught us that the guns should be a part of us. If we loved them, they would love us. If we stuck with them, they would serve us, and it would be improper for a real man in a position of responsibility not to know how to handle a gun. He brought many varieties from the storeroom and started training us on them one by one, persistently and attentively. A small minority had some previous experience, but for most of the boys this was the first time they had handled guns.

When we were together, Emad never tired of telling us that having a weapon in your hand was like having a gang for back-up. Whenever he wanted to chew us out for pulling out of a fight we were losing, or if we had failed to support him, he raised his voice so that Youssef could hear: "If I have a friend behind me, fighting with me, I never retreat or run away. If I have a gun in my hand with just a single bullet, I don't need the friend. I don't need anyone. The gun will keep me safe. When you have one there's no need to fight with your fists or feet or teeth, or sticks and stones, or even with knives. Your gun is a hand you can trust. It doesn't let you down, or abandon you and run."

The head stood with his left hand on his hip and an automatic rifle in the other hand. "Hold your arm steady. Look before you fire. Hold your breath and don't let it out until you need to breathe. Focus hard, body, and don't misaim."

Bang. The bullet hit the picture of a boy in the circle, as surely as if Osman had punctured the target with his finger. Bang. Again in the circle. Bang. The same for the third shot.

"Stand aside, body, and don't move. That's a miracle."

I met Osman after watching him from afar. He was a better shot than all the other boys, and maybe than the heads too. I was convinced that if he had a contest with them, he would beat them hands down, but he was the kid who was always being told off for not running fast enough. I couldn't understand how he combined the two: an ignominious failure in the gym and shooting skills that amazed everyone. At the end of the day I asked him bluntly why he moved like a cripple.

"Aren't you afraid they'll dump you in the desert if you can't keep up with the rest of us?" I said. I refrained from saying the rest of what I wanted to say: I had forgotten for a moment that he was a recent newcomer and didn't know our secrets. No one had told him about the lame boy and his buddies and how the desert had swallowed them up.

Osman was busy watching television until the program cut off. Pictures of colored baubles appeared on the screen and the call to evening prayers began. Without looking in my direction, as if speaking to himself, he said he had been run over by a car while crossing the highway and people had taken him to a clinic. With difficulty I gleaned from him that they had stitched up his leg and his shoulder there, and when he was about to run back to his life on the street, there was a titan waiting for him. The titan brought him to the camp without much resistance from Osman, who was frail and weak, and the doctor had also turned against him when he tried to slip away. He said Osman had better go with the titan. His injuries were still bleeding when he joined us, and later they filled with pus, but he survived. There are plenty like him, I told myself, because the big government hospitals and the health centers are in contact with the camp and the titans. I had heard the same thing from kids who were added to our group after doctors reported them to the authorities. They are all the same, doctors. And barbers and people who have coffee shops and restaurants. They're all the same, except Amina. She was the only one who stayed loyal to us until they caught her. But did she really never report us? Did she let slip a word or two to them under coercion? I thought about her absent-mindedly, as the television broadcast more images of stars, the sky, and more colored baubles. Then I remembered Ramadan and the lanterns she brought us once, and out of the blue I told Osman what I was thinking.

"Those decorations are like Ramadan decorations. Are you going to fast when it comes?" I asked.

"Have you ever fasted?" he replied.

"When I was young I used to fast like Firdous, my mother, and I'd break the fast alone in the middle of the day."

"My mother fasts two days a month all year. She says it brings good luck, but I know she's really saving the food for me and my sisters."

"How many sisters do you have?"

"There's Fatma, Maryam, Iman, and me: Osman."

I almost danced for joy. That was when I found out his name. He had almost forgotten it, as the others had. He said his name confidently, as well as the names of his sisters. I thought he might agree to join me and Saad, and that would make three of us, three boys sworn to remember people's names. I trusted he wouldn't report on us and that, if he wasn't keen on the idea of joining us, he would at least keep it to himself. May evil never enter this house, as Firdous used to say. I mentioned my name to him and kept on using his name as I tested his trustworthiness.

"Did you arrive here last week?" I asked.

"Yes, and I went to the lecture by Sheikh Abdel-Gabbar the next day. You were in the hall, too. I saw you sitting there. Didn't you hear what he said? He told stories about the religious holidays we celebrate: the Prophet's Night Journey, the Feast of the Sacrifice, and the Night of Destiny, and he also spoke about fasting."

I didn't tell him I had been busy daydreaming the whole time. When he saw how slow-witted I seemed, he repeated what he had heard in the lecture.

"When one boy asked him, the sheikh gave a fatwa that in the camp we're serving the country, like mujahideen fighting in God's cause, and so we don't need to fast. He said we're excused from fasting on all occasions, in Ramadan or not, because we're under intensive training and we need to eat. If we fasted we wouldn't be able to follow the heads' orders and so we would be disobedient. Basically, we won't be fasting here, Rabie."

"I'm not going to fast, Osman. Nothing new there. You know, me and my friends used to call the heads by another name. Between ourselves we nicknamed them the titans."

Our conversation resumed over the following days, and I understood that Osman had to move slowly when he was in pain. His injuries had healed, but they left pains in his body that we couldn't see. So he continued to train with us, but sometimes he felt weak and couldn't keep up with us. Things soon changed and he was scolded less harshly after Head Salim noticed what an exceptionally good shot he was. From then on Salim forgave him his disability and didn't talk about it when he found it hard to run or jump, or when his legs let him down.

6

The Heart of the World

A LARGE NUMBER OF MEN were sitting on the ground shoulder-to-shoulder, many of them wearing galabias and skullcaps. Their brown faces looked exhausted and their eyes gazed into the distance as if waiting for the unknown. That scene suddenly disappeared as the camera switched to the face of Nanice al-Nahhas reclining on her sofa, running her fingers through her auburn locks and inserting an earpiece into her ear.

"We now have an interview with one of the people who live in the protest area," she announced. "Hello, hello. Yes, can you hear me, sir? Go ahead, we're all listening in the studio, go ahead."

The caller's voice came through clearly, as if he were sitting next to her. "Good evening, and my greetings to everyone. I live in a building that overlooks the Space, and I'd like to give my testimony, if I may. I do hope you don't cut me off. There are some very dubious things happening here, things that obviously count as unacceptable under sharia law, in fact, the kind of things infidels do, God forbid. I've been sitting by my window day and night and I can almost hear the breathing of the people sleeping on the ground and I know precisely who is visiting each tent, and I'm well aware of what they are doing inside. In the last few days their sheikhs have issued a fatwa allowing what they call 'marriage jihad.' They put men and women who are not married in the same tents, and they can do what they like without constraint! I apologize if I've offended any viewers but I see their women coming every day with a different man. The men go in looking tense and impatient and they come out exhausted, with a strange look on their faces. We local people fear for our children, our women, and our morals. We can't take it any more!"

Aida sat up straight in her comfortable chair in the sitting room. Her face was flushed and her heart was racing. Nanice gasped in shock and covered a sharp intake of breath with her hand. Then, in alarm, she started to check she had understood the caller properly: "Are you sure about what you're saying?" she said. "I have to warn you on air, in the presence of the millions who are watching, this involves questions of honor, so you have to be certain."

"I am certain!" the man cried. "I swear, this is what's happening in front of my eyes, and more. I couldn't help seeing things, and I asked around and found out that they're selling, pardon the expression, condoms every day close to those tents."

Covering her face with her hands, she interrupted him before he could finish. "Unbelievable! I really can't believe it. Personally, I'm speechless. You said there was a fatwa? We're expecting senior sheikhs and eminent religious scholars to comment as soon as possible on this . . . I don't know how to describe it." Addressing one of her guests, a religious scholar, she asked: "Give us your own fatwa, please. Is this possible? Was that fatwa sound?"

Before he had a chance to answer, she turned defiantly to her guest, who kept his cool in the face of her histrionics. "Professor, what do you think?" she asked. "Are you also going to tell us that this is one of the human rights you defend? Does the right to protest against some political position give the protesters the right to commit these heinous acts? I want you to be honest with me. Can one defend the scenes you have seen and the appeals for us to help that you have heard?"

The guest cleared his throat, leisurely adjusted his smart jacket, and replied calmly: "Anyone who defends this shameful situation must be biased. The residents have a right not to be subjected to material loss or emotional distress. What we have seen today, and what we have seen over the past weeks, is definitely an outrageous violation of their right to privacy, which is enshrined in many constitutions and international conventions. And I tell you here and now, and this is a sincere personal appeal, that the state must intervene, do its job, assert its authority, and put an end to this travesty. No fair-minded person could accept or justify the current situation. Human rights are not an absolute. I am a citizen and I have rights, but I should not encroach on the rights of others."

Nanice leaned forward a little and looked pleased. "Well said! At last you admit there are limits. So please do us another favor and be frank with me, and impartial on the point I'm going to raise, a point that has been a source of controversy: have these people been able to live this way for almost a month without being financed by someone?"

"The question of financing is as clear as day," the guest fired back. "Anyone who's sane and, first and foremost, honest with himself, wouldn't dispute it. The state has to investigate the sources that have been pumping in millions to keep the protest alive, and see whether the sources are legitimate or illegitimate, though I think the latter more probable."

Aida turned off the television and sat still for a while in the hope that her nervous tension might subside. Then she went and stood under the hot water to wash off the sweat of the long day. She hoped it would also wash away the traces of the stupidities she had just been listening to. She felt slightly numb and a sense of relief coursed through her body at the tingling sensation of the water from the shower head. She thought about Murad. When she'd finished her shower, it occurred to her to go to sleep early, but then she changed her mind. She wanted to watch some more television and her mother was still in the sitting room. Throughout the two weeks they had spent in the Space, Aida had found some time on her way back from school to meet her mother, see her sister, use the washing machine, and have a leisurely shower without anyone hurrying her. Then she would organize the things she needed for the protest and grab the chance to watch the programs she couldn't watch in full on her cellphone. While switching from channel to channel, she chatted with her mother and asked about family news.

Her channel surfing took her to a new channel owned by well-known businessman Qadri Abdel-Hakim, where a dignified-looking guest was holding court. He was being interviewed with great deference by a young broadcaster she didn't recognize.

"Dr. Abdel-Samie, we know you're very knowledgeable about the phenomenon of street children," the interviewer was saying. "What do you think of the rehabilitation program that the general has announced? Are you contributing to it with your vast experience?"

Abdel-Samie replied seriously and with a frown, "I'm honored to be one of the people who laid the foundations for it. The situation was extremely difficult—complicated and convoluted. You know, of course, that the existence of these children has been troubling the state for a long time. They pose a danger to society and place an extra burden on the national economy. The prevalence of street children has even led to a decline in tourism, but thanks to the general's interest, and with God's help, we have managed to find systematic, successful solutions. We refused to follow the execution method adopted by some countries, and decided to go with the Chinese approach. We've raised the financing we needed, but that's a long story perhaps for another time."

The interviewer nodded appreciatively and turned to the audience. "After the break we'll come back to Dr. Abdel-Samie Mukhtar and bring in an official from the Ministry of

Social Welfare to talk to us about the budget and the steps that have actually been taken."

Short advertisements followed and then a shiny bright truck appeared with the slogan "The Heart of the World" painted on the side. The door carried a picture of a little boy with his right hand raised to his forehead, and a large sun disk behind him. Aida was too distracted to work out whether the boy was giving a formal salute or shielding his eyes from the light. The screen glowed with the words "National Street Children Rehabilitation Project: Children at the Heart of the World." The advertisement then introduced the team that went around in the truck and examined street children one by one: a doctor in a white coat, an elegant woman who acted as psychologist, and a handsome young social worker.

The advertisement immediately reminded her of the kids who lived near the house. She knew some of them by sight and had decided some months earlier to give them the clothes Adam had grown out of, but unfortunately she had been too busy with school duties and half-year exams, and she had lost track of them. The protest had come to dominate her concerns. On the few occasions she had come back to the house she had tried in vain to find any of them. She imagined that the change in her schedule was the reason, but she soon realized that it had nothing to do with her. The children weren't in the places where they usually gathered in the morning and evening. She hadn't spotted a single child at the nearby traffic lights, which had been one of their regular haunts, or on the faded wooden bench that they liked to sleep on close to the corner of the main street. The bench now lay empty in front of the railway tracks. No kids clutching bags of tissues to sell hassled her when she went past the market. No one tried to elicit money from passers-by outside the nearby cinema complex. She thought of trying again the next day to see if she could find any of them. It was after midnight when she kissed her mother goodnight and snuggled into bed.

In the morning Aida deliberately walked down a couple of streets to test out her theory: she turned off a side street into the main street, then stopped at the old station. She confirmed that the kids who had once lived there were no longer around, neither were the kids who had lived next to the large trash cans. After turning into a backstreet that was a dead-end, she realized that they had all completely disappeared. There was no trace of them in the area. What she had heard on television might be true this time. At last they would find someone to take care of them and give them some attention.

Aida went back to the Space with plenty of news of her own and looking forward to hearing Murad's news, but he didn't have anything interesting to tell her. He laughed at her curiosity and wondered what she expected when she had been away for less than twenty-four hours.

"You haven't missed anything at all," he said. "Today was just like yesterday. The protest is digging in, turning into just a fact of life and, as you can see, people are organizing themselves, finding their way around and getting things done in innovative ways. The people with jobs here in the city are the same as they were. They don't have a problem. They go to work during the day and then come here for the night. But the people with jobs in the provinces have to deal with bosses who are reluctant to approve long periods off work. Shakir says there are strict instructions to give them a hard time and put black marks against their names in the register if they sign in just a few minutes late. Even so they find ways to stay in the Space as long as they can. In this country a civil servant isn't short of ways to get off work, and now the day has come when we encourage such behavior as a great virtue!"

"It's the same with us at school. The principal was very rigid yesterday when I was preparing to leave. He refused to let me go even five minutes early," Aida replied.

"Have you seen the Heart of the World adverts?" she asked as she took the pins out of her headscarf, her eyes sparkling with interest in his reaction. "Qadri Abdel-Hakim has sent out trucks to help street kids. Didn't I tell you a while back that I noticed a fancy car driving up and down our street with his name on it? Yesterday afternoon I saw an ad on TV for a charity called Heart of the World, which collects donations for the kids. Then I found out that he's in charge of it. I think it's already started work."

"Don't judge by appearances. I expect he sent out the car you saw to make a tour just for show, to catch the attention of passersby so that they come to trust his organization and throw money at it. Qadri's a big conman. I've known him since university days and I've never heard of him being interested in charity work or helping the poor. Never in his life has he reached out to someone in need or contributed to any useful economic project. He's a tycoon. His business is consumer-based through and through, and the goods he imports wipe out the local competition and drive small factories into bankruptcy. On top of that, in all his years in parliament he's never come up with a single proposal unless it serves his own business interests or those of people like him."

"You're unfair to him, Murad. Even if he is as you say, this project would be enough to make up for his mistakes and earn him plenty of credit. Today I checked for myself and I couldn't find any of the kids I used to meet in the streets, and don't forget that you always used to get upset about the terrible state they were in. You were always on about their faces and bodies covered in dirt as if they weren't human. For God's sake, I don't know where the officials have been all this time. Anyway, I'm happy they've finally woken up. The newspapers have also been writing about the national plan to look after these children. They say the state intends to draw up a whole rehabilitation program for them, and the general's busy working on it."

Murad's face changed. He looked disappointed by the last remark. "The general, you say? Does any good ever come of that man?" he said. "Maybe once in his life he did something good in an unguarded moment, but aren't we here because of him, Aida? Anyway, there are plenty of imaginary plans, and the media hype doesn't mean anything has really been achieved. Do you think the program has been launched and has produced results this quickly just because you couldn't find the kids you're used to seeing? They simply might have left our neighborhood for another area where they can make a better living. Anyway, don't worry about this now. We have more than enough to worry about, to be honest. I forgot to tell you—tomorrow drop in on the theater the young people set up close to their stand. You'll like the idea. They're doing comedy shows and the people who've seen them have liked them. Have a look. We might find time to attend one of them."

A loud voice boomed out from the main podium, addressing the protesters.

"Strength, resolve, faith. . . . Our men are everywhere," said the speaker. "Stand firm, Brothers! And be patient till we carry our abducted leader to the presidential palace on our shoulders. Stand firm and be patient, for the morrow comes soon for those who wait. His legitimacy will not lapse even if they try to deny it, in which case there will be rivers of blood. Let them take heed. If anyone dares to harm our ruler, even with a splash of water, we will respond with a torrent of blood!"

"*Allahu akbar, Allahu akbar,*" the audience chanted.

"Do they imagine," the speaker continued, "that by abducting the ruler they have proved they are men? Since when was there ever a man among them? We do not recognize the perfidious general, or his cronies or his judges or this man they have installed in office instead of our ruler. We will hold our ground here, well entrenched, and we will not move until we have achieved our objective, and there is nothing we would like more than to die for the sake of God and His prophet!"

Murad frowned and turned to Shakir, who was sitting beside him in a tent chosen for a meeting of the group's leaders. "That sermon's bound to seriously annoy the System," he said.

"They have to keep the protesters enthused, or else they'd lose interest and leave the Space."

"But what he's saying is so irrational, it's stupid. It's the kind of thing that people who've lost their common sense say. Doesn't anyone point that out to them?"

"And is it logical what we're doing? Stupidity has got the better of everyone and the podium is no exception to the rule."

"All the more reason for us to watch what we say and not compete with the regime to say stupid and reckless things."

"I don't know, Murad. If we up the stakes, ratchet up the rhetoric, we might gain ground."

"Come on, Shakir, is there the slightest hope we'll carry the abducted ruler to the presidential palace on our shoulders, as if nothing has happened, as if there hasn't been a coup, or as if all the signs don't suggest that the whole state machinery has been mobilized against us?"

"That's precisely the reason, if you want to examine the reasons. The hope is slight, so we have to crank up the tone as much as possible, frighten the System, and make it feel uneasy about how the current situation will end. We might win ourselves some room to negotiate. They have to reinstate the ruler, if only in a token role, by having him appoint a prime minister for example, or holding early elections and then we'd see what happens, but we won't get to that stage with the kind of soft, polite talk that you favor."

"But what the Brothers say on the podium, and the reckless discourse of war that they put out without thinking, might help to make the System more intransigent and defiant, and then we'd lose more and more, not to mention the fact that the general is using our own methods. We're not the only ones speaking in the name of Islam. He's doing so too and the sheikhs are supporting him and his discourse in a way that improves his image. Before we came I read an article in *The Economist* that said the general had blended nationalism with Islam. He includes plenty of Quranic verses in his speeches. This hadn't caught my attention, there's nothing new in it, but the writer used it to paint a frightening picture. He describes the general as pious, and says that people like him and see him as a source of security and dignity by having saved them from rule by the Raised Banner. In short, the general comes across as a devout, religious man who obeys God and enjoys overwhelming popular support, and whose strength is appreciated abroad. His discourse works, Shakir, while our discourse backfires on us."

Murad paused a while to get a grip on himself, then he continued, "Besides, how can we trick the thousands of people who have abandoned their homes, their work, their livelihoods, and their families and have come here in response to the call from the Raised Banner? Many of them are simple and well-intentioned and believe every word that comes out of the leaders' mouths. They think the top leaders speak only truth and wisdom, and always choose what is right. Should we enthuse people by telling them lies, Shakir?"

"The political differences between you and us won't disappear overnight, Murad. Ever since you were young you've had a vision that's different from ours, though the only thing that kept you apart from the Raised Banner was your obstinacy. Even so, you're here with us today."

Murad sighed, looked up at the roof of the tent and noticed a sign saying "Shoura Council, Freedom Square in the Space." He looked around outside the tent and noticed a slogan painted on a tent nearby: "Sovereignty belongs to the people, who are the source of authority." He read it and smiled, but he was reluctant to resume the discussion, aware of how difficult it is to change people's attitudes. The wheel had started turning and now it was impossible to stop it.

At the women's entrance, a woman stood carefully searching those coming in, as usual. She picked out Aida with her books from afar. She let her through quickly, along with a small boy who was tagging along at her coattails. The woman never imagined that the boy didn't know Aida or that Aida would allow him to tag along with her unless he was her son, her nephew, or a close relative of some kind.

The boy, Halim, slipped into the Space and disappeared into the crowds. He walked around for hours exploring the place warily, learning the routes, remembering possible hiding places, and making a plan to settle in. Like a puppy drawn to the home of its first owner, his feet led him close to Aida and Murad's tent. He adopted it as a landmark, like the garbage dump. He went to the fairground area, which was full of people and their children, and dashed from one swing to another, amazed to discover that they had left it open to everyone and no one was collecting money from the children using it. When he had had enough, he started picking the tops of mineral water bottles off the ground and made friends with a boy with whom he could play the game *siga*, which was like checkers. At the end of the day he went back to the landmark and found somewhere to lie on the ground.

Within two or three days at the most, Halim had blended into the place, heart and soul. He instinctively became part of the Space, like a member of the Raised Banner and indistinguishable from the other Raised Banner children. He mixed with them and shared their toys. He got hold of a plastic gun that was the color he liked. He also learned some of the songs. Whenever there was loud singing from the podium, he swayed his head in time with it and started singing along, unwittingly contributing to the process of enthusing and energizing the protesters. He didn't understand most of the words, but he liked the strong rhythms, so he joined in. Often he was so carried away that he started singing the songs to himself. He would stand up straight and shout, "We are the brave, *Allahu akbar*! We have sworn an oath not to be defeated!" He soon found other children to join in. At the tent he had chosen as his landmark, a tentative friendship formed between him and Adam because they were close by and got used to each other's presence. They didn't play together but they knew each other and sometimes chatted.

As a professional electrician of known competence, Saber Abdel-Mawla regularly visited many parts of the Space, fixing faults, adding lights, or maybe taking on bigger tasks if needed. If the podium broadcast a request for electricians, he would head to the problem area whatever the time of day and volunteer to solve the problem, even if it wasn't an emergency. He could respond easily because he was nimble and had only his son Hussein for company—a boy in the first year of middle school who spent his time sleeping, too lazy even to play. He had told his wife to stay at home and had undertaken to work hard enough for them both as an active member of the Raised Banner. He visited her with Hussein every weekend, changed his dirty clothes, and then went back to the Space holding the boy's hand. Since the protest had started, she had been happy they were out of the house and she was spared the noise, the endless demands, and the arguments over homework and waking up early. At the same time, she had tried many times to persuade the boy to stay with her, for fear his father might neglect him and he might get lost in the crowds.

Unluckily for Halim, Saber was observant and distrustful. One evening he was assigned to fix a minor short circuit in the area that included Aida and Murad's tent. When he arrived he came across Halim stretched out on the ground close to the tent, staring at the sky, and discretely playing with himself. Saber cursed fathers who neglect their children, and thought no more of it, but he remembered the details of the place and of Halim. Luck would have it that he caught sight of Halim the next day too, near the fairground. He had taken Hussein to the big wheel and was standing watching him with eagle eyes to make sure he stayed in his seat and held on tight as Saber had repeatedly told him to. Halim was there riding in one of the gondolas of the big wheel, clinging to the two metal posts, his eyes sparkling with excitement. Saber couldn't see Halim's eyes, but he could see his arms, and he was shocked to see that there was a tattoo on the inside of one wrist. He couldn't be sure exactly what the tattoo was, but he naturally suspected it was the kind of cross tattoo that many Christians have. The wheel was turning and Halim loved the feel of the warm air against his face. He was laughing, sitting up straight, standing up and sitting down again, oblivious to the operator's instructions that people stay in their seats for safety reasons. Halim got out and Saber expected to see Halim's father admiring his courage or his mother smacking him for his reckless behavior. He expected to see a man with a beard or a woman in a hijab, but no one came up to Halim, who left in a hurry and melted into the crowd.

The same day, Saber ran into him again at the urinals, again alone, and he walked after him. He saw him standing in front of the stage making gestures like a circus performer. He was increasingly indignant about Halim's behavior. The boy didn't have anyone to control him. At iftar Saber deliberately chose a place near Aida and Murad's tent, and he was not disappointed. He found Halim as he expected, sitting alone and waiting for the sunset call to prayer. Then he tucked into his meal ravenously and finished it all off. Saber felt that his suspicions about the boy were sound. He had never seen him in the company of any adult, male or female. He moved around constantly and never called out to a mother or a father, and no one called him. And Saber was now certain that the greenish tattoo on his wrist was a Christian cross, God forbid.

Halim caught on to the fact that Saber had been monitoring him all day. He decided to make a break for it before he was exposed. He kept out of sight till the evening of the next day, when the time came for evening prayers and the protesters formed lines to pray, and he was among them. He bent down and prayed like them, repeating the prayers after the imam: "*O God, protect us from tyrants, O Lord of the Worlds. Give us victory over them, thwart their wiles and guide us to the right path.*"

When everyone went their separate ways, Halim went to the podium wailing and speaking with difficulty between his copious tears. He said he was looking for his parents, who had brought him to communal prayers. He said he had let go of his father's hand in the packed crowd and he had got confused. He couldn't make out his father among all the men who looked similar and couldn't find his way back to their tent. The podium announced that a lost child had been found and his parents should come to identify him. Half an hour passed without any response, and Halim moved on to the next stage of his plan.

He went up to the man holding the microphone, his eyes bathed in tears and said, "I'm worried my father might have left the Space. I heard him and my mother saying they were going to visit a relative of ours in the hospital in the evening. What shall I do without them? How can I get home when it's dark and they might not come back today?"

Halim cried even louder, thinking back to painful memories to help himself along. The man took pity on him, had him sit on the edge of the podium and brought him some candy while he sought a solution. Halim's only purpose was to obtain official recognition that he was alone and waiting for his family, whose existence was proven by the boy's tormented weeping.

Another announcement was made: "Halim Rizk, a lost boy, is at the podium. He's wearing a blue t-shirt and brown trousers. Please come to collect him."

After the podium had repeated the appeal several times, Adam leaned over to his mother and asked her to go to the podium with him to buy some cotton candy from the cart that was parked there. Aida looked up from the biology book and begged him to wait until she had finished her work, but he nagged her again minutes later. She put the book aside and stood up. No harm in a little exercise after iftar, she thought. Adam led her straight to the podium, and the appeal was repeated. She soon put two and two together. She had noticed a boy sitting on the edge of the podium, ignoring the candy lying on the wooden stage. His eyes were like two red balls and his face was flushed and drenched in tears. She recognized him immediately as the boy who had been staying near them and who had used her as cover when he sneaked into the Space. For some minutes she wondered what to do. Adam held her hand in speechless silence and didn't even ask her to move on to buy the cotton candy. She made up her mind, went up to the official on the podium and said she knew the boy and could look after him until his relatives turned up. She wasn't lying. She had seen him before, and that was enough when it came to a child the same age as her son who didn't have anyone else to look after him. As soon as Halim caught sight of her and Adam, and heard what she was saying, his face lit up, as if he had been waiting for her in particular.

Halim said nothing all the way back to the tent. He didn't try to make conversation, explain anything, or resume his crying, which he might have done given that he had supposedly lost his family. Aida asked him his name and he said, "Halim."

"Your father?"

"Rizk."

"Brothers and sisters?"

Halim clammed up again, as if testing what she would do after saving him despite knowing from the start that he was lying. Of course she knew he wasn't lost, since she had seen him every day: sitting alone, playing, and sleeping. Now he had to explain things to her. Would he just say he had a mother in the slums? Or that he lived in the street most of the time and rarely went home?

Aida refrained from asking. She didn't want to press him, in case he was frightened and ran off. When they were close to the tent, she asked him if he needed anything: a blanket, a pillow, or some food. He shook his head and opened his fist to show her he had picked up some candy from the podium floor before coming with her. Then he put his hand out to Adam to offer him what he had. Adam looked at Aida, seeking her approval. She pushed Adam gently to accept Halim's offer.

"Have some and say thank you to Halim," she said.

Aida went into the tent deep in thought and resumed her seat. She started to look through the pages of her biology book and write notes in the margins. She looked up for some moments to watch the Archipelago Channel on her cellphone. It was showing scenes of a march with large banners reading: "Free women—martyrs to truth, pride and dignity." The camera zoomed in on a woman in black robes, leading lines of women, raising her arms in the air and shouting, "*Allahu akbar*! God is most great, you infidels! God is greater than you!" Aida put her book aside and turned to Murad.

"They killed some Brothers this morning," she said.

Murad didn't reply. Meanwhile the announcer started to describe shaky video of the demonstrations that had broken out in several provinces southwest of the capital. Thousands of people had come out after nighttime Ramadan prayers to condemn the latest massacre, this time of women shot while on a peaceful march calling for the return of the abducted ruler.

"Now we can hear the strident chants," the announcer said.

The demonstrators were shouting slogans such as, "Kill again, kill again! Then you call the victims criminals!", "Down, down with the gangster!", "Either we'll do them justice, or die like them!", and "Where are you, justice, where are you? The general's killing women!" The voices died away and the picture changed, and Aida went back to Murad. "What's going on, Murad?" she asked. "I know you hate blood, but giving in to evil is also horrible."

"It shouldn't happen this way. Our blood is being shed to no purpose. We gain nothing in return, not even sympathy. I think we should stop the protests outside the Space. There's a danger the street will turn against us because of those protests, but the Raised Banner leaders can't see that danger, or else they see it but only care about their own interests."

"The leaders are very friendly toward you. Speak to them and warn them."

"They're not listening now. Did the abducted leader listen before them? At this stage God alone knows where this will end."

Murad turned to the screen of Aida's cellphone and his mind wandered a while with the sounds and lights coming from it. He didn't watch or listen in detail.

Then he turned back to Aida and said, "I share memories with them that go back a long time. They have always been very close to me in hard times, as you can see for yourself. But this frenzied war of words has made them slightly crazy."

"You were optimistic when we came, so what happened?"

"I don't feel comfortable. They're escalating their rhetoric in a way that's out of control. It's emotional and ill-considered. And at the same time the people here aren't questioning what they say and the things they organize. They don't hold them to account for the consequences. Look around you. You'll find an amazing level of confidence, and a mood so full of optimism that it's almost naive, without a trace of doubt or caution, despite the repeated attacks on them and the rising death toll. Imagine, some of my assistants at university are arranging to meet their friends in the Space during the weekend break, as if they were going to have tea together at a downtown café."

"Are you thinking of leaving the Space, Murad?"

"No, Aida, no. We took a decision after a long discussion. We based our decision on principle, not the interests of the Raised Banner. We won't be able to dream of better days for Adam if things go on as they are and we have a succession of generals in power, or people who rule in their name. Even if the Raised Banner leaders slip up and make the wrong choice, all we can do is support them, and I think we have to stay at least until the abducted leader reappears or negotiations produce an acceptable result. So let's take advantage of our flexible work schedules during this period. You have the end-of-year vacation, and my college is in turmoil, with classes one day and fighting the next."

His mind wandered again, as he thought things over and worked out what more to say. Then he looked into Aida's face and saw that she seemed to agree. He bowed his head and said, "We'll have to go back to our usual routine sooner or later, when school starts and the universities calm down, but let's stay with them till then."

Aida looked at Adam and Halim sitting on the ground facing each other with a square for playing *siga* drawn in chalk between them. They both looked exhausted.

"You know that boy we've been seeing around here for a while?" she said, almost casually. "No one knows where his family has gone. They left him and disappeared. Maybe we should look after him till someone comes looking for him."

When Saber saw Halim talking to Aida on their way back from the podium, he assumed the boy must be related to her, but he still felt an urge to ask her about the puzzling aspects of his story. The next morning he sought her out, setting aside the irritation he had felt when she and Murad had said what they thought of the Archipelago Channel. When he found her, he looked down at the ground and was as polite as he possibly could be.

"Good morning, Sister," he said. "Is that boy part of your family? For several days I've seen him roaming around in the Space and sleeping on the ground at night. And what's more, I noticed he has a tattoo on the inside of his wrist. Do you know what it is? I have my suspicions that he's spying on us. If he's not someone you know, we should hand him over to the security official in the area to take the appropriate measures. We don't need any more problems than we have already."

Aida recalled Saber's face immediately from when he opened the cover on the lamp post and reached inside to find the electrical connection that Shakir wanted. The fact that she knew Saber didn't mean she wasn't troubled by his suspicions. She felt he was implicitly accusing her of being an accomplice. She had no reservations about having the boy stay with them out of compassion, or about admitting that he was an intruder on the protest, and Murad had no objection to him staying close to them either, but the matter of the tattoo was very upsetting. She was the only other person who had noticed it and she might be held responsible. No one else would understand that Halim was just a street kid and his religion didn't much matter. It didn't affect him, or her, or anyone else in the Space. She took a deep breath, asked God for forgiveness and lied to protect Halim from any suspicion.

"His name's Halim and he's from a poor family. I know his mother and father. They were here in the beginning, but they have to work. I think they're farmers and they can't stay away from the land for long. Now he's standing in for them in the protest, and we shouldn't deprive him or them of the chance to campaign in a righteous cause, for which God will reward them," she said. She spoke as if she was resentful that Saber distrusted Halim and misjudged her assessment of the situation.

Saber backed off grudgingly, but didn't seemed reassured. "Be careful, Sister. God alone knows what these days might bring. They'll hold the slightest mistake against us and find any excuse to clear us out. Don't let your good intentions pave the way for a disaster that does us harm."

After her conversation with Saber, Aida decided to speak to Halim. She found him behind the tent, lining up bottle tops on the ground and imagining he was playing *siga* with someone else, or maybe waiting for Adam to come back from visiting his grandmother. She went up to him and gently tried to engage him in friendly conversation.

"How are you, Halim?" she asked. "I'd like to talk to you about something important. Dr. Murad and I are not responsible for you. Don't be afraid to tell me the truth, because it's just between me and you, and no one but us will know. I know you've been alone in the Space since I let you come in through the gate with me. I also know you're a good boy and you wouldn't harm anyone. I don't have any problem with you staying here, but some other people don't like you being here. I'm going to explain what all these people in the Space are doing, and if you want to stay, I'll teach you how you ought to behave, and what you have to watch out for when you speak, so you don't have any problems."

Aida told Halim about the protest. Using all her versatile skills as a teacher, she did her best to help him understand, as she had done with Adam. Halim seemed to get the idea quicker than she expected, and he was impressed. His eyes lit up and he finally spoke.

"So the adults, the kids, and the old people are all here against the titans?" he said.

Aida was taken aback by his strange expression. "They're all against. . . . They're all against the titans," she repeated after him with a laugh.

"You and Adam too?" he asked.

"Me and Adam too."

"Me too. I'm like you, against the titans."

Halim declared his position with simplicity, dividing the teams as if he were playing football and choosing his own team. To him it was simple, and didn't need to be discussed. Using his own terms, Aida agreed with him. She liked this concept of 'titans,' but there was something else she wouldn't have enjoyed bringing up under ordinary circumstances: "You know, Halim, everyone has their religion. All the people here are Muslims and you're Christian. Listen carefully. Don't let anyone see the cross on your wrist. Never say you're Christian, and never swear by the Virgin or Christ to any of your friends, and keep away from the dark man you saw me talking to a while ago."

"Uncle Saber?"

"You know his name? Uncle Saber exactly. Don't approach him and maybe he'll forget you. Don't let him see the tattoo on your wrist, even if it means running away from him, and if he asks you where your family are, tell him you're waiting for them, but don't say much."

Soon after coming to the protest, Adam started preparing for the new school year. Aida always got him into the habit of reading his school books for a while before the school year began, so that he would be a step ahead of his classmates. She reminded him he had made a promise and that he would be moving up to middle school, which would require greater concentration. He didn't avoid school work often: he was eager to excel and naturally inclined to be studious. She set aside a fixed time of day, went over the lessons with him, and made good progress with the curriculum. She tested what he had learned. Adam had stipulated that they should sit outside the tent. He sat cross-legged on the ground beside her, comfortable with the activity around him and hopeful he would get a break and an ice cream at the end. After one or two sessions, Halim joined them. He approached several times to follow her explanation, without showing any signs of being bored or distracted. She noticed how committed he was and invited him to sit down next to Adam. He was delighted by the invitation and didn't hesitate. In fact, he put his thin finger on a word in the textbook and pronounced it in his own idiosyncratic way, determined to show her that he could decipher the word. He achieved his purpose: Aida was surprised at how well he pronounced the letters, and his curiosity about the words led her to bring him into the conversation and give him some attention.

Adam's insistence on sitting outside the tent meant other people were drawn to the group. Around midday a woman in niqab came up to Aida just after Adam came back from the fairground and started preparing the mats, papers, and pens, helped by Halim.

She said hello and announced her purpose: "God bless you, Sister. I'm the inspection official. We've only spoken a few times, but I know you well. You often come through the checkpoint close to the shopping center. After seeing you I gathered you work as a teacher. Then I heard from your neighbors how interested you are in teaching and how good you are at your work. You're famous around here. It's amazing. If it's not too much trouble, I wish you would take on my daughter as a pupil."

"She's about the same age as them," she added, pointing at Halim and Adam, "and I won't hide the fact that I don't understand her school work at all. I can't follow it. She failed two subjects last year and has to redo the exams. I'm worried she might fail again and have to redo the whole year, and there are only a few days left before the retakes."

Aida didn't see the request as too onerous. She felt she owed the woman a favor, since she had repeatedly helped her at the entrance to the Space and was pleasant to Adam whenever she saw him, so she agreed without hesitation. The girl turned up the following day: she was dark and thin with fine features, wearing a modest dress and an ordinary hijab with a colored design.

She had a backpack full of books and was holding the straps as she walked, bending over under the weight. Aida had her sit to the right of her while the boys sat to her left. Adam read and Halim read after him, while Aida listened to them with half an ear and went over with the girl what she had learned and worked out what help she would need.

The very next day another girl appeared, tripping over her long dress. She approached the small study circle gathered in the shadow of the tent and then spoke to Aida in a high-pitched whisper.

"I'm Sara Adel al-Sabbagh and I'm in the second year of middle school. My father asks if you'll let me listen to your lessons," she said.

From her voice and body language, Sara seemed shy, but her face was hidden behind a white niqab. Aida stood up to make her feel more at ease.

She went up to Sara and put a hand gently on her shoulder. "Wonderful. You're welcome, Sara. Where are you staying?"

The girl pointed at a tent in the distance that was covered in slogans and pictures of the abducted ruler. At the entrance stood the Raised Banner flag and around it the flags of many neighboring countries had been planted in the ground. The shiny posters reflected the strong sunlight, making it hard to see clearly, but Aida had a long look at the tent. She was impressed, since it clearly showed how enthusiastic Sara's parents were about the protest. She went back to patting the girl on the shoulder, which helped to reassure her.

"Sit down next to your sister, Sara," said Aida. "She's in the same year at school, and it'll be easier if I explain things to you two together. But later you'll have to introduce me to your wonderful mother, so she can follow your work with me like the others. She's in the tent, isn't she?"

Aida acquired a reputation in the nearby tents because of her classes, which continued regularly for days, especially as they were no longer limited to Adam. Some of the women nearby came and asked if their children could join the group, imagining that Aida was being paid for her work and anticipating that it would cost less than they paid for private lessons. In response to the insistent parents who came by throughout the day, she agreed to take on more students and treated it as a hobby. The news spread amazingly fast, along with comments on her skill and her easy manner. She didn't know where the comments came from. When the daughter of the inspection official was receptive to Aida's method of teaching, and her mother declared Aida to be a genius, it added to the aura that had rapidly developed around her. Eventually Saber himself came to her and begged her to let his son Hussein into the group, setting aside his suspicions about her. He begged her desperately, as if she were his last recourse. She accepted his request reluctantly, driven only by a sense of duty. Overnight Hussein became a classmate to Halim and Adam, but Aida was even more wary of the family. She monitored what the boy had learned, while avoiding any conversation with his father.

She didn't need to publicize her free lessons, but some members of the Raised Banner sensed the importance of her initiative and how useful it could be for the protest. The man in charge of the area contacted her and tried to work out a more rigorous educational plan. Her idea soon spread and she became responsible for coordinating free extra classes across the Space. She was pleased with this unexpected development and felt as if she were running her own private school where she didn't allow any laxity. Her workload increased. She worked like a bee and started to prepare an extended educational program. She spoke to people she thought would be capable of teaching and would want to help, with a view to giving out course material and sharing out the students during the year. She had decided to keep a small group for herself and give them her own fuller explanation of the course material. This group of lucky children included Saber's son Hussein, the inspection official's daughter, along with Adam, Halim, and Sara.

There were several headline stories in the news bulletin, primarily the news conference at which Sheikh Abdel-Gabbar announced that a considerable amount of donated money had been set aside to help educate street children, teach them the principles of Islam, and protect them from the evils of life on the streets. He ended his announcement by saying there was an urgent plan to send special outreach teams to the places where former street children were staying. The television showed a friendly handshake between Sheikh Abdel-Gabbar and businessman Qadri Abdel-Hakim, who were said to be cooperating successfully with the state institutions working to save the children from their wretched surroundings. It then showed shots of a visit that the head of the National Industrialization Council had made to the office of the minister for social welfare in order to strengthen the partnership between the two organizations as part of the Heart of the World project. The children would receive vocational training, including in manual trades, so that they could join the labor market and increase production capacity in the future. The newsreader added that the state had allocated more than a hundred million pounds to this integrated project as a grant from the Our Country Is Here To Stay Fund, which was overseen by the general.

Aida turned to her mother, asking whether or not she and her sister had made a donation to the fund, as they had intended. The subject had been discussed, and they had wanted to donate, while Aida had doubts about whether it was serious and whether the people in charge of it could be trusted. Now that there were signs that it really existed, she had started wondering whether it might be possible to make positive use of it. She wasn't reassured by the involvement of Qadri Abdel-Hakim, given what Murad had said about him, but why shouldn't Halim benefit from the advantages that the project offered? If the money donated didn't reach the intended recipients, then the money had no doubt been stolen. It occurred to her to put the idea to Halim: maybe he would like it and would look forward to leaving the Space.

7

The Assignments Office

THE REDNESS ON MY HANDS gradually faded and I no longer felt any pain when I swung on the bar and lifted myself up. My hands grew tougher and the veins on the back of them stood out. My shoulder muscles bulked up and looked more manly. Sitting cross-legged and leaning forward in the camp mosque as Friday prayers were about to start, I stretched out my arms and saw my fingers: they were no longer as thin as they had been. Now they were long and rough and good to look at. I looked at them instead of looking at Abdel-Gabbar in the pulpit, but this time I decided to listen to him properly, because the mosque is one thing and the lecture hall is something else.

"My boys, the Mulid of the Prophet Muhammad, blessings and peace be upon him, is upon us, and this is an invitation to reflect on his life and the example he set us. In order to guide us and improve our lives, he told us that Muslims are like a single body. If one part is suffering, the other parts respond by going on the alert in defense. In this hallowed camp of yours, you are connected to each other like the parts of a body. The camp itself is part of the larger body that is the country. If any disease attacks the camp, you will all take a stand to fend it off. You have defended everything that is dear and precious, your unity and cohesion, your security and your country. The Prophet teaches us, my boys, the meaning of belonging and cohesion. When you consider these concepts, you strengthen your attachment to your religion and your community. You have nothing to fear now that you have reached safe shores and your lives have been put right in the camp and you are like sons to the great leader, who is judicious and honest in his intentions and his faith. You have nothing to fear, but I urge you to think hard, preserve what you have gained, hold fast to the rope of God that has been offered to you, rally around your leader '*like a solid structure*' and treat him as the Prophet was treated by his companions and followers."

I came out of the mosque deep in thought, as Abdel-Gabbar had suggested, but I didn't come to any particular conclusion. I left Saad and Osman behind me as I daydreamed. I imagined myself in a galabia and wooden shoes, with the Prophet talking to me about an imminent military expedition and how I had to stand firm against the infidels. Then suddenly Emad's face appeared in front of me. Actually, I had heard from Head Allam that some children from other camps were going to join us in batches, but I hadn't considered the possibility of Youssef and Emad being among them. I had been on my own for so long that I had forgotten many things. I was startled when I saw him and, for a moment, thought I was still dreaming, until he punched me in the chest and brought me around with a laugh.

"Don't pass out. You're looking at me as if you've seen a ghost," he said. "Fetch a glass of water for him. There might be something stuck in his throat."

I stared at him, then burst out laughing too. Emad had hardly changed, but I was surprised to see that a mustache had sprouted above his lip. It was light down, but obvious to me. Two boys older than him had come with him and they had mustaches and were tall. Youssef wasn't with them. I was the only one whose mustache hadn't appeared yet.

Emad introduced me to them and we shook hands like men. I couldn't hug him while they were there. I suppressed my desire to do so, in case they had suspicions about me. I didn't have to make much effort to suppress my desire anyway, because a moment later I realized I was less excited about his reappearance than I had expected to be. The pleasure was half-hearted, like the remains of something that has lost its savor. His friends soon went off while Emad and I walked slowly outside the dormitory and past the training ground. He kicked up gravel absentmindedly, while I was impatient to find out what had happened since I had last heard him swearing, the night they took us from the garbage dump. He didn't say much but he reassured me he was well and asked how I was.

He then spoke hurriedly about the camp where he had been living. "They're going to close it down soon and move everyone here. Sometimes they say it will be turned into a government school sponsored by the general, and sometimes they say it's going to become an international hospital specializing in liver diseases."

Based on his description, there wasn't a great difference between the camps. The dormitories were similar, the regime was similar and so were the heads. General Ismail was their boss, of course, ruling over the two camps and maybe all the camps on the face of the earth. Anxiously, I asked him where Youssef was, and he said he was fine.

"We overlapped at the camp for some time, but the head decided against him coming in this group because he hadn't managed to do what they had asked of him and he hadn't proved he was competent. So he stayed there with some other kids. They're all losers and failures and the heads see them as useless bodies. They haven't responded to training so far, but he will definitely come, don't worry about him. There won't be a body left there within a few weeks."

Body. Emad was saying *body*. I would have to bring him into the group that remembered people's real names and introduce him to Saad and Osman.

I asked him about the two boys he had come with and he said they were new friends. They had lived in a hostel run by a charity, two streets from the tunnel exit. The security forces raided the hostel at dawn, took the kids from their beds, put them in trucks as they had done with us, and dumped them in the camp. Their story was no different from ours, except that they had lived most of their time within the walls of the hostel. Walls alone are always enough to make me feel sad and put me in a bad mood. I often thought back to the damp walls of my mother's house, which had soaked up the smell of her cooking constantly for years blended with sewage smells. It ended up as a strange mixture that made my throat feel full. The smell clung to me whatever I did. I had sudden memories of the whitewash peeling off and the cracks in the ceiling. The whitewash came down on our heads in thin flakes and got caught in my younger sister's hair. It also found its way onto the pots and pans, which were covered in it. Although the walls were annoying, I still had a soft spot for them in my heart until I met Emad. He rejected school before me and decided never to take orders again. He flouted orders brazenly—at school, at home, everywhere. When I tried doing the same thing, I very much enjoyed it, so I joined up with him. There was nothing to stop me and I ended up preferring the dump to the house and the walls. I started feeling claustrophobic in places that don't have a way in or a way out. Now I don't know if I miss it or hate it, but I envied the two boys their stay in the hostel. I didn't let my envy show, because it's pointless now.

The four of us met at lunchtime and we went to the same dormitory when night came. The dormitories were chock-full, so we had to move the beds closer together to make room for each other. I was not inclined to grumble, as Youssef, Emad, and I used to sleep side by side at the dump. An arm might hit my head, or I'd get someone's finger in my mouth, but I wouldn't get upset. I knew that someone had rolled over unwittingly in their sleep.

Emad reserved a whole bed for himself so one of the boys ended up sharing mine. I happily conceded the bed to Emad, though I had been there longest and had the right to choose. When we shared our stories and compared them, one of Emad's new friends told me how the security forces had opened fire and knocked down an iron gate to reach them. Out of the window he had seen the armored vehicle that led the attack, completely unscratched. It just pushed the gate to the ground, making a tremendous noise. The vehicle stayed where it was, without coming any deeper or demolishing the hostel. Police trucks joined it, once the path was clear. The trucks turned and the back door opened to swallow up the half-asleep kids from the hostel one by one. He told us the details, but never admitted in his account that he had screamed and cried like us. He didn't talk about himself until Emad elbowed him.

"I stayed calm," he said gleefully. "I watched what they were doing with a smile, without losing my nerve. I didn't budge from my bed. They pulled the cover off and I didn't cling to it. I let them take it and kept smiling. Suddenly someone slapped me, my head shook and I saw flashing stars. Then I heard a loud angry voice insulting my mother, but I didn't care. I've never seen my mother, though at that moment I was curious to know whether their insults were on the mark. Someone pulled me by my underwear, which was all I was wearing, tearing them into long strips. All he had left in his hand was a ragged piece of cloth. He looked at it in disgust and reeled backward when the cloth gave way, which made me split my sides laughing. That made him furious. His eyes flashed and he lashed out, digging his fingers into my arm. Then he landed some powerful punches on my chest and head. I just laughed even louder. He and another man carried me to the police truck and threw me inside. I landed any old way, colliding with the bodies of my friends, who were heaped on top of each other, and I went on laughing my head off. Then, on the way to the camp, I heard guys groaning with pain and envying me. They realized I had swallowed a whole bunch of pills before the attack. That was a piece of luck that comes only to those who know God, to imbeciles, and people in deep despair."

The second boy didn't say anything, either on the first day that we met or in the days that followed. He seemed to be watching me from behind a wall of silence he had created. I was worried his silence might be a sign of danger and I warned Emad to be on his guard. In our camps the silent ones were the snitches, the eyes that recorded everything—what we said, our jokes, our grievances, our boredom, our fears, and suppressed desires to escape. The desire to escape especially was a constant nightmare and source of alarm to me, because few of those who tried to run away ever managed to escape for long. Many tried and sometimes we received news they were dead, such as the boy I called Rice Grain, my would-be friend who escaped when we first arrived. Some of them came back after a while, but they didn't come back to the camp the same. Escapees were taken somewhere for re-education and rehabilitation. The process took days and we didn't know exactly what went on there, but when they came back their behavior showed that something seriously frightening had happened to them while they were away. They were rare cases anyway. Emad had known the boy for a while and had never gotten any words out of him, and the boy hadn't done him any harm. I tried to ignore the subject and deal with him straightforwardly. I soon realized I was mistaken, when they announced one day that Emad's friend had tried to escape and they had caught him after another boy gave him away. They sent him to a place where they analyzed his deplorable behavior. It was only a few days after we met, and I realized that to carry out his plan he had taken advantage of conditions in the camp, where there was serious overcrowding, order was lax, and the monitoring was sporadic. He must have planned it well in advance and waited for the right moment. I very much envied him, but I felt sorry for him and for myself too. I was also angry: why hadn't he brought us in on his plan, or at least Emad, who had been his friend for some time? Once my thoughts had calmed down, I went back to finding excuses for him and consoling myself. Maybe he thought his chances of success would be greater if he did it alone rather than with others, or maybe, like me, he was worried one of us might be an informer. My experience of fugitives had expanded: now I knew two of them and neither wanted to take me along and neither trusted me enough to let me in on their secret.

Osman, Saad, and I sat at the same table, while Emad and his friend who hadn't escaped yet sat at another table nearby. Speaking in an unremarkable tone to avoid attracting the attention of the other kids, I said I'd like to have Emad join our group. I didn't like him not using his own name, my name, and the others' names when talking. I wanted him to promise to use our real names between ourselves, as we had done. Saad was against the proposal and Osman strongly supported Saad. They argued that Emad was different from us. He wouldn't like the idea. They said he didn't feel nostalgic for the streets and the dump. Instead, he liked the camp, and he was keen to be like the heads. He didn't disapprove of the things the general said, so why would he challenge their system?

Saad slapped the table and declared: "Emad's a body."

I defended my friend and his wishes. I didn't go along with what they said. Whether he was Emad or a body, what harm was there in imitating the heads? They were there whether we liked it or not. We were at their mercy and we had no recourse against them in any case. As for me, I hoped the heads would just disappear without me having to lift a finger, and in secret Saad and Osman made jokes about them and the general, but Emad wanted to rise to their level. All our lives were in their orbit.

I was happy to postpone bringing up the subject with Emad for a while. There was no harm in being patient. None of us were going to leave the camp any time soon. We now had strong ties to the place.

*

The assignments office lay in a remote corner of the camp, far from the dining hall and the dormitories. It was separated from the lecture hall by a low wall built of white stone. If we stood on our tiptoes in the hall and looked out of the side windows, we could see the office standing alone as a separate building. There was rarely much activity around it and it gave the impression of being detached from the rest of the camp, except that it was built in the same style and had the same dingy color as the other buildings. The building, where the two heads lived, was in fact the only building we had with more than one story. The camp had plenty of land, and we didn't even know where it ended. We had nothing to do with the assignments office when we arrived, and we didn't visit it until we'd been in the camp for more than a month. We could see it in the distance but we didn't give it any attention. I automatically assumed it was reserved for the heads, to receive important and influential visitors, and maybe for the general to stay as a guest whenever he came to visit us.

Emad was the first of us to go into the office, on orders from Head Salim, and at the time we didn't know why they'd chosen him. He stayed there about half an hour, then came out elated, with a self-confident smile on his face. Those of us who were waiting on tenterhooks, terrified at the various possible reasons why he had been summoned, realized that he hadn't been reprimanded or punished, as we had initially imagined. On the contrary, based on our first impressions of the look on his face, he had received some kind of promotion. We noticed a certain haughtiness in him—we no longer saw him as one of the outcasts and reclassified him as a rising star.

Emad told us the head had given him an important secret assignment, but he refused to satisfy our hunger to hear the details. The little he did say was enough to make the kids envious of him and consider him lucky. The head had spoken to him alone, and he had looked the head straight in the eye without fear. Maybe they had even had a back-and-forth conversation. Each of the boys imagined him playing the role they wanted for themselves: to be on close terms with the adults and stand in for them in some of their activities. The adults would let him loose and he would do what they wanted, and in return he would gain prestige and influence. Emad liked this image and promoted it. He embellished it by giving us mysterious and condescending looks. For a while he became a bright star in our sky, so much so that I thought of him as someone who might defend me if necessary and I boasted that we were old friends. The status Emad had acquired certainly suited him well.

As we were going to the dormitory one night, after all the kids had gone off to their beds, Emad told me it was Head Allam he had met in the office and Allam had given him the details of his assignment, but he didn't reveal much else. I was surprised that he seemed so composed, unfazed by the surprise. He showed no sign of being frightened or tense. I had a strong impression that the head hadn't specifically told him to keep quiet, but he was instinctively afraid of the consequences of speaking out. He was afraid of failure if he told people what had happened in the office or gave out information that only he had received. On the afternoon of the following day, however, he started talking. He came to see me and described proudly what he had done on his first assignment.

"I didn't have breakfast with you this morning, as you may have noticed. I went straight from the dormitory to the office and got on one of those security force vehicles, which took me to the gates of the camp. Then I got on a big bus and took a seat near the front. There was a body next to me, and he offered me his hand as soon as I sat down. 'Awali,' he said, but I didn't know if that was his name or where he came from. Awali. The bus was full of bodies. I don't know where they came from. I think there are other camps, but I don't know anything about them. I didn't say much to the body next to me.

I preferred to keep my eyes shut until we reached the mosque that Head Allam had described to me, but I didn't doze off. I listened to the conversations between the bodies in front of me, behind me, and to my right. I found out that they were friends who lived in the same place and some of them had taken part in previous assignments. That was reassuring, because experience makes a difference in these situations. I planned to look braver and more daring than them. The bus stopped and we saw the mosque to the left in the middle of a wide street. Before the door opened, a man who had been sitting next to the driver during the trip turned to us and shouted, 'We're here. It's over to you, heroes. The banners, flags, and sticks are in the baggage compartment. Take them all, and other people will join you. Hold the banners high and chant as you cross the street to the mosque. I want you to make the place ring and the ground shake. You have three hours. Don't forget: most of the chants are in support of the general and a few for the ruler, and all of them are against the Raised Banner. Those of you who can read have pieces of paper with the chants you should use. Don't let anyone chant anything that's against the state, or the System, or any of our leaders, of course. Anyone who does that must be a Raised Banner member, and you have to shut them up immediately. The driver will come and drive you back to where you came from at the end of the three hours.' I didn't bother to find out who the man was, but he definitely worked for the heads. The only thing that bothered me was that I wasn't one of the bodies who were given pieces of paper, though I had geared myself up to play a bigger role than they gave me. I jumped off the bus determined to take any possible opportunity to chant and lead the demonstration."

Body. Body. Body. I let the word pass without openly objecting. Emad no longer remembered people's names—they were all bodies now. It didn't bother him and he didn't notice that the names were missing. When it came to names, he wasn't on the same wavelength as Saad, Osman, and me.

"We closed down the street at both ends, puffed out our chests and competed to shout the loudest. We brought the cars to a halt by deliberately dawdling in front of them, on the alert for signs of opposition from anyone."

"Did you get into a fight with anyone?" I asked, enthusiastic to hear more.

"No, at least not at first. Most of the cars cheered us on, honking their horns in time with our chants, and the passengers started waving and clapping out of the windows. Then women in minibuses started trilling as if we'd won a major battle. The owner of a cigarette stall even gave us bottles of cold water because it was very hot. The demonstration soon got bigger as other groups joined. Some passersby were sympathetic and stood with us, but we were leading everyone: we were the bodies in the front lines, carried on people's shoulders, holding flags and controlling the situation. The other people followed us and they were very enthusiastic about the new ruler and the general. You wouldn't believe it unless you'd seen it for yourself."

I was taken aback by Emad's account. What was the point of him and the other kids demonstrating? There was no battle, no conspirators, and no need for us or the demonstration. I kept the question to myself and let him continue with his story. He had been fired up by the crowds that had gathered to support them and cheer with them. If he had been chanting alone, a sense of weakness might have got the better of him. I could see he was thrilled by the experience. And why not, when it had made him a role model for me and for all the other kids in the camp?

"What matters is that we took control of the place and filled it, and did what Head Allam wanted. We held up banners and pictures of the general, and when the body holding the piece of paper started croaking from so much chanting, I climbed up onto a large advertising hoarding with a picture of a child and a sun and stood on top of it, shouting as loud as I could. I didn't give up my place as leader of the demonstration until we had finished. The only fight was with a man who had a little girl with him, a toddler, and she had her hair covered, even though she was only about two feet tall! The man came up to us and shouted that the old ruler would be restored to power and the general would be put in jail. Imagine that! He said the general would spend the rest of his life in jail. But the madman didn't get to finish what he wanted to say. A body who's bigger than me took care of him. He punched the man in the face so hard he knocked his skullcap off, and you could see he was bald underneath. He let go of the girl and tried to grapple with us, swearing and cursing. Anyway, the girl screamed and cried and the other people pushed the man back and made him leave. He didn't have a choice. Either he left or we'd have killed him. The people with us were encouraging us to grab him, and some of them wanted to take it out on him. If we had cut his throat no one would have cared. Not at all. They would have urged us to tear his body limb from limb. You know what? From up on the hoarding I saw a girl who looked like Hanager but she was a long way off, and I was busy chanting so I couldn't speak to her and I couldn't find her when I climbed down."

"Wow, Hanager!" I replied.

"In the bus that came back to pick us up, I leaned my head against the window, so exhausted that I didn't notice who was sitting next to me. I didn't realize it was the body who'd been chanting before I took over. But then he leaned over and whispered like an expert that he had been outside the same mosque just one week earlier. I sat up, all ears. Trying to look important and pleased to have caught my attention, he went on to say that Qadri Abdel-Hakim, who's one of the general's main supporters, sent a bus every now and then to take bodies from the camps to the streets, and he had been doing that regularly since the change of ruler. I could hardly make out what he was saying, because his voice was muffled. It sounded as if it was seeping out from cracks deep inside him. Clearly in pain, he pointed to his throat and said his voice was no longer what it had been, even after he had used warm herbs to treat it. He's an impressive guy and he was the permanent cheerleader on most assignments. They choose him again and again because he's shown a remarkable ability to attract people and lead the other bodies. He's been out on demonstrations more than ten times in the past month, and almost always, he'd never failed to shout from the first minute until leaving time. But he confided in me that there might be a downside to it. 'It looks like I'm going to stop chanting and lose my voice forever,' he said. I was delighted: fate had offered me a chance to take his place."

The assignments continued and Head Salem brought in more boys to take part alongside Emad, whose star continued to rise and who took on the lion's share of the assignments. They were soon the focal point of our lives in the camp: most of our conversations were about them and they provided most of our jokes. The rules for being chosen to go out on an assignment were established and everything became as clear as day, which made us more and more involved in our own little world. We continued the usual training exercises under Head Salem and if there was a new assignment coming up he paid more attention and made sure to monitor us more closely. He wrote notes in a little book and then chose the boys he thought most suitable—the ones in whom he detected the skills needed to do everything required without mistakes or confusion. He would take one boy or more, sometimes even five or ten, and those he chose would accept his decision without any hesitation. There was no longer any reason for the others to murmur or spread rumors. Head Salem took those selected to the office, where Head Allam personally laid out the details of their assignment and made sure they had memorized their instructions properly. Most of us looked forward to receiving assignments and proving ourselves. A competitive spirit developed in the camp and we grew antennae that sensed the mood and intentions of Head Salem. Each kid tried to highlight his competence, his strength, his toughness, and his eligibility to go out on an assignment. But I wasn't in a hurry. I kept out of sight and didn't try my hardest. I did just enough to spare me from getting into trouble or being punished.

Once Emad appeared on television and we held a little informal celebration. He was perched on the shoulders of another boy, chanting through a megaphone and waving his arms. The people behind him were chanting the slogans they had learned by heart. He shouted them out as if they were sharpened arrows. He looked funny to me, with his neck muscles corded and straining. Emad had no interest in politics or in the ruler he chanted for. I'm sure he didn't understand what he was saying, but his chants shook the television and reverberated around the hall and the kids started shouting with him. They went up to the television screen and adopted the same stern, sophisticated expression as Emad. The hall heaved with emotions that were extreme but heartfelt, without a trace of pretense. I could see that most of the kids would in fact have been willing to die immediately for the ruler or the general. They were really serious and genuinely loyal to the titans too. But I think Emad was pretending to be loyal to the general and to believe in the new ruler. He obeyed the titans and rode their wave in pursuit of his own ends, not out of love or hate or loyalty. I started watching him and I gave up the idea I had held for a while—that he was a true believer and ready to die for the country. I remember that he fell asleep in the mosque when Sheikh Abdel-Gabbar spoke to us about belonging to the camp and to the general. I wonder if he heard the sheikh say that we are all parts of the camp's body, stones that are laid side by side to form part of the buildings. In the middle of the racket we were making, Head Allam appeared and asked us to go to the lecture hall after the program was over. We obeyed. It looked like he was going to say something important, since he wasn't in the habit of addressing us on his own in the hall. Normally he would just say what he wanted to say anywhere at any time.

"Clean your ears out for me and I won't take more than three minutes. You have moved on to a new phase. You are now active bodies and you've been assigned missions outside the camp. Society has been hostile toward you, but now society needs you. Respectable people support you all across the country and thank you profusely. They constantly recall the ruler's virtues and incessantly sing the general's praises. You mustn't let all these people down. You must meet their expectations. From now on, you must also be as careful and alert as possible. There must be no loose talk and you mustn't let power go to your heads. You, body (he pointed at Emad). You were on television and the pictures appeared on both local and satellite channels. Of course you're happy and proud, and you're right to feel that way, but you're not thinking about the consequences of being famous. From now on you're a hero, but you're also in the line of fire. Whenever you go out on the streets, you face the possibility that you might be recognized by some traitor, a member of the Raised Banner for example, or one of their supporters. No one would blame you if you defended yourself. In fact, you have a duty to keep yourself safe, because now you're worth something, and when it comes to the crunch, a scratch on the tip of your finger would be worth more than the head of one of those people. You must also bear in mind that information about the state, the System, and the camp is classified, and you mustn't pass it on to ordinary people. That would pose a real danger to the country we're protecting. The only option you have is to live up to your responsibilities, endure hardship, and do your duty selflessly, as the general has asked you to do. I congratulate all the bodies who have achieved success on past assignments, and I want you all to prove your worth as loyal camp bodies in the days to come. Now go to your dormitories, think about what I've said, and make sure you've understood it."

We followed Head Salem into the room, where we were welcomed by Head Allam, who was reclining in his chair. He moved back a little and looked at us as if thinking, then sat up with his elbows on the desk.

"How have you been doing in the training, you bodies? Is it true, Head Salem, that they've done well in running and jumping? If that's the case, it's time to test you out. Tomorrow morning, you're going to the old university hospital. You'll take the bus with the security forces and join the demonstration that starts there as if you're part of it. Head Salem will give you weapons and clothes that won't attract any attention."

As I listened, I looked down at his feet under the desk, and wished I could have boots like his: black infantry boots with soles as thick as tank treads.

"At the right time, when you're out of sight, fire some shots toward our forces. Are you listening? Toward our forces, three or four stray shots. Then run off as fast as you can into the confusion. Run without stopping until you get to the bus that brought you, and when the security forces arrest you, resist for a while, and then submit. Absolutely don't surrender to those traitors. If you fall into their hands you'll be beaten to death. We know they have weapons and are planning to use them against us, so there's no point in waiting. We have to go on the offensive against them and force them to bring out their weapons against us. Then we'll destroy the weapons and punish them for possession as harshly as we can. Understood?"

"Understood, Head Allam."

When we came out of his office, we weren't the same people who had gone in. Saad was eager to see the streets again, but as usual I was anxious. What if the traitors in the demonstration caught us? What if we shot one of our own forces by mistake?

Saad stood looking out of the open windows at the back of the police truck. Since no one told him off, I stood up too and looked out at the road. We stopped at the edge of the camp for security procedures. There was a metal gate between two towers, each with a soldier armed with an automatic weapon, and a wall higher than the back of the truck, with coils of barbed wire along the top. I had a good look and noticed that the top of the wall had sharp pieces of glass embedded in cement. How had Rice Grain escaped? If he had, he must be able to survive anything, however difficult. I wondered what had happened to Emad's friend and hoped he wouldn't end up like Rice Grain: a rotting corpse on the television screen. Maybe a kinder fate awaited him.

We left the camp behind us and an endless stretch of yellow desert appeared. I scanned the dunes for signs of the lame boy and the people who were with him, but all the dunes looked exactly the same, like clones of each other, and there were no footprints on them. After a while a wall like the wall of our camp appeared but the truck was moving too fast for me to make out what was written on the sign above the gate. We drove for about another hour until we reached a built-up area and I started to prepare myself, my palms moist with sweat.

After we got back, we stood at Head Allam's door. I was smiling as I remembered the face of the man at the demonstration who pointed at me and shouted, "That's the guy who fired the shots, the dark guy in jeans and a white t-shirt. I saw him getting out of the truck with the police. He's with them, the son of a bitch, the pig. Grab him." I hoped the head would ask me why I was smiling, so I could tell him how I had run as fast as I could, with dozens of them running after me, and how one of them had pulled out a pistol and aimed it at me, but I had rolled onto the ground before he fired, then jumped up and kept running until I deliberately fell into the hands of the soldiers, who surrounded me and handcuffed me. Then, as I pretended to resist, they pushed me to the back of the truck. Saad was already there.

Head Salem went in alone, while we stayed outside and heard him declaring, in a loud voice, "Mission accomplished, Head Allam. The bodies did well and we killed five members of the group. The television channels are breaking the news now on their tickers. They're saying the security forces were shot at with live ammunition while securing an anti-government demonstration, and they responded decisively. They're saying they managed to eliminate some of the ringleaders and arrested some others, and secured the weapons used in the attack. Would you like to meet the bodies?"

I smiled broadly as I prepared to claim my first victory.

8

Halim

AIDA KNEW SHE SHOULD GO to visit Sara al-Sabbagh's family as soon as possible. She had no idea what the parents were like. Neither of them had passed by, even once, to ask how Sara was getting on in the study group she was attending regularly. They hadn't passed on any queries or comments through Sara, as other parents had done, and Aida didn't even know what they looked like. They might as well have been an imaginary family. She believed they existed, but their behavior made her uncomfortable. Aida always tried to stay in touch with her pupils' families and thought that the Sabbaghs' attitude suggested indifference and disrespect. This meant she had to step in and make inquiries but her increasing responsibilities distracted her from monitoring the girl properly. Nour, Sara's elder sister did, however, visit Aida one quiet morning before the lesson had started. She said hello shyly and introduced herself.

"I'm Sara's sister, Madame Aida, Nour al-Sabbagh," she said. "I've come to thank you for helping my sister and the other children. You really are an example to us all, and people desperately need what you provide."

"Welcome, welcome, Nour. Your name suits you perfectly. You've lit the place up. If you hadn't come by the end of the day, I would have come and found you," Aida replied.

Nour wiped her forehead with a tissue. Her face was sweaty and flushed. "Really? You would have come by yourself? Sorry.

I didn't want to disturb you when you have so many pupils and you're really busy. I really don't want to waste your time, but just to check up on Sara. I'd like to help if I could have a chance. I know that there might be opportunities to teach as a volunteer. I'm a graduate from teacher training college and I've been looking for work for several years. I have spare time when I'm not doing anything useful, so if you'd be so kind and agree to let me contribute, I could teach English up to high-school level."

"God bless you. That's very noble of you. You must come from a good home with a generous father. Consider yourself a teacher from now on. Give my regards to your mother and the whole family. I'll take good care of Sara and make her a priority."

Aida beamed. Someone from Sara's family had finally appeared and a weight had been lifted off her shoulders. A task that had been nagging her was done. Nour's visit had been belated, but it had gone very well. Aida felt reinvigorated and eager to finish off the tasks she had put off in the previous days. She was delighted that Nour had turned up. The children would definitely get along with her: a well-mannered young woman with a face that looked friendly and reassuring. But there was something else she wanted to sort out as quickly as possible and it seemed appropriate to finish it off the same day, after she had gone over the schedules and made sure that everything was in order.

Halim turned up with a green balloon and a tiny booklet no bigger than a child's hand. He had been given them both after the last prostration at prayers, where he had followed the ritual practice of the other people praying, ending with a turn of his head to the right and then one to the left with his eyes closed. Aida saw him from a distance and waved at him. He came running up to her, with the balloon flying behind him. She pulled over one of the three plastic chairs that were always at the door of the tent, and invited him to sit down and catch his breath.

She took a deep breath too, in readiness for what she was about to tell him. She had thought about what she would say several times and was intent on making it interesting for him.

"You're very clever, Halim. You have talent that isn't common in many children your age," she said.

Halim smiled, but didn't respond.

"I imagine your situation makes it impossible for you to go to school. That's a shame, of course, but there are other possibilities that might make up for it."

Halim still didn't say anything. He just looked at her quizzically, knowing there was something she wanted to say and waiting to hear what it was that had made her call him over. Aida realized he was more intelligent than she had thought, so she abandoned the long preamble she had prepared and told him straight about the rehabilitation program and the Heart of the World project. She laid out all the information she had spent weeks gathering and sorting out, and in the end she pitched her idea.

"I don't know much about your situation or your family," she said, "but the schools they're planning to open don't require that you have a family. They'll give you full board and take care of your food and clothing. They'll even provide recreation facilities. You'll find sports teams, I gather, and in the end you'll get a useful qualification. Murad and I are willing to help you go to one of the schools, if you decide to try it."

With enthusiasm Aida elaborated on the advantages of her proposal and embellished it for Halim. His silence gave her the impression he was moved by her interest in him. She stopped speaking and waited for him to jump for joy, but Halim turned pale and shuddered, not at all what she had expected. He seemed to be on the verge of tears, and his obvious distress pulled at her heartstrings. She could see that his face was flushed and his eyes scrunched up. Aida didn't understand what had come over him, but she backtracked immediately. Her enthusiasm subsided and she was at a loss what to do.

"What's happened, Halim?" she asked. "For God's sake, tell me what's wrong. If you don't want to go, you don't have to. Rest assured you're among family here. It's just that I thought the opportunity might give you a good start in life and I didn't want to hide it from you. Why are you so upset? Don't be so miserable, and don't worry. I'm sure you'd do well in this school, or another one."

Halim said nothing, but stared at the balloon, which was gradually deflating. He withdrew into himself and seemed detached from Aida and his surroundings. She said nothing, leaving him space to calm down and take in what she had said. She withdrew into herself too: what was wrong with what she had said? Maybe the boy was so sensitive that he thought her proposal meant she wanted to get him off her back. Was he a burden in any way? He didn't cost them anything and they didn't take responsibility for him. He just hung out around them and approached only when she or Murad called him. Adam was now a close friend and they often played together.

Halim looked up at her, summoning up his courage and seeking assurance, or that's what she felt. He began to speak in a low voice, as if talking to himself. He told her how he had left home for the street, how he had moved from the street to the Space. His story about home life was familiar and Aida had heard similar stories many times: poverty, a cramped apartment, a meager life, and those painful daily details that drive a child onto the street. His story of living on the street began mundanely but then took her to unexpected places and to things she had never dreamed of. He told her of incidents, some pleasant and some unpleasant, as is the way with life. Halim talked and talked, while Aida listened patiently. Sometimes she gasped in shock or put her hand over her mouth in horror, but he didn't stop talking. His voice was steady most of the time, until it suddenly grew more intense and loud when he told her about the barber. He admitted to Aida that one day he had gone to a barber called Sayed Halawa and pestered him to give him some work. Sayed wasn't a charitable man and Halim's request was nothing new. The same scene had recurred dozens of times. The man wasn't interested in Halim and wouldn't think of hiring such a dirty child to work in his shop. Halim started harassing the barber for money and the barber lost patience. Repeated disturbances by Halim and others had annoyed him, and he didn't want to hear another word from any of these street urchins or see their faces. After the barber persistently ignored him, Halim bent down to pick up bits of cut hair and beard from the floor. He was planning to take them to the dump and make a mustache and a beard out of them for use in acting out Youssef's stories. At that point Sayed Halawa put down what he was holding, went over to Halim, his eyes throwing sparks, picked him up off the floor and threw him outside. But he wasn't that rough, as he usually was. When he went back to remove the white towel from around his customer's neck, Halim heard him muttering. 'Tomorrow they're going to clean you off the streets, you sons of bitches,' he said."

Halim was out of breath and his eyes were wide open, but he resumed the story: "I was worried when he said that. I was used to him shouting at me and swearing, or maybe kicking me to the ground and throwing the trash can at me, or jumping on top of me and burning me with the iron, but this time he didn't do anything like that.

"His low voice was more frightening than when he shouted, and he was more threatening when calm than when he was angry. I sensed he was planning something, or knew something he didn't want us to know. I thought about what he and Amina had said. On her last visit Amina had advised us to go back home, if only for a month or two. She said they were preparing a campaign that included this thing you mentioned—the Heart of the World—and she wasn't her usual self. I walked away from the barber's shop very worried, and when I met my friend Emad at the dump I told him what had happened. 'You're worried about the barber, Halim?' he said with a laugh. 'You're young and easily frightened. You'd better go back to your mom. What made you come and join us anyway?' I left them but I didn't go home. I wandered the streets, steering clear of any trouble with the barber. I went to other rubbish dumps and swore I'd never go back to hanging out with Emad. I was annoyed with him after he made fun of me and told me to go home. I said I'd never speak to him again. Days passed, and I wasn't happy on my own. I thought Youssef and Rabie should leave him and come with me. I spent the night working out what I would tell them, and when I reached our old dump I saw the titans in the dark carrying off my friends, like the chicken man carrying chickens to slaughter. I saw the kids being beaten up and wailing, but I couldn't help them. I stayed in hiding till the trucks took them off, and one of the trucks looked different, as if it didn't belong to the titans. I watched it but no one got into it or came out of it. It just stood there till dawn and on the door I saw the words 'Heart of the World.'

"I ran, but I couldn't see anything in front of me and I tripped over. I lost the sandals my mother had given me and told me to look after. I was dead tired and I didn't have any food, but I was so frightened I didn't stop. I lay low for days, moving around carefully and never sleeping in a garbage dump at night. In fact, I stayed up all night and when day came, I would nod off and then wake up in a panic. I walked to our shantytown, then jumped on the train, thinking I would try my luck, and I got off only when everyone had got off. I walked in the crowd and saw the big river and I also came across garbage dumps that looked like the ones I'd lived in, but they were empty. Many months passed without me seeing any friends and it was boring. I didn't get into fights with anyone and I didn't find anyone to protect me. I jumped on the train again and went back, but I got lost and went down streets I didn't recognize. Then by chance I reached the Space and saw lots of kids like me, though I don't know if they had families, and endless people moving in all directions. No one shouted at me, so I stayed in the area till nightfall. An old woman came by and gave me lots of food and candy and pressed me to take it to my mother and brothers inside, and I didn't know what she meant by 'inside.' I nodded and stood up. I was worried she might take the food back if she found out I was alone, so I walked away, and on the way I ate up the food she had given me. I kept looking at people from a distance and then I got into the Space behind you. I haven't seen my friends at all. Maybe they took them back to the dump, I don't know, but I'm frightened of going there again, because the titans might grab me, too."

Aida's thoughts were all over the place while Halim was telling his story: the dump, the barber, his friends, the security trucks with Qadri's vehicles. His story was a tangled web. It may have been full of contradictions, but they formed a picture that was radically different from the one she had imagined. She closed her eyes and thought back to what Murad had said about Qadri Abdel-Hakim and his work. Then she remembered what a senior official had said: he had appeared in person to deny rumors about children being held in an underground prison. She also remembered the general saying there weren't any secret camps holding minors. Was it possible that the obvious conclusion from all this information could be the right one? Like Halim, Aida was lost in thought, each grappling with their own preoccupations. Aida tried to piece the scraps together to form a full picture and make some sense of what she had heard, while Halim tried to prepare his defenses against any possible development. The minutes passed languorously and Halim started playing with the booklet he was holding and looked at the colors on the cover. Aida caught a glimpse of the title, *Jihad for the Young Muslim*, and laughed despite herself. She had to smile at the paradox. Halim was a story in himself. He unintentionally added a comic touch to everything he did. She sighed, trying to shake off her bad mood.

"You did well to come to the Space," she said. "As long as you stay here no one will hurt you. Forget what I told you and go and play now, or read Adam's stories for a while before they start giving out the meals."

Halim went off and she sat there a while, shaken by her thoughts. She needed to give Halim's story careful thought, but hunger, her headache, and the new information she had received all combined to make her feel terribly tired, so she put it all off till Murad came back. Then she stood up too and picked up some magazines to amuse herself until iftar time. She took off her headscarf and her stockings, then lay down and turned the pages, but her attempt to escape was futile. In the middle of the *Whole Picture* magazine she found a long article calling for a national committee to combat the phenomenon of street children. She braced herself and started to read the text. There was a proposal from the woman who chaired the National Council for Children to persuade the children to join military institutes that would teach them discipline and patriotism. She folded down the corner of the page so that she could find it again easily. The subject had completely drained her. She picked up a tabloid newspaper in the hope it would help her relax a while, and started to skim the headlines, then she turned to the back page to find the cartoon. It showed the general laughing in the square frame, with a peasant woman in a green galabia laughing beside him. Aida scowled. The laughter wasn't infectious, and the cartoon didn't raise even a transitory smile on her face. Underneath the cartoon, a news story said the executive council of some province in the west of the country had decided to set aside several acres of land on the edge of the remote village of Talabib to build a special settlement, financed by the state and supervised by the Ministry of Youth and Sports, to accommodate street children. At the end of the story it said the general had issued strict instructions that similar projects should be set up on the edges of all other provinces.

Aida threw the newspaper aside and put her head in her hands. That was her fate today and there was no avoiding it. The coincidences couldn't have piled up in this extraordinary way unless there was more to it than they had announced. Before speaking to Halim she thought she was on top of the subject, but now she couldn't make heads or tails of it. Who was working with who, and why, and how far did it go? And what exactly were their aims? Qadri Abdel-Halim had a finger in the pie, and the fingerprints of government agencies were obvious too. Public figures had joined them one by one, and the general was in the background of the whole thing. At that moment Aida had a profound sense that there was something disturbing about the Heart of the World project, especially as it was being vigorously promoted by the newspapers and television stations. Despite appearances, it wasn't just a matter of providing education, healthcare, and social services to children in need. There was an aspect that people couldn't see, and that she herself would not have seen unless Halim had spoken out. Her thoughts wandered and she felt dizzy. Apparently, as Murad had said, Qadri Abdel-Hakim's trucks were just a front and the security force commanders were sending their own trucks to pick up the kids by force, as had happened to Halim's friends. There were whole areas that were being cleared of street kids overnight. So that was why they had disappeared from her area. They were holding them in penal institutions, maybe even underground, and collecting donations from people as part of the act they had prepared. So it wasn't innocent or humanitarian, but yet another disaster to be added to all the other disasters and, to her disappointment, she had been keen to send Halim to join them. As she awaited Murad's arrival impatiently, she questioned herself, wondering if she was being too suspicious and jumping to too many conclusions.

*

Adel al-Sabbagh stretched out his legs and put his feet on a small wooden chair he had brought from home. He took a pack of cigarettes from his shirt pocket but then remembered it was daytime in Ramadan, so he pursed his lips, put the pack back and turned to his daughter, in the hope that talking to her might distract him from a strong desire to smoke.

"How are you, my dear?" he said. "And how's Auntie Aida? Have you made friends with her and her son?"

Nour turned to him reproachfully, but it was Sara who answered. "Auntie Aida sends her regards to Mom after every lesson," she said. "And Adam takes part with us but he doesn't speak to me. He only speaks to Halim and the electrician's son."

"No matter. The important thing is Auntie Aida," said the father. "And have you seen Uncle Murad? How's his clinic doing? Tell him that if he needs anything I can help. If he wants to get hold of any supplies that he's missing, anything from drips and imported ointments to the latest Lasik equipment, then I'll be there for him, and that would be at very special discounts that I don't give anyone else. We're brothers in the Space and we have to help each other out and provide whatever people need, or else they'd go looking for it somewhere else and we'd lose. I mean, lose having them among us."

He went back to his other daughter, who hadn't taken part in the conversation but had buried her head in a book.

"And you, Nour," he said, "did you and Auntie Aida agree today on what you can teach? You have to help her enthusiastically. I want her to rely on you and trust you so much she makes you her right arm. By the way, I'm sure you'd gain her trust more if you wore a niqab like your sister."

"Madame Aida doesn't need anyone's help," Nour replied, with a trace of disapproval that she tried to conceal. "In fact, she's the ones who helps us. May God help her in the good she does."

Adel's wife Jehan put the last touches to her hairdo and had a good look in the small mirror she kept with her wherever she went. Then she turned to her daughters and said, "What do you think of the color? Do you like how shiny it is? It's much better than the henna I used last month."

She continued without waiting for an answer: "I think Dr. Murad might need a range of contact lenses, or maybe you could show him a new range of glasses. Most people here wear ordinary glasses."

She adjusted some strands of her hair and added, "Are you looking for a fan for us like the one they have in the tent next door? The sweat's going to ruin my hair."

Adel laughed. "Your hair will be pressed against your head as soon as you put on your headscarf, my dear," he said, "and no one will see it. Have you forgotten you're wearing a hijab as long as you're in the Space?"

Nour closed her book and got up to perform the afternoon prayers. Sara went up to her father endearingly and asked him for the new cellphone advertised by Samsung.

He gave way easily. "Okay, Miss Sara. I can't deny Your Highness anything for long. You're the only person here who treats me kindly. Show me how clever you are and the phone will be yours."

Murad looked exhausted when he came back from the clinic in the Space. Aida wasn't used to seeing him like that. He was worn down by the pressure of work and the number of patients, even after Ibrahim had joined him, supposedly to relieve him of some of his workload. He threw himself down on the mattress with a groan, without changing his clothes. Aida was sure he was really tired, since for the past fifteen years, as long as they had been married, he had come through the door of the house, taken off his shoes, changed into comfortable clothes, washed, and then prayed. He had kept up this habit in the Space for three straight weeks. He might have made some slight adjustments because the place was so cramped and there wasn't a bathroom in the tent, but nothing more. Before she could ask, he volunteered an explanation for the state he was in: "Today was the hardest day of work I've ever had. I handled more than fifty patients, besides the simple procedures. There was a child who got a splinter of wood in his eye while playing, a young man whose eyelid swelled up as he was unloading some stones, and an old woman who wanted glasses so that she could read the news ticker on the Archipelago Channel on her son's cellphone, but she didn't respond when I pointed to the sight chart and behaved as if she couldn't see me. I spent half an hour talking her into closing one eye and opening the other, but she refused. I can't even remember the number of people I sent to the hospital for major surgery."

Aida raised her eyebrows. "And where's Ibrahim?" she asked. "Wasn't he at the clinic today?"

"He was right beside me, but he was working at half-strength. He's volunteered for the self-defense groups and he spent the night on duty at the main entrance, next to the shopping center."

"Seriously? I wouldn't expect a doctor like him to spend the few hours of rest he has standing guard!"

"Nor me. I thought he must have been up all night with books, working on his thesis. When I asked him I was surprised by his answer. He signed up with the area official and he's going to guard one of the entrances two nights a week and on those days I'll have to make up for his slowness and lack of concentration."

"But I heard that they choose the least educated and most junior people to do front-line security. They usually come from the provinces. I don't think the group would let the children of a leader, for example, do this kind of job."

"I don't know, Aida. Maybe you're right, but that was what he asked for."

"Murad, they say vast amounts of weapons have come into the Space: rifles, Kalashnikovs, high explosive bombs, and anti-aircraft missiles. On one program they even said that the protesters have a tank ready to resist the security forces if they decide to clear out the area."

"A tank? Do you believe that, Aida, or are you joking? Ibrahim told me today that the equipment he was given when he went on duty, or the weapon if you like, was just a club and a helmet for his head. He was fairly disgruntled. The most I can imagine is that there are some light weapons, and knives of course. And by the way, Ibrahim told me he was trying to get hold of a weapon, anything he could find, a revolver or a pistol or even a sword, and I think he will find one soon."

"I can well understand that the Space can't be completely clear of weapons. Even at the time of the first revolution there were weapons around, especially when the security forces withdrew from the streets. I saw people with quantities and varieties of rifles and pistols I had never imagined. But that's not the core issue. I'd like to know where the Raised Banner really stands on carrying weapons, whether they've left it to individuals to decide, based on their own personal judgment, or whether the leaders have taken a decision that applies to everyone, either to reject weapons completely or to allow them. It's essential to resolve this issue. The responsibility cannot be shirked now. It can't be left up in the air. I heard an extraordinary story that involves Halim and Qadri Abdel-Hakim. Would you like to hear it now, or can it wait till after iftar?"

Murad sat up, took off his shoes and undid his shirt buttons. "Of course I want to hear it. What makes you think it can wait till sunset?"

The elements of the story tripped chaotically off Aida's tongue—something someone said, a public statement, a program half of which she had seen at home, a campaign on the radio she had heard while taking a taxi to school, a story spread by colleagues in the staff room, though she didn't know how true it was, and of course she didn't leave out Halim's account. Murad didn't interrupt but his facial expression changed as she jumped from one point to another. He dived into the sea of details and tried not to forget any of them. He was impatient for the conclusion but Aida, who had already aired her suspicions and pessimistic expectations to him, did not have a conclusion to offer. She just peppered him with questions and he didn't have any easy answers—only more doubts than she had had in the first place. He agreed with her that Halim should stay in the Space, and she started to praise the boy, including the amiable disposition that she sensed in him during lessons.

"Children have their own way of understanding things," she finally said. "I explained to Halim what people are doing here and he understood that they're working as a team against the authority that he fears and hates. He seemed to like the idea and felt that taking part in the protest with us was one way to challenge them. That's what he told me in his childish way. Imagine."

"So now you're recruiting a young boy, Aida," said Murad with a laugh. "Are you going to enlist him in the ranks of the Raised Banner?"

"He came to the protest by himself. No one invited him. He had nowhere else to turn and the Space took him in. Where else do you think he should go?"

"I think this generation is different," replied Murad, seriously again. "It might offer some hope. It might win the freedom for which we failed to pass the test. The generation of Halim and Adam will make up for our shameful failure, one way or another."

The meeting broke up and Shakir set about making his calls. He had taken on some tasks that could not be delayed. Organizing the protest and sustaining it during the month of Ramadan posed a real challenge. The Raised Banner had managed to do it adroitly. Naturally that was gratifying to Shakir, but he also had major responsibilities for maintaining that success in the coming days. The start of Ramadan had served them in a way neither they nor the System had imagined. The spiritual aspects of fasting gave people certainty that their anxieties would soon be over and victory achieved. At the special prayers in the evening, all the men stood in line with their skin tingling in the belief that the thousands of people around them could never have come together in a mistaken cause. The Raised Banner would lose an important aspect of its influence over people when the month came to an end, but there were preachers and sheikhs who could keep people fired up and even whip up their emotions further. He started thinking of ones that he knew. He was well aware of the powerful effect they had when they mounted the podium. He had some names in mind and could call on them to fill the need in the coming period. As he strode along, he started working out a plan to proceed along two parallel tracks. First, there were protesters who were satisfied because they felt they were campaigning to please God, were not concerned with minutiae and were willing to give up even a minimum of comforts as long as they felt that someone was leading them to their objective. But a percentage of the thousands of protesters would have no incentive to stay if they received nothing in return. Some of them hardly had enough to live on, and providing food and the necessities of life did attract many people of all kinds. Prominent people, on the other hand, needed a little more, and for them some comforts would do no harm. Members of the abducted ruler's advisory council, for example, might like special food and a comfortable place to sleep. Some of them might not object to sitting cross-legged on the ground, but some of them were used to their home comforts and their bodies wouldn't tolerate anything less. So he would have to give each category what they needed to ensure continuity, because backing down was not an option.

Shakir stopped a few steps from the door, cleared his throat and said hello loud enough for the people in the tent to hear. Adel al-Sabbagh's face lit up as soon as he heard Shakir's voice, and he jumped to his feet.

"Welcome, welcome, delighted to see you, Brother Shakir," he said. "Why haven't you been visiting us? I hope you're not upset with us for some reason. We've really missed you."

"How are you, Mr. Adel? You know how organizing things can be an endless task."

"I swear, if it wasn't Ramadan, I'd ask my wife to get some food ready right away. Would you like to sit here or shall we go over to the council tent? I'm with you whatever you prefer. Sara, bring two seats over quickly."

The men sat outside the tent in the shade of a big picture of the abducted ruler that was attached to the top of the tent. Shakir looked at the picture for a moment and Adel turned to look too, then he smiled and pointed upward.

"Those glasses our ruler's wearing came from me," he said. "I mean from the optician's where I'm a partner."

"Congratulations," Shakir murmured. "We pray to God to bring him back safe and sound."

"Amen. Tell me, how are the Brothers outside? I mean outside the Space of course. Are they managing okay financially?"

"So far so good, though I'm worried some discriminatory economic measures might be taken against them, as a way to put pressure on us and force us to leave."

"Don't say that! You'll get me worried. I'm sure they've thought it through and in the end it will sort itself out. The protest is very strong and the Raised Banner is in control of the place."

"In any case, I came to advise you to stock up. We don't want any shortages in the shops around us in the last few days of Ramadan, especially tea, coffee, herbs, tinned goods, nuts, dried fruit, and stuff for children. Of course you know we'd have no problem feeding the whole protest for months to come, but some of the protesters like to do their own shopping and don't like to have particular meals imposed on them. The ruler's deputies are here with us, and his advisers and their families, and those people have special requirements, as you'd understand."

"Whatever you say. I'll do what I can and I'm sure there'll be no problem providing what you want. I promise you that no Brother or Sister will see a shortage of any product in the supermarket or any other store within twenty kilometers of here. I'll ask Qadri to provide three or four times as much to cover the Eid period too, and after. To be honest, that man never denies me anything, as long as the wheels are turning and there's business to be done. Don't forget us when it comes to the arrears. I know the ready cash that's moving now is enough to satisfy the whole country till the Day of Judgment, and the side channels for donations are pouring more into your coffers. And there's no harm in a little love coming our way."

Adel laughed again. Shakir got up from his seat and, without making any comment, put out his hand to shake Adel's, with just a smile that played on his lips and a hard squeeze on his host's shoulder, as a message of reassurance unalloyed by doubt.

Near the fairground Halim came across many children who had had their faces painted, as at the annual Sayeda Zeinab fair. He liked the way they looked and followed the path they were coming from until he reached the big wheel, where he spotted some small red, blue, and yellow cups. Intrigued, he went closer and saw a young woman sitting on a crate that had contained bottles of water, with her painting equipment on another crate. She had several brushes of colored paint in her hands. Boys and girls were lined up in front of her, awaiting their turn. He didn't know if having your face painted was free, like the swings and the other rides, or if you had to pay. For a while he watched her running the brush over their noses and cheeks, painting beards and mustaches on them or putting circles or squares around their eyes. Then he hurried off.

He went back to tell Adam about his important discovery. He wanted to take him by the hand and show him the place, but the daughter of the inspection official turned up, followed by Saber's son Hussein and finally Sara. Then Aida took her place in the middle to start teaching. For the whole hour Halim and Adam were fidgeting in their seats, dying to stand in line to have their faces painted. Finally Aida put her pencil in her book and closed it. As at the end of every lesson, she urged them to come on time for the next lesson. Adam stood up and took her aside to tell her he planned to have his face painted as Superman. He asked her if she would come along with him.

Aida was hesitant. She had nothing against painting faces in itself, but she wasn't comfortable with the whole situation. The paints might not be safe and she didn't know how careful they were about keeping the brushes and other things clean. She tried in vain to make her case to Adam, and the negotiations between them dragged in Hussein and Sara. The daughter of the inspection official left, uninterested in the face-painting. Halim stood at a distance, awaiting the outcome of the discussion. Moments later, Aida raised the white flag. She gave Adam permission to go, and handed him twenty pounds, enough for both Adam and Halim to have their faces painted. Hussein arrived a few minutes later and hurried after them with two pounds in his hand. Sara followed him, holding up her long dress and trying to run too. When Hussein saw her behind him he stopped and turned to her with a scowl.

"What do you want?" he said. "Don't follow me."

"I'm not following you. I'm going to have my face painted too."

"It's not for girls."

"Mind your own business. My father agrees, so I'm going to have it painted."

"You're wearing a niqab, so how can you have it painted, eh?"

"That's nothing to do with you. I'll have my hands painted, and around my eyes."

Halim and Adam stopped at the sound of the argument and went back to find out what it was all about. "I'm coming with you," Sara told them. "I have my father's permission and some money."

"No, you can't come," shouted Hussein. He was impatient and her insistence had made him angry. "Why are you always butting in on us? Go and look for some girls like you. I bet your father doesn't know who you're going with."

Sara couldn't understand why Hussein hated her so much. She didn't like him either, but she hadn't lied to him. Her mother and father didn't object to her going: in fact they welcomed the idea. Anyway, she wasn't going to give in so easily. She stepped away and stood defiantly next to Halim.

"I'm not talking to you. I'm going with Halim," she said.

Hussein expected Halim to turn against her and take his side out of male solidarity. But Halim, who had no preconceptions about gender or religion and had learned his principles on the street, disappointed him and agreed to go with Sara. They walked on side by side. Halim slowed his pace, allowing Hussein, who was fuming more than ever, to overtake them. Adam walked beside him. He hadn't expressed support for either of them. It was all the same to him and all he cared about was looking like Superman before the day was over and before the face painter was gone. The four of them stood in line. Halim chose to be a cat with whiskers. Hussein asked for thick eyebrows and vertical lines on his cheeks, like an ancient warrior, while Sara got red and yellow flowers on the back of her hands and made sure that everyone could see them.

When the cannon fired for iftar, Adam gulped down a glass of apricot nectar, still jumping with delight at his new face, which the young painter had worked hard on. Then he started telling his parents about the argument that had broken out on the way and that had continued until they reached the fairground. Even in the line to be painted the argument kept them apart, though it ended when Hussein left them angrily, after getting his face painted and failing to exclude Sara. He went off alone, heading for his father. The three others came back together, but split up after a while. Sara went on to have iftar with her family and Halim went back to have a ride on the swing. Murad looked at him questioningly and Adam, sounding like an expert, described the swing that Halim had chosen.

"It's the one that looks like a boat with red and green waves, and it makes a full circle in the air," he said.

Aida noticed that Halim wasn't around and assumed he was going to have iftar in the fairground area, so she finished off her food wondering why Sara's family had left her with the boys for so long, especially as the girl was wearing a niqab. Maybe there was no call for a niqab at her age, she thought.

The time passed quickly. Adam finished his stories, repeated some of them and made up others. He was bored of staying in the tent, especially as he had no extra homework that evening. His mother had let him off homework as a reward for working hard. He went out, hoping to go for a walk with Halim and to show off their painted faces, but Halim didn't show up even after the special Ramadan prayers, so Adam just sat there, annoyed that he had missed the chance to go out and worried that the paint would come off before their neighbors and acquaintances and their children could see them. Aida was worried about Halim's mysterious absence, as it was almost midnight. When it was one o'clock in the morning, she anxiously begged Murad to go looking for Halim, and he agreed, although he wasn't as worried as she was. He went out in his galabia and trainers. The weather was slightly warmer than usual and there was a light breeze that made the night pleasant and cooled the skin. The moon was still just a sliver. The boy might have fallen asleep. Maybe the slight breeze and the excitement of playing all day had gone to his head and jumping and running around the Space had tired him out. Murad thought he would probably find him stretched out in some corner, his eyes closed and having pleasant dreams, much as he slept outside their tent. Murad was away for half an hour or a little more, but he did come back with Halim in tow. Halim looked pale and trembled in the August heat, and Murad's face was covered in sweat.

"I found him on the other side of the podium. I think he lost his way back to the tent in the darkness. No great surprise—people didn't pray eleven *rakaa*s today. They only prayed four, so that they could go to the demonstration announced from the podium. They came out in large numbers and Halim wasn't the only person who got lost. Don't move around alone at night, my boy. What with the crowds and the changes to the routes during the Ramadan prayers, it's hard to find your way."

But had Halim really lost his way? He knew the place better than she did, thanks to his extensive wanderings and a memory for the smallest detail. She looked at him in silence in the hope he would satisfy her curiosity by saying something, or disprove Murad's hypothesis, but he turned away with the *suhour* meal he had been given, walked a few paces, then lay on the ground with his back to the tent and began playing with a thin stick. He didn't even stare up at the sky, as he usually did. Aida watched him and noticed that he didn't touch his food. He was in a strange mood. Maybe he'd fallen off the swing and hurt himself, she thought.

In the morning Aida opened her eyes alongside Murad. Only half-awake, she asked if he knew when Ibrahim was on guard duty. He begged her not to remind him of the extra work he expected or of Ibrahim's thoughtlessness, saying he had no idea why he deserved them. She sat up in bed.

"When you meet him," she said portentously, "could you ask him if there were any incidents last night?"

"Incidents? What do you mean?"

"Arguments, fights, any major problem that caught people's attention."

"Go back to sleep. You're still dreaming. I'm late for college and today I have lots of operations to do. After that I take over the Space clinic. Let's speak in the evening. I'll have finished work and you'll be awake."

"Don't joke, Murad. Halim didn't get lost last night. What really happened is he saw some protesters stop a man who was wandering around. They took his ID card off him and asked him what he was doing in the Space. Then they tied him up and gave him a beating till he had multiple injuries. Halim was horrified. Then they took the man to the podium, bleeding and with ripped clothes. Halim hid away for hours and didn't dare came back here till you found him. After you and Adam went to sleep, I quizzed him on what had happened and he told me the whole story. He was deeply troubled and asked me what would happen to him. He wanted to know what people would do to him if they caught him here, since he has no family and no ID card."

Ibrahim came into the clinic primed and on edge. As soon as he saw Murad he launched into his own account of what had happened the previous night. In his impatience he even forgot to say hello. He confided in Murad that while he was on guard duty they had discovered an informer and the protesters would have killed him if the security officials hadn't saved him and held him in custody for interrogation. The news had an electrifying effect on the mood in the tent.

"The incident worked on Ibrahim like magic," Murad told Aida in amazement. "I wish you could have seen him.

He was so energetic and took such an interest in the patients, unlike last time. He was efficient and alert all day long. He didn't force me to work harder to make up for his exhaustion and his eyelids weren't drooping from lack of sleep. He was many times sharper than when he comes on ordinary days. He looked like he'd finished some Herculean task."

Aida shook her head, imagining the emotions Ibrahim had been through. She knew he was more enthusiastic about confrontations and other challenges than he was about his job, which had little to do with political battles. Anyway, Murad hadn't told her anything new. The informer everyone was talking about seemed to be the person Halim had seen. She heard the same story when she visited neighbors around noon. The news had spread. Based on what she knew about the inner working of the Raised Banner and on what Shakir himself had said, Shakir's wife Fayza said the System was sending loads of informers to mingle among the protesters, collect information, write reports, and try to demoralize them. When Aida looked anxious, Fayza quickly added that the Raised Banner had its eyes wide open and was gradually clearing them out of the Space. She said the one who was beaten up was not the only one. Similar incidents had happened before and some of the System's agents were indeed being beaten to death in punishment for their deeds.

A discussion broke out over the strict measures needed to protect the protest. Murad didn't approve of the Raised Banner making its own laws and enforcing them inside the Space. That would allow the leaders and the security committees to try, detain, and punish people at will, like a replica of the government against whose acts they were protesting. Several times he told Shakir he was opposed to this practice, but he wasn't eager to be dogmatic about it, because the situation had grown more complicated as time passed and it was impossible to be categorical about anything.

"Everyone sees things from their own point of view," he told Aida, trying to sound level-headed despite his anxiety. "Take Ibrahim, for example. He doesn't think there's any sense in treating informers well, or spies as he calls them. He thinks it's weak and irresponsible, and he doesn't favor throwing them out of the Space, either. He wants them detained here indefinitely or until they're got rid of, on the grounds that they'll misrepresent the protest if they leave. I can't deny there's some truth to what he says, but I disagree with him, because even if they spread rumors about the protest and deliberately exaggerate and make up lies, that doesn't justify us proving them right when they make accusations against us, as is happening now. If we were to swear right now to people outside the protest that we don't mistreat anyone, we'd be lying."

Aida didn't have a clear idea what procedures should be followed that would provide a measure of security but could not at the same time be exploited against the protesters. Yet because of the negative impression most people had of the protest, she didn't think it would make much difference whether the Raised Banner adopted violence or peaceful methods.

"In both cases the result would be the same," she said, in a tone that was a mixture of bitterness and defiance. "The protesters will continue to be maligned and accused of horrendous crimes. That's just normal practice and it isn't about to go away. People will deliberately paint a hateful picture and dismiss everything that's positive."

Murad interrupted her with a wave of his hand. "There's a big difference between ordinary people, who are led and blinded by the media and become easy prey," he warned, "and the government that's in the know and the obedient goons that it lets loose every now and then against those who don't submit. Don't confuse the two categories. Don't equate those who deliberately deceive with those who fall prey to them."

"You're right, but the victims in this case volunteer to block their ears and shut their eyes. They completely abandon their reason and take the side of the general and the government, which in its turn has no scruples about inventing lies, as you said, with a brazenness that is unprecedented. Murad, they're saying in the media that there are prostitution rings and secret torture chambers and that the toilets are just a facade that hides all that from sight, like we were living in a slaughterhouse and a brothel at the same time. They portray us as a composite of every mortal sin. Doesn't that make you angry? And besides, aren't they the ones who torture people? Who are they kidding? Watch Nanice and you'll be shocked by her show."

"Nanice is one of the people in the know, of course. She's well aware of what she's doing," Murad said curtly.

Aida responded, "Yes, and she controls millions of people who watch her show, including some of our close family members. She's a chameleon who's created two opposing camps in every home. Each camp finds arguments and justifications for what it says. Sometimes they use the same event in their debates, with each of them framing and adapting it as they want, using whatever information that they have and contesting what the other camp says. She has brought us close to avoiding and hating each other, against our better judgment. But I don't think this means we should back down to prevent confrontation, however hard that is, or that we should make peace and give way when we know right from wrong. Nor does it mean we should make excuses for those fighting against us on the grounds that Nanice and her likes have managed to brainwash them and mislead them with the rumors and nonsense they invent."

"Aida, although there's plenty of solidarity on our side, we still disagree on hundreds of points and sometimes we have to do extensive research to find out whether a report about us on the news is really true. Everyone's liable to be blind, to lie and twist the truth, so would you expect anything less from the people on the other side? Don't you hear what they're broadcasting from the podium every day? Don't you think that what they say shapes what people say about us outside the Space? Didn't you hear the sheikh who was given the microphone to shout and insult the general and say his supporters were a tiny minority that could be stamped out with one blow? Do you think the thousands of people who came out and asked the general to intervene and demanded that the ruler resign would now believe they're a tiny minority and wait to be crushed? They'd say only one of two things about us: that we're mad or we're liars. After that they won't accept anything we say, even indisputable facts."

"You're in a strange mood, Murad. You're still angry with the people in charge of the protest. In fact you get angrier day by day, instead of understanding and accepting their motives. If you think there's no point in us being here, let's leave."

Murad became unusually agitated. "I've told you before, Aida," he said sharply, "our being here has nothing to do with the podium or what the people say there. Some of them are arrogant idiots and some of them are hungry to be leaders. Others are exploiting the situation for gain, but we are here among ordinary people, not above them. You and I aren't on the podium, but among friends and acquaintances, and we're going to defend the ruler we chose, because that's how we can defend our right to determine our own destiny."

The discussion lasted a long time but ended as soon as Adam came into the tent with something that he was folding and unfolding in his hand, and that he finally put over his eyes. Murad could then see it was a pair of glasses. Adam adjusted them on his nose theatrically to check that they had noticed. Then he pointed to the watch on his wrist, indicating to Aida that she was late for a lesson with the children. Aida picked up her papers hurriedly, aware that the conversation had distracted her from the group. Murad called Adam over to show him his toy, but Adam told him gravely that it wasn't a toy but a real pair of glasses. He handed them to Murad, who examined them closely. He was curious: they were glasses of a new kind, very flexible and strong, and they could be folded several times to fit into a very small space. They looked expensive too, beyond the means of ordinary people. He wondered how they had ended up in the Space, and in particular how they had come into the hands of his son. He didn't have long to wait. Adam announced proudly that Sara al-Sabbagh had brought them and given them to him. Murad and Aida exchanged glances and thought it over without comment.

Then Aida called Adam as he left the tent. "Take them off, Adam. They might damage your eyes. You don't wear glasses and they're not yours. Give them back to Sara."

The Sabbaghs were extraordinary, Murad thought with a smile. Obsessed with promoting the latest gadgets.

The daughter of the inspection official looked at Sara's hands as she took out her exercise book. It had been days since Sara had them painted, but the flowers were still visible. The colors had faded but the effect was still striking. The girl reached out to touch one of the flowers. "How did the paint stay on all this time when you wash for prayers five times a day?" she asked, without looking at Sara.

Sara wasn't interested in replying or in the question of ablutions, which meant nothing to her. But she had a warm feeling that she was several steps ahead of the inspection official's daughter, not just with the flowers but also through her sister Nour, who had started teaching a group of children in the square, just like Auntie Aida. Then there was the new cellphone that was on its way. None of the other children had anything like it, not even an older model. The other girl didn't give up just because Sara was snubbing her. She asked her which group of Girl Scouts she belonged to. This time Sara wanted to answer but she didn't understand the question. She didn't know anything about Girl Scouts, either inside or outside the Raised Banner. She didn't know of the Raised

Banner system or its principles, and she didn't know anything about flowers or trees. She choose to say nothing in the hope it would save her the embarrassment of admitting her ignorance in front of the other children. She started acting the studious child that opens her mouth in the presence of the teacher only to ask questions about the lesson. Aida, whose mind was still wandering, appreciated Sara's politeness; she was a well-mannered and strictly brought-up girl who didn't chat frivolously and listened attentively to the teacher's explanations. She might have a natural childish interest in painting and amusements but the niqab definitely gave her sound morals not often seen in girls these days.

Fayza, Shakir's wife, visited several tents to invite the women to take part in a march inside the Space. It was very hot and people's throats and tongues were parched, but the woman's enthusiasm soon worked on Aida, who put on her headscarf and told Murad she would be with the demonstrators until it was almost sunset and iftar preparations began. He agreed, but stressed that if the march went out of the Space, she shouldn't go with it. Then he lay back in bed, reading the newspapers that had piled up on the low table next to him. He had taken time off from university until things calmed down and the clashes ended between the police and the students—or, to be more precise, the clashes between students and students, because the Raised Banner students were on one side and the police and the rest of the students were united on the other.

Aida joined dozens of women marching in lines. The number gradually increased as they passed through various parts of the Space. Women arrived from the provinces too, with obvious rural accents, chanting more fervently and more effective at motivating other women. Aida walked alongside Fayza, and Nour soon joined them, trying to drive her parents' voices out of her ears. When she left her tent, they were still arguing with each other over whether there was any point in demonstrating. Fayza noticed that Nour looked a little overwhelmed, as if she had never been on a march before. She held her hand to encourage her.

"Today we'll march here, revive people's enthusiasm, make them more determined, and tomorrow you can come out with us on a march that is bigger and hopefully more important," she said.

Nour nodded and looked at the women's faces. She wished she had some of their daring and courage. As far as she was concerned, they were indisputably heroic.

Adel didn't despair. He kept trying to persuade Jehan to take part in the march, but she refused on various pretexts: she had a headache, the sun was too bright for her eyes, her hormones were acting up, the only clothes she had were expensive and wouldn't look right at a demonstration, and her nail polish might get chipped accidentally. He cajoled her and begged her.

"But don't worry, my dear," he said. "There you are. You can hear them loud and clear, repeating the same thing almost every day. They'll walk around a while and then come back. For God's sake, go and join them, if just this once. If you start preparing for tomorrow's demonstration now, you can choose the clothes you'd like people to see you in, and it would be a chance for Nour to feel that you're with her."

"Your daughter doesn't care if I take part in the demonstration," Jehan replied indignantly. "Nothing I do will make her change her mind. She's not our daughter. She's her grandparents' daughter. Your mother and father spoiled her for us by bringing her up so strictly that she no longer has anything in common with us. Now she's a member of the Raised Banner, and she doesn't have a brain to think with like us. If I could turn back the clock, I would never have left her with them and I would have taken her with me when I traveled."

Adel looked down but didn't object to what she said. He wanted to avoid going back to a discussion that he knew would end nowhere, but as usual his silence looked like tacit agreement. He waited a while for her anger, which flared up from time to time, to pass. Then, in a lighthearted tone that suggested he had not accepted her refusal, he said, "It's a chance for us to show our faces and prove we're firmly on the side of the protesters. You might meet the wives of some big Raised Banner businessmen too. They would obviously get special treatment, so don't hang around at the back. Stay at the front so that people can see you, and if you manage to pray in the front row that would be great. Some journalist might take a picture of you that shows you in the march and maybe we could stick it on the door of our tent, next to the picture of the abducted ruler. Actually, maybe there's no need to have your picture taken. Pictures might cause us trouble outside the Space. You can't be too sure these days and it's always wise to be cautious."

Nour took a liking to the chant, and worked out the words. She gradually felt emboldened and it wasn't long before she was chanting loudly, drowning out the voices of the women alongside her in the march. She was thrilled to be able to join them. For hours she chanted, stopping only for a moment now and then to clear her throat, when she let go of Fayza's hand to raise her arms in obeisance and prayer. Then she went ahead alone and joined the front row. It wasn't unusual that women should form groups and move around the Space, with an initial nucleus made up of tough young women incited into action when they heard some news. The core group would then expand like a sponge absorbing water. Hundreds of women might join in, and their chanting wouldn't die down until the muezzin gave the call to prayer. These groups of women had adopted a standard practice: as they went past they would urge men to stage larger and more violent demonstrations outside the Space. "Why are you sitting there? Arise to jihad! Activity is good for you. Ramadan is the month for work, not for lazing about. I answer your call, Islam, I answer your call!"

The march went past the mosque, then past the medical services area. From her place at the front, Nour noticed a young man walking casually out of the eye clinic. Their paths almost crossed, with the young man just a few paces away from her. He was of medium height, with dark eyes and long eyelashes curled like those of a woman who takes great care of her appearance. Down his chest hung an uncut beard as black as her dark eyes. His gait gave Nour a striking impression of confidence and fearlessness. He looked as if he were going to war and about to make a sacrifice. He didn't look at her in the crowd, but she kept half an eye on him and kept the other eye for the demonstration.

The sun sank in defeat and the demonstrators started to tire. The woman in charge of the march stopped the chanting and asked the women to stay two minutes to hear about the program for the next day.

"Tomorrow, God willing, we're going to join a sit-in the Sisters have called in the city center. Those of you who want to take part, go to the entrance close to the shopping center right after noon prayers. May God reward you well for your jihad, and make every step we take together a blessing and a means for remission of our sins."

9

"Hanager"

THE CAMP WAS IN TURMOIL. Nationalist songs were broadcast through loudspeakers and the screens showed scenes of official celebrations in deserted streets. Many guests arrived at the camp and the number of cars that brought them suggested they were very important. I heard talk about the Eid, about liberation, a leader, and a revolution. I didn't know what liberation, leader, or revolution they were talking about. All I knew was the first revolution, which I had taken part in a while back with Youssef and Emad. No doubt the head would tell us. When the security forces appeared, lined up in the squares, with tanks rolling slowly behind them in a vast open space, I remembered the time when I chose a day as my birthday, after I decided to stay in the big garbage dump.

The big garbage dump lay in al-Dawaran, not far from the houses next to the old station. After staying there only two nights at the invitation of Emad, I found his way of life irresistible. The area was full of lovely things. There were countless restaurants, and the carts selling liver and sausages there were as numerous as the flies. It was easy to find scraps of bread that smelled of grilled meat and sometimes they were soaked in gravy and hot pepper. There were also many sources of amusement, and the dangers we faced there were fewer than in other dumps I had visited, where the children would fight over a pancake. I had decided to stay in the big dump with Youssef and Emad, so I went to settle in and work out a routine for myself: I would sort through the rubbish at the dump all night, setting aside whatever was usable, and then sleep for a while, holding on to whatever I had picked. In the morning I would go to the station carrying the food and snacks I had prepared in advance. I sat on a bench in the shade and tried to appease my hunger by watching people until the others arrived. Youssef joined me first and Emad followed. Then we left together, heading for downtown areas as best we could, walking or taking public transport. There I searched the rubbish bins near the hamburger restaurant, looking for fruit juice at the bottom of a cup or a lick of an ice-cream cone that someone had thrown away. Often luck was on my side and I had a reasonable dessert. We'd spend the days in the streets and squares, and split up when the area got crowded, when children came out of school and hung around between the carts, arguing and harassing girls, and when the office workers came out of their offices and hung out in the streets, the women among them looking at clothes and handbags in shop windows, as we did too.

One day there weren't any carts in the streets. We met on the bench and there was none of the usual activity around us. Small groups of people arrived in colorful clothes—children and people of all ages. They walked to the park and filled it until not a single blade of grass was visible. They set out bowls of food and strings of onions. At noon, our dump had a pungent rotten stink and it was full of fish remains. I don't like fish. I gathered pieces of squeezed lemon, while Emad stuffed the grilled fish heads in his pocket and sucked the meaty bits off them with his eyes closed, as happy as a sandboy. Then we'd make fun of his appearance and start rolling around in laughter. We also got hold of orange-colored heads that looked like fingers and Youssef introduced us to them as "shrimps." He suggested we celebrate Emad's birthday on that day to make his happiness complete, as none of us knew when his mother had given birth to him. Such things don't matter at the dump.

We agreed casually, then the idea started to grow in our heads and we got high on pills and agreed that each of us would choose a day to celebrate as their birthday. Youssef said he would choose Cake Day as he loved the smell of cake. I waited a long time before telling them which day I had chosen. I wanted it to be a day that had nothing to do with food. I chose the day on which they cleaned the downtown streets, sent the water truck out, and put up lots of notices. I didn't know what to call the day, though I recognized it easily whenever it came. People stayed at home and armored vehicles roamed the streets instead. We couldn't even find anyone to harass or play vicious tricks on. On that day the place was a wasteland.

We met Hanager on the day I was celebrating my birthday. We guessed she was about our age, or maybe a bit older. She was a little stouter and taller. The titans were all over the streets, downtown and around the old station. The police were lined up as usual, but there were people gathered on the pavement in the distance, shouting in unison and holding up banners. A titan came up to us and told us to harass them. There was a girl standing near us in silence. He asked us our names and then turned to the girl.

"Hanna Girees," she said without hesitation.

He looked at her irritably, then went back to writing things down. He put her name on a small, separate piece of paper.

"You there, Hanna, girl, get behind those women on the corner and grab them. You there, Hanna Gir Ees, hit the thin woman in the front row. Hanna, grab her hair and pull it out."

Hanna proved she was better at this than us boys. Her strong body worked like magic: she attacked, took people by surprise, and did what she wanted. We met her on other occasions, and her name was always right there on the piece of paper. The titan would say, "Hanager, shout louder than the bitch that's carrying the flag." Hanna shouted and drowned out everyone else. She was louder than anyone had ever been. Hanna slept on the sidewalk outside the hamburger restaurant. In the morning she left for the traffic lights nearby holding bags of tissue packets and knocked on the windows of waiting cars. Sometimes she ran after them to get whatever she could off them. When the titans summoned her she turned up immediately, willing and on fire. She would go into battle against any number of women and pull off a victory without fail. She had passed every test and proved that she was the fittest, without any disability in her arms or legs. She didn't sniff glue or take pills. She had never gotten pregnant and none of us boys had touched her. Like others, we were afraid of her and her strength. The titans knew her and trusted her. They had her name on the lists they kept and they called on her whenever they wanted a voice that no one could silence, or strength that could no one could match.

Youssef spotted her name on their list one time. Since it wasn't a familiar name they had reduced it to simply Hanager, and then they added Yassine as a family name. Whether or not Hanna's name had been changed deliberately, it suited her and stuck to her. It was easier to pronounce and safer, because she didn't have any religious affiliation, childhood stories, or old memories. She was simply the product of the poverty, the hunger, and the bustle of the streets. She accepted the new situation and her new name. When we met her and later spoke to her, we learned that indeed she had no address. Hanager belonged only to herself and to her vocal cords.

Emad later changed his birthday to Eid al-Adha, when people slaughter sheep. He said that he could find more food then, and that he no longer liked fish, so he started celebrating his birthday whenever the streets were full of livestock for slaughter.

A long time had passed since then, too long for me to work out precisely, but I thought that day was my supposed birthday, the day the three of us invented. They changed the traffic system in the camp and smartened up the roads, and there were motorcades cruising around. Flags were flying on both sides and all the buildings displayed a picture of the general. There was lots of activity around us: senior titans coming in and going out, moving between halls, flaunting their status and their power. It was definitely my first birthday in the camp. I tried to celebrate it when Emad was around but it wasn't the right time. He was too busy watching what was happening. The atmosphere of pomp and grandeur suited him perfectly and he really identified with it. It made him stand tall, stick out his chest as much as he could when he walked, and look down on people as if he had his own motorcade and bodyguards. I didn't know whether it would be best for me to keep this day as my birthday, or choose a new day that's less noisy. I wondered how Emad was going to recognize his birthday when it came since we've been eating meat regularly since coming to the camp. I wondered whether he'd celebrate his birthday every time he had a meal.

We heard that the ruler was coming in person to celebrate with us. Then news spread that he had already been to the camp, made a short speech, and then left in a hurry. When all the other guests were there, they took us into the large lecture hall. The sun was shining and the spotlights were so bright that even the remote corners were lit up, and not an inch was dark. The platform had been properly prepared to honor such prestigious people and so many titans. Head Allam sat in the middle, with Head Salem on his right and to his left someone who was said to be a senior official in the Ministry of Social Welfare. Silence fell and then Head Allam opened the session. He told us in a few words that the general sent his regards and apologized that he couldn't attend because he was busy opening a new project. The ministry official stood up in his place and started talking about history and the greatness of the revolution that the army had carried out more than half a century ago. He listed the benefits they had bestowed on ordinary people. Then he touched on the second revolution and the general's role in it. He said we had encountered many obstacles but had managed to overcome them and free our country from predators that had been lying in wait. He greeted Head Allam and Head Salem, then looked at us admiringly and announced that his ministry had decided to double the support it gives to the rehabilitation program, because through success after success it had thwarted the wiles of the country's enemies and disproved the nonsense put about by skeptics.

At the end, cheerfully and with a faint smile, he said, "I'm also pleased to join you in honoring some of the boys in this camp—outstanding beneficiaries of the rehabilitation program who have stuck to the program, performed well in all fields, and shown tangible excellence."

The children looked around inquisitively and exchanged looks across the hall. What did this man mean? And what form would this "honoring" take?

Head Salem was next to speak. "Today we are honoring two bodies who helped to secure the university," he said with his habitual roughness. "During their mission they proved their manliness and honor, which raises the camp's name high. With unwavering determination we were able to eliminate students who had been hired to stir up unrest and disturb public order. There are students who have sold their futures to the devil and incited people to demonstrate against the System and the general. They have even attacked fellow students who tried to appeal to their consciences and prevent them from carrying out acts of sabotage. If those bodies hadn't behaved the way they did, we wouldn't have been able to reimpose control on the university. I'm sure that many bodies, maybe all of you, are eager to prove that you deserve to be honored and that you are looking forward to the right opportunity. Let me assure you. There will be plenty of such opportunities."

The two boys, apparently prepared in advance, walked up onto the platform by a side passage and received certificates from Head Salem, who shook them by the hand. Head Allam and the man from the ministry also shook hands with them. Then they walked back down to join us in the hall, trembling with pleasure and proud to have obtained this recognition.

Osman beside me was speechless, stunned by the award. "Those are the first kids that we know have killed anyone," I whispered to him. "They're the first kids in our camp that have aimed their guns at live targets and killed them instantly without missing. They're bound to honor you soon. You're the best shot among us."

We were no longer eating ready-made meals in boxes. We had plenty of food. Large refrigerated trucks came and unloaded food at the end of every week. They brought packs of pasta, rice, cans of corned beef, luncheon meat, sardines and tuna, and frozen vegetables, as well as meat, beans, and lentils. We tried out many kinds of food and became experts. We had a chance to taste things we had seen as scraps in the dumps but hadn't actually eaten. We took turns moving the food into the kitchen and handing it over to a cook who was as massive as the heads. He set aside what he decided to cook the next day and put the rest in storage. The food came out of the kitchen in large steaming pots. Then, drooling at the mouth, we ladled it out into bowls and gulped it down. Each of us had a metal bowl instead of a cardboard box, and with bowls we acquired a permanent right to ask for seconds.

The trucks always came at night, and their arrival was the starting signal for a competition we had invented. We would bet on what kind of food they were carrying, and wait to hear the answer from the boys who did the unloading and carrying. Usually the winner didn't win anything. In the camp no one had anything to set him apart from any other boy, other than his performance on the assignments, and that was decided by the titans. None of us were greedy and there was no fighting over spoils. We were equals. I liked to watch the trucks with their thick wheels and the lips of the pretty girl painted on the side. I had a long look at her face and my mind wandered. Emad made fun of me for being attracted to the picture. One evening he put his hand on my shoulder tenderly and pointed to the trucks. "All of them, including the food in them, belong to Qadri Abdel-Hakim," he said, sounding like someone privy to secret information. I was stunned. I suddenly realized what a small world it was, like the eye of a needle, as Firdous always said. Once I'd been on an assignment that was connected with this man. Qadri had bought some land from the government and was planning to start a large investment project there. He wanted to build an enormous shopping mall and employ lots of young people. But the land had been appropriated for communal use: the local people had built a school on it and had occupied it for years. The school wasn't legal or recognized by the Ministry of Education but the children went to study there instead of going to the government school, which was about to fall down. Our task was to help the man get hold of his land, so that his project wasn't held up and he didn't lose his money. The local people who had taken over the land called for a protest against Qadri Abdel-Hakim, to stop him demolishing the school, and Head Allam told me to take part in a counter-demonstration in support of the businessman, with chants in favor of his development plan.

In fact, I was less interested in the project than excited about the idea of demolishing the school, and I did everything I could to thwart the protest by the local people. I shouted, "Tell the truth, Qadri's right. Tell it straight, Qadri's great." Suddenly I seemed to have acquired enormous strength and alone I managed to pull down the door to the principal's office and destroy some benches in the classes. My performance was outstanding. Qadri Abdel-Hakim seemed to be a decent man with the magnanimity of a local man who had done well for himself. Despite his repeated successes he didn't forget the favors the heads had done him, so he decided to take on the task of providing the camp with whatever foodstuffs were desired. The man recognized what we had done for him and he returned the favor properly. I kept what I knew to myself and didn't tell Emad.

Youssef turned up unexpectedly. I saw him walking alone to the training ground, aimlessly as if he couldn't hear or see anything. I couldn't help using his name when I called him. If I had said "body" for fear the titans might hear me, Youssef wouldn't have turned or replied. He did turn to me and looked hard, as if he didn't believe the voice, then he loped toward me in amazement. When he was sure I was his friend Rabie al-Mahdi, he opened his arms wide without saying anything, and I did the same. We gave each other a long hug that reflected the loneliness and desolation of the past months. I looked at him gratefully and noticed that his eyes were glistening with tears.

"When did you get here?" I asked. "Emad said you'd be staying in your camp for a while."

"I just arrived with the last group of kids," he replied. "There were only seven of us left after they moved everyone else out. I think they're going to close our camp down completely, or they want to use it for some purpose that has nothing to do with us. They've emptied it out and cleared all the chairs and tables from the rooms. Even the cook left a while ago and we were left to eat whatever we could find."

"What matters is you're here. I envied you and Emad when I heard you'd been together since the start, while I've been alone. I had some hard times without you, Youssef, but I have lots of stories to tell you that you'll definitely like."

There could be nothing to equal my delight at seeing Youssef. I had always imagined I would prefer to be friends with Emad, but after we were parted I discovered that I missed Youssef more and that I liked to have him around more than Emad. I kept saying his name aloud, putting it into every other sentence, even without good reason. Out of us all, Youssef most deserved his name, because he was a decent guy like Youssef the prophet in the Quran.

"I've been out on three or four assignments so far," I said. "And what about you, Youssef?"

"None at all. The titans don't think I'm fit to go out yet. I'm a loser."

I laughed at the way he described himself, since it was very far from the truth. "You've missed lots of things, then," I said. "You've missed seeing the road from the camp to the city. We're basically in the middle of the desert. There are no buildings within sight of us here. Your camp might be the only thing between us and the urban area. You've also missed seeing the police deployed along the camp wall, and the most important thing you missed, man, was the sense of authority, of enjoying control over people, or being in authority yourself. It's a feeling you've never experienced, Youssef, the feeling that you can control other people. They obey you, or you force them to obey. You attack those who disobey you and you're not afraid of the response. I'm telling you, so you can see for yourself. After my success on the first assignment, Head Salem chose me for the group of kids to go and help clear an area of the people living there. He explained the situation to us in brief. He said the people were refusing to leave their hovels to allow for redevelopment, although the government had an integrated plan to get rid of shantytowns and dangerous areas. The government had provided them with better houses built of reinforced concrete and with proper roofs that wouldn't let the rain in. They argued that they had been born there and had grown up there and didn't want to leave, but Head Salem explained to us that these people made their living through illegal activities and used their shacks as hiding places. Most of them lived off thuggery, theft, or drug dealing, and if they'd had good intentions, they would have been delighted with the new buildings, which let in the sunlight, had doors that could be locked properly, and were far away from any piles of rubbish, stray animals, or pools of stagnant water. The sewers overflowed day after day in their old houses. We reached the hovels but the trucks couldn't get down the narrow lanes, so we got out on the outskirts. The security forces surrounded the place and put on gas masks. We slipped in ahead of them. The commanders used megaphones to give the inhabitants orders to leave immediately, but they refused, both men and women, and armed themselves with sticks and stones. A battle broke out between us and them. It only took us half an hour to level their shacks to the ground. Their kids choked on the tear gas: some of them came out timidly and we dealt with the ones who resisted. One kid from a nearby camp, maybe your camp, got over-enthusiastic. He was firing a gun and the bullet hit a woman in the chest and she died instantly.

"You know what, Youssef? When the woman collapsed I remembered Firdous, my mother. It's true she didn't look much like her. Firdous was plumper, and older, but the woman was wearing a patterned galabia like her and holding a carpet beater. She might have been beating our green carpet a few minutes earlier. The situation escalated when she died. They regrouped and started resisting again, although the kid never meant to kill her. We had to fire many rounds to subdue them because the situation almost got out of control, but in the end they surrendered.

"I'm telling you the truth. When the security forces led them away and the bulldozer came to crush everything that was still standing and I saw the people's cowering faces, I felt my chest seize up like on the day they grabbed us from the dump. There were old men and women and many children. All of them were crying and screaming. None of them managed to save even a change of clothing from their hovels. Yet a feeling that was stronger than their grief came over me. I felt fulfilled, satisfied with what we had achieved and eager to go back to the camp as a hero. These people were stupid, or maybe they had vested interests, as Head Salem said. If they had complied at the start, they wouldn't have come to any harm, but they insisted on belittling us, belittling the state and the System, Youssef, and we had to respond. Now they know how insignificant they are, and how strong we are. The television filmed us and a local government official came and said that the leases for the new houses were ready and they were going to move the people who had lost their houses to them there in special buses. I was even more convinced that what we had done was right, especially when the official spoke about the development plan. It was indeed a massive national project and big businessmen were part of it. It was a big deal and it shouldn't have to wait on people's nonsense. On the way back I was full of pride. I felt sure that in future I would always know the thrill of winning and subduing troublemakers. Head Allam's words rang in my ears: 'Hold your heads up high before you leave to carry out an assignment,' he said, 'and don't look down until you're back. Remember, people see you as a symbol of the System and representatives of the state, and the state never bows its head.'"

I stopped there. I had been trying to ignore the irritation on Youssef's face, but it had become more and more obvious and now he seemed to be in pain.

"You've changed, Rabie," he said. "You used to stand up to the titans, and now you're screwing over poor people who have no one to help them. It's only by chance that you recently ceased to be one of them and they have to suffer without you. You used to enjoy defying the government and harassing the rich and powerful. And now you're picking on people who live in slums? What's wrong with you, Rabie? Where do you stand now? Which side are you on? Our dump or theirs? Don't you remember how they grabbed us?"

Youssef had tears in his eyes again as he remembered being abducted from the dump. But I didn't, and I tried to conceal my indifference. The night we were abducted was just an ordinary memory for me now. I didn't even shudder when I thought about it. In fact, I sometimes had a laugh about it.

"They're stronger than us, Youssef," I said to placate him. "Do you doubt that? I'm sure you haven't forgotten the abandoned mansion near the city center. Don't you remember when the titans let loose those vicious dogs to drive the children out of it. The children pissed on themselves and died of fright. Didn't you see one of the kids with me? He was running and screaming like a madman after a dog bit his fingers off. They even knocked down the orphans' home and brought the kids who'd been there. Besides, they're always right in what they say. Can you imagine Head Salem being wrong about the slums, for example? I swear I can't. I heard that Qadri Abdel-Hakim himself had a stake in the development project. He spoke about it on television and revealed that for the project he had bought from the government the piece of land that we had cleared. You must know him. His photo's all over the newspapers and we see him on television every now and then. He also owns the group of satellite channels we watch in the camp and he's the president of the Heart of the World association. So he's a serious man. He doesn't cheat or sell fish that haven't been caught yet. They don't deceive us, Youssef. Don't be taken in by the stories you read that are very different from our own experience. The titans know what's in our interests. They see things we can't see. They control everything. We've never seen any failure on their part, or any shortcoming in any field of activity we've come across. There's no reason for us to challenge what they say."

I didn't tell Youssef the idea that was taking form inside me, in case it irritated him and put him in a bad mood—the idea that the heads think about us and for us. They get into our heads and before long they can even read our hearts. They seem to run in our blood. We see things and understand things through their minds. In fact, we feel as they feel. Have we turned into titans, or have they turned into bodies?

I was worried Youssef would avoid me and choose to keep to himself. I couldn't do without him, however much we might argue and disagree. I was frightened, so I didn't tell him we had been learning to fire guns and had been happy and enthusiastic doing it. We never asked why. We had been taught that it didn't matter what crime the target had committed, whether it was a sick man or an old woman. When we received the order, what mattered was seeing the blood flow and the body fall and shudder. I didn't tell Youssef that the area we had cleared included Halim's mother's shack. I didn't tell him that in Emad's eyes I had seen the satisfaction of the true killer, the pleasure of the bang as the bullet left the chamber, the sight of a thin trail of smoke at the end of the barrel, the raised fist of triumph when the bullet hit its mark, and the sign of a sniper's success: victims falling in endless succession.

I walked at Youssef's side, weighing my words before I spoke in case I offended him. We went into the dining hall and Emad was there, filling his bowl for the umpteenth time. Our normal meal was no longer enough for him. Emad seemed to have grown in size because he had a strong desire to grow, in order to impress the titans and others. But we were smaller than him, and we didn't share that deep desire. He waved at us and shouted, "Hey, you body, and him!" We waved back and headed toward him involuntarily. I wasn't inclined to pick a fight. He wiped his hand and shook Youssef's hand energetically, congratulating him on his arrival.

"At last. Welcome, you lazy body. We had doubts you would make it. You must have acted stubborn and gone on behaving stupid, so they held you in the other camp till they were fed up with you. Look, man, the camps give us food and a place to sleep, so be good and do what you have to do."

Youssef was annoyed to hear Emad talking to him about being good. He took a step toward him, more passionate than I had ever seen him. He was scowling and his high-pitched voice showed the first signs of rage.

"Well, I'm not happy about your good deeds," he said. "I think that's the kind of behavior you'd expect from criminals.

Being good and having a conscience doesn't mean you attack people and intimidate them."

Emad chortled scornfully and pushed his chair back. "What do you mean?" he said. "Haven't you heard Sheikh Abdel-Gabbar talk about conscience? Conscience means you do the job you've been assigned to do as well as possible. If you fail to do it, or do it carelessly, you don't have a conscience."

Youssef screwed up his face in disapproval. He pursed his lips but said nothing. I felt he was assessing the situation to see if there was any point in saying anything more. Meanwhile the boys around us were following the altercation. Youssef was silent for some time, while Emad moved his empty bowl aside and sat up as if he were going to make a speech to us.

"I'll give you a clear example that you can't dispute," he said. "My first assignment came up when I was still in our old camp, before all of you, that is. There were some filthy women who regularly gathered and stirred up trouble in a small province in the countryside. We went specially for them, to the main square, then turned into Bahr Street, which the women had closed off. They were standing and clapping and chanting and insulting us and the general. With my own ears I heard them chanting, 'Hey crackpot general, why are you protecting the thugs?' I couldn't believe it. Who did they mean by 'the thugs'? You tell me, were they talking about us? Aren't they the thugs? Anyway, we kept quiet and decided to keep our cool and wait for orders, but a minute later one of them started shouting insults about the general that were ruder than anything I'd ever heard in my life, such as, 'Hey general, you creep, our brothers' blood does not come cheap!' Does that make sense? I controlled myself the first time, and then she repeated the insult, with all the other shameless women behind her. I put it to my conscience and decided I had to take a stand against what was happening right in front of my eyes. I aimed at her mouth to shut her up, and she fell, and then two others fell, shot by a fellow body, a real man. A decent body who doesn't like to see the situation deteriorate. Just like me, he wasn't happy with this insolence, this shamelessness. Anyone who insults the general should have their tongue cut out and those women were acting without conscience or honor, and my conscience didn't allow me to let them go on living."

Emad laughed and Youssef's face clouded over and turned pale. He didn't answer.

As the assignments proceeded, they reorganized us according to our ability to read. I could hardly make out the letters of the alphabet and when I tried to string them together, I was as slow as a tortoise. My group was the largest group. I was terrified they might force us to study to improve our reading, but they didn't do that. Quite the opposite. They put together kids like Youssef, who were very few, the ones who could read well, and started providing them with newspapers and magazines, and sometimes books, without putting any pressure on us or paying any attention to our ignorance. They exempted the ones who could read well from almost all assignments, though they made sure they worked as hard as us when it came to the daily training. Some of the good readers even turned out to be good shots, and the real surprise was that Youssef was among the highest scorers when it came to sniping, like Osman. Most of these kids wanted to go out and try out their skills. Only Youssef didn't want to leave the camp on an assignment of any kind.

Nothing in the camp pleased Youssef, not even the reading or the arrival of magazines and books that he liked and carried around wherever he went. Unable to understand, I asked him why.

"The books here aren't like the books there, Rabie," he said. "At the dump I could choose what I wanted and if I couldn't find anything that was useful I went and looked for it. And if I failed, I wouldn't read anything until I got my hands on what I wanted. Here they force me to read stories I hate and boring newspapers that repeat the same old stories, like the television programs we watch."

I slapped him on the shoulder to make fun of the way he was setting conditions as if he were a king in his castle, with servants and retainers to bring him whatever he wanted. "Take it easy on us," I said. "The things you're complaining about are definitely better than nothing, and don't forget that when we arrived we only had the water hose to amuse us—no magazines, no pictures, and the television only came recently. You're a body now and bodies don't care about these minor details."

Youssef gave me an angry look, maybe one of reproach, and despair too—a look I had never seen from him before.

"Rabie, I'm Youssef," he replied. "Don't forget my name, and don't refer to me by that word ever again."

I quickly corrected myself. "Don't be upset. I don't like the word either. In fact, I've gone even further than you. I'll tell you a secret that will cheer you up."

Youssef's eyes lit up when I told him about the pledge to remember names I had taken with Saad and then Osman. He offered to join us immediately. If I had guessed he would be so happy about the group we had formed, I would have told him about it as soon as he arrived, but I had forgotten about it myself and had simply been following the rules of the group. There were now four of us: me, Youssef, Saad, and Osman. We met in the dormitory to renew our pledge. We should never address one another without saying the name the person grew up with and, if possible, his father's name. We should also remember the names of their mothers and siblings and grandparents too if the person knew them. We should never use the word "body" and in our conversations we should use the names of the other kids if we had found out what they were, whether by chance or because someone had said it through a slip of the tongue.

Youssef gave me a meaningful look and asked me if I had told Emad about the group. I said that, sadly, I hadn't. "Saad and Osman stopped me from inviting him," I added.

Youssef didn't object, and Osman settled the matter. "We thought Emad wouldn't like the group and wouldn't give us any promises," he said.

Saad interjected, supporting Osman without hesitation. "Yes, we agreed it should be limited to us. Emad doesn't share our interest in names. He's integrated into the camp separately from the group, and, except for you two, his friends have given up their names, like him or even more so."

Youssef shrugged his shoulders in agreement, understanding the reason and aware that he had to accept the exclusion of Emad. I saw an unmistakable look of relief in his eyes. I didn't try to persuade him to support me.

Meanwhile, Saad went back to reminding us of something from the past. "Do you remember what the heads said about identity cards? They said we would get them when we grew up, with addresses and jobs on them. I already know what the address will be and I can guess the job, but where's the name? I often wonder how they'll get hold of my original name, when I don't even know it myself. The only answer I could come up with was they'll make up their own names for us."

Picking up the same theme, Osman said the doctor who looked after him in the hospital didn't write down his name in the register of accidents and emergencies. When the titan came, the doctor just pointed at Osman, who was laid out on a white stretcher, and said, "Another kid from the streets. We're having more incidents with them these days. We're really tired of them."

"When I was very young and understood nothing about the world," Saad said, "I went to school with the kids in our neighborhood. I woke up early every day and watched them setting off with bags on their backs and in their hands, few of them new, many of them old and most of them torn, with books sticking out and sometimes falling out. I would open our door, which never closed properly anyway, and follow them. I went into class with my friends who lived in the rooms next to our room, and listened to the teacher. I understood some of what he said. I went to school regularly for a whole year, until exam time came, and then they discovered I wasn't registered at the school. Then one day he asked me my name and I used the name the other kids used when they talked about me. 'Saad bin Nagda,' I said, using my mother's name. Then he asked me what my father's name was, and I said I didn't know. He waved his hands and kicked the air and shouted, 'Get out of here. Your mother's a fraud. Fetch your papers and your guardian, and then we'll see what to do with you.' I went home to my mother to give her the good news that I was going to sit the exam, but she laid into me, scratching me and hitting me and cussing me. 'You loser, you son of a loser. You don't have any papers in the first place. Do you want to embarrass me in public? Most kids play hooky from school but you lounge around at school instead of helping me.' I didn't care what she said, and I didn't understand what papers they were talking about. I kept going to school, moving up from year to year. I didn't sit the exams until I learned to read and write and do arithmetic. Then my mother got me a job that I hated, and I refused to do it. I insisted she get me a birth certificate, since I had grown up by then and I'd gradually realized that this was an important piece of paper. But my mother shouted and slapped me and made me choose between doing the job and being thrown out of the house. I walked out, with just an exercise book marked with my name: Saad."

So Youssef joined the name preservation group and started to research in secret the names of all the other kids in our camp. Then he suggested we expand our activities and form a new group that would remember events we had lived through and their dates. The four of us were walking along after shooting practice when he put his idea to us. He explained that the news we saw on television was very sparse and brief. It didn't fully describe what was happening outside the camp and it couldn't be relied on. "No doubt we would have a better understanding of events if we gathered them together, sorted them out and then read them all at once," he said. He took on the task of collecting cuttings from the newspapers and from rubbish bins too, and organizing them. The project obsessed him and he started to appropriate the cardboard boxes that had contained cans of food, cut them into rectangles and squares, and used them to store the cuttings that caught his attention. Sometimes he wrote notes in the margins. He monitored news about Sheikh Abdel-Gabbar, Dr. Abdel-Samie, and Qadri Abdel-Hakim, and pulled together everything relevant to the Space, the new ruler, and the general. His mood was more stable after that. His interest in reading increased and he went back to how he had been. In fact, he was even more enthusiastic and energetic. Saad shared his interest and the two of them took turns telling Osman and me what they were collecting. We regularly received *al-Ahramat* and *al-Anbaa* newspapers and the *Whole Picture* magazine. Previously we had made cones out of them or wrapped our food leftovers in them, but then we started keeping them from the other children and making sure they reached our friends in good shape.

In the morning, as we were still opening our eyes, Youssef would take us by surprise with a pile of papers he had made into a kind of magazine. He lifted them up to make sure we could see them. In a confident tone, he then said, "Qadri Abdel-Hakim is like the general, and maybe more important." We looked at him in surprise. Judging by his swollen eyes, he seemed to have been up all night researching Qadri. It was true that Qadri was said to be outrageously wealthy, but he would never be a general. He didn't control any security forces and he wasn't going to build any camps and he wasn't going to rule the country. So how could Youssef think he was more important than the general?

"The fancy dinner you ate last night seems to have gone to your head," Saad commented sarcastically. "It's given you the impression that Qadri is more important than anyone else since he's the source of the food."

Youssef didn't notice that Saad was joking. Youssef pushed his blanket aside and replied earnestly, "He is really important from the food point of view. I read that he brought a consignment of livestock from a nearby country, Sudan or Somalia as far as I remember, but he doesn't stop at food. He has a thousand businesses or more. Every time I open a newspaper I find him."

I had no idea about livestock, or about the countries Youssef had mentioned. Saad and Osman hadn't heard of them either but we shared his impression that Qadri was important. Personally I was grateful to Qadri.

"Maybe they'll award him a military rank one day," I said hopefully.

All day long Youssef talked to us in amazement about Qadri Abdel-Hakim and his projects, his businesses and his connections, until we were bored. We weren't at school and they weren't going to test us on what we knew about him. When we went back to the dormitory, we asked him to tell us some interesting news that didn't include the name Qadri. He replied that a major event had taken place a few hours earlier and was reported in that day's edition of *al-Ahramat*. That silenced us and had us in suspense.

He waved his finger, as lecturers do, and said, "King Ptolemy had a cartouche and this cartouche was stolen yesterday morning."

We watched him wide-eyed as out of his clothing he took a small newspaper cutting the size of his hand and read, "A man in Minya who was digging for antiquities inside his house never expected to come across the foundations of a Ptolemaic temple with a depiction in relief of Ptolemy V, alongside cartridges of Ptolemy IV."

Youssef didn't go on reading. He folded up the cutting and put it carefully among his papers. He said the man in

Minya stopped digging on the orders of the officials in charge of antiquities, who had taken steps to find out how far the temple extended, and that the "cartridges"—apparently this was a mistake and they were cartouches—had been taken to the big museum. I laughed and rolled around on my back until I was out of breath. Saad clapped his hands together, and Osman laughed till he cried: a temple and antiquities? He was talking as if disaster had struck. So we were great kings and maybe they'd build a pyramid for us one day, and then we would have enough cartridges for the whole planet and no one would dare to steal them, as well as live bullets and grenades, and automatic weapons too if they liked. We would also have a vast camp with clearly marked borders, and we could also make a temple in it. There would be no difference between us and their king.

I no longer had the slightest doubt that they had taken Amina. Youssef came across her on the front page of *al-Anbaa* newspaper. He cut out her picture and brought it to me immediately, but we didn't tell Emad. The story didn't say where Amina was, but Youssef was very sad and lost his appetite for some days. He was sure she was being tortured and beaten. He thought they would be electrocuting her with their prods. He read that she had denied the charges against her, hadn't confessed to anything and hadn't given them any information. He also read that there was plenty of evidence against her: in the headquarters of her organization they had found t-shirts with banned slogans printed on them, as well as marbles and darts that children had shot at the security forces. So Abdel-Qawi wasn't lying to us in his lecture: she had been in their hands ever since that day. They got kids to testify against her. We were sure she wasn't far away from us, maybe held in solitary confinement at the far end of the camp. We didn't ask the kids who had seen her where she was, so as not to arouse suspicion about us and our connection with her, but he heard that Head Allam showed them a lineup of pictures, and asked them to identify her. Then he taught them that, if they were questioned, they should describe how she gave them money to carry out her instructions.

As we were coming back from training at midday, with a scorching sun over our heads, a woman in the distance waved at us, and our mouths gaped in surprise. She came closer and we started walking toward her, without knowing who she was. Soon we could make her out with difficulty—it was the girl with the loud voice, Hanager. We nudged each other to show our surprise. She had grown up to become a large woman with awesome breasts and an ass that could carry me and Youssef side by side, with enough space spare for nine other kids. We looked at her in amazement at her size, which had doubled in a matter of months. She seemed to be years ahead of us. She spoke first, in her jangling voice, well before she reached us.

"How are you?" she asked. "I never imagined meeting you today. Have you started working here? Congratulations."

"And how are you? What are you doing at our place?"

"I do any assignment they give me. What else can I do?"

"We've also gone out on lots of assignments. I've been to demonstrations and sit-ins and shantytowns. And you?"

"I came specially to beat up this filthy whore woman. No doubt you've heard of her case—Amina Shaaban, the spy."

Beat up? Did she say, "Beat up"? Hanager reduced us to silence. Amina wouldn't survive a single punch from Hanager or even one of her shouts. We tried to think of something to say that wouldn't make her suspicious. We walked along with her, across the camp. She didn't stop talking. Emad ran up to join us, and spared us the embarrassment of saying nothing by yelling at her and giving her a high-five. They exchanged welcomes and broad smiles and said how much they had missed each other. With his pubescent mustache, upright posture, and broad shoulders, unlike me and Youssef, he seemed to deserve such a greeting. Beside him we still looked like children, even though our muscles had grown.

"Hanager, we've missed you, I swear," said Emad. "I heard what you did to that woman. They say you didn't lay off her till she was almost dead."

"She deserved it. Don't you know what she did to the little kids who lived on the dumps downtown? She locked them up in her organization's offices, took off their clothes, and took pictures of them doing disgusting things to each other and passing syringes around. She went even further. She had the pictures published in foreign magazines."

"Are you sure about that, Hanager?" asked Youssef, his voice timid and croaky.

"Of course," she replied. "It's hardly a secret. The children gave evidence against her and they all picked her out instantly from a line-up of nine women. I was at the line-up a few days ago, and I saw with my own eyes how they shouted when they saw her. I also heard that she forced kids to demonstrate against the country and throw stones at the security forces. She had threatened to embarrass them by publishing the photos and sending them to their families. If they'd asked me to tear her into little pieces, I wouldn't have hesitated."

Hanager walked on fast, as if the time she had allocated to us was over. She said goodbye to Youssef and me from a distance, shook Emad's hand and advised us to keep working hard. Then she headed to the assignments office, as energetic as ever, committed to the task she had been given. She would go the extra mile and never overlook the smallest detail.

In the evening Youssef's only interest was to plant himself in front of the television to catch any passing reference to Amina. He stayed long after the other kids had tired of watching and gone off to bed. I stayed with him under duress: her name might yet come up.

In the middle of the night, when I was so tried my eyelids were drooping, Youssef sprang to attention and, in a crackly voice that sounded like it came from under a pile of rubble, told me that the main defendant in the street children case, Amina that is, was being treated in hospital after suffering a sharp drop in blood pressure while under interrogation. The news ticker on the screen was carrying the report. I read it again and again. The wording was repeated without change, but Youssef insisted on waiting for it to come round for the fifteenth time, and then insisted on waiting even longer in case they added some new detail. I begged him to turn the television off, because nothing new would happen and it was almost dawn. He started arguing in favor of staying till the morning. When I firmly refused and stood up to leave, he gave in, but he made me promise to try to find out where she was.

As we prepared to go to our dormitory, Youssef mumbled gloomily. "Stupid Hanager beat her up because she was told to," he said. "They're going to kill her. She didn't say what the titans wanted her to say."

"Maybe they'll make do with what they've already done to her," I said, trying to allay his anxiety.

"Are you two friends of hers?" said a distant voice.

This time we trembled together. At the end of the empty dining hall a small boy with sunken cheeks was crouching, watching us in awe and curiosity and weighing the effect his question had on us. We were dumbstruck and there was a long silence. The boy decided to take a risk and speak out again. He told us his name and I thought to myself that maybe he'd take the pledge too, making five of us. Then he told us in brief how the titans had grabbed him off the street a few days earlier. Under intense pressure and extreme intimidation, they forced him to memorize a story about Amina giving out money and inciting him to set fire to government buildings. They also told him that Amina had abducted him, starved him, and sexually abused him. Then they'd put him on a television program to tell the story. Finally they told him that her foreign assistants were on the lookout for him because his confession incriminated her and would lead to her being sentenced to life imprisonment. He believed that he might be murdered at any moment and the titans were offering to save him. When they gave him a choice, the boy decided to move to the camp under their protection. I don't know what persuaded him to speak to us. Maybe he was moved by Youssef's emotional reaction to the television report. Maybe he felt guilty about what he had done and wanted to get it off his chest.

In the dormitory, I turned to Youssef angrily: "They only detained him," I said. "They didn't beat him up or tie him up like an animal for slaughter. They didn't blindfold him and leave him in total darkness, as they did with us."

"He was already blind, Rabie. He didn't understand what they were planning. He didn't know anything about Amina and he'd never even seen her before."

As we lay stretched out in our beds, unable to sleep, Youssef continued in a low voice, saying that the boy was just a body in the hands of the titans, and they controlled him as they controlled us. All the kids in the camp were a natural extension of the titans, an intrinsic aspect of their power and a sign of their prestige, but the bodies would forever remain lower in status and less influential.

He turned to me and, in a voice that was quavering and emotional, he said, "Now we're part of the System, Rabie. That girl Hanna Girees has turned into a big strong woman, much stronger than she was, and yet they use her as they like. They'll keep us in our place forever—us and her."

Osman woke up at the sound of our voices, left his bed and sat at the end of my bed listening. I thought back to the past because of Youssef's saddening remarks and the pain Amina must be going through.

"Youssef," I said, "you remember that incident when you and Emad and me threw empty bottles and stones at that big building and at the titans' trucks. Do you think that was why we got into trouble later? Maybe we shouldn't have taken part in that. At the time we were eager to throw stones at the windows, but how were we to know it meant they would bring us to the camp as punishment?"

"No, Rabie," said Youssef, "they didn't pick us up to punish us. They did it because they liked our style and wanted to use us for their own purposes. They wanted to take advantage of our skills. For us it was just a game, but it turned into something serious, and now there's no way out."

Osman joined the conversation in support of Youssef. "That's true. They're not punishing us like at home or at school. They're inciting us to attack the people they want attacked, to grab girls' breasts and asses in demonstrations, and light fires here and there. In short, we do what we did before, but under their protection. Now we belong to them. Now we're their willing tools." I was convinced that Youssef and Osman were right. We were no long free to choose where we went, what we did when or who we argued with or tormented. The titans didn't give us a free hand. Now everything was worked out in advance. It didn't matter anyway, because my memories were receding into the distance and fading. I no longer had my old dreams. They had all died away and camp dreams had replaced them, because the camp was all there was now. My old life and my feelings had faded away. The camp took their place, with its rules and its methods, as well as its various goals and aspirations, with consequences that seemed saddening.

Looking though the bars of the window, I said, "You know what, Youssef? Grabbing girls' breasts, throwing stones at windows, and jumping on cars isn't as fun as it used to be. Was the fun in the acts themselves? Not at all. What I enjoyed was challenging the grown-ups, seeing them in a rage and desperate to get their hands on me."

*

The boy who was Emad's friend came back. I had forgotten his name since he ran away, or maybe I'd never known it. He came back safe and sound, without any signs of injury, not even any bruises. He turned up near the dining hall, as if he had never run off. There was a cold and slightly cunning smile in his eyes that I hadn't seen before. He put out his hand and I put out mine, cautiously as usual, keeping some distance between us, but he pulled me toward him and almost shouted, "How are you, body?"

He gave me a firm hug. Emad opened his arms wide and hugged him in turn. He was more like Emad than he was like me. Osman and Saad were right. As soon as we sat down the boy opened up a little, though he didn't immediately tell us what had happened to him when he was away. He made a few offhand remarks, which didn't satisfy our curiosity, about the fate that awaited those who escaped the camp. When we asked him for more details, he twisted his mouth and fell silent again as if he were thinking.

Then he said, "When we were little kids they told us an orphanage was better than the street, and a family home better than an orphanage. But that's rubbish. What family were they talking about? Before I went to the orphanage my stepfather used to chain me up in the stairwell of the building we lived in and leave me to writhe there for days, licking the water that seeped out of the wall. All my crazy mother did was try to make sure the neighbors didn't notice. 'He's a little devil. It's the only way to make him behave,' she said. The scar on the side of my neck, can you see it? That's from when they branded me with an iron rod. It was as thin as my finger but as long as a corncob. The bastard hid it on the top shelf of the cupboard. Whenever I asked for something, he would burn me, with her help. I knew where the rod was but I didn't steal it. I wanted them to stop burning me because they wanted to stop, not because I wanted them to. I was stupid and deluded. I ran away and they took me in at the kids' home, where the supervisor gave me only enough food to keep me alive. He said I was naughty. When I tried to leave he slapped me about, confiscated my clothes, banned me from watching television and refused to give me any allowance. He told the woman who visited me from time to time that I had attacked the kids in my room. He made some of them lie about what I had done, so she stopped asking to see me and adopted a kid who was younger than me. The horrible man was worried I'd tell her what had happened to her donations, which he took home with him, so he kept me in isolation and gave me hell."

He looked around at us for a moment, and then continued, "I suspect you've all been through some of the same things as me. When you were weak, you were abused and humiliated. The weak are pushed around. The strong push them around as much as they like. They tell us the truth here: the camp's better than the street and better than the kids' home and the pimps there, and better than being at home and the people there. And I tell you: going out on assignments to protect the heads is better than anything else in the world. Now we're the masters, the masters of the country. No one will dare to harass us. No son-of-a-whore driver will look down on us, no lousy waiter will shoo us away from outside a restaurant or a café. No one will dare call for help or report us. We'll report on people and wipe them off the facc of the earth like straw. If some bastard shouts, we'll shut him up and in future he'll open his mouth only to obey us. If he speaks out of turn he'll get such a punching and kicking he'll be on his knees at our feet begging for mercy. If we want, we'll forgive him, and if we want, we'll finish him off. Personally I won't forgive them, even if the guy on the ground was my father. The camp's the best. There's no doubt about it."

Youssef listened to Emad's friend till the end. Then he walked off sadly without saying a word. He didn't disagree with him, or agree with him. Saad was upset that Youssef had left, so I later explained to him that Youssef liked home, his own home of course, and he had left home unwillingly. His mother had left him at school one day and hadn't come back to collect him, and when he managed to get back home by himself, she wasn't there. She had died in a minibus accident. The landlord gave him his books and his clothes, not all of them of course, then locked the door until a new tenant came. In Youssef's experience a family was more loving than a hostel, and a hostel was better than the camp, but he wasn't going to argue with the boy. "By the way, do you know his name?" he said.

Lecture on Morals

When there were more of us, because boys from other camps had joined, they started to give us lectures in the hall, which was big enough for all of us. Head Allam summoned us one day and we filled every seat in the hall. He came in alone, unaccompanied by the guest, and told us we were about to meet Suleiman Abdel-Malek himself.

"Professor Abdel-Malek is the most prestigious psychologist in the Arab world. He is, in fact, world famous and one of the general's few close associates. The ruler also consults him and gives weight to his opinion," he said.

From what Head Allam said, we sensed that this man was more distinguished than the others who had given us lectures before. Not everyone had the chance to meet him. He traveled often and was always busy with the invitations he received from abroad.

"Listen and learn as much as you can, be guided by the professor's profound insights and his analysis of the psychology of the sham movement that is meddling with the security of the country and its people. Don't hesitate to ask questions about anything you find hard to grasp," said the head, who left once he was sure that we were all in our seats and no one was missing.

The guest had arrived exactly on time. He was an old man with long silver hair brushed back like a film star's. Like foreign tourists, he had white skin flecked with red. He wore a light blue jacket, gray trousers, and a blue tie dotted with little shiny suns. The fact that Head Allam didn't accompany Dr. Abdel-Malek to the platform, as he had done with other speakers, came as a great surprise, which showed on our faces, though it lasted only a few moments. The professor commented on this as if he could read our minds.

"I know you're used to Head Allam attending your regular lectures," he said, "and I know you're surprised that he isn't here now, but I wanted to address you alone and let you say what's on your minds without inhibitions. Don't worry, don't be afraid. Head Allam agreed with me that you should have space to speak without reservation. We're now living in a truly democratic climate, a climate that allows people to express their opinions, even if they disagree with the state and the System. The important thing is not to be destructive and to stay within the bounds of decency. What matters most is upholding morality in dialogue and in stating one's opinion, even if you are in opposition. Civilized nations are built on moral principles. The countries you see on television that look like heaven on earth got where they are today by paying attention to morals. Morals don't require a budget, financial resources, or a strong economy. They require real faith and commitment to lofty principles. What are courage and virtue, for example? What are magnanimity and altruism? They are all values that are essential for any society to progress, and of course there are people who are in a hurry to eliminate them from the national consciousness, and hence to sabotage people's morals and demolish the state itself.

"Let me give you a simple example so that you don't confuse the concepts. Let's take shame, for example: if someone has no shame, an important component of their character is missing. All religions speak of shame with approval. It is an aspect of faith. The prophets themselves felt shame. Great leaders and scholars felt shame and modesty. Take me for example."

Abdel-Malek laughed and we laughed with him. I looked to the right and saw that Youssef wasn't laughing. He didn't look at me, so I went back to listening to Abdel-Malek.

"All of you, or at least some of you, must be following what's happening in the country. Some of you must have seen the demonstrators in the Space. The behavior of the people there is hard to accept. They are thumbing their noses at all and sundry, as one might say. Decent people find this behavior repugnant and disgusting. Humans are different from animals. This is a scientific fact. Animals only follow their instincts. They don't care if there are other animals around them. They urinate, defecate, and copulate openly and without shame in front of anyone who's coming or going. But we are not animals, and we should never be, not to ourselves or to those that see us and see what we are doing. We live on a planet inhabited by people who have to live together. The kind of barbaric behavior that the protesters indulge in is extremely dangerous because it is not governed by any measure of insight or balance. It may act like a germ, spreading through the body of society, undermining and destroying the pillars of society. In this case intervention is inevitable before we're overrun by an incurable epidemic, in which case the only remedy would be surgical excision. The iron fist of the state would be called on to restore good order, and there would be no alternative to the decisive use of force. There might be some collateral damage but saving society as a whole is worth the sacrifice and it requires firm decisions. When great nations have risen from decline, they have all left many casualties behind, and we are no less than them. In fact, we are in the forefront. This is a duty, and let us bear in mind that killing one saboteur who is protesting could save a hundred people because that saboteur will not have a chance to reach them. Listen carefully. If there's pus in a wound, it needs the surgeon's scalpel. Every one of you is like a scalpel, and there's no harm done if a little blood flows when the pus comes out. It's a sign that the body is healing, the body of the nation."

Dr. Abdel-Malek left the hall and, stunned, we watched him leave. Then we followed him out and saw him heading to a fancy black car. We could see our reflections in the shiny metal surface without even needing to look at the windows. As soon as the doctor appeared, the driver hurried to open the door for him. Head Allam was waiting for him by the car in person. They shook hands warmly and exchanged a few words. The driver then drove off as if he were piloting a plane. I went back to the hall and found Youssef still sitting on his chair as if Abdel-Malek was still speaking. I called out to tell him the guy had left, and he stood up.

"Did you notice, Rabie, that he was almost describing us?" he said.

"Describing us?"

"Yes. Describing us before we became bodies."

At dawn one of the boys had crippling stomach pains and started vomiting and shivering. We were alarmed at his groaning and the cold sweat on his temples. Then a second boy and a third showed the same symptoms, and in the end there were more than ten of them in all. Emad went over to the assignments office to tell the guard. Head Salem hurried over with a doctor. The doctor examined just two boys, gave out enough medicine for everyone and then had a private talk with Head Salem outside the dormitory. Head Allam joined them a while later. I saw him from the balcony and I pricked up my ears to catch any news. The doctor soon went off, leaving the two heads. I held my breath to pick up any word in their conversation. A minute later I overheard Head Allam talking firmly and rapidly to Head Salem. But he wasn't discussing the disease: he was talking about our education.

"Salem, we're going to step up the religious lectures going forward," he said. "We have to get them a hundred percent ready. It's been decided that we're going to carry out a more serious experiment to evaluate the effect the rehabilitation program has had on them, mentally and physically. They've been here almost a year now, and their performance needs to be tested in particular situations, as you know. And in light of the results, some of the lectures and training exercises will be adjusted to make them better suited for future batches of kids. Our orders have come and our camp has been chosen to take part in the next operation, which is great. The bodies at the other camps will get their turn later, though they may have assignments that are different from the traditional ones that have been done so far. We want some of them to mix with people."

"Great," I heard Salem reply. "We could cut some time from the training to make time for extra lectures. Sheikh Abdel-Gabbar will have to devote his time to us until this issue is over. We don't want any empty excuses now."

They were going to bring Abdel-Gabbar every day and we were going out on a new assignment, because we were better than the others. I'd now established that there were other camps like ours, as Emad had said. But what about the kid who was still moaning? We didn't really need to know the diagnosis, because food poisoning is common and most of us had been through it. We weren't from one of those fancy resorts they advertise on billboards or on television, and we hadn't lived in palaces. We'd eaten out of trash bins. In fact we'd eaten the trash itself, and we'd often had these symptoms and gotten over it. We'd come to tell the difference between the pain from rotten meat and the acidic burn from leftover *koshari*. The question no one answered was how and why we came to have food poisoning in the camp. We'd eaten only the food prepared by the cook and it was impossible to bring in food from anywhere else. If the food in the camp was rotten, then how come we didn't all fall ill?

Youssef slipped away while everyone was busy, and headed for the kitchen. He retrieved some sardine and luncheon meat cans from the main trash cans, then went back to the dormitory before I even noticed he had disappeared. Breathlessly he pulled me by the arm, took me aside far from the noisy kids and the pervasive smell of vomit, and took the cans out from under his clothes.

"I wanted to make sure, and my intuition proved to be right. Most of the cans are past their expiry date and only a few of them are fit to eat."

"How can that be?" I said. "So the rotten cook gives us rotten food? Take the cans to Emad. Have him take it up with Head Salem."

"Are you crazy, Rabie? Salem wouldn't do anything, and neither would Allam. You've seen the food trucks when they come. You know who they belong to."

"So give me the cans and let me talk to Emad."

"No, I'll take off the labels with the dates on and keep them with my cuttings."

I was impatient and angry, and eager to shock Emad with the news before he fell asleep. "Give me one and keep the other one," I said.

Youssef agreed grudgingly. I took the can of luncheon meat, ran to Emad, and sprang the news on him. He grabbed the can from me sullenly and ran out, as stiff as a ramrod. I watched him disappear into the darkness.

In the morning we made sure to smell the boiled eggs carefully. I sniffed one, bit into it warily and started to chew slowly. Head Salem came in and I stopped chewing.

"One of you bodies told us yesterday that rotten food has appeared in the camp. Don't be upset. I've ordered an urgent and thorough inquiry into the incident, and the perpetrator will receive the severest punishment. There's no need to remind you that the enemies of the country are adopting vile methods to bring down the System and that your strength is a threat to their existence. Now finish breakfast, and the results of the inquiry will soon be announced."

I stuffed the whole egg into my mouth and looked right into Youssef's eyes. I wanted to see Youssef admit that his suspicions about Head Salem had been misplaced. Head Salem had been fair to us: they weren't going to ignore what had happened, and for our sakes they would take revenge on the culprit.

The Lecture on Strife

Sheikh Abdel-Gabbar said our society had always been loving and compassionate and that no one would ever be able to stir up strife between us. From his seat in the front row, Head Salem nodded in agreement.

Abdel-Gabbar continued, citing the Quran: "'*Tell them that the life of this world is like water We have sent down from the sky. Then the plants of the earth mix with it and turn into chaff that is blown away by the winds. God has power over all things.*' These arrogant people, my children—God will turn them into chaff that is blown away by the winds. And what is chaff? Have you seen the ground when the plants have died? That's chaff, dried up bits of plants. It breaks easily into little pieces and it's simple to pull it up and get rid of it. This also involves breaking the head off the rest of the body, and the head is of course the most valuable part. If there's no head, there's no life, so turn our enemies and the enemies of the country into chaff. Fight them in God's cause. This is the true jihad, not jihad as the modern Kharijites portray it—those people who are sick at heart and who spread corruption wherever they go. Never cease to fight them, and God will give you strength to challenge them and grant you victory over them. They are like chaff that is eaten by animals—those people who lay claim to the whole Earth, which belongs to God, and who harass the people who live around the Space as they come and go, intruding on their privacy, giving them body searches and humiliating them. Such acts have nothing to do with Islam. In fact, Islam detests and prohibits such acts. It prohibits us from living at the expense of others and from obstructing people as they go about their business. In fact, Islam urges us to eliminate wrongdoing and offers a great reward for doing so. This would definitely apply when these deviants from true religion are blocking off streets deliberately, preventing children from going to school and young people from universities, and obstructing sick people who are seeking help. If an emergency arose, it wouldn't be possible to react. If a fire broke out there, God forbid, the fire department wouldn't be able to do its work if they were blocking the roads, and so because of them, people would be burned to ashes. They also persist in their extremism and their sedition, by falsely assuming authority, laying ambushes, blocking traffic, checking people's identity cards, arresting people, mistreating and torturing them, and discriminating between those who belong to their movement and those who do not. The sins of these people are grave, their deeds have been in vain, their wiles have been thwarted, and, I assure you, God willing they will turn into chaff thanks to you and your weapons, you soldiers of God, because the One, the Almighty and His angels and prophets support you in your fight, and you will receive the greatest possible recompense, and they will go to hell to meet a miserable fate."

Emad stood up from his seat and started chanting, "*Allahu akbar*! *Allahu akbar*!"

The hall behind him took up the chant: "*Allahu akbar*! *Allahu akbar*! With our souls and our blood we're willing to die for the general!"

Head Allam took over from the sheikh. His eyes throwing sparks and his face contorted with anger, he thundered. "Some people imagine they are powerful and can be hostile to the country and the System. Their imaginations run wild and they think that time can go backward. These people are deluded. If we have been patient in recent times, it is because our ideology requires us to act prudently and wisely. But that does not mean we are ignoring them. Not at all. Or that our hands are tied and we cannot reach them. Absolutely not."

He clenched his fist and raised it in the air, bellowing: "We can crush these people in the blink of an eye!"

Unconsciously we clenched our fists with him and raised them in the air. Then we burst into applause that shook the seats and walls. Head Allam asked Head Salem to come up onto the platform, where the award ceremonies began. These ceremonies were repeated from time to time, depending on our achievements.

I was surprised when I saw the first award winner, who had never been out on an assignment. He was a quiet boy who almost never spoke to us. He floated around amongst us, listening carefully to our chitchat, but he didn't ever offer an opinion or tell any stories, even made-up ones.

Sheikh Abdel-Gabbar put on his glasses and started to read the boy's award citation: "He has set an example of sound morality. He has been attentive to his colleagues, solicitous of their interests and of himself, never failing to give them good advice, and even taking risks to correct their behavior if he thought they had gone astray, acting on the instructions of our noble prophet, when he said one should wish for one's brother what one wishes for oneself."

I discovered that he was the boy who had recently snitched on Emad's friend. He had enabled the titans to catch him and send him back to us. I only became aware of his identity when Abdel-Gabbar went into more detail about his praiseworthy achievements. The boy headed proudly to the platform, as prize winners usually do. In the meantime I looked around for Emad's friend: I very much wanted to see the effect the award had on him. I found him sitting at the end of the row and noticed that he clapped when the boy went up to receive his certificate. Was he really happy, I wondered, grateful that someone had informed on him?

The second award wasn't for one of the kids, but for Qadri Abdel-Hakim the businessman himself, in all his pomp and glory. Head Salem said he had served the nation magnificently in ways that were too many to enumerate.

"This patriotic man is a pillar of our economy. He has set up massive projects and he is a strong ally of the state. He has spared no effort to answer the country's call and has put his institutions and finances at the services of this camp, and from those finances he meets whatever needs arise without counting the cost. The regime never denies loyal and honest people their due."

Qadri Abdel-Hakim went up on the platform and it was the first time we had seen him in real life. I had imagined him as a man who had traveled the world and made a vast fortune, as Youssef had said, but he didn't match my expectations. I had thought he would be old but in fact he was about the same age as Head Salem. His clothes were not obviously smart, he wasn't strikingly fit, and he didn't move with any grace. Instead he was broad-shouldered with a flabby chest and an enormous belly that stuck out in front of him. He looked like he was carrying all his possessions inside him: his land, his companies, and his apartment buildings. On his plump fingers he wore thick silver rings and the strong perfume he used smelled like the incense those crazy men carry around the streets in censers, offering to fumigate shops and cafes.

"In the name of God, the Merciful, the Compassionate," he began, "distinguished sheikh, leaders. I offer my thanks to you and to the great father of all citizens, General Ismail. I am proud to be here among you today. I have only done the duty that anyone with a conscience must feel toward the country, and no one should be thanked for that. I shall remain at the service of the state and of honest state officials as long as I live, and I hope I can always be well thought of."

He didn't speak long and I was pleased he was brief. His appearance had undermined half of the admiration I had felt for him before he spoke. I thought of the rotten can of luncheon meat, but then I remembered that it wasn't just about Qadri but part of a wider conspiracy of which he was a victim, just like us.

Finally, they honored Sheikh Abdel-Gabbar. He stood up from his seat on the platform and shook hands with the heads, so vigorously that Abdel-Gabbar's caftan almost came off. For him, as for Qadri Abdel-Hakim, they had made a crest with the eagle emblem on a wooden plaque and a certificate of appreciation. As soon as they gave the sheikh his award, the hall burst into applause and he turned to receive the acclaim with a subdued smile that preserved his dignity. He looked down at the floor, anxious to appear grave.

When the awards ceremony was over and the guests had left, we were asked to stay where we were. Head Allam produced a black, medium-sized electronic device and plugged it into a socket in the wall. I racked my brain trying to think where I had seen a similar device before, but I couldn't remember. The sheikh's lecture and the talks by the heads had driven everything else out of my brain. Everything seemed dull in comparison.

The hall was completely dark except for a tiny light as small as a pinhead that showed us where the device was. Then the massive screen, which looked like a cinema screen, began to show a sequence of images. Each picture had a caption, which Head Allam read out to us. We saw a picture of a column of trucks carrying strange things we couldn't make out properly. The head said the Raised Banner falsely claimed that these trucks were carrying food and drink, when in reality they were taking weapons to what he called the Space. He gave us secret information about the amounts of ammunition and explosives that gunmen were smuggling to the protesters through tunnels that had been dug specially for that purpose. He said that twenty thousand armed men had entered the country illegally to carry out attacks on us in support of the Raised Banner movement. After that, there appeared a picture of a group of people wearing short galabias and each pointing one finger of each hand upward. The head explained that they were chanting that they were willing to die in order to free the old ruler and destroy the state and that among them there were suicide bombers who were willing to blow themselves up, along with us.

The screen went dark for some seconds, then lit up again with a video, rather than still pictures, with a solemn voice explaining what was happening. At the beginning we saw a clip in which the protesters detained a number of people and started torturing them. We could hear the torture going on under the wooden platform from which they made their speeches, which they called the podium. Then we saw another clip of a man with a big beard jumping onto the veranda of a house and stealing a cell phone, a pair of glasses, a tape recorder, and some clothes, and then running off. The third clip showed some protesters of about our age vandalizing the cars of the people living around the Space by puncturing the tires, throwing trash at windows, and writing obscene words on walls. Finally Head Allam froze the projector on a picture of a young, muscular man dressed in jeans, a shirt, and boots. His hands were tied and one of the protesters was slapping him on the face. The head said the man was from the security forces and they had caught him at one of the entrances to the Space. The man hadn't been able to escape them, and he was still being held there. The sight angered us and made us more receptive to orders. We stood up immediately, burning with rage, and some of the kids shouted out vulgar insults and made whistles of protests. How could they do this to one of us? If we had been in his place we wouldn't have submitted. We would have brought the place down on their heads. I felt the blood rushing to my head and boiling, and I whistled with the other boys. I wanted to take revenge myself for this poor guy who'd been caught. I couldn't take my eyes off the screen and a new feeling overwhelmed me—the sudden realization that in the past we had been completely detached from the real world. We had been aware only of our own immediate needs, and the battles we had fought had all been small and insignificant. Sheikh Abdel-Gabbar may have been right in his first fatwa about us, and Dr. Abdel-Samie Mukhtar may have been right too. We served no purpose until we came to the camp.

10
The Light of My Eyes

THE WOMEN ARRIVED AT EXACTLY two o'clock in the afternoon. They made the trip from the Space to the city center in special buses. Fayza, Shakir's wife, was in charge of coordinating with groups outside the Space so that all the women would converge at the agreed landmark—a tree that had been pruned to the shape of a hand missing a finger, in front of the Ibrahim Hamed mosque. It was a quiet spot and scorching hot. There were between a hundred and maybe a hundred and fifty women. The security forces had started taking steps to cordon off the area and their vehicles were lurking nearby, taking shelter in the sparse shade of the trees. As soon as the chanting began and the demonstrators held pictures of the abducted leader over their heads, another group of women appeared from nowhere, wearing black galabias and colored headscarves knotted at the back of their necks, muscular and built like tanks. They had come off trucks under the protection of soldiers armed to the teeth, and clashes soon broke out.

Aida took her fair share of blows in the early stages of the battle. A ferocious woman attacked her, grabbing her shoulder with fingers like a trap that closes on its prey and will not let go. Then she deployed her teeth as well and gave Aida a head-butt. Aida tried to repay her in kind, but she hadn't been trained for a contest of this kind. She spent most of her time trying to keep her scarf on and, while she was trying to escape from the fray, she noticed Jehan, Adel al-Sabbagh's wife, who had been with her all along the way, turning her back on the mosque, taking off her shoes, picking them up and running away from the scene. Nour began at Aida's side, but she soon fell to the ground and the women attacking didn't take any interest in her, since it was obvious that she wasn't a leader and she clearly wasn't about to stand back up. Fayza tried to fend off the women's well-practiced assaults whenever the chance arose, in order to protect herself and Aida, but there were too many for them and in the end it was clear that they could not continue. The same applied to all but a few of the other women in their group, and within half an hour the organizers had ordered a retreat. The injured women were helped out of the way, as the attackers continued to punch, bite, and curse them.

Murad and Ibrahim were busy seeing patients in the clinic when news of the attack arrived. Murad left his assistant anxiously and hurried to the entrance to the Space, expecting to meet the bus when it brought the women back from the demonstration. He started to have a bad feeling about what had happened to Aida. He stayed around, asking the women coming through the gate if they knew anything about his wife and looking around in confusion. As soon as he saw her, leaning on Fayza and hobbling slightly, but with no obvious signs of bullet wounds, he calmed down, because he had been worried a bullet or shotgun pellets might have hit her.

He strode toward her without hiding his anger and shouted, "Thank God you're safe, and the other women too! How were you hit? Do you have any pain other than your foot?"

"Thanks. It's nothing serious, Murad. It's very minor. It's just that I pulled a muscle trying to defend myself when they attacked us."

Fayza chipped in, reassuring him and praising Aida's resilience. "Don't worry, Dr. Murad," she said. "Aida's fine. She put up a good fight today against those bullies. May God preserve her and help us all to stand firm."

News of the attack dominated the conversation at most gatherings for the rest of the day. Shakir and Fayza joined Aida and Murad outside their tent to discuss it, while Aida dressed her right foot with a support bandage and lifted it up in front of her on a mat folded over several times.

"Hello, hello," said Shakir, catching sight of Ibrahim walking toward them. "Come and join us, if you don't mind of course, Dr. Murad."

Ibrahim came up to the group with his eyes on the ground as always. "Peace be upon you," he said. "I've finished at the clinic and I thought I'd pass by to see how the Sisters are doing after what those criminals did."

Murad made space for him to sit down and pulled up an extra chair. If Aida hadn't insisted on renting some chairs just in case, there wouldn't have been room for visitors to sit.

"Thanks, Ibrahim, that's good of you. Luckily we don't have any serious injuries."

"Thank God for that. But no one's listening to reason. I've said what I think several times. We need to get hold of some weapons immediately. We can't go on like this."

Murad was annoyed that Ibrahim insisted on bringing up weapons whenever a clash occurred. He didn't think the subject should be open to discussion, though Ibrahim kept trying to convince him.

"Don't get carried away by your emotions," said Murad. "I've told you before that they could exploit it. In the current situation weapons aren't a solution. It would give them a pretext to crush the protest immediately."

"So how do you think we can protect our people? Should we just leave them to die in the streets whenever they go out to demonstrate? Dozens of our people have been killed, including women. More than seventy Brothers were killed last week alone. I was in the Space myself and they kept firing at us for hours and they deliberately shot the journalist who was filming them when they launched the attack. All that and you talk about 'exploiting'? We should be exploiting what they are doing. We need weapons now. If the System knew we were armed the security forces would think a thousand times before they aimed their guns at us."

Murad sighed in irritation at having to repeat what he had said before to no avail. This young man wouldn't give up, and nothing would change his mind.

"If they found us with weapons," he replied impatiently, "they'd treat us as outlaws and we'd lose all the advantages we have. No one would sympathize with us, even those who are still neutral. Do you think we could go into an armed conflict with them and win? Whatever we do we couldn't get weapons that match the ones the state has or enough of them for us to hold out against the state for even a few hours. Do you want to declare war on them? The battle would be lost before it began, so don't judge by your emotions and think of the consequences."

"Listen, Dr. Murad," Ibrahim replied. "Our sheikhs have told us it's better to fight in the Space than in the streets and that going out on demonstrations with the protesters is better than staying in the Space, and that dying on a demonstration is the most glorious thing possible. I'm now prepared to give my life if it would be good for the others, but I can't accept being abused and humiliated. What can we achieve by this sterile approach? They've beaten up the women like brutal thugs. They've beaten up your wife, Doctor, and trampled on Sister Nour's dress, and no one lifted a finger. If we didn't have a duty to obey under these circumstances, we would have something else to say."

Murad didn't reply. He was upset that Aida and her ordeal were being mentioned in this way, as if anyone could now talk about her casually. He knew that Ibrahim was mild-mannered and amiable, as long as the conversation was nothing to do with politics. But his manner turned acrimonious when political disagreements arose, especially if the discussion was about choosing between peaceful demonstrations and arming the protest movement. Then nothing would deflect him from his advocacy of violent options. The speeches from the podium had definitely influenced him.

As for Shakir, he suppressed his emotions, drew a deep breath and said, "We're ready to die in the Space if they try to break up the protest by force. We won't give the place up whatever happens. The thousands of people you see around you won't budge an inch if we tell them to stand firm. Now, when things are going smoothly and negotiations are under way around tables—and in secret too, I won't lie to you—between our representatives and their representatives, there's no question of arming people. We've lost many martyrs over decades and we've grown used to handling it prudently. We're used to resisting the urge to do stupid things that could undo years of work. Put aside the enthusiasm and recklessness of youth and come to your senses, doctor. You show the potential to become a determined and courageous leader and, besides, some of the protesters really do have weapons but we don't approve of it openly, because we are peaceful and the protest is peaceful."

Adel al-Sabbagh arrived looking energetic, with the same smile he always had, whether he was awake or asleep. "What are you arguing about?" he asked. "I could hear your voices from my tent. Thank God you're safe, Madame Aida, is your injury any better?"

"We always thank God. It's not a real injury compared to what happened to other women."

"I heard that the people who started beating you up were wearing civilian clothes. The police say they were local people and some newspapers describe them as thugs—foul-mouthed, abusive women of the kind they bring from the slums. My wife—she was with you and I think you saw her—told me she almost fell into their hands, but she miraculously escaped. Just point out the criminal who hit you and I'll make sure she's punished. And you, Ibrahim, don't get worked up, and bless the Prophet. I've got a good-quality gun for you and at half the real price, or just take it, man, and don't pay anything unless you like it and decide to keep it."

He broke into a loud chuckle that took the edge off the intensity of the discussion, though the others joined in the laughter reluctantly. His last remark sounded awkward despite his laugh, and none of the others shared Adel's jovial nature.

Aida took seriously what he had said about punishment for the woman who attacked her and took the occasion to have her own say on the subject: "The criminal who hit me is a helpless woman. It's true she was twice my weight and she had hands like sledge hammers, but she was of modest appearance and simply dressed. Her accent, her behavior, and the words she used suggest she was from the slums, maybe even the shantytowns. She looked much poorer than the people who live in the area where we were, which is known to be wealthy. I'm sure she's been brainwashed. She didn't know who we were or what we were doing or why we were demonstrating. She didn't even know what we were shouting. I think I've seen the woman before in the company of the security forces. She was shouting so loud it was deafening. She was attacking some of the demonstrators, hitting them and pulling their hair and even trying to pull their clothes off."

Shakir welcomed the change of subject. "They're raising a parallel army they can call on to deal with their opponents. Murad, did you know that the leaders of the security agencies sometimes incite people like that to commit crimes, then they blame the crimes on us? A few days ago, in a speech from the podium, one of the Brothers mentioned a particular incident of violence when the general used ex-convicts and then blamed the Raised Banner for what they had done. I think you heard about that fiery sermon. News of it got around, thank God, and the Brothers both inside the Space and outside were talking about it. I think it influenced a large cross section of people."

Murad took renewed interest in the discussion and tried to forget Ibrahim's irritating remarks. "What people say on the podium no longer has an effect on anyone outside the Space, or else it has an effect that's the opposite of what we want. What you say, Shakir, only appeals to the people here. They're easy to influence. But people on the other side are listening to another story that's more convincing. I agree with you on the thugs, though. The System is creating a generation of thugs who are loyal to them and have a grudge against society in general. It's pushing them to carry out tasks that the regular forces don't want to get involved in, either because they're dangerous or barbaric. Most of those tasks undermine the image of itself that the System wants to project. These wretches serve the System, but it usually sacrifices them and never admits it has anything to do with them. If necessary it offers them to the masses as scapegoats. They are caught between the anvil of poverty, ignorance, and necessity on one side, and the hammer of oppression and control by the System on the other side. They turn out when the System wields its stick and then they look forward to the carrot, even if it's limp and rotten. Humiliation dogs their wretched lives. If they try to resist or disobey orders, they will find no rest on this earth. I think the only recourse they have is to stay under the protection of the System and give it their full obedience and loyalty, simply to avoid its vengeance and so that the System at the same time protects them from the vengeance of other victims."

Shakir shook his head dismissively. "You make me weep, I swear," he said. "Wretches and victims? You're still as kind as always, Murad! You always find excuses for weak people who act in defiance of God. The System asks them to ignore their reason and their natural instincts, and obey it blindly and follow its orders whatever they might be, and they voluntarily do its bidding."

Angered by the response, Murad tried to turn the tables. "That's true, but doesn't the Raised Banner demand the same, Shakir?" he said.

Shakir shook in his chair. "Are you comparing us to them?" he shouted. "We don't force anyone to do anything. We don't threaten people or abuse them. People join us out of love, not out of hatred, and you've seen that as well as anyone else."

"You expect them to obey, and you give them money and benefits so that they stay attached to the movement. I don't deny that the System's methods include a level of coercion and oppression that you don't adopt, but people respond to one side or the other depending on their circumstances and their needs as the opportunity arises. You can't deny that you also mobilize them in other ways, and you have an example of that in what's happening here. Most of the sheikhs who speak on the podium these days deliberately play on the emotions of the protesters. One of them talks about seeing the Prophet with the abducted ruler in a dream and says this is a sign he will soon return. Another swears that something big is going to happen in two days' time and the ruler will be with us on the third day, and no one asks what is going to happen or how. They listen and shout *Allahu akbar* as if in a trance. Their emotions are aroused and this naturally has an effect on their decisions and choices. But none of that is true and you know it. I don't mean to offend, Shakir. You in particular have known what I think for a long time, and you know that I greatly respect the Raised Banner and have friendly relationships with its leaders, despite our differing visions. I'm just pointing out that the situation is exceptional now and the cause for which we have come together is bigger than anything, but what they are doing on the podium may not end well."

Shakir looked away, preferring not to continue with the conversation. Aida sighed. Murad turned to her, sharing with her a sense of sorrow at the course the conversation had taken. He waved his hand, recalling what had happened at the demonstration.

"The way we live in this country, you're either an oppressor or oppressed. If you don't oppress others, you'll be oppressed to death. The poor woman who attacked you, Aida, is irrefutable proof of that. If you could offer her a decent life and provide even half what the other side has promised, she would abandon them and take your side."

After a long silence, Ibrahim mumbled angrily. "They're not poor, doctor," he said. "Shakir's right. This woman and others like her have been blinded. People threw dust in their eyes. They easily yield to temptation in return for any gain, and don't tell me they don't have any choice. She willingly chose to obey the System's orders. She could have joined your group or any other group that tried to recruit her, as you said. But she chose the System, which is a criminal gang, and she and all the others who joined her group are responsible for the situation we're in now. You can see how heated the climate is right now. There's plenty of blood between us and when blood is boiling only revenge can cool it down."

"By God, you're right," Adel al-Sabbagh interjected. "This heat is unbearable. It's like living on the equator. With all these people, maybe the Space has grown so much we've actually reached the tropics. But thank God for his blessings."

A number of clean-shaved men gathered, the oldest of them apparently no older than forty. They formed themselves into a silent march and started to walk through the barricades that the protesters had set up on the main road leading to the Space. Their march was a little disorganized but this didn't detract from their staid and dignified appearance, which was accentuated by the turbans, gowns, and caftans they were wearing. They swerved to avoid the blocks of stone, car tires, and sandbags that stretched as far as the eye could see, installed to stop the security forces if they attacked from this direction, especially after the previous Friday's attack, in which much blood was shed. They reached the entrance with their clothes covered in the dust kicked up by their feet. There they were given a respectful reception. The young man in charge of searching them gave them a special welcome and asked a boy to show them the way. They went into the Space and planned to wander around in support of the protesters. They shook hands with people who knew them and were greeted by people who simply knew from their religious dress that they were students from al-Azhar University. They ambled aimlessly and ended up near the clinics, where Ibrahim spotted them through the window. Unable to believe they had come, he took a close look to check, and then his face lit up and he hurried off to ask Murad if he could have a break for a few minutes. As they came close, he went out in jubilation.

"Welcome to the brave men of the world's greatest mosque," he shouted. "We've been waiting for you!"

"Good to see you!" replied one of the students. "We thought you had something against us. As you're here, we now know why we haven't been seeing you recently. But you've made the right choice, no doubt about it, Brother."

"How are you all?" asked a third voice in the crowd. "What's up with the big sheikhs, the ones everyone makes such a fuss about? Why don't they say anything about the System's crimes against us? We're used to prisons and detention camps but it's a major sin when Muslims attack Muslims and create rivers of blood. Aren't Abdel-Gabbar and the people around him ashamed of themselves? Won't they take a stand against the sultan?"

A young man in the march bowed his head and said, "God asks no one to do more than they can. We all know how Abdel-Gabbar thinks and it's no secret what goes on in the corridors of power between him and the government. But he has issued a statement on the events of last Friday that we consider to be acceptable."

"Really? Tell us all about it. Maybe he's found his conscience and come to his senses."

The man put his hand in his top pocket, pulled out some folded pieces of paper, and picked out two of them. "Here are two copies, not just one," he said. "Read it carefully at your leisure, when you think the time is right. Then get in touch to tell me what you think, and don't forget us. We knew you're now an important doctor, but you still have obligations to your friends."

Ibrahim took the pieces of paper with a cheerful laugh. "How about we agree to have a proper catchup on the last day of Ramadan? We haven't had an iftar together yet, as we used to every year, and Ramadan's almost over. So come and break the fast with us here, then we can stay up till dawn and perform the Eid prayers together. It will definitely have a different flavor in the Space, different from any other space you might choose."

"Great. It's a deal, inshallah. We'll see you in the next two days as well. We've made up our minds to stay in the Space until Eid comes."

Banners were fluttering around the podium and the protesters who had been waiting for the venerable sheikh stood up in anticipation. The officials had announced he had come unexpectedly and that he had plenty of news. The sheikh appeared moments later, picked up the microphone and greeted the crowd. Then he started talking in a deep voice that had a calming effect on his audience.

"My Brothers," he said, "I come to you today with some excellent and extraordinary news, news of a vision granted to a virtuous and committed young man from a good, devout family that reveres Islam and the Muslim community."

There were murmurs of acclamation, which the sheikh silenced with a wave of his hand. "This young man fell asleep in the mosque after prayers, and in a dream he saw the general sitting in a plane, surrounded by a red sky with red clouds. Red, the color of blood that is."

The audience gasped, in suspense to hear what more the man might have seen in his vision. "The young man screamed in terror at the sight of the sky. The general looked down from the plane and said, 'Don't worry. The abducted leader is coming back.' 'When?' the young man asked him. 'When I've shed enough of your blood,' the general replied."

Some of the protesters chanted enthusiastically for the ruler's return, while others cursed the general as a murderer. The crowds were in uproar, and the sheikh called on them to calm down, and then continued his speech.

"The young man was at a loss what to do and prayed to God. The clouds started to rain blood, and the blood came through the steel body of the plane and filled it, and the blood swept away the general as he sat in his seat. Yes, brothers, our blood will sweep him away. He has shed much of it and, if he wants, let him shed more, for he will definitely drown in it. Our ruler is coming back, while the general is doomed to disappear. By God, this dream tells the truth. It tells the truth, *Allahu akbar* and God be praised."

Before he finished the audience broke into chanting and raised their arms in the air, imploring, calling for help and threatening. Some of them burst into tears, and the sheikh started nodding his head to acknowledge their favorable reaction to his speech. He gave them several minutes to express their feelings. His account of the vision had reassured them. Then he called for their attention so that he could recite the iftar prayer to them, and they obeyed. As soon as he had finished he left the platform with a faint smile on his face, confident in the success of his mission.

Murad waved a folded piece of paper at Aida as they headed to the stage. He wanted to tease her for her obsession with the statements put out by Sheikh Abdel-Gabbar. Aida took the piece of paper and unfolded it, imagining at first that it was the program for the play they were going to see. Surprised by the title, she started to read the statement with great interest. They went through the door and sat down side by side. Even when the young actors arrived and the lights were dimmed she didn't stop reading. She was well aware that Abdel-Gabbar had been extremely active in recent times and had joined Qadri Abdel-Hakim in the Heart of the World project. He had started to arouse her dislike by becoming more and more active in political matters, to an extent that was completely unreasonable. What exactly was the sheikh doing? she wondered.

Three young men appeared on stage. One of them was short and moved unnaturally. His eyes wandered and his fists were clenched to suggest nervous tension. Suddenly he opened his arms, closed his eyes, and moved forward on the stage.

"Come to my arms," he said amorously, "I'm sure you want a hug. Hugging is the cure for brainwashing, so don't shy away from it."

The audience burst out laughing at his performance, and Aida chuckled too, though she was still busy rereading the sheikh's statement.

"His Grace the Sheikh condemns and strongly deplores the death of so many victims," read the first line. Meanwhile two other actors appeared on stage, one of them whipping the other, who was bare-chested.

"Have you ever seen such compassion and gentleness as mine?" commented the short actor. The room rocked with laughter again, and this time people whistled.

Meanwhile Aida read on: "My heart was racked with pain at the rivers of blood that flowed across the country in Friday's violence."

The young man put on dark glasses and walked like a blind man, stumbling into his colleagues and shouting, "I told you you were the apple of my eye but, as you can see, I don't have any eyes."

As the actors lined up, took a final bow to applause from the audience and in their turn clapped for the director, Aida turned to Murad, pointed to the piece of paper and said, "It's really odd. Have you read this statement carefully? I can't make it out. He condemns, he deplores, he denounces, he calls for dialogue and describes the general as a criminal? How can he do that when he was with him in the early stages of the crisis? Do you believe him now, Murad? What he says doesn't seem logical, given his previous positions."

"That man dances to all tunes," Murad replied tetchily as he watched the actors walk off the stage. "I gave you the piece of paper to show you that the man has a thousand and one faces. Spare yourself a headache and don't read anything more by him or about him. That man is just an apologist for whoever's in power. All he believes in is his job and his only religion is self-interest and power."

"If he really is an apologist for the general, then why would he denounce the killing of protesters, and in such strong language too?"

"Some of the language you're talking about is just words for media consumption. He's trying to take the wind out of the sails of people who criticize the positions he takes. You can't deny he defends the System as much as he can and justifies whatever the general does, or else how come he's still in his job? He has openly put a positive spin on the abduction of the ruler, and has even said he's grateful for what happened. He hasn't missed an opportunity to endorse the continuation of the status quo. He talks as if life has gone back to normal thanks to the general and that everyone's happy now."

Murad paused a while and then resumed, "But to tell you the truth, Aida, I think he had reservations about all the bloodshed. It's true he's openly taken the government's side, but in the end he always thinks twice before saying it's legitimate to kill people. It may be a relic from the past that he hasn't been able to shake off yet. There were principles he was brought up on and he knows he's got caught up in something that should be anathema to him. Endorsing murder isn't easy for someone brought up in a household where people perform their religious obligations and respect the pillars of Islam, for someone who has the learning to tell right from wrong, even if he appears to deny it."

Adel left the Space, then came back in a pickup truck a few hours later. He called Shakir for help getting his goods in but refused to divulge the nature of the goods on the phone. They met close to the mosque and Shakir got into the pickup with him. At first he thought Adel had fulfilled his promise to bring in foodstuffs that were in short supply, but Adel shook his head at that idea.

"This is a surprise," he said. "Take us somewhere where there's plenty of space where we can arrange a place for women to sit."

Shakir raised his eyebrows and guided the driver to an area that was relatively free of tents. He sneaked a few glances at Adel, impatient to discover what he had up his sleeve. Two minutes later the driver got out slowly, lifted the cover, untied the ropes and unloaded a large crate and some gas cylinders. Then he asked permission to leave, waving away the money that Adel tried to slip into his hand and wishing them a happy Eid. At last Adel broke the good news, beaming from ear to ear.

"This is an oven made of sheet metal," he said. "I heard from some of the Sisters that they were sorry they wouldn't have a chance to do any baking for Eid, so I said I had to do right by them. After all, they've abandoned their kitchens for the sake of our ruler."

"You've brought an oven for the women? You're incredible. May God reward you in every possible way. They'll be so happy they won't be able to sleep tonight. You'll be wildly popular and maybe you'll be able to stand in the next parliamentary elections. But how did you get the oven at such short notice?"

"I visited the Qadri Abdel-Hakim organization this morning to buy some household stuff and I saw the oven right in front of me as soon as I went through the door. It seemed to be calling out to me. I swore I'd buy it straight away, and when Qadri found out what it was for, he swore he would pay half the cost from his own pocket and also cover the cost of transportation."

"Qadri will always have a special place in our hearts," said Shakir. "God bless you, and him, and every Brother who supports our struggle to see justice done, even if they give only moral support. I promise you the sacks of white flour will arrive today, after the evening prayers, and tomorrow God willing the women can start baking."

"So we'll eat Eid cake two days before Eid," replied Adel. "As long as we don't have any uninvited guests I'll send Sara and Nour to help you prepare. They might learn something that'll be useful to them in the future. I know your wife's led the way. She was the first to put forward the idea, and she'll lead the team of course."

"Where've you been, boy?" asked Saber. "I looked for you at the fairground, and at Auntie Aida's. God damn you, did you leave her and go off to play?"

"No, I was with Halim," replied his son, deliberately provoking his father.

Saber's face changed instantly. He clenched his teeth and his face looked like a piece of cloth that had just gone through a mangle and come out full of creases. With much effort, he refrained from hitting his son as punishment.

"And where were you, if I may ask?"

"We were at a class memorizing the Quran. Halim goes there every day and I'm going to go with him."

Seething with rage, Saber said nothing. What's up with this Christian learning the Quran, he wondered. You have taught us to be patient, Lord. I've said nothing about it out of respect for Sister Aida. Unwillingly I've kept the secret. Isn't that enough?

"Good. It's your cousin's wedding today," he said. "They're going to do the marriage contract on the podium. Go and wish him well and meet the rest of your family. Go by yourself."

Saber's nephew stood among hundreds of young people, receiving congratulations and prayers for a successful marriage. His thin brown face showed signs of poverty and anemia. The bride's face radiated an excited pride that affected everything around her. She wanted everyone to see that she had outdone the other girls in her village by having her wedding in the Space. The groom took hold of the microphone and hailed the leaders of the Raised Banner movement, although he looked a little embarrassed addressing such a large gathering.

"Please God, may our meeting here today be the prelude to good things, Oh Lord of the Worlds, in the name of God the Merciful, the Compassionate. I've come from my village specially to have my wedding here among you. Praise be to God that He has answered my prayers and fulfilled my wish to come up on the podium alongside our great ulema and blessed leaders. This is an honor that God has bestowed on me, and I take the occasion to announce that I am joining the protest today. I thank God for His grace, and I thank you profusely for the generous help you have given us, and I swear to God, the only god, that we will remain committed to our ruler and to the Quran, never abandoning our position until the Day of Judgment. *Allahu akbar* and praise be to God! *Allahu akbar* and praise be to God!"

As soon as the young man and his bride left the podium fireworks soared into the sky. At the same time religious songs were broadcast, and women brought the wedding to a climax with trilling noises that added a rustic flavor quite distinct from the constant speeches designed to enthuse the audience. Some of Ibrahim's friends from al-Azhar, in gowns and caftans, joined in the celebration. Ibrahim came with them, bad-tempered and reluctant to respond, even in passing, to the displays of joy that marked the gathering, since he didn't approve of excessive merriment. Halim and Hussein had a wild time in the noisy atmosphere. They caught the candy and sugared almonds that some of the young men threw in the air and went around jumping and shouting ecstatically. Then Halim started singing the songs he could remember, as his contribution to the celebrations.

"We obey you, Islam of heroism. We are ready to die to protect you. We obey you, so climb to glory over our skulls."

He repeated his song at the top of his voice, swaying from side to side, and Hussein followed him, repeating the last lines as if he were the chorus. Later they noticed a young man approaching them and listening. Delighted with the words of the song, he slipped his hand into his pocket and handed them some shiny new coins and a handful of peanuts.

The men in turbans gathered a few dozen yards from the podium. They still seemed to be in a celebratory mood, while Ibrahim was scowling. As soon as the noise died down a little, Ibrahim launched into a little speech.

"For your information," he said, "this podium where people have been partying and dancing does not represent us at all. Most of what it broadcasts to people day and night does not speak for us. The fiery speeches you hear and see on YouTube are just so much hot air. They don't mean what they say and they don't do what they say. I was in the Space before you and since I've been here I've heard nothing but nonsense. Protesters lose their lives for no purpose and none of the people who make these impassioned, bombastic speeches carry out any of their plans and don't even have plans that they can explain to us. They froth and foam, but all they manage to do is put on a show, hang up decorations and repeat empty phrases in their songs. It's all rubbish."

"Take it easy, Brother Ibrahim," replied his friend. "Don't be so stiff, or you'll snap under the pressure. The protest is succeeding by every measure. I read a report by some international organization that estimated that there are at least seventy thousand protesters in the Space alone. Do you realize what that means? They can't force us to leave unless we do so willingly. Take it easy. The situation looks encouraging and people don't need to look as gloomy as you all the time, and they don't need to stand up and fight, as you want. There has to be some balance in politics. You know that better than anyone. And don't forget that if you look down on the people you see around you all the time and deny them the few modest pleasures that you despise, you'll lose them and you'll lose your real strength on the ground. The protest would collapse within minutes. You know this better than we do."

Adel sat on a metal stool awaiting his turn because the doctors were busy. His cell phone rang, playing his ringtone: "My eyes have grown used to seeing you" by Umm Kulthum. Ibrahim's hand, which was holding a bottle of saline solution, froze for a moment, along with the rest of his body. Murad remained engrossed in his work, unimpressed by the song and indifferent to his assistant's fidgeting. Adel sighed in admiration, then looked at the screen and decided to take the call before Umm Kulthum had finished the line of her song. Ibrahim suppressed his desire to comment until he had finished examining his patient, while Adel set up a business meeting after evening prayers in the Space.

"You listen to songs?" Ibrahim mumbled, without looking up from the floor. "I mean songs that are not the movement's?"

"Don't you listen to other songs?"

"No, I don't. How could you ask when you're senior to me, and older than me too, and you know the rules better than me? You know what's allowed and what isn't. It's true that the movement allows anthems, but this isn't the kind of song they allow. They allow anthems about the mothers of mujahideen or ones that praise the Prophet."

"Don't get angry, Ibrahim. I'm just joking. This phone belonged to a friend who isn't in the movement. I bought it from him yesterday and I haven't changed anything yet because I'm hopeless with the technical stuff that you young people are so good at. You can change the song and replace it with whatever you choose when you've finished with the clinic."

Ibrahim went back to his work with a troubled mind. As soon as Adel left, with a prescription for his red eyes, Ibrahim turned to Murad and tried to draw him into conversation.

"We don't know how to have fun!" he said. "All our songs are about sacrifice, imprisonment and martyrdom, or battles and jihad, or sin, repentance, and forgiveness! Remember when the ruler we overthrew two years ago was gone and people came out on the streets singing songs by Sheikh Imam, Shadia, and Abdel-Halim Hafez, and we didn't have anything we could sing? Our sheikhs and your sheikhs think that songs of that kind are haram, but we don't have any alternatives, and neither do the sheikhs."

"You're not a member of the Raised Banner, are you, Ibrahim?" asked Murad.

"No, I'm not. I chose a different path in my youth, not very different from you in the ranks of the Raised Banner but stricter in some respects. To be honest, I didn't choose between one and the other. Me and my whole family followed the same way of thinking. We've been strict Salafis for generations. The sheikhs that taught me said that music and singing were haram. I obeyed without discussion. Sometimes I'm not convinced by their views on religious law but obedience is obligatory and essential to a righteous life. I think you'd agree with me on that."

"You're right. We have a duty to obey those with knowledge. Only the ignorant and the arrogant dispute that, but there are times when it's possible to disagree and when there's no objection to people choosing the easier option."

"I've read lots on the subject. There are various views, ranging from allowing music to prohibiting it. You may be aware that the leaders of organizations that seem more strict than us don't ban anthems. Al-Qaeda itself allows them. Al-Awlaki said anthems inspired the early Muslims and weakened the resolve of the infidels. It's a means of waging jihad and a factor that helped to achieve victories in the time of the Prophet. You have, for example, the organized Salafism that follows jihadi thinking, and that has adopted certain anthems in order to promote a warlike spirit and help members endure hardship calmly, but those anthems are very different from the songs of Umm Kulthum."

"Forget about Umm Kulthum and tell me what you were saying to Adel al-Sabbagh. He's not a member of the Raised Banner or a Salafi. What's with you and him these days?"

Ibrahim was surprised and his face turned red. Murad's questioning shocked him in a way he hadn't expected: "I didn't know he was an outsider! Where did he come from? Which group does he follow? I imagined he was a long-standing member of the movement, although I'd never seen him before and his name didn't ring a bell with me. But his relationships with senior leaders in the Space, as well as the way he and his family look—everything suggested he was one of us, and one of you."

"Who are we, and who are you?" asked Murad.

Ibrahim looked for the answer in Murad's face, but soon revealed what he was thinking. "Don't be offended, Dr. Murad. I've heard lots about you, ever since I came to college as a student, and you also taught me, although you don't remember me. But I know you well. I used to see students hanging out with you and being friends with you, and you showed them every attention and interest, but I still don't understand where you stand. You're definitely not a Salafi, but I don't understand if you're really just an ordinary member of the Raised Banner or a leader at the heart of its hierarchy."

"What brought the movement into our conversation now? You started with singing and Umm Kulthum and you ended up talking politics again. Anyway, I'll give you an answer. I'm not in the leadership or even an organizer. I have no official status in the movement, but I have strong connections with members, some of them childhood friends and school and university friends, including some who were in the same year as me. The only reason you see me in the Space is that I do believe we need to take a stand on what has happened. I believe in the importance of the protest and in the justice of our demands. Other than that, don't bother your head with appearances and superficialities, and don't let them sidetrack you. Save your effort, doctor, for useful activity, like your work in this clinic. That's my advice to you. You can listen to whatever songs or anthems you want, and it won't make the slightest difference, as long as you follow in God's path and fear God in your work."

Murad left his young assistant confused and thoughtful. Information that had never occurred to him before had imposed itself on his consciousness. Murad and Adel were both from outside the Raised Banner! He had only just learned this, after more than a month in the Space. And Nour too? She looked and behaved like a committed Muslim, yes, and yet she wasn't a member of the movement and she didn't follow its rules and wasn't bound by its principles. In other words, she didn't follow any particular sheikhs or other religious authority. Did Dr. Murad also listen to whatever music happened to be playing, like Adel al-Sabbagh? No doubt Nour did. She followed her father's path, of course. If the head of the household plays the drums and sings, the rest of the household automatically follow suit. People like that do their own thing and have their own way of analyzing what they want, even if it contains a hint of the forbidden. He felt like an outsider: maybe he was one of that minority of people that still took a deep interest in their religion and stuck to the rules—a minority that didn't listen to their hearts and didn't waver or go soft. What could be done when both approaches led to irreparable loss? Ibrahim left the clinic mystified and sunk in his thoughts, looking for a straw to clutch onto that would keep him afloat.

*

Adel al-Sabbagh picked one of the electronics stores around the Space and browsed through the cell phones on display on the shelves. He bought one for Sara, gave his old phone to the salesman and asked for the ringtone to be changed. The salesman carried out his requests, stealing a glance meanwhile at Adel's clothes and face. He had come to the store in a galabia and hadn't shaved for days. Surprised and unable to restrain himself, the salesman asked Adel whether he was part of the protest or just a reporter covering the news.

"A protester of course," he replied.

"And you listen to Umm Kulthum songs? You don't look like one of them, despite your beard. Did you have a change of heart during the protest and decide to join the movement?"

"What's up with people these days?" Adel replied. "Why does Umm Kulthum make them so angry? Didn't she sing 'Contentment and light' in the film *Rabia al-Adawiya*? Listen, er . . . what would your name be?"

Adel knew from his answer that the man was a Muslim too, so he resumed speaking without fear of giving offense. "I'm just like you." he said. "I say there is no god but God, I pray and fast, and my youngest daughter even wears the niqab. I like the movement, in fact I respect all such groups, but at the same time I don't deny myself worldly pleasures, and for me music is the first of those. I listen to music and I adore Umm Kulthum in particular. Who on earth doesn't love her? Honestly, don't you listen to her? I trust your conscience and I don't mind how you answer, but do you see yourself as an infidel, God forbid?"

"God forbid. I would never say anything like that, but now you're removing the Umm Kulthum song and replacing it with an anthem. A minute ago you said you wanted Sami Yusuf, and of course you know he's their type and he sings religious songs the way they like and he never crosses the line. If it wasn't for the criticism they would get, they would bring him to their podium."

"Well, the thing is I heard him recently. I like his voice and his songs are suitable for the holy month. That's all there is to it, no more and no less."

The salesman didn't look convinced, but Adel quickly changed the subject. "Tell me, what goods are you short of? I'm a wholesaler to the market and I have experience in the electronics business and other sectors too. I can provide you with what you need, in the quantities you want. Your colleague on the next corner spoke to me and I helped him get hold of what he needed, without the company taking the usual cash advance. I'm sure you've seen an increase in demand and that'll keep rising as long as the protesters stay where they are. I can tell you with a clear conscience that the big suppliers think the quantities they are distributing in the area around the protest are running out, and all they need is a word from someone they can trust, and I'm at your service. Take my number and feel free to call me at any time."

When her day was done at school, Aida turned to home, after buying Eid clothes for Adam. This time he would be far from his cousins and from the family celebration he took part in every year, so at least he deserved to have new clothes and a nice toy. She sat cross-legged on her favorite sofa, enumerating to her mother the reasons for spending the first day of the Eid in the Space, and the following days too, instead of having a family get together as they usually did. She started laying out the justifications, appealing to her mother's emotions by describing the atmosphere of spirituality in the Space, reminding her that the protesters had a duty to stick together and support each other at this stage, and then apologizing to her and assuring her that she and Murad had decided to leave the Space a few days into the Eid holiday and come home, since the protest had gone on longer than they had initially expected, negotiations were still under way, and it was impossible to predict when they would end. Aida didn't forget to invite her mother to visit the tent, if only to spend a few hours with Adam. Her mother, who had taken a neutral position in the conflict between the protesters and the government and who had lived through the rituals of Eid without change for dozens of years, merely pursed her lips, unconvinced, and busied herself with the television. She was waiting for Nanice al-Nahhas's program, while Aida listened to the washing machine, waiting for it to end its cycle.

The program began with a man with a calm, dreamy look. He wasn't shouting like the others and he seemed to be soft-spoken, almost poetic. He distracted Aida from the washing machine and she started to watch him, while Nanice heaped praise on him and his project.

"It takes a great musician to look for creative abilities among street children—something that would never occur to any government official. It's definitely a stroke of genius and it might change the behavior of those children and develop their love for things that are good and beautiful," she said.

"Tell me, dear," she said to a boy seated nearby. "What do you feel when you do your music practice in the center for talented children?"

"I'm very happy," replied the boy, without any sign of emotion.

"What do you dream about? What do you hope to be when you grow up?"

"An officer."

"Wonderful. May God protect you and make all your dreams come true. A moment while we take a phone call from an official. We seem to have a surprise."

The studio loudspeakers carried the voice of the Minister of Youth and Sports. Nanice beamed and her cheeks glowed. The minister praised the young musician, who stared at the floor, and announced that the ministry was adopting the project, expanding it on a national level, to improve the artistic awareness of street children and strengthen their sense of loyalty and attachment to the country.

He soon finished off his speech by bellowing enthusiastically: "They're not street children. They're Heart of the World children."

Nanice waved her arms in the air and shouted too, in the same declamatory style. "That's what all officials should be like! This is the best news we've heard today. It's our Eid gift to you. And in my turn I'm sending a letter to His Excellency the General, asking him to invite these children to an official celebration and to attend in person to listen to them, encourage them, and confirm that they are children of the state, Heart of the World children."

Aida got up to hang out the washing, convinced that the musician, who timidly whispered words of thanks, was goodhearted and a man of honest intentions, but at the same time living in another world. Did he think that knowing the rudiments of music would improve the lives of street children? When they sang, would the piles of trash around them be magically transformed into gardens full of singing flowers? It was absurd to think that music could bring about any real change for Halim and his friends, however miraculously beautiful it was. Clearly the man didn't understand what the state was doing to them in secret. This was a government that pushed nastiness and depravity to the limits, exploiting people's good opinion of it and playing on their feelings, especially those who longed to play a role that would make them feel their lives were useful. It lured them in and took advantage of them to burnish its image and then tarnished the reputations of those same people by associating them with its filth. The program made her angry and reminded her of the children's sufferings. Her skeptical instincts came to the fore and she gradually reconsidered her partiality for the musician. Maybe the man wasn't as naive as she had assumed. He might have been complicit and aware of what was happening behind the scenes, but he was playing his part with skill. She hung out the last sock and dried her damp hands. She didn't rule out anything these days.

She cast a glance at her mother, who left the sitting room and went off to bed when the program ended, so she turned off the light and went to sit in front of the computer. She hadn't checked her email for many weeks. She seemed to have forgotten about it: it was no longer as important as it had been. She found many messages that she didn't want to waste time on. There was one message from her sister and she clicked on it to open it, drawn by the strangeness of the headline: "Call for help from inhabitants of the Space." She was confronted with a statement with the same headline. She expected a diatribe that was hostile to the protesters, but the contents did not match her expectations. It was a succession of quotes from residents who said that, even if they agreed to publicize their complaints about the protest, they were not giving the security forces a green light to use excessive violence and that those responsible for shedding blood must be deterred. As for the simple people who had been deceived, they should be treated gently. "We are in a situation that no one has experienced before. We can't live a quiet or normal life, but at the same time we can't allow ourselves to be used as a pretext for bloodshed," one of them said. She read it again and tried to work out how she felt about it. The statement didn't reassure her, but it didn't make her angry either. The residents were taking a balanced approach, and the proposals that some of Murad's colleagues were trying to put into practice had had an excellent effect. The free medical examinations they were offering to the people who lived in the blocks of apartments around the Space and their house visits to the elderly must have reduced the anger toward them, but the inconvenience described in the statement and the disturbance caused by the leaders' speeches must be giving a bad impression to people who read it. Only the day before, one of the sheikhs on the podium was shouting into the microphone, vowing to divorce his wife if the abducted ruler did not come back and saying that to doubt he was coming back was similar to doubting the existence of God. What were people supposed to do when they could hear such talk in their houses? Aida had tried to suppress the relentless struggle inside her between her desire to stay on in the protest to the end and the resentment that she felt and that made her think of leaving whenever she heard the protest leaders speaking. She couldn't deny that some of what they said was mindless nonsense, but she kept her opinion to herself and kept working. The situation could not tolerate any dissent. She remembered what Murad had said about the stupidity of the preachers and the reckless behavior of the Raised Banner leaders. She closed her email and went to some opposition websites to catch up on events she had missed that were unrelated to the Space. A story only three lines long caught her attention, about expired foodstuffs being seized in the warehouses of a well-known businessman. She did a quick search and found another site that gave the news more coverage and revealed the man's name: Qadri Abdel-Hakim. Intrigued, she started looking for references to the incident on the websites of the main government and independent newspapers, but she couldn't find anything at all, not a single reference, not even a sentence in the brief news section.

As soon as she got back to the Space, Aida admitted to Murad that her defense of Qadri Abdel-Hakim now looked misplaced. "I think your opinion is closer to the truth, Murad," she said. "I've grown more suspicious of him since I told you about the Heart of the World project. The more I've heard about him in the news and the more I've looked into it, the more question marks there are in my mind. Yesterday I discovered yet another shocking new fact about his businesses."

By chance, Adel al-Sabbagh happened to be nearby. He was just a few yards away from where they were sitting, giving out dates from a large sack he had just brought. He came a little closer and insinuated his way into their conversation, letting out a laugh as if he were asking permission to take part.

"Why do you say that, Madame Aida?" she said. "He's an honest, hard-working man and he spares no effort to help people."

"That's what you think, Adel, but Murad could tell you endless stories that show the opposite. Leave aside the old stories. They're ancient history. But what do you have to say about recent allegations of fraud and corruption? Today there's a story about expired foodstuffs they found in his warehouses and stores. It's hard to wriggle out of that."

Adel stopped laughing and his face turned red. He tightened his grip on the neck of the sack. For the past few weeks Qadri had provided him with most of the goods on sale in the stores around them. Even these dates were from him, and the people here, neighbors and Raised Banner members, knew that he and Qadri were partners. It's true that their dealings were insignificant compared with the overall volume of business Qadri did, but in cases such as this the value didn't matter. There were official papers on which their names appeared together. He swallowed his apprehensions, preferring to stand his ground first, rather than being frightened to take any decision. He forced a smile but it looked tense.

"Where's this news story, Madame Aida?" he said. "I haven't come across it, though I'm careful to read the newspaper from start to finish. I even do the crossword and the sudoku for fun before breakfast."

"You won't find it in most of the printed newspapers, because news like that isn't allowed to be published of course. You know the man has close relationships with the government and the newspaper chiefs. Go to the opposition news websites and you'll find it easily."

Adel looked grateful. Aida had unexpectedly offered him a lifeline and he gave another broad smile.

"Ah, the opposition," he said. "But how can you be sure they're telling the truth? They often exaggerate and make up sensational stories to attract readers. Anyway, I'll ask him directly when I speak to him, though I doubt the reports are true. In fact, I bet you they're fabricated to discredit him. Of course someone like Qadri Abdel-Hakim is bound to have many enemies. You know what the business community is like, and the games and tricks they play. Do you know what I'm saying, Shakir?"

Shakir had arrived toward the end of the conversation, so Adel repeated the story to him, adding expressions of disapproval and surprise. He went around the group one by one, handing out Qadri's dates and asking them to taste them. Shakir took one and seconded Adel's disapproval and incredulity.

"I really think the man's been maligned," he said, scowling and speaking in a sorrowful voice. "Qadri Abdel-Hakim has a good reputation among us and in the market in general. He does a lot of business on all seven continents. Recently his operations have stretched from the countries of North Africa to southeast Asia. I know he imports stuff from Libya, Vietnam, and China, and I don't think someone with that kind of business would put it at risk for the sake of the insignificant extra profit he might make from trying to sell shoddy goods. A damaged reputation can soon lead to ruin and he's not stupid enough to fall into that trap. Besides, he's a man who fears God and doesn't like to make Him angry. So if he hasn't been convicted of anything, then it's God who will hold him to account and he'll be judged by his intentions and his deeds, which may be known only to God."

Sara leaned against the back of her father's chair, pestering him playfully. She asked if she could go to swim in the new pool that had appeared that morning in the fairground area near the big wheel. They had inflated the sides of the pool and filled it with water, which spilled over the brim whenever a child jumped or dived in. The pool was very crowded. The children had taken off their shirts and galabias and were wearing just shorts or, to be precise, their underpants. Barefoot, they jumped from the edges of the pool to the middle, sending up great splashes of water that soaked passersby. No one objected or complained, because it was the last day of Ramadan and happy children were a welcome sign that it was almost Eid. Having wet clothes and water on the ground also alleviated the intense heat.

Adel stared at his phone and answered Sara robotically. "Very well, my dear," he said. "Call your mother and ask her to get the swimming things ready, and I'll bring them for you tomorrow when I come back."

Nour was annoyed. The conversation had distracted her from her prayers, so she put down the prayer book she was holding and turned to her sister and father.

"What are you saying, Dad? And you, Sara, what do you think you're doing? We're at a Raised Banner protest. You're going to wear a swimsuit here? Have you lost your mind?"

Adel slapped his forehead. He realized he had overlooked the fact that they were in the Space. "Oh my God. Good for you, Nour. And you, Sara, what your sister says is right. When we go to the beach in the summer you can go in the water as much as you like. But here, it's impossible. And besides, it won't be clean and chlorinated like it is in the club, and you might catch some skin disease and your mother wouldn't like that at all."

Sara was angry. She was totally bored with staying there. She didn't move from her place at the back of her father's chair and started to sob in frustration and disappointment. Nour had thwarted her and deprived her of an opportunity that had come to her on a silver platter. She had hoped her father would take her to buy some new clothes from the shopping center, but now there was no chance of that whatever she did. It would have been easier to persuade her father, because she knew her mother would never let her swim there. Sara had turned up her nose at the whole Space ever since her first visit and she loathed the people there. She had lost a treasured watch in a demonstration and she could no longer bear talk of the sit-in. In fact, she had decided to stage her own sit-in at home, refusing to spend the Eid holiday with them in the tent. Their attempts to persuade her to stay would founder on the rock of what she judged to be her dignity and pride.

Sara went to the lesson angry, her eyes still red and wet from crying. She sat down but didn't answer any questions or show any interest in Aida's teaching. This led Aida to interrupt the lesson before they were halfway through and take Sara aside to find out what had happened to her. Sara willingly explained why she was upset, in the belief that Aida was bound to take her side. She told Aida the details of the dispute, confident that her logic was sound. With the best of intentions she believed that her teacher, who seemed to know more about the Space than anyone else and to be more committed to it, would be able to persuade her father to relent. She might tell him that swimming helped children learn and think, along the lines of the adage she had been taught at school: "A sound mind in a sound body." Aida was bound to have a strong argument.

Aida was tongue-tied in amazement as she listened to the story. She looked hard at Sara to see if she was joking, or maybe lying to hide the real reason why she was upset. But Sara's eyes said she was telling the truth and Aida could no longer hold back. "Sara, you wear the niqab!" she said in outrage. "Do you want to undress in front of everyone?"

Sara started to weep loudly. She was horrified that everyone was telling her off, and in her emotional attempt to defend herself in front of her teacher, her confessions poured out unfiltered, like a broken faucet spilling water. She said her father had forced her to wear niqab just one day before they had come to the Space. She had never worn it before, or any kind of head cover. She didn't want it, she added, but her father was tempting her with a trip abroad that the club organized every year, but only if she obeyed him.

"Next year, I can go to Italy with my friends," she said.

Aida was dumbfounded. There was no way she could console Sara in this particular situation. She handed her a tissue to wipe her eyes, and muttered, "Let's put off talking about the swimming till after the lesson. I'm going to meet your sister in the evening and we'll talk about it, Sara. The other children are waiting."

When the lesson resumed, Sara's grumpiness affected the others. It made the time drag and meant they didn't make jokes as they usually did. When they finished, all the children left. Adam went off with Halim to wander around the neighborhood, and Aida sat outside her tent absentmindedly. People walked past, but she hardly noticed when they wished her a happy Eid. She remembered how Sara had insisted on going with the boys when they all had their faces painted. She also recalled Sara's conversation with the daughter of the inspection official, which showed that she had never heard of the Raised Banner's scout groups, and maybe she hadn't heard about the Raised Banner either. Then there was the extraordinary behavior of Adel's wife at the demonstration, when she kept bringing out a small mirror to touch up her makeup, even while chanting slogans. The worst thing was when she suddenly disappeared—behavior that could be described as despicable and cowardly, were that not too disparaging. How could she not be ashamed to have left the other women to their fate as soon as the fighting started and before anyone had even touched her? And Nour, the sensible elder sister, how could she justify leaving her face uncovered when Sara was wearing a niqab? There was something strange about the Sabbagh family, from the eldest to the youngest. She moved her chair inside, thinking aloud and unaware that Murad was there.

"Maybe Nour's the only one that's in harmony with the place and with herself," she said. "When it comes to the others, there's something I don't understand."

"Are you talking to yourself? About the Sabbagh family? Don't bother yourself with them. You only have to know what a close friendship Adel has with Qadri Abdel-Hakim. Then you can judge him and find out what he's really up to. You can tell a lot about a man by the company he keeps."

"Your friend Shakir is a friend of Qadri's, just like Adel al-Sabbagh, and maybe even more so. They seem to share several interests. Did you see how vigorously he defended Qadri when his name came up in the scandal over the expired food? The problem's not his relationships or friendships, but Adel's character and behavior. I find him incomprehensible, especially when you add in the behavior of his wife and daughters."

"Don't bother trying to work him out. Adel is simpler than you think. His family has belonged to the Raised Banner movement for generations. They have a strong presence and a respected position in it, and Adel's brothers all have organizing roles in the movement. But Adel was irresponsible at university and scraped through the end-of-year exams, not because he was stupid but because he spent his time on other things that interested him. He didn't even take part in the Khaled ibn al-Walid group that the movement had been running and sponsoring for decades. In fact, throughout his university years he went to the mosque only sporadically. His relationships with female students were criticized by Raised Banner members who knew him and his background and his father's sensitive position. Imagine, Adel never joined the hierarchy of the movement or even had strong links with it or its leaders until he went into business and needed help. He took part in some successful business projects here and in some Gulf countries, and I think he realized it was important to retain strong ties, at least with members who were involved in economic activities. He's on the margins of the movement, morally and ideologically, but he's at its heart in other respects."

"By the way, tell me, Murad, why doesn't the movement give regular updates on the amount of money it's received in donations for the protest, and where it comes from, instead of leaving the television stations to speculate, and leaving people to guess and spread rumors?"

"Shakir doesn't think they should disclose the names of the people supporting them, because it might put them in danger," said Murad.

"But there are some questionable people who are said to have donated billions of pounds. Don't try and tell me that someone like Qadri Abdel-Hakim supports the movement for selfless reasons, without expecting anything in return."

Murad moved closer and leaned over to her, laughing sarcastically. "You've completely turned against Qadri," he said, "and abandoned Adel al-Sabbagh. There are dozens, maybe hundreds of people like him, and some of them spend more money. What matters most is knowing how the money is spent and where the donations go."

The muezzin gave the call for noon prayers and Aida set her thoughts aside and stood up. God works in mysterious ways, and the only member of the Sabbagh family she was really interested in was Nour. She wasn't pretentious and didn't speak with any affectation. Aida went over to Baking Square and sat down cross-legged next to Fayza, who was busy making dough. She picked up her own mixing bowl and began to help enthusiastically. Nour soon joined them and Aida greeted her with a friendly smile, eager to include her. She gave her another bowl before the bowls ran out. Women had started to arrive one by one: for some, it brought back sentimental memories, while others looked forward to an amusing gathering and had no objection if some chat and gossip came with it. There were others who only wanted to give practical help, because it seemed impossible that the three thousand women at the protest would have enough Eid cakes otherwise. Among them was a good-looking woman in her fifties with a warm voice.

"I haven't baked since my mother died," the woman said, "and many years have passed since then. She used to get us all together, me and my sisters, and give each of us a job to do: making the dough, shaping the cakes, putting them in lines and filling them with dates, Turkish delight, a honey-sesame mix, or walnuts if there were any in the house. At the end of the process the boys had to carry the trays of little golden cakes to the bakery. Those were the best cakes I ever tasted and after that Eid, they never tasted the same again for me."

Fayza was sympathetic to the sadness in the woman's voice and wanted to cheer her up. "At least you had a chance to bake," she said. "Baking's only fun as a group. None of us would like to sit at home alone to make cakes in the kitchen if other people couldn't smell it and share the work. That way they'd only appreciate the result when they bit into it and it melted in their mouth."

A third woman joined the conversation, in a confident voice that suggested long experience. "That's true. Making the dough and arranging the cakes should be group activities, and the start is definitely the most important part. If you get that right it ends well. There are secrets known only to serious cooks, the ones who don't approve of ready-made food, especially cakes. Personally, I love baking together. I enjoy it much more than actually eating the cakes."

They laughed and their laughter attracted more women. Nour wasn't the talkative kind, however. She started playing with the little cakes on the black baking trays, then she arranged them next to each other to spell out the name of the abducted leader. Her neighbor noticed what she was doing and started to copy her. Then all the women began to do the same thing, and then to spell out protest slogans in cakes. Their work caught the attention of some boys, who stood watching their prodigious output. Some of the boys were so enthusiastic they started chanting the slogans. They set up a miniature protest march that circled around the baking women in a celebratory mood. Aida caught sight of Saber's son Hussein proudly leading one group of children. He stood upright and stretched his arms out in front of him, holding a folded piece of white cloth to represent a burial shroud.

"Victory! Victory!" he shouted, in time with a whistle blown by one of his friends. like a cheerleader at a soccer match. The chant soon changed to "*Allahu akbar*" and then to insults aimed at Nanice al-Nahhas, which made Aida smile despite herself.

"We'll sit here a thousand years until they let him go," shouted Fayza. "We won't leave whatever they do. What were they thinking? That they could simply turn against him as if he didn't have any supporters or helpers? Say after me: 'Determined, faithful, strong! We don't care how long!'"

11

The Dusty Cake

Murad woke up to metallic clanging noises. After dawn prayers he had closed his eyes for less than an hour. He came out of the tent yawning, annoyed at what he thought must surely be a poor joke, but he soon realized that the Space was in imminent danger. Young men were banging on the electricity poles as hard as they could, and the people around him were scattering to the main entry points. The clanging was both a desperate call for help and an alarm to wake up those who were still asleep. He went back into the tent and told Aida to wake up Adam and get ready. He didn't know what exactly she should get ready for, but the increasingly loud and rapid banging had pumped bursts of adrenaline into his bloodstream. Was it possible they would attack now? Aida pulled Adam out of bed half-conscious and got dressed. She put her bag on her shoulder and joined Murad outside the tent. Halim joined them, looking pale, his chest rising and falling rapidly.

At exactly six o'clock, the tear gas hit the noses and eyes of those in the area, and then filled the air until it was difficult to breathe. People started to grab pieces of cloth, soak them in vinegar, and put them over their mouths and noses to counteract the effect of the gas, but the vinegar didn't have any significant effect. Some people, young and old alike, started having convulsions, and some vomited repeatedly or frothed at their mouths and noses. A woman carrying a baby girl collapsed on the ground, waving her arms in the air and struggling to catch a breath. Murad ran and tried to help her but she began to deteriorate rapidly, and not much later she was making gurgling noises as if her lungs had filled with water. Soon she was dead and within a few minutes her baby died in Murad's arms. Murad brushed off the shock and laid the baby's body on its mother's chest for Aida to cover them with a sheet, her hand shaking at the horror of the scene.

"Aida, I'm going to the hospital now," Aida heard Murad say firmly. "We're definitely going to need lots of doctors. You stay here. We're roughly in the middle of the Space, and I think it's safer here than at the edges. Send me anyone you think could lend a hand in any way: nurses, pharmacists, doctors, even vets."

"Take Adam with you then," shouted Aida, trying to control her emotions as he left. "You'll be better able to protect him, and if anything bad happens, you could handle the situation better than me. Halim and I will stay here until you come back or call me and tell us to come and join you. May God protect you."

Murad picked up Adam and left. They made their way past tents that had been hit by gas canisters and caught fire. Clearly the situation was serious and the attack was going be devastating. He held Adam tight and pressed his face against his chest to protect him from the effects of the gas. Adam was clearly alarmed at the sight of people running in all directions. Some of them were calling on each other to organize defenses and shouting "*Allahu akbar*" to keep their spirits up. Adam started crying and Murad tried to calm him down, though that was hard when Adam shuddered at the sight of every body they passed along the way. Some of them were clearly dead, and an hour had not yet passed since the assault began.

The tear gas was followed by deafening bursts of gunfire, but no one knew where the bullets were coming from. Before long helicopters appeared overhead and opened fire with automatic weapons, mowing people down like dry grass.

They were backed by special forces troops that deployed on the roofs of buildings and started firing sniper rifles, aiming at people's heads. Halim looked up, fascinated by the helicopter that came down so close to the ground that he thought it was going to land nearby. Aida gasped to see him standing immobile beneath it. She gave him a tug and started running.

The young men hurried to the entrances, where barricades had been set up after the previous attacks, aiming to stop any heavy weaponry from advancing. Some of them were carrying sticks and tent poles, and others were holding swords and chains. One man with a pistol in his hand went ahead of the others and cleared a path for them. After covering hundreds of yards with snot and tears pouring from her nose and eyes, Aida spotted a man waving his left arm to guide the people who were fleeing. His right elbow was bent across his chest to hold the top of a small round table, with its metal legs folded over, like a shield protecting his side. The people hurrying toward him didn't know where he was telling them to go, but they followed his directions like blind people desperate for guidance. She told herself that in the confusion that had overwhelmed almost everyone, someone at least was still behaving as a leader. She reached an area where the tents had been flattened and large numbers of women had gathered. Busy as bees in a hive, they were breaking up the pavements with whatever implements were at hand and gathering up pieces of stone and rubble. They arranged the pieces on food trays, leveling them out to fill them as full as possible. Men arrived, took the trays from them and hurried off. Aida slowed down a little and then stopped to help them. She found it calmed her down to be helping to collect the only ammunition readily available at the time.

Close to the crowd of women she came across three young women in a cluster. They weren't moving around much and they weren't bending down to pick up stones. One of them looked up at the sky, cupped her hands around her mouth like a trumpet, and started shouting "*Allahu akbar*" at the top of her voice to encourage the others to stand their ground. Another one of the three started praying to God to give strength to herself and her brothers, who had set off to defend the entrances. The third woman collected children who had lost their relatives in the chaos, sat them down behind a barricade and sat next to them on the ground. She tried to put their minds at ease by telling them stories. Halim saw the children, who were about his age. He let go of Aida's hand and ran to listen to the stories, ignoring what was happening around him. Aida stopped and watched him go anxiously. The woman was calmly sitting cross-legged, praying and smiling as she started a new story. It seemed to Aida that the three women hadn't yet grasped the gravity of the situation. They might have thought the Space would hold out against the attack, that the men could easily resist security forces backed by helicopters, armored vehicles, and possibly tanks. Or maybe they did understand what was really happening but they had decided to stay and were trying to control their fear and the children's fears in this way. No one knew at that point whether staying in one place would be safer than moving, or the other way round. Everyone was thinking on their feet. A short while later a young girl collapsed next to Halim, her skin and lips blue, unable to breathe from the effects of a tear gas canister that had landed a few yards away. The woman who had been praying rushed over, picked the girl up and broke into a run past Aida on her way to the field hospital. Aida followed her with her eyes until the woman disappeared, and Aida prayed to God to save the innocent child. She wished with all her heart that she could close her eyes and open them again to find that the men had discovered the weapon stashes she had heard about for so long.

Aida prepared two trays of stones and rubble and handed them to a middle-aged man with a beard. He balanced them on his bare head and ran off to the shopping center. Then she collected more until there were no stones left on the ground and her hands were bleeding. She decided to continue on her way as she might come across Fayza or Nour. Maybe they were helping give first aid to the injured or protecting old people and children, in which case she would join them. Halim resisted: he didn't want to leave while the other boys were still sitting listening to the stories. He was even more insistent on staying when Hussein unexpectedly joined him, barefoot, covered in dust and coughing incessantly. His father wasn't with him and the two of them wanted to be together without anyone to supervise them or spoil their time together. They were enjoying the situation, treating it as a challenging video game rather than a frightening reality. Unable in her confusion to take Halim with her by force, she decided to leave him there. As she turned to walk away, she urged him to be careful and not to go near any vehicles or helicopters.

"If you're in danger, Halim," she said, "run away. Don't stand around to watch."

As she walked off, food trays shot by her, sagging in the middle because of the pieces of asphalt they were carrying. They reminded her of the heat of the oven and the cakes they had made just a few days earlier, and she imagined the smell of baking. The sounds of battle grew louder. Men called for help by shouting "*Allahu akbar*," and she realized she was very close to one of the entrances and she had no choice but to turn back. She quickly changed direction, and a few feet away she caught sight of a girl in her late teens, her headscarf covered in dust, bending down and picking up a handful of dust and throwing it at something. When Aida turned to see what the girl was trying to hit, she found a bulldozer approaching and heading for a tall building where dozens of young men had hunkered down and were trying to fend off the attacking vehicle. Some of them were shooting at it, but it appeared to be armor-plated and their bullets had little effect. The bulldozer came closer and closer but suddenly backed off because it was being hit by so many petrol bombs and parts of it were on fire. When the fires died down, the attack resumed.

Back where Halim was sitting, there were frequent bursts of gunfire and the men warned people that the security forces were using live ammunition. After a third tear gas canister landed only a few yards away, the woman who was reading felt that the place was no longer suitable for children. Besides, there were now so many children that the metal barricade, supported by plastic barrels full of sand, was too small to protect them all. The woman had them stand up in an orderly manner and organized them into pairs like schoolchildren walking down the street. Then she led them away in search of a new shelter. She made sure they didn't run, in case they panicked or were split up. Halim and Hussein held hands and moved along step by step, laughing together as if they were boy scouts on a hike, but Hussein couldn't take the walking for long. He started to weaken, found it hard to breathe, and coughed up vomit mixed with blood. He leaned forward with his hands on his knees. Halim stayed back with him and they lost contact with the rest of the group. After a while Hussein leaned on Halim and they went to the mosque together for help. A young man, alarmed at how pale Hussein looked, sat him on the mosque steps, took off his own mask and put it on the boy to stop him inhaling any more gas. The mask wasn't enough by itself. Hussein was already coughing his guts up, his eyes were wandering, and he could no longer hold a conversation. After a while the coughing stopped, the boy's body began to go limp and there were long gaps between each breath he took. A few minutes later he passed away. His head slumped onto the young man's shoulder and there was no longer a smile on his face. The man put his hand on the boy's neck to check for a pulse, then closed his eyes gently. He recited the declaration of faith. Halim jumped to his feet and ran off.

*

Adam was holding Murad's hand but he was extremely confused. They had taken shelter behind a barricade of sandbags at some distance from the hospital, which was full of tear gas. There was so much gas around it that it was hard to see, and as the gunfire intensified, the idea that the sandbags were protecting his son began to seem delusional. Bullets were streaming in from all directions and Murad couldn't see that anywhere was safer than anywhere else. A young man collapsed beside him, bleeding from several high-velocity bullet wounds in his chest, and maybe in his heart. Murad pulled the sheet-metal bucket off the dead man's head, since he clearly no longer needed protection, and put it without hesitation on Adam's head. The living take precedence over the dead, he said to himself. The bucket covered Adam's head to the shoulders, but he didn't object. His little body was shaking violently but he wasn't making any sound. This wasn't the moment to cry: this was death's moment. Murad noticed a knife in the young man's hand. He eased it out from between the limp fingers and held it in his hand, his heart pumping.

After a while the attacking forces announced on loudspeakers that there were safe exit routes, but no one knew where they were or if they even existed. Whenever people tried to get out of the Space they were caught in gunfire, and if anyone did manage to get out, they were grabbed and thrown into trucks. In reality, there were no routes out. Most of the people on the move inside the Space were carrying injured bodies, or were injured people themselves crawling in search of medical help, but snipers were watching them, and to move along the main routes was to dice with death. Purely by chance Shakir ended up close to Murad and Adam, but he didn't recognize them in the fog of gas and smoke. At just that minute Adam lifted the bucket off his head with one hand to see what was happening. He spotted a sniper aiming at them from the roof of a tall building overlooking the Space.

In panic Adam grabbed his father's arm with all the force he could muster and tried to pull him out of the way, but it was Shakir who was hit: he fell to the ground but didn't scream. Somehow human voices seemed irrelevant amid the violence. Blood was pouring from Shakir's thigh and running into the dust. Murad jumped up to help him and gestured to Adam to stay where he was behind the sandbags. Murad knelt on the ground, wrapped Shakir's arm round his neck and tried to stand up, but Shakir gave him no help at all. His body felt heavier than expected and he was mumbling in a weak voice, begging Murad to save his son and promising him that they would meet in paradise. A third man bleeding from wounds on both sides of his left shoulder threw himself down next to them and volunteered to help. Murad assumed a bullet had gone right through his shoulder and come out the other side, maybe without the man noticing, in the heat of the moment, that he had been hit. From the amount of blood that had come out, Murad reckoned that the man would soon collapse. The two men struggled to their feet and rose to the challenge. It proved easier to lift Shakir, but as they stumbled toward the barricade the volunteer took a bullet in his back. He sunk to his knees and Murad, already injured on the side of his neck, fell on top of him. Then Murad took a bullet in his forehead and finally, Adam screamed.

They woke us up at four o'clock in the morning and this time no one told us where we were going. Youssef leaned over to me and whispered that we were going to break up the protest by the Raised Banner movement and clear the Space. I didn't believe him at first, but I had learned to trust what he said. We received orders to get dressed immediately, put our boots on and pick up some heavy weaponry we didn't usually handle. They assembled us in the lecture hall in an atmosphere of suspense and high alert. No one spoke or made jokes. Then the national anthem began to reverberate throughout the hall and we realized that this was serious. This must be a major event. The mood was so tense you could cut the air with a knife. We were definitely going out on an important assignment, and it could only be what Youssef had guessed. A few minutes later Head Allam walked in wearing his uniform and fully armed. His face was strained and severe, much more so than we were used to.

"Today you're going to put into practice what you have learned in the last year, from A to Z," he roared. "Your camp has been chosen for the honor of going out on the most important assignment ever. Those traitors protesting in the Space are persisting in their error. We have been very patient, as you know. We have given them good advice and there has been no response. But we're ready to take them on, aren't we?"

In unison, our hearts quaking at the shock, we shouted, "We are ready, Head Allam!"

"You are well aware that they have plenty of weapons, brought in by truck, as you saw on television, and they have trained snipers and dangerous foreign elements. Don't give them a chance to prepare themselves for resistance. We are taking the initiative and only the general and the senior security men know when we will start. These people are the real enemy, and this will be the decisive battle between us and them. You will cleanse the country of their evil deeds. Everyone will appreciate the service you have done them, because not a single one of you bodies will come back without having performed honorably and to the satisfaction of the general. Not a single one of you bodies will come back without having earned the right to be called a hero. I am looking for lions that will hunt down these rats. Don't leave the place until it's been cleansed, until the sources of evil have been eliminated and those who stand in your way have been exterminated. We will free our country from the hands of the traitors. We will win back the territory of the Space. When this assignment is over I don't want to hear that any of them are still able to operate, reorganize, or plan further machinations. Do as Sheikh Abdel-Gabbar said: turn them into chaff that can be blown away by a baby's breath. Arise, bodies, and prepare to move! Everyone will move immediately to the trucks, and I personally, along with Head Salem, will be close by. In the Space we'll join up with various combat units and large numbers of fully equipped security forces. The ruler and the general are monitoring events closely and receiving updates minute by minute. *Allahu akbar*! Camp! Duty! The general! Long live the country!"

I felt a rush of fear and excitement coursing through my veins. My body trembled and my voice boomed out when we chanted after Head Allam. We stood up, impatient to join battle and achieve victory—all except Youssef, who moved his lips but did not chant with the rest of us. They put us in trucks and we filled twenty of them. Youssef came in the same truck as me. It was the first time we had gone on an assignment together and I was certainly pleased to be with him, but I was uneasy when I saw that he was distracted and still sullenly silent. I could see that he didn't share my emotions. Before we went through the camp gates, they gave out identity cards to the older ones among us, with their pictures on them. I didn't get one and neither did Youssef. I was curious to see the names written on the others' cards, but I stayed where I was, immobilized in awe at the drama of the situation and primed to face danger.

The truck stopped on the edge of the Space. It couldn't go any further because of the barricades those dogs had built. They took us off the truck and told us to get ready. We formed into parallel lines and started running on the spot. At exactly six o'clock, we took up the attack positions we had learned in training. The ones with tear gas launchers started firing canisters nonstop until I thought that the rats hiding inside must have died of fright and asphyxiation. One of our helicopters appeared, spewing bullets and bombs onto their heads. My fear completely evaporated, replaced by an impatience to launch the assault. I started playing with the trigger in my eagerness to pull it. We were given the order to advance and we set off to battle. We ran with our guns raised and began firing in the air at random. A few minutes later we heard Head Salem ordering us not to waste ammunition and only to fire directly at targets. Before he finished speaking a stone hit me in the stomach. I realized that now it was for real and I expected a bullet would follow the stone. It was a matter of life and death. I held my ground and without hesitation I aimed at the legs of the people who were running back and forth. Youssef was the only thing holding me back, I thought. He wasn't in his right mind. I could see that his eyes were wandering and that he couldn't concentrate. He didn't know what he was doing.

I stayed behind Youssef to protect him as we moved in among the tents that our forces had destroyed, attacking anyone who was still standing, spraying them with bullets till they looked like sieves. I fired bursts at a large group that was throwing stones at us. Youssef was in a daze. He wasn't firing his gun and he wasn't even holding it up. I was worried that in this state of mind he might get shot, but God protected us and all we faced was waves of stones, against a din of shouting, the roar of the helicopters, and loudspeakers giving orders to us and to them. I heard them screaming for jihad for God and Islam, but what do those infidels have to do with our religion now? Only we have the right to shout *"Allahu akbar"* and call on God's help against them. I shot two of them and saw them fall to the ground, then crawl into hiding behind some massive tires they had put on top of each other to obstruct us. I'd seen them on television and now I was seeing them for real. I aimed at the tires and just as I was about to pull the trigger Youssef grabbed my arm to stop me. I didn't much care about him stopping me, or about hunting down the two men. I just started looking for another target. Despite all the noise, which almost deafened me, I could hear Youssef whispering to himself, or maybe to me.

"We're not going to do what Emad is doing," he said. "There are little children running in panic and they're unarmed."

After a few hours the sun was shining bright and the situation was even more heated. The ground around us was covered in random items: pots and pans, packs of tea, torn clothes, empty, crushed water bottles. It looked like someone had thrown the contents of their house into the street. The scene reminded me of the day they moved us out of the rubbish dump. The ground was covered with the inhabitants' possessions, like rubbish waiting to be buried in landfill. I felt something breaking under my boot as I dragged Youssef forward. I lifted my foot out of curiosity and saw a colored pistol, a children's toy that I'd trodden on and smashed into little pieces. I kicked the remains away and looked around for another target. To my right I spotted some swings like the ones I often used to ride at fairs. Are these people mad? I wondered.

Youssef moved away from me a little and started to examine something that had caught his attention. Then he bent down, ignoring me when I called him, and picked it up. I went back to him and found a half-squashed Eid cake in his hand. The titan couldn't believe what he saw. Head Salem had come up behind us without us noticing. He looked at the remains of the cake and shouted angrily at Youssef in a voice that cut through the clamor of battle.

"What are you doing, body?" he asked. "Are you stupid? Are you hungry? Never bend down, you idiot! Is that what I taught you to do?"

I was nailed to the spot as I watched the two of them together. No one on the face of the earth would have understood what Youssef had done, except for me and Emad. Head Salem wouldn't have known that the cake meant it was his birthday and however loud he shouted, Youssef wouldn't forget that. Youssef didn't drop the cake, but in his confusion he squeezed it so hard that it broke into crumbs and slipped through his fingers, leaving only a light powdering of sugar. Head Salem was busy on his walkie-talkie meanwhile, shouting that an officer had been shot and then assuring the person on the other end that the bulldozer was already making its way deep into the Space. I gave Youssef a big push to move him out of the titan's sight. Next to a building we found an excellent spot where we had a good view of the scene. I looked up and saw the sharpshooter kids from our camp firing from the rooftops and hitting people in the head and chest with precision. Then I looked down to check on Youssef and was surprised to see him sniffing the sweaty hand that had held the cake crumbs, with his gun lying between his feet. I aimed my gun again, started shooting, and begged him to do the same. He picked up his gun, stretched his arm out as far as possible, and swung it right and left without firing a single shot.

"I'm not Emad, Rabie," he said.

"Be Emad, just for today, for my sake," I shouted back like a madman. I didn't have time to argue.

Hours passed and we didn't rest for a moment. The sun blazed down on us. Fires had broken out here and there and the battle lines were still shifting back and forth. Fighting flared up again on the news that seventy officers had been killed. I was frightened and fought harder, especially when one of their men dug in behind a large barrel and raised what looked like a machine-gun above his head. They must be preparing some heavy weaponry on the other side of the Space or maybe they had taken over the roofs of some buildings and would open fire at us from there. I heard Head Salem ordering us to go to the mosque, and I set off immediately.

Some of the protesters had set fire to car tires not far from Youssef, filling the air with black, foul-smelling smoke, in the belief that this reduced the effects of the tear gas. They had no other solution: they had run out of vinegar and there were hundreds of cases of asphyxiation. Some mothers had even started telling their children to inhale the smoke in the hope that it might give them some more minutes of life. Youssef looked at the fires in silence and, through the thick smoke, saw women and children hurrying about blindly in confusion.

"Rabie, Rabie," he said. "Look, right in front of your eyes."

I didn't reply. I just ran off to obey Head Salem's order that we stop the protesters setting up barricades and then regroup with the rest of the bodies by the big wooden door of the mosque, ready to take on the snipers and gunmen among the protesters, who were thought to be holed up in the building. Youssef left his hiding place and shouted at me again. He thought he had seen the ghost of someone he knew. He had seen Halim running in the distance with a food container upside down on his head. He was holding it with both hands like a helmet for protection. It was definitely Halim. Youssef imagined that Halim had spotted him, but he didn't have the time or wasn't brave enough to shout at him or join him, and they wouldn't have been able to hear anything anyway against the noise of the frenzied slaughter.

Aida couldn't call Murad. She moved from area to area, large numbers of protesters were killed in front of her eyes and she gradually came to grips with the level of destruction inflicted on the Space. She came to realize that she probably wouldn't get out safely. Everyone was being attacked mercilessly, even old people and children, and nothing was safe, even the ants under the ground. She was walking around aimlessly, sick with worry for her husband and son, but she held out hope. Murad and Adam may have reached the hospital safely, or they might be stuck in a place where the bullets and grenades hadn't yet wiped out everyone. My God, yesterday life was so orderly and now it had fallen apart and turned into chaos run amok. There was no sign of Fayza or of Nour, but she had to keep moving. There were no options now. After hundreds of attempts to contact Murad, she suddenly received a short call from Ibrahim. In a hoarse voice interspersed by panting, he gave her the news that Murad was dead. She didn't have time to extract any extra information from him. Receiving the shocking message had consumed the remaining seconds of charge in her cellphone battery and the phone went dead. The screen was now totally blank. In her agitation, Aida wavered between denial and acceptance. As if detached from the reality of it, she imagined many ways she could react—screaming, slapping herself in the face and throwing handfuls of dust, or performing two prostrations to God and wailing in grief, or maybe recklessly standing in the middle of the Space in the hope that she too might die a martyr's death. But she set all that aside as soon as she remembered Adam's face. Ibrahim hadn't told her anything about her son. What had happened to him? Might he have escaped? Was it really Ibrahim anyway? Was he afraid to give her two shocks at the same time and so he decided to hide the news of Adam's death from her? It might have been someone else who called: she hadn't been able to identify his voice for certain through all the gunfire, the explosions, and the screaming. Maybe he didn't mean her or her husband Murad. Under the circumstances it would be very possible to make a mistake. She set off single-mindedly, aiming to reach the hospital to find out the news with her own two eyes. She didn't notice how uneven the path was or what she was stepping on. When she arrived, the destruction was worse than she could ever have imagined and she wasn't even certain she was in the right place. Adam filled her thoughts, to the exclusion of everything else: his voice, his smell, the feel of his hair, his eyes looking for her and seeking her help. As soon as she managed to enter the hospital, she bent down here and there, examining the dead bodies and what was left of their faces. The sight appalled her, and the number of bodies was shocking. She tripped over an old man sitting cross-legged among the bodies, his head bowed, screwing up his eyes because he wanted to cry but was too ashamed to do so. Then she saw two women side by side, one with her arms wrapping around an open coffin with a man lying in it, while the other threw herself on the dead body of a young man in a shroud. Her face was stained with his blood and the shroud was soaked with her tears. Aida looked around in horror but she couldn't find Murad. She asked the doctors, most of whom she knew. After asking them all one after another, she was sure that none of them had seen him. He hadn't been there since he left her at dawn with Adam. Neither of them had reached the hospital and the report that they had died on the way was very credible. At this point all she wanted was to see her son, if only for one last time. She had imagined that Adam, under Murad's protection, was more likely to survive than she was, and now, in the blink of an eye, he was lost. She left the hospital in a daze, unable to see more than a few inches in front of her nose, and her body was racked by an anguish that was irrepressible.

Tongues of flame could be seen from the podium area. Many of the protesters were cowering behind sandbags or tires that were spread around the Space and hadn't caught fire yet. They thought they were protected, but bullets went through the tires and came out the other side like knives cutting through butter. The bulldozer was shoveling corpses and crushing the ones that got caught up in its tracks. The crushing machine was working at full strength to wipe out every trace that might remind people of the protest. More than forty days had to be erased from the face of the earth. The bulldozer pushed out the pegs of one tent, drove into another and crushed what was left of it. It did not stop for a man hidden between the twisted chairs and the shredded blankets. It mangled his flesh and bones along with pots and pans, copies of the Quran and assorted household objects. Aida picked up a stone from the ground and threw it at the raging beast, then a second stone and a third.

Head Allam turned up to see how things were going. Youssef was in an even more pitiful state now. Allam told him to pull himself together and aim properly when shooting. He stood and watched him but Youssef missed time after time and the targets got away. After a while the titan ordered him to aim at a flag that was still flying among the ruins in the distance. He finally succeeded: he hit the flagpole spot on, fragments of wood flew in the air and the flag fell to the ground. One of the protesters picked it up shouting *Allahu akbar*. The titan raised his gun and shot the man in the leg. The man collapsed with the flag. The titan shouted at Youssef to blow off the man's head, but in ten attempts in close succession Youssef couldn't aim straight. The man clung to the flag, holding it high as he tried to get to his feet, but with his wounded leg it was a struggle. Another body who had been following the situation from the start volunteered to have a shot. At his first attempt he blew out the man's brains, which spattered all over the flag. In the meantime Youssef was still pulling the trigger and shooting to no avail. Everything about Youssef refused to take part in the killing: his eye didn't want to see people, his arm didn't want to hold the gun steady, and even his finger didn't want to pull the trigger at the right moment. But he could hit inanimate objects.

The titan walked away a little, clearly displeased at Youssef's performance, but one of the bodies called him back: "Youssef isn't killing anyone, Head Allam. Youssef isn't killing anyone."

The titan squinted and looked into the distance, then lifted up his gun, held it steady and fired straight at Youssef's head. I was so shocked I didn't even hear the sound of the shot. I saw the titan looking at me out of the corner of his eye and Youssef slumping to the ground. I bit my lip to stop myself screaming or crying. I tasted blood in my mouth but I swallowed it so that it wouldn't give me away. I raised my gun and when I heard the order to fire, I aimed at people and shot them down one after another.

Aida eventually found Adam at the bottom of a pile of sandbags. By then she had convinced herself that he must be dead and that his body, riddled with bullets, was lying in blood-stained sand somewhere. She recognized his shoes between the sandbags and started to pull at the bags one after another, grinding her teeth until they almost broke and coughing at the dust she stirred up. She wept a flood of tears that she could not stop. When she reached the last bag on top of his little body, she stepped back and her hand hesitated, unable to face reality. She didn't know if she would scream or just accept the loss of her son in silence and with resignation. Someone else's hand reached out to finish off the job, grabbing the end of the bag and pulling at it firmly, though not with the same strength as Aida's hand. It was Halim's hand, trying to reach his friend. She was startled. Should she let him remove the bag, at the risk of finding Adam dead? Could she take the shock of two deaths on the same day? Or maybe she should grab a weapon and aim it at the invading security forces in the hope that they would shoot her dead before she could pull the trigger? That way she would join in death the people she loved most, Murad and Adam. Halim's voice brought her out of her musings.

"Wake up, Adam!" he said, "wake up. Your mother's here. There aren't any bullets in you. They didn't shoot you, Adam. Come on, let's go. Your mother's right here."

Adam looked up with eyes as red as blood. Aida knelt beside him and held him to her breast. Then she pulled Halim to her and hugged him too.

Supported by his mother and holding on to Halim's shirt, Adam stood up. None of the three could take in what was happening and there was no time to talk. Aida headed automatically for the residential buildings in less dangerous side streets, to keep out of sight and safe from fires and sniper bullets. She walked some way with the two boys, dragging her feet from exhaustion and shock. Sometimes she pushed the boys to the ground and threw herself on top of them to protect them from a hail of bullets, sometimes she hid with them in the lobby of an abandoned apartment block and sometimes she just sat on the ground without taking any precautions, and then the panicked boys would persuade her not to give up. Around them there were people, alive and dead, with faces as white as sheets, their clothes and skin stained with blood. After hours of dodging and toing and froing Halim heard what sounded like a loud "*pssss*." He stopped walking, looked around for the source of the sound but couldn't see anything. The sound came back when he resumed walking, louder and clearer now, as if the person making the noise wanted to attract their attention. Aida heard the noise too and Halim's behavior led her to believe that it wasn't just hallucinations playing with her tired brain. Amid the smoke and the tear gas they were able to make out someone trying to catch their attention from a balcony above them. It was a woman with her head covered, gesturing at them to come upstairs. Aida was hesitant and the woman knew what might be going through her mind to make her anxious, so she called her daughters over to show Aida a large picture of the abducted ruler. They were waving their arms and welcoming people who had survived the massacre. Reassured and with few other options, since she had no cash and her phone battery had run out hours ago, she went to the door of the building, holding Adam's hand and with Halim behind them. The woman spoke to her on the intercom and told her to come up to the fifth floor without using the elevator, in case the noise alerted the doorman, who might ask difficult questions. Aida understood the possible sensitivity of the situation and began to notice the marks their shoes were leaving on the stairway. She bent down to wipe away a drop that looked like blood so that none of the residents would be suspicious. Adam started reading the small nameplates on every door: Counselor So-and-so, Colonel Such-and-such, Judge So-and-So, while Halim dawdled behind them. Before they reached the fifth floor, Halim turned and ran down the stairs. Aida called after him, trying hard not to shout too loud in case she alarmed the residents, but he didn't come back.

"Thank God you're safe," said the woman. "This is your home now. Don't worry. Come into the girls' room, Sister. I'll fetch you some clean clothes right away and get the bathroom ready. Then we can have dinner together. I'm sure you haven't had a bite since the morning. Do you have any injuries, my dear? Are you in pain?"

Aida wanted to stay as she was, and she wanted the same for Adam. She asked the woman not to fuss over her. She did drink some lukewarm water and eat a very small amount of food, and she used the toilet. But she couldn't remember her normal routines; the fragrance of perfume in the bathroom troubled her in some mysterious way. Did such things matter now? She didn't care how clean the bathroom was, or how beautiful, or how glamorous or well-maintained, not when all she could smell and taste was blood. Washing seemed pointless when she felt the dust and the bitterness deep inside her, under her skin, in every atom of her body. God decreed, but he certainly didn't always achieve what he wanted. Victory today belonged to the tyrants and their henchmen. The Space was theirs, and a whole world had died. Aida spent the night in a stranger's house, in an unfamiliar bed, with her son in her arms, trembling constantly even when Adam fell asleep. She got up at dawn to pray, but she didn't want to wash. Something strange prevented her from removing the lingering traces of the previous day's horrors.

Saber Abdel-Mawla sat in the mosque weeping. Next to him a woman tried to console him while simultaneously stitching up an open wound in someone's abdomen.

"There is no strength or power other than in God. Fear God and seek his help," she said. "Remember that your son is now in His care. Those who die as martyrs live on with God and tomorrow he will intercede on your behalf, when no one will be wronged and everyone will receive their due. Today you should be celebrating, not sad. Dry your tears, be brave, submit to God's will in the hope of recompense, say that you're content with the lot that God has given you and do not squander your heavenly reward."

Saber covered his face with his hands and sobbed. "What shall I tell his mother? How can I take him home dead in my arms, a body with no feelings and no soul, when yesterday he would race me to the door and pull at my clothes in his impatience to go out. How can I go back when I have no other son? He is my only child and neither I nor his mother have a life after he is gone. What shall I tell her? What shall I say?"

He wiped from his dead son's cold blue mouth the white foam that filled it and spilled out from the sides. The mosque was crammed with more than three hundred bodies. The doctor and the medics who were still there had started laying the corpses on their sides to make some space where they could help the injured, especially those they thought had a reasonable chance of survival, though those ones were an insignificant minority among the seriously injured people pouring in. As the dead piled up, there was no solution other than to pile the bodies on top of each other to make room for the newcomers.

Bursts of gunfire smashed the mosque windows and ricocheted around the room. Then came the sound of boots kicking down the wooden door. One doctor was still trying to stitch up the chest of an injured man when the attack began. The people in the mosque tried to fend off the invaders. Saber rushed to help them but their efforts were in vain. Most of them were exhausted and bleeding from multiple wounds. What strength they had left wasn't enough to take on ferocious men with rippling muscles and minds bent on a single objective. The heavy door fell in under the pressure of their blows, as if it were made of paper. The masked men invaded the room, treading on some of the corpses. They aimed the muzzles of their rifles indiscriminately at the people inside. Everyone froze. Unexpectedly, a young woman came forward with her hands raised in unconditional surrender and asked for some time to evacuate the wounded. The masked commander looked at her, then pulled the trigger, firing a rapid burst from the machine gun he was holding, making a deep hole in the wall opposite. Everyone ducked. The woman closed her eyes until she heard him give the order: "Ten minutes and no more, and then we'll clean you all out of the place." Saber withdrew to the back door and the next thing he knew he was running away. He didn't look back.

Saber saw fires burning in the distance. He was still looking for a good place to hide until the invaders left and he had an opportunity to go back, pick up his son's body, and take it out of the Space. He looked around to check out the situation. The unpleasant smell of burning hit his nose. He emerged from behind a cart that once served hot fava beans and that had lost most of its paintwork. All that remained of the faded decoration was the Quranic word "*la'azidannakum*," which means "I shall give you more." He started running toward the black clouds that filled the air, his heart quaking with doubts, and then suddenly he was watching the mosque as it started to burn. The cruel bastards. O Lord, you are not happy with this, O Lord, put out the fire. O Lord, O Lord. When he reached the mosque, it was just ashes. He lost his son in a matter of hours, yet within just minutes he lost the chance to give him a dignified burial, wrapped in a shroud. It had never occurred to him that they would set fire to the mosque to cover up their deeds. If he had known he would have stayed where he was and burned to death alongside his son and countless others, their bodies charred, nameless, and without bones that could be buried. O Lord, why, O Lord? He fainted and when he came around, he saw Halim sitting nearby. Opposite them an old man was dangling the blackened remains of a Quran. Many of the pages were missing and charred fragments lay scattered on the ground like chaff.

Saber sat there lost in his own thoughts until darkness fell in the Space and the sound of shooting died down. Then, without changing his position, he asked the boy what his father was called.

"I'm Halim Rizk," Halim replied.

"Rizk? Do you pray, Abdel-Halim?"

"In the Space I used to go and pray every day."

Saber pulled Halim's arm toward him and turned it over to see the inside of his wrist. Halim didn't want to move away or hide his wrist, so the green cross tattooed there was easily visible. Saber frowned and resumed his silence. Halim also kept quiet: he didn't say a word about everything that had happened since he had woken up before daybreak, or about Aida and Adam and what had happened to them. He didn't say he had spent the whole day with them until he had faced his moment of choice. He didn't say that in the end he was very frightened, even more frightened than during the killing in the Space. He was frightened when he went up the clean, polished stairs and when Adam read the names and titles of the residents, and when he saw the wooden doors and the golden door handles, and when he saw from Aida and Adam's faces that they were comfortable with the place. He was frightened and thought that the woman on the fifth floor might refuse to let him in. He felt claustrophobic and decided to run away. He didn't tell Saber how he managed to get back to the Space and how he came to be sitting next to him when Saber came around. Finally Saber looked away. "I'm going home," he said to Halim. "Your friend died today, so will you come with me?"

Halim nodded and just said, "Coming."

Saber stood up and took Halim by the hand, avoiding any contact with the cross. The boy's hand was cold despite the heat. Saber pressed it gently to warm it up, and when they drew closer to Saber's neighborhood he let go of Halim's hand and held him by the wrist to hide the cross.

Saber's wife opened the door anxiously. She had heard reports that the protest had been dispersed and had put herself in the right state of mind to welcome her son home and set his mind at ease. She vowed she would never part with him again, having gone through the worst of all possible agonies all day long. She wanted to give him an endless hug and she was startled when she was confronted with a face she didn't know. She jumped back a step, tongue-tied for a moment. Then she launched into a tirade of questions, sensing that disaster had struck and that all her fears had come true.

"Saber, my son?" she said. "My son, Abdel-Mawla? Where did you leave the boy?"

"Shh, shh, I don't want to hear a sound, woman. Today we're going to celebrate a martyr, and this is his brother. Rejoice and bring the drinks."

The woman screamed and wailed and burst into torrents of tears. Then she turned on Saber and cursed the Raised Banner movement. She lambasted the movement's leaders for failing to protect their followers as they had promised. She pushed Saber in the chest and shouted that she had heard the preacher on the podium vowing that the security forces would never touch a hair on their heads. She shouted so much she went hoarse and one neighbor after another came to find out what was happening in the house. Halim stood there without flinching. He didn't even think of escaping. The woman didn't seem to see him. She tore her dress and uncovered her hair, ravaged by emotions that no creature on the face of the earth could have controlled.

12

Speak Without Fear

Aida said goodbye to her hosts early in the morning and went straight home, troubled and exhausted. Her eyes were red and swollen. Her clothes were crumpled, torn in several places, and stained with soot and dried blood. In one hand she had Adam and in the other she had a stone she was still holding. She wasn't annoyed that the land line had been ringing off the hook since the moment she came through the door. She didn't seem to hear it. Without a word she pushed Adam into the bathroom and started washing his face and pouring plenty of water onto his eyes. She went out for a few seconds and came back with a bottle of alcohol and a towel. She checked his minor injuries and then picked up the phone, which was still ringing. At the other end it was Fayza, who launched into condolences for Aida and pity for herself.

"Only God lives forever, Aida," she said. "We belong to God and to Him we shall return. We're in this disaster together. Shakir is dead and Dr. Murad is dead as well. They are martyrs in the paradise of the immortals and they shall be given the greatest reward. God may grant us victory over the unjust through their martyrdom. Your cell phone has been turned off since yesterday evening. Tell me you're okay, and your son too. How is Adam?"

She didn't wait for an answer but continued without pause. "Don't risk going anywhere near the Space. They've arrested hundreds of people. When I have news from the Brothers on where the bodies are, I'll call you immediately."

With great difficulty Aida managed to get out a few words, to the effect that she was ready to go out as soon as someone told her with certainty where Murad's body was and that she would then complete the burial procedures. She hung up feeling miserable.

Someone banged on the door loudly and repeatedly. It sounded as if fate had come knocking. Aida looked through the peephole to find a police officer in uniform. She didn't ask him who he was and she didn't waste time arranging her thoughts or adjusting her appearance. What might he want? Nothing was any use any longer. She opened the door and he asked to come in. He was accompanied by another man from the security forces. He took two steps forward and then stopped.

"Dr. Murad Fathi Mahmoud, your husband, is in the morgue at the university hospital where he was working," he said impassively. "An ambulance took him there after one of the medics recognized him."

Frowning, he looked down at her and his voice took on a tone that was callous, unpleasant, and brimming with arrogance. "It would be best for you and for his memory if a simple death notice appeared in the newspapers," he added. "In *al-Ahramat* newspaper, for example, without any details. And if everyone was told that Dr. Murad passed away from some chronic disease."

The message contained a threat that was implicit but unmistakable.

Aida wasn't up to engaging in conversation. What he said made no sense. It wouldn't change the reality if she agreed. She didn't seek to argue, or make any objection. Happy with a quick nod from her, the policeman left her to pick up the pieces of her life. Adam still hadn't finished dressing but she dragged him off and headed out of the door to the university hospital.

*

Many mourners joined Murad's funeral procession. They fell into two main groups, with very different backgrounds and perspectives on Murad. The doctor seemed to have several personae. One group included most of his students in the Faculty of Medicine: after the burial rites they discussed the circumstances of his death, convinced he had died after days in bed incapacitated by an unknown fever. Then there were his faculty colleagues: they said he had died when his heart stopped because of the intense emotions he felt when watching television coverage of the killing during the operation to break up the protest. He was known to reject violence and to be of a gentle disposition, and on top of that to sympathize with the protesters. His close friends and a tiny number of colleagues made up a third group: they kept quiet about the fact that he had been killed in the Space by a bullet that penetrated the frontal lobe of his brain. This group included his young bearded assistant, Ibrahim, who acted as one of the pallbearers. Ibrahim's face was tense and stormy at the funeral. He walked with slow, embittered steps, then went down into the burial chamber, constantly mulling the reasons for the massacre and who to blame for their failure to defend themselves.

"If only we had been properly armed!" he said to himself. "If only we had had at least a hundred guns. People went through hell to sneak guns into the Space, and in the end there were only dozens of them and they acted in isolation against thousands of soldiers armed to the teeth. If we young people had been assigned to defend the protest and if we had been free to build fortifications for the Space as we saw fit, they wouldn't have been able to break in. I swear, they wouldn't have got in, even if they'd besieged us for days, and we wouldn't now be sending Dr. Murad off to heaven to join God, whose eyes never lose sight of criminals. We heard and obeyed. We said 'Yes!' to our leaders. Obedience plays an important part in building up an organization, but in this case it backfired on us horribly, and this is the result."

The one fact everyone agreed on was the simplest and easiest to prove: that Murad ascended unto his Creator on the day the protest was dispersed, within the first few hours to be precise.

Aida's face was frozen. She found it impossible to express any emotion in her response to condolences from the mourners, but from time to time she would overcome the numbness of her pain and come out with a phrase or a sigh, or try to fill the silence by asking after the close friends she had met through the protest in the days before the massacre. The first person she asked after was Nour. Shakir's widow, Fayza, who was sitting beside her, shook her head in sorrow. In a tone of voice that combined derision, bitterness and sadness. she said that the whole Sabbagh family had left the Space a few hours before the attack began.

"Adel's excuse was that his wife suddenly felt unwell and was alone at home, so he took his daughters and stripped their tent bare of its contents."

She turned her face aside and coughed a constant dry cough, then she put her hand on Aida's hand and whispered some fresh news to her that might cheer her up, if only a little. "The day before yesterday the League of Sunna Defenders said it's haram to work in the security forces, and I heard from reliable sources that some officers and men are asking to leave the service after what happened in the Space. This is not the end."

Halim held his silence during his first days at Saber's house. Saber and his wife also kept quiet: they were both thinking hard, looking at all the possibilities from every angle. Saber himself was also afraid to speak in case his wife flew into a rage again. Halim slept on the old sofa in the sitting room for several nights. Saber brought him food on a tray, rather like he did in the Space. Sometimes he asked him to help with simple housework. He fetched him a nail and a hammer to fix the spice rack that was askew in the kitchen, or he handed him a strip of soldering iron to repair the light fixture that had shorted in the bathroom. Halim went along with him. He never refused a request for help or made a fuss.

Saber's wife was bewildered for some time. She didn't know where her son was buried, or if he even had a grave, and she could find no trace of him, not even his smell. She might as well never have been pregnant or given birth to a son. All she could see was Halim, who was the same height and the same age, with a soul she thought was close to her son's soul. She started watching him closely throughout the day: he was thinner and fairer-skinned, and he had nice bright eyes. Yet she didn't understand what she was meant to do with him. Saber watched her and didn't say anything. This was an unfamiliar boy, a stranger to her, to the house, to their relatives in the countryside, and to the people around them in their area. But her broken heart would fall to pieces completely if Halim went on his way and left the place empty. She would well and truly die.

Saber's wife tested Halim several times. Halim neither passed the test nor failed. He didn't show any obvious attachment to anything: not to the church, or to the mosque, or to any religion. After making an effort and getting through the first stages of shock, she realized that Halim was attached only to where he was and the people he was with, and to food and security. At noon one day she had him sit at the table with her, and Saber didn't object. Then Saber took him into the bedroom of their dead son, and his wife didn't object, though she looked a little uncomfortable. After wavering, she accepted him and overcame her doubts and fears. She felt calmer. She convinced herself that God had sent Halim to compensate for her son. She thought up many possible ways to hide the cross from her neighbors, but her ideas were impossible and naive. Saber thought along the same lines: it wouldn't be right to pretend that the boy, with the cross on his wrist, was a relative, a distant cousin from Upper Egypt for example. He would have to conceal the cross by some means if Halim was going to stay in the house, but how, when it was tattooed indelibly onto the boy's wrist?

For his part, Halim was happy to live with Saber and his wife. He trusted them and thought he had become like them; they had a shared memory, since they had all borne witness to the massacre. In the Space he had created a life that was to his liking, gained new friends, and found food, toys, and stories. He had stayed until it all disappeared overnight. On top of that, he had been with Saber's son till the end. It's true that he met many people and that he liked Aida, Adam, and Sara, but Saber now seemed closer. There were no other children at his place, so Saber would give him his undivided care and attention, and the house was very much like his old house. At least the staircase didn't shine and the door handle didn't sparkle, as in the building Aida had taken him into. Saber's wife was also rather like his mother. All she knew about him was what he told her. Aida knew his background and where he came from. She knew he came from the street. He wouldn't be going back to his family after everything he had been through and the things that had happened to him. There was no room for him there anyway. Nor could he go back to his friends at the garbage dump, even if they had gone back, after seeing Emad killing people and Rabie following his example. They must have changed, just as he had changed. From his pocket he took out the bottle tops he played *siga* with, sat alone in the living room, and arranged them on the tiled floor.

Adel al-Sabbagh got in touch with some big businessmen who were members of the Raised Banner movement. He found an excellent opening in the Gulf and flew off there. His wife didn't go with him as she preferred to stay at home and spend her time in her usual way: going to the club, visiting her women friends in their homes, trying out new hair styles, and taking part in gossip sessions. He failed to persuade her to join him, though he tried several ways to tempt her: the affluent lifestyle she could expect, the daily shopping trips, and so on. But she wasn't interested in such inducements.

"Why move now when your businesses here are doing fine?" she said. "We don't need the hot weather and I couldn't bear having to wear that stifling shroud they wear there."

"My dear, can't you see that the situation here isn't stable?" Adel replied. "Do you really want me to hang around and wait for this madman to take decisions? I might believe his sweet talk and decide the future looks promising, only to end up at the mercy of some brutal decision he suddenly takes. He has all the cards in his hands now. He controls both wings of the security establishment, and he has Abdel-Gabbar. I would be a complete fool to sit around feeling safe, only to find myself in prison with my all money frozen."

"So off you go then, maybe we'll join you for the mid-year break. Don't forget that we can't move Sara to another school right now."

"Think about it. As soon as I get there I'll send you pictures of the house. Maybe you'll like it and decide to come. I know it's grand and spacious, with a swimming pool and a private garden. It's in a closed compound and you can wear what you like there."

Sara took off her niqab and went back to her old look. Her long hair hung free over her shoulders and she wore interesting earrings and necklaces to prove she was now a proper adolescent. Her mother stopped wearing the hijab every day, as she had done temporarily, and treated it as just one possible fashion option. She wore it when it suited her outfit, but not if she thought she would look better with her hair freshly styled. Meanwhile Nour kept an eye on her and, without expecting a response, made occasional comments such as, "That isn't the Islamic way. That's a joke." Without great difficulty, Adel soon arranged to stay long-term in the Gulf. He found a commodious house waiting for him, big enough for his family to live in and entertain lavishly. He had soon installed every possible comfort and convenience, as a precaution in case a security crackdown forced his family to leave the country and join him. Adel took the first opportunity to sort out the paperwork for his new business deals in the Gulf. He went back home about a month later, with gifts for his wife and daughters, hoping they would change their minds and decide to move with him. He didn't tell them he was coming, so when Sara opened the door to him and saw him smiling on the threshold, she screamed in excitement, hugged him, and planted kisses on his cheeks. She didn't wait to let him recover from the fatigue of traveling. On the contrary, even before he had time to get his breath back, she started criticizing him for abandoning her and begging him to save her. She didn't let her mother or Nour get a word in, while a torrent of words poured out of her. When the four of them sat down at the table for lunch, she brought up the subject of moving to the Gulf and insisted he take her with him so that she could go to a foreign international school. She didn't disguise her reasons and felt no inhibitions because of her sister's presence.

"I'll go with you. Nour's started behaving silly. She's always depressed. She hasn't laughed since we left the tent and she doesn't want me to listen to songs. She says we have to mourn those who died in the Space. She always refuses to come to the club with me and doesn't approve of my friends visiting me. She never stops criticizing what I wear. We have arguments every day. She wants me to bury myself away and turn into an idiot like her. We can't share the same room any longer."

Adel had no objection to sorting out Sara's passport and other papers and taking her with him when he went back, to keep him company and listen to him rather than her mother, to share with him the McDonald's meals he always ended up eating. Maybe luck would be kind to him and she would learn how to cook his favorite dishes, saving him from going to restaurants. He welcomed her suggestion and started to lay out the advantages of her coming with him. But he ran into stiff resistance, which no discussion or pleading could overcome, because his wife could no longer stand Nour's behavior—her surliness, her black moods, and her anti-social practices, such as her refusal to leave the house for weeks on end. She shouted at Adel when he tried to discuss it with her.

"Take your elder daughter to live with your father and mother," she told him. "Maybe they can handle her. Take her. I'm fed up with what she's doing to us and to herself."

Nour no longer felt at ease and decided to get out of the house more. She looked for work and did in fact join a charity, but she wasn't happy with the way it was run, so she left after a short period and stayed at home again. She spent most of her time daydreaming, thinking about what she had been through for the weeks in the Space, remembering Aida and the group of children, and going over the experience she had gained from the teaching. She pondered the experience that had brought her together with thousands of people seeking the same goal, although they disagreed openly on other things. It had taught her many things. She had heard friends who took part in the first revolution talk about the spirit that had inspired the movement. It had changed people's behavior, purified and united them, and turned the physical space into a virtuous city, better than Plato's Republic. She listened to their stories about the sense of solidarity, determination, and self-sacrifice, about how their magnanimity came to the surface, about their high-minded ethics, about the example that was set during the protests in the streets and in the squares. But at the time she hadn't taken in what they said. Their stories hadn't touched her. She wasn't impressed by them. She didn't understand why they wrote poetry about it and dreamed of reliving the experience. She didn't understand what they were describing in the first place. She thought it was all naïve and childish. But now she understood. She understood clearly what strength in numbers could mean. She also understood what defeat meant.

The idea of contacting Aida nagged at her. Maybe Aida would know how to get her out of her shell and save her from a sense that she was trapped and her life was empty. But she hesitated to make the phone call because she thought it might be impolite. She had had the same feeling since they left the Space on the eve of the massacre—a persistent and pervasive sense of guilt that brought a lump to her throat, especially when she realized, belatedly, that her father knew that the attack on the protest was going to happen the next morning, through a businessman in touch with the government. Her father had insisted they leave immediately, but without mentioning the true reason. "Your mother's unhappy about our absence," he said at the time. "She gets up and goes to sleep alone, and she doesn't have anyone to talk to or anyone whose opinion she can consult. She even spent Eid alone. Let's spend two or three nights with her and then come back." He didn't bother to tell the people in the neighboring tents. He didn't care about the lives of thousands of protesters—old people, women, and children. He didn't even warn his close friends. He was only interested in saving himself and his little family, and let everyone else go to hell. It took her days to pluck up courage and dial the number, but finally she did it. She heard Aida's voice at the other end, worried and hurt, but as friendly and generous as ever.

"Hello, my dear," said Aida. "How are you, Nour? Haven't heard from you for ages. I asked after you but I couldn't find a way to get in touch. I do hope you're well."

"Hello to you, Madame Aida. Sorry I haven't been in touch but I've hardly been showing my face. My condolences on your terrible loss. God alone knows the state I've been in, and only today did I push myself to pick up the phone and call you."

"It's okay, Nour. We all feel that way. These are difficult times. I hope your family are all well."

"We're all well, thank God. I was hoping to visit you, if your time allows, if only for half an hour."

"You'd be welcome, of course. Come over to the house, have a cup of tea and tell me your news. Write down the address."

Nour got out of bed and walked around the room. Then she picked up the niqab, which now hung on the wall. Nour brushed the dust off it and stood in front of the mirror to try it on. Her parents hadn't cared much when she refused to obey them and wear the niqab in the Space. But now she felt an urge to hide her face. If only she could manage to hide her eyes too. They looked leaden through insomnia, downcast in shame, and weighed down by the defeat in her heart.

Nour wavered in front of her wardrobe, uncertain what clothes to choose. She had an hour till she was due to visit Aida. In the end she settled for her old jeans. She put them on, with a loose blouse on top that reached down to her knees and almost hid the curve of her breasts. Then she chose a plain gray headscarf that came down to her elbows. She had a final glance in the mirror and went out to hail a cab.

The mood in Aida's house had an obvious tinge of sadness. The centerpiece was a photograph of Murad on the wall facing the door. His name was written on it in a decorative Arabic script, preceded by the title *shahid*, martyr. Yet Aida looked delighted to see Nour. Many weeks had passed since they had last met in the Space, and they each had a close look at the other to see how they had changed. Aida had lost weight and seemed exhausted. Nour was depressed and had changed her appearance. Her luster had faded and she had lost much of her vitality. They sat down and swapped news. There wasn't anything to be optimistic about: just one misfortune after another in rapid succession. Time apparently refused to relent and give people a chance to recover their strength and patch up their disagreements. Aida spoke about Murad only in passing, and Nour avoided reminding her of her pain and sorrow. Adam and Sara were at the center of their conversation, and Nour felt the need to apologize to Aida for leaving the Space the way they did. She wanted to come clean about the truth, which continued to hurt her and give her sleepless nights: the fact that the Sabbagh family was in the Space under false pretenses, as part of a charade that she couldn't prevent, and that her father had used the protest as a means to pursue his own interests as usual, in the belief that being there would be good for business and confident that the Raised Banner movement would maintain its economic strength whatever happened. He didn't care much for the abducted ruler but, whenever the subject came up, he repeatedly insisted that he had to take precautions for future possibilities. He was her father, always the same and never changing, always behaving shamelessly and adapting to the needs of the situation. Whenever an opportunity arose for him to build up useful relationships and expand his business, her mother was happy to go along with him, as long as the goal was achieved. It was an ordeal for her to speak about such things, but she had been determined to get it off her chest, rather than hide it and ignore it. She had wanted to tell Aida what was troubling her and keeping her awake at night, but in the end she held back: it could wait and what had happened had happened. The important thing was that the way things had turned out had disappointed her and crushed her spirit.

Aida felt it and didn't need any explanation or justification. She knew enough about the characters of Adel and Jehan. People like them don't change. They follow the money and their whims wherever they lead and they defend their shameful decisions till the end. Indeed, within the circle of her close acquaintances there were people who were instinctively prepared to compromise and make concessions of every kind in return for rapid advancement. She could sense for herself how they grabbed at every opportunity and how anxious they were not to miss out. She wasn't even surprised when she heard from Nour that her father had gone to the Gulf so soon to manage a project. The news just made her wonder to herself how many of the movement's leaders and officials were like Adel. How many of them were prepared to exploit people and their belief in the cause for their own personal benefit? How many cared only what they could gain and were interested only in adding to their wealth, even if it meant trampling over the dreams and dead bodies of others? How many of them knew when the massacre was going to take place but kept it secret and left people to face their fate with whatever defenses they could get their hands on? She shook her head sadly and swallowed. Then she threw a sly smile at Nour, who hadn't said anything for some minutes, not wanting to break the calm.

"You look like your father," Aida whispered, as if she could hear what was going on in Nour's head. "You look like him in many ways. Of course you have more of your mother's features. But when it comes to personality traits, I think Sara inherited them all from both of them, and you didn't inherit any of them at all."

The conversation moved on spontaneously to the Space. They couldn't avoid it for long—who was injured, who was killed, and who had miraculously survived. Aida provided most of the answers, while Nour merely asked the questions. The friendships Nour had made had been disrupted by her family's suspicious disappearance. Aida assured her she was in touch with Fayza every now and then.

"Her only news is that she's had these painful coughing fits since the day they broke up the protest," Aida told her.

She added with gratitude that the inspection official who wore the niqab had come to see her a few days earlier to give her condolences. "She was well. Neither she or her daughter were hurt, but she lost her personal papers and now she's trying to get copies of them."

Finally Nour asked about Ibrahim, and Aida had no idea what had become of him. "I haven't seen him since Murad's funeral. He promised to visit to check up on Adam, but he hasn't shown up since. It's good of you to remember him. We should ask after him and see how he is. He seemed angry and vengeful when we spoke. It wasn't the right time for me to find out what his plans were."

After two hours chatting they shook hands warmly and felt they had renewed their friendship. Nour left the house intrigued by the idea of looking for Ibrahim, and maybe not just Ibrahim: they were definitely others like him of whom she had heard little news. In the days right after the attack on the protest there was a succession of reports that people who tried to leave the Space had been arrested and that some unnamed people had been killed. She had also heard that there were hundreds of charred bodies in the mortuary and no one had shown up to identify them or take them away. She might find some of the people she knew there. Thinking about it, although it was horrible, relieved the feeling of impotence that had previously overwhelmed her and reduced her to passivity. There was a responsibility that had to be borne, if only as a way to make up for her family's well-timed escape, for which she was ashamed although she was not to blame.

Nour kept up her phone conversations and meetings with Aida. Sometimes she asked after her health and that of her son. At other times she would pass on news that someone who hadn't been seen for a while had turned up somewhere, sometimes alive and often dead. On her own she launched a project to trace missing people and she gradually expanded her activity. Her time was filled with phone calls, interviews, and strategies to discover the fate of hundreds of protesters. Days went by without her finding a trace of Ibrahim, but finally Aida made some progress when she visited his colleagues at university, taking advantage of their friendship with Murad.

In secret, some of them told her that Ibrahim was probably in detention, but they didn't know where. She passed this news on to Nour straight away and felt guilty that they had neglected him. Nour took the news with a confusing mixture of feelings: sadness and anxiety, fear and also pleasure that she was making progress, but she put her emotions to one side and set about looking for more useful information. She obtained his full name, including the name of his grandfather, his date of birth and the date he had started work. Aida helped her and obtained a photograph of him. Then coincidence took care of the rest: while searching through newspapers, she came across his name among a group of young men accused of trying to overthrow the System. She followed up on the lead, confirmed the report, and identified the place where he was being held. After consultations with Aida and some lawyers she had met in the course of her project, she applied for permission to visit Ibrahim in detention at a prison described as "high security."

Ibrahim sat cross-legged, daydreaming, with beads of sweat on his forehead. There wasn't enough space between him and the men on either side for him to spread out. The place had been very crowded since the latest batch of prisoners had arrived. His voice sounded frail and crushed, indifferent to the people around him.

"We went to the protest and spent many days there," he said. "We slept and ate on the ground. We fought against the things that could lead to defeat and were haunted by fear of failure. We often had misgivings about the outcome and we had nightmares when we were in the tents—for example, that the regime would take revenge on us one by one if we failed, but we tried to ignore them. We were furious that our dream of better government had been dashed so soon and with so much stupidity and shortsightedness. We were also tormented by a sense that we had been deceived. They had all conspired against us: our leaders, our allies and friends, and the state. None of them had told the truth, but we hadn't told the truth either, even with ourselves."

One of the men next to him looked away. He didn't want to hear Ibrahim. The other turned toward him. Ibrahim had piqued his curiosity.

Ibrahim resumed his soliloquizing: "When should we stop? Some of us asked this question early on, and some of us are still asking now, I believe. There's no answer that pleases everyone. The ideal answer is just an illusion, and the easiest thing to do is run away from the questions and stop seeking answers. Most of us trusted the path that the Raised Banner leaders had chosen. They listened and obeyed without argument or critical examination, but apparently the leaders took us down a one-way street from which there was no return. In fact, the worse and more complicated the situation became the more they insisted on pressing on, until it was too late and all their gains had gone to waste. And now most of the Brothers have stopped work, I hear. Their aspirations have been dashed and we have reverted to somewhere short of square one. The gates of hell on Earth have opened in our faces, for us to burn in."

Ibrahim looked at the man, suddenly aware of his presence: "Tell me, what do you think of what happened?"

Ibrahim didn't believe his ears when news of a visit came. It had never occurred to him that anyone could come in person to see him in this tomb. His family didn't live in the capital and probably didn't know what had happened to him. His friends were either in hiding, on the run, or lying low in some way. When he saw his visitor he jumped up, wide-eyed with surprise. He was both alarmed and delighted. His heart pounded. He was about to put out his hand to her, but then he backed away and wanted her to leave the room immediately, to spare her the horrors of the prison and the people inside it.

"Miss Nour!" he cried. "I must be dreaming or God has taken mercy on me and let me die! There's no power or might other than in God! What brings you here? I mean, aren't you worried for yourself and your family? Does Mr. Sabbagh know about your visit?"

Nour bowed her head to hide a smile that escaped her at his emotional outburst. She assumed a gravity that she didn't feel at that moment.

"Good day to you, Dr. Ibrahim," she said solemnly. "Thank God we found you. Madame Aida has done everything possible to find you, and here you are, not in the best of circumstances, I understand of course, and I don't envy you your situation, but we'll do what we can for you and for the Brothers detained with you."

Nour stayed with Ibrahim for as long as the prison warder allowed. Unlike people familiar with prison visits, she didn't keep track of the time, so she couldn't tell whether her time was really up or whether they had cut it short for some reason. As she was about to stand up, Ibrahim advised her to lie low and watch out for the big detention campaigns, which took no account of who you were or what your role had been: they would round up active leaders, insignificant members, and people whose only fault was bad luck. Reluctantly he asked her to refrain from visiting him.

"They take everyone and his uncle, and then they beat them up," he said. "They deliberately act tough to show who's boss. For God's sake don't let them get their teeth into you."

Adel al-Sabbagh wasn't yet wanted by the security agencies, despite the stake he held in the Raised Banner's institutions and companies, so Nour tried to convince Ibrahim that she was in little danger.

"Don't worry," she said, "and don't trouble yourself thinking about me. I'm not a familiar face to them and I've never had any kind of connection with the movement. I wasn't an activist at university and the police don't have a file on me."

She tried to reassure him further, saying that her father had many contacts, and if there was any reason to worry in this respect, he would have moved her and Sara and her mother, without delay, to the Gulf, where he was living. As she was leaving and the warder took Ibrahim back to his cell, she took the opportunity to tell him she would be attending his next appearance in court.

The First Session

Nour dropped in on Aida's school at the end of her classes, and they left together. They chose to spend some time walking in each other's company. Nour rarely had a chance to take a walk that didn't have a clear destination and wasn't part of a prearranged plan. Outside a small juice shop, sugar cane stems stood in a bundle, tempting passersby to approach. Aida invited Nour to have a glass of sugar cane juice with her: maybe the sweetness would take some of the bitterness out of their conversation. Aida pointed inquisitively at a magazine that Nour was holding in her hand because it wouldn't fit in her small handbag.

Nour launched into an animated explanation: "It's an issue of *National Geographic* magazine that I picked up on my way. I was about to tell you about it. Don't laugh at me, Aida, but I was crazy about it when I was at school and I liked to read it even after I started university. Then in my last year I was too busy studying and I almost forgot about it when I graduated. I came across it yesterday when I was Googling the gas that the police use. I was thinking about it after we spoke about Fayza and the chronic cough she's had despite the antibiotics and the herbs. I thought the two might be linked: a bad chest and exposure to large amounts of tear gas. But I came across something more interesting: an article in the online edition of the magazine on research by a doctor at an American university. I think his name is Dr. Tedridge. This man analyzed and tested weapons that are approved for crowd control internationally and he came to some frightening conclusions. The magazine quoted him as saying that tear gas has an effect on nerve tissue. The chemicals in the gas don't affect only the eyes and the mucous membranes but also the nerves that transmit pain. That means that there are long-term consequences. In fact, they might cause serious diseases. I wrote down the date it was published, June this year, and I managed to find a hard copy and buy it this morning. It might be useful to lawyers."

Nour handed the magazine to Aida, who browsed through it, having gone back to thinking about her own troubles. After just a few minutes together their conversation had strayed into sensitive territory, so they finished off their glasses of juice and decided to go back to Aida's house, for fear a malicious ear might overhear a loose word from them. As soon as they were through the door, but before it was closed behind them, Nour impatiently poured out everything she had been reluctant to say outside. "I attended the session in court. He looked haggard when he came out into the glass cage, Aida, much paler than when I saw him in prison. As soon as he settled down, and despite what he's suffering, he shouted, 'Down with the general!' in a hoarse voice. 'Down with the general's government! Down with the new ruler!' And his colleagues chanted after him. They could be heard in the courtroom because the microphones were turned on, and the judge was very upset. I was upset too and I wished he would shut up. He was ordered out and the guards took him out immediately. Then the prosecution read out the charge sheet, and I managed to write down the charges: organizing an armed gathering, closing the Space, helping to close down roads, restricting people's freedom of movement and planning to murder them, premeditated murder of forces assigned to disperse the protest. Imagine, the protesters killing the security forces and civilians as well! The prosecution also accused them of damaging public buildings, private property, and electricity wires, terrorizing the population and lots of other things. There may have been some other charges I didn't have time to write down, because it was a very long list. After that, the prosecutor showed video of the security forces finding some bloated corpses and said the bodies had been taken from under the podium—our podium in the Space, Aida! Our lawyers argued that there wasn't any evidence, but the judge didn't look convinced."

"My god. Those are charges that could lead to hanging," said Aida. "But, the lawyers have their ways to disprove them. All we can do is wait and pray to God that things don't get too complicated for us, or for them. This morning I read a news story that might soon affect Ibrahim and the other detainees. The prison department is going to organize lectures by senior sheikhs, starting with Sheikh Abdel-Gabbar, of course. As I understand it, these lectures will take place before the ideological tests that the regime is trying to impose on members of the Raised Banner and allied groups. The newspaper said the National Security Agency was planning to give the lectures to young prisoners who have no political or religious attachments, as a precautionary measure to prevent them being influenced by mixing with our young men and adopting their ideas. They want to brainwash everyone all at once, with no one slipping through their fingers. I don't know how the men will be able to stand all this pressure."

"It's not just that, Aida. Conditions in the prisons are awful. The walls are in very poor condition and could easily fall in on those inside. When I visited, Dr. Ibrahim told me the prisoners were piled on top of each other and the smell was disgusting and gut-wrenching. Sorry to be graphic, but that's his description. They can hardly breathe in the cells, which are infested with insects and mosquitoes that bite. Infectious diseases spread from one prisoner to everyone else in the cell and to the cell next door. It's not a prison: it's more like the gas chambers that Hitler set up. With their crimes, they're competing with the most villainous criminal in history."

*

"I went out to stand near the big shopping center and check out the situation," Ibrahim said. "We had set up plenty of barricades there and we started handing out rubber goggles for protection against what we thought were shotgun pellets. The shooting intensified, so I took cover. There was an old man standing beside me and on my right there was a young boy, two women, and a young man who had a gun with an empty magazine. We all kept low, behind the sandbags. We could hear the sound of bullets but we couldn't see where they were coming from. We could see people throwing stones and setting fire to car tires, trying to stop the security forces from breaking into the Space. The old man shouted that they were just making noises to frighten us. He suddenly stood up to his full height and he was massive and well-built and looked like he might even be impervious to bullets. I begged him to keep down but he started trying to pull me up and overcome my fear. Suddenly he took a live bullet and collapsed, soaked in his own blood. We picked him up and rushed him to the hospital."

Ibrahim didn't stop talking. He was in the mood for the kind of spontaneous story telling that his cellmates were accustomed to. His companion was constantly drawn to his endless monologues and always curious to hear what else he might be about to narrate. Ibrahim never disappointed him. He would end one story only to start another one, moving from memory to memory. This was how he had been since they arrested him.

"The snipers weren't trying to frighten people or make them move away, but rather to kill them, just kill them. As I stood in the hospital trying to save as many people as I could, I saw an old woman with a wound from a sniper bullet. Her son was standing beside her unable to move. There was also a young man in his death throes. He had been shot in the head, and his brother was begging us to save him. I said he had to be taken out of the Space at all costs. The brother went looking for an ambulance willing to take him, then he came back to me: dead like his brother. If you were shot, you died. There wasn't any room in the hospital and there was no emergency care outside. When they attacked the hospital itself, I had a man whose thigh was split in half. I was about to run out to fend off the attack with the other people, and he looked at me as if to say: 'Are you going to leave me?' I stood up and laughed, I don't know how, and said, 'I'll stay with you and what happens happens.'"

As he told the story, he acted out the laugh, and then the laughter spread to his companion, who was still listening, although Ibrahim's voice was rather weak. He was used to Ibrahim and could hear what he said even when it wasn't clear to the others.

"I'm a doctor. Are you a doctor too?" Ibrahim asked him on the spur of the moment.

"No, not at all, I've always been frightened of doctors," the man said evasively, as if denying he had committed a crime.

The guard pushed Ibrahim into the visiting room. He looked tired and pale, and his eyes were dull. He sat down with difficulty and started criticizing her immediately.

"Why did you come, Nour? Didn't I ask you to be careful?" he said weakly.

Nour didn't want to waste any visiting time in a fruitless argument. "You did," she snapped back, "and I told you I'm not in danger, and here I am in front of you. I haven't been arrested or come to any harm yet."

"Don't be so sure," Ibrahim said. "No one's immune, even if they're right at the heart of the System. They don't have any qualms about arresting people in the army or the police."

Ibrahim bent down a little and leaned toward her. He wanted to get something off his chest before the guards noticed. "There are rumors that three officers who took part in the Space massacre have seen the light and come to their senses, thanks to lessons from one of our sheikhs. They decided to atone for the crimes they committed. They're here now, held in a special cell. They've tried to hush it all up and imposed tight security around them, but the news is the talk of all the cells and there's no smoke without fire. And it's not only them. Even people who know absolutely nothing about politics or religion, and have nothing to do with government, aren't safe from the brutality either. I met a guy that no sane person would have imagined should be here: a man roughly in his early thirties who's lived his life like any ordinary person. He graduated from the social services institute and was appointed supervisor in an orphanage. He was planning to get married and have a family and he was paying instalments on an apartment, and then suddenly, overnight, he's here. They haven't charged him with anything and he hasn't done anything. All there is to it is that he was on duty in the orphanage when the security forces attacked it, and he witnessed children being arrested there. He didn't understand what was happening at first, because the orphanage belonged to the government. There was nothing said, no discussion, no agreement, no papers, no procedures of an official nature. They just attacked and carried the kids off like livestock. He spoke to some of his colleagues and discovered it was part of a larger campaign and not confined to that particular area. It included other orphanages. He didn't do anything more than what I told you, but they realized he was a witness and thought he was gathering information. So they brought him here just like us, and I don't think he'll get out soon. Listen to me carefully: you're not safe from harm. Not you, and not anyone living in this country."

Nour leaned back in her chair. She felt as if she'd just been hit on the head. She said nothing for a while. She tried to stay calm and arrange her thoughts. Then she said, "It's horrible what you say, Ibrahim. Things are going from bad to worse.

It's one disaster after another. Tell me, should I get a lawyer for him? If there's any way I can help him, please tell me how. Or you could consult him and tell me on my next visit. That story about the children is another matter altogether. Does he have any idea what became of them?"

"I don't think so, but I'll ask him. By the way, the prison management told us we'll have to attend all the lectures by Sheikh Abdel-Gabbar and decisions on pardons will be tied to that. Imagine, they forced the orphanage guy, who didn't understand anything, to listen to them. At the end of the last lectures they even called us in for interrogation sessions, him and me and most of the Brothers and the other inmates. They wanted to assess how much we had changed! They asked us about our attitude toward the present system and our position on the use of violence against the state, what we intended to do when we get out of here, and if we were still committed to playing a political role. It's crazy. How could anyone play a political role under these conditions anyway? Would we speak openly about what we believe in when we're in their hands? These questions are so stupid they're maddening. The whole session lost direction. I don't think the interrogator was satisfied, at not least with what I told him."

Nour bowed her head. "The general will only pardon people who respond positively to Sheikh Abdel-Gabbar and change their ideas to match his," she said, speaking softly as if embarrassed by what she was saying. "But Madame Aida thinks he's a big hypocrite."

"God bless her! These lectures and tests aren't designed to combat violence, as the government claims. They're designed to co-opt the regime's opponents and bring them back into the fold of obedient servants. Obeying them, of course. If they wanted to fight against violence, they would start with themselves."

"Even so, Shakir's poor widow thinks we should now pretend to conform, until the clouds pass." said Nour.

Ibrahim said nothing, as if it was too painful to speak. Then finally he muttered, "That's between her and the movement. They got us where we are, and now we're in God's hands."

"While we were busy stitching up people's wounds," Ibrahim narrated, "a man walked up with his hand on his jaw. 'That's a minor injury,' I thought to myself. One of the nurses was handling the admission process, and as soon as the man took his hand down off his jaw she screamed out loud and didn't stop until I came over and moved her aside. I saw a sight I'd never seen in my life: the man didn't have a lower jaw. All I could see of his mouth was his tongue and his upper teeth. How he reached us, I don't know. He was the one who calmed the nurse down and helped her get over the shock. I gathered some gauze and rolls of cotton wool, and gave them to him as they were without undoing them or cutting off pieces. I just tied them together with some tape so that he would move away. I was worried they might come back and kill us all."

Ibrahim's face froze and he began to hit the wall he was leaning against slowly and repeatedly with the back of his head. He might have been trying to activate his memory or maybe to knock some memory out of his head for relief. Meanwhile, his friend gritted his teeth and buried his face in his hands: he wished he had been struck deaf so that he couldn't hear any more of these horrible stories. He tried to listen to the conversation of some other inmates but he couldn't ignore Ibrahim: he was familiar with his accent and the timbre of his voice, and there was no longer any barrier between them. He could make out the slightest mumble, without Ibrahim having to repeat himself or give an explanation. The man withdrew into himself: his hands and feet felt freezing cold and he was worried he might have a breakdown.

In the meantime Ibrahim went on banging his head against the wall and laughing scornfully. "I wasn't hit by a bullet or by shotgun pellets there. I was hit by the bullets of despair and despondency, and they riddled my soul through and through."

The Second Session

Ibrahim came into the glass cage with his arms around the shoulders of two fellow defendants, his feet barely touching the floor. His face looked jaundiced and pale. His chest was rising and falling as he drew rapid breaths, like a man with a fever. Seeing him in this state set Nour on edge. Maybe he was ill, or maybe they had tortured him. Before the judges mounted the bench some of the prisoners chanted, "Long live the country! Down with the Raised Banner!" Three of them didn't join in, including Ibrahim, who sat still with his legs crossed. Then several Raised Banner leaders came into the courtroom in chains and the prisoners started denouncing them.

When the trial began, Nour watched the few gestures Ibrahim made. The prosecutor submitted a letter from the head of the public transport authority in the capital as evidence that the protest in the Space had caused the authority massive losses in the surrounding area, reducing its revenue by more than ten million pounds. He then attached the letter to a copy of *al-Ahramat* newspaper with an indistinct picture that he lifted up in front of the judges' bench, and read out the caption: "Protesters place wooden planks studded with nails to sabotage private cars." The prosecutor finally asked the judges to listen to the city mayor and to the director of education in the Space area. The mayor said the protesters were responsible for massive damage to the trees, grass, and lamp posts, and even to the asphalt on the roadway and to the walls of the houses, which were defaced with graffiti and pictures in support of the Raised Banner movement and hostile to the state and the System.

"I visited the area myself on the day after the protest was dispersed and I was very angry. The people who did this do not like this country and do not care for it, and they deserve to be executed," said the prosecutor.

The Director of Education noted that the protesters had occupied the government school until the security forces intervened to disperse them. While there, they had disrupted exams and damaged some furniture. "I saw them sleeping all over the place, using the benches improperly, putting leftover food on the desks and removing the blackboards."

Nour smiled as she remembered the school. She had visited it and had taken fruit juice and yogurt to some of the women who were staying there. She had even given their children lessons in one of the classrooms. Maybe she deserved to be in the dock along with the other defendants. Next the defense gave its opening statement, and when it was finished, the group went back to chanting. Ibrahim stayed as he was, bowing his head and not saying a word, and the guards turned on the microphones so that the court could hear the defendants. One of them shouted that he recognized the new ruler and supported the general and hoped to get out of prison to help make the country great again.

"Long live the country! long live the country!" people in the courtroom chanted and applauded, while the chief judge smiled, maybe for the first time since the trial had begun.

Ibrahim came back from the court hearing in a daze. He made no comment on the judges or the court proceedings. He didn't criticize or argue with any of the other defendants. He settled down in his tight little space, pressed up against the shoulder of his neighbor, who also seemed distracted and content with his lot. Ibrahim's breathing calmed down a little, though his bones and muscles were stilled racked with pain. He finally summoned up the energy to speak, but the words came out slowly and in confusion, in the gaps when the pain died down for a moment.

"I saw the officers firing their rifles at us, aiming at our bodies in cold blood as if they were shooting rats. They targeted journalists, cameramen, and photographers, and we had little but slingshots and stones to defend ourselves. I saw that some Brothers and others had knives and swords. The ones with pistols or automatic weapons could be counted on the fingers of your hands. They were an ineffective, insignificant minority. None of this was enough to fend off the attack. Men kept falling, one after another. I carried over my shoulder one young man who had two bullets in his forehead. His father came to take his body from the mosque, which was soon like a graveyard. The father shouted at us to wail for his dead son on his final exit. There were only men standing there, but he repeated his request: "A wail, a wail for Mustafa my son." The female doctor looked up from the wounded woman she was treating and let out a wail that shook the building. At that her patient couldn't help but muster the strength to add her own, even louder, wail, although she was bleeding profusely. So Mustafa left the mosque to the sound of women wailing. If I had known how to make the sound, I would have done so too. No one thinks about what's halal or haram at a time like that."

Ibrahim's companion kept rubbing his hands and forehead and plucking at short hairs on his chin. Then he chewed at his finger nails. In the end he made up his mind and spoke. His voice sounded grating, as if he needed to cough to clear his throat of saliva and overcome his shyness. He cleared his throat once and then again, and finally looked Ibrahim in the face. "The interrogator told me that none of their investigations proved I was affiliated with you or with any other group like yours. It was all about the orphanage, and I assured him I had completely forgotten about it and it didn't matter to me in the least. I promised him I would go out to work as a taxi driver with my father or buy a *tuktuk* on instalments. Maybe you heard that the prisoners who don't have anything to do with your group are writing a joint letter, asking to appear before an investigating magistrate separately from you. They refuse to take responsibility for the positions that some of you have taken. You are stubborn and arrogant, and they can crush us and crush you. You shout in court and then they crack down on us all. You go on hunger strike and we suffer the consequences. A hundred times a day I feel like I'm dying, and unlike you, I don't have a cause I'm willing to sacrifice my life for. No offense, but I also heard that some of you have changed your minds and repented and will soon be released. Dr. Ibrahim, I'm going to sign that letter, and please don't get angry with me or hold it against me."

Disconnected memories started to flash through Ibrahim's mind. Sometimes they came to him uninvited and sometimes he summoned them up by an act of will. Then he could explain what was troubling him. He was trying to keep his memories alive and patch up those that were fading, before the detention camp could erase them.

Without showing any sign that he had heard what his neighbor said or was paying attention, Ibrahim continued with his story: "There were hundreds of dead bodies piled up in the room, and when we were trying to clear them out I was so tired that I dropped one corpse three times."

Nour arrived early, to be told bluntly that Ibrahim wasn't allowed to have visitors and all she could do was wait for the next session to see him. Banning visits, the lawyers told her, was a way to punish prisoners, so he must have done something to provoke them. She started racking her brains, wondering whether his contempt for the ideological tests and for Abdel-Gabbar's lectures was sufficient reason for punishment, or whether there was something worse he had done. She spent all of the next few days thinking about it and it almost drove her mad. Maybe *taqiya*, pretending to conform for safety's sake, was an approach that had its logic. The Earth wouldn't stop turning if he obeyed them and was flexible, just enough to stay safe. His hard-line attitude wouldn't be much use if he came out with a chronic and incurable disease, or if they kept him in jail in a helpless physical state. In fact, he might be tortured to death or die from neglect. But lying is hard, for those who aren't used to it. She told herself that in all honesty, if she was in his shoes, she would have done the same thing. She wouldn't have given in and obeyed. She wouldn't have cheered for the general, even if they had buried her alive. That was a difficult choice that could be made only from a person's own convictions. It couldn't be decided by some statement or declaration and it couldn't be prescribed by some permit or order. Nor should the decision be influenced by obstinacy or arrogance, or fear of subsequent blame or criticism. Everyone finds it easiest to do what they are cut out to do, as the hadith says. Ibrahim was stubborn, but Nour worried about him because he had become frail with the passage of time. The decision was up to him alone. Of course he had his Lord to protect him, but not knowing what was happening to him was almost killing her.

The Third Session

In the third session of the trial Ibrahim didn't appear in the cage. Nour was heartbroken and felt that something bad must have happened to him. She hung around in the courtroom wondering what to do and who she could ask for help. Then she went up to the cage in the hope of speaking to Ibrahim's fellow inmates, but she was too frightened to ask. She dropped the idea completely when she heard them chanting: "We're behind you, general! Our country, our motherland, is what matters most! The security forces are a hundred percent and the movement members are thugs!" She couldn't believe her ears. They had all started flashing victory signs and repeating, "Long live the general! long live the general!" Not much had changed in their appearance, though their faces struck her as less desperate and less hungry. Some of them had shaved off their beards and were wearing ordinary white t-shirts similar to the ones issued to prisoners except that they had a picture of the general's face on the front. At the end of the session, the judge ordered the release of a large number of Raised Banner members, but Ibrahim wasn't among them.

Ibrahim stretched his legs out on the damp ground, which gave off a dizzying stench of shit and steamy decay. His head slumped back against the rough, cracked surface of the wall and he looked up at the drab ceiling, which was covered in stains that he imagined were moving. He swallowed some saliva but it tasted as bitter as gall and was so sticky it was hard to hold down. Unconsciously he spat it up again and put his index finger into his mouth in an attempt to get rid of the horrible taste. His other hand explored the damp floor in the corner of the cell. A small chip of stone came loose in his hand. He lifted it up level with his eyes and looked at its color and shape. Then he leaned forward until the tip of his nose touched a bulge in the wall. He felt the surface with his hand until he chanced upon a flat area. He sat up straight a little and, his hand trembling, wrote out a statement that had been haunting him for days. When he had finished, he ran his finger over the thin scratches he had made on the wall and read it to himself in a mumble.

"Compromise may be a way to get out of prison and seek vengeance. Tricking you may be a way to achieve revenge, but you're so insignificant that none of us would lie to obtain your forgiveness. Other people do that, but it's beneath us. One can wage jihad only by standing firm."

He spat out a thick sticky gob and went back to mumbling. "What should one do when standing firm doesn't work and brings only contempt and humiliation? Answer me! Why don't you say something? So now you like to be silent?"

He had a good look at what he had written, then shut his eyes and started to repeat it from memory: "Detain as many of us as you like. Lock us up as long as you can. Set up prisons to your heart's content. There may be a high price to pay and the possibility of revenge persists as long as those who shed blood remain alive. Torture us in your torture chambers. Assassinate men in their homes so that you feel safe. You are only an arm's length or less from perdition. Give us more grief and suffering, because the greater your crimes the bleaker your fate will be."

Rabie went back to the camp on the day after the attack on the protest. Youssef wasn't on the bed next to his and didn't come to the dining hall. Rabie felt it as another loss, and this time he had to believe it was forever. He wouldn't live on hopes any longer or dream of a possible reunion, because Youssef was gone for good. He removed the blanket and the pillow from Youssef's bed, slipped his hand into an opening in the mattress and took out a bundle of papers from the stuffing. He looked through the papers, trying to read what his friend had written. He picked up the pieces of cardboard that Youssef had torn off the crates of tomato sauce and the packs of cheese triangles, but he found it hard to separate the words from each other and decipher what was written. He put the pieces of cardboard aside and picked up the newspaper cuttings. He managed to read some of the headlines and looked at the pictures that went with them. There was a picture of Qadri Abdel-Hakim and Sheikh Abdel-Gabbar, and several pictures of the general: a broad smile, a clenched fist, and closed eyes. In the end he sat cross-legged on the floor with his back to the room, bent down and chewed his mattress with his teeth. Soon he had made a similar opening in his own mattress. He folded up the papers and slipped them inside with the yellow cotton that stuck out of the tear in the mattress. He restuffed it to hide it. Then he sat on it to make it level with the rest of the mattress.

All he meant to do was preserve the only memory left to him. He thought of giving all the papers to Saad to keep him company during his convalescence from his injury, but he was worried they might get lost or fall into the hands of another boy or reach one of the titans, so he decided to keep them inside the mattress, safe and sound, unlike their unlucky original owner.

Rabie stood up when he detected soft footsteps approaching—Emad's footsteps if his hearing hadn't deceived him. The voice soon confirmed it was him.

"What are you doing by Youssef's bed? Crying like a woman?" said Emad.

Rabie turned to him, and Emad continued, not waiting for any reply, "They killed more than four or five of us bodies, but we wiped the floor with them. Don't think about him too much. Death was his fate, yesterday, or tomorrow or even the day after tomorrow. Youssef wasn't man enough to live like us. Let go of him. Get up and celebrate victory with us."

Rabie didn't budge an inch. The words he wanted to say stuck in his throat and he couldn't argue back. Emad didn't insist. He turned and walked off as if he had done his duty.

In his daydreams Rabie wished he had some of Emad's daring and composure, at least enough for him to stand up to Emad. He started pacing up and down the dormitory, shaking his head and looking at the floor with his arms linked behind his back.

"Why didn't we save Youssef, Emad?" he repeated, reproachfully and in desperation. "Why couldn't we protect him, you body? Only you could have kept him safe. The titan who shot Youssef in the head, doesn't he have special respect for you, and not for us? Aren't you one of the chosen ones, Emad? You know them all. You know lots of people, starting with the general and down to the most junior titan. Maybe the ruler knows you too. Couldn't you have saved Youssef? You're capable of anything. Remember when I joked with you and told you that soon you would run the camp. At the time you boasted, 'I can do anything. Nothing in the world is beyond me. I can lay it waste. And I'm above all this anger and hatred. Just like the titans, no one refuses any of my requests and nothing living stands in my way.' I believed you at the time. I didn't doubt a word you said. And I still believe you, but that means you didn't want Youssef to stay among us. Youssef shamed us without intending to, Emad. Youssef didn't become like us. He didn't give in, so you started to avoid him, and his death was good for you, and maybe for me too, so that we don't have to think too much."

Rabie leaned against the wall at the end of the dormitory, then he collapsed in a heap in the corner. His legs had gone weak on him and his mind drifted back to the past.

"Before we came to the camp, we used to look out for left-over food and beg from people. We didn't know what would happen to us on the next day, any next day. We took life day by day and we survived as best we could. It had nothing to do with what had gone before or what was to come. If we had lived and died the way we were, I wouldn't have been so torn up about Youssef. I don't think it would be possible to leave the camp after all this. The streets are no longer ours in the same way they were, or they are ours but on the terms set by the titans. If only we could overcome our fear of the people outside the camp, of the titans and their troops, and of the vastness of the desert, then we'd run away. Ah, Youssef, if only you had come back with me, but now we're crying as we've never cried before. Dr. Abdel-Malek told us about morals and honor, about giving priority to the interests of the country and other people, but he didn't tell us about the blood we would shed. He didn't tell us about the dead, Youssef. We sacrificed people for the sake of the country. And we sacrificed you for our own sake. We sacrificed ourselves to please them. It's just a single bullet, as the body Emad said, Emad the body. A single bullet ends everything from a distance, without fuss or bother, provided it knows exactly where to go."

"They finally allowed visits," Nour told Aida. "I met him, but I wish I hadn't gone and seen him. They're dying a slow death,

Aida. Ibrahim is just skin and bone, and he's let his hair grow long, like his beard used to be. All you can see of him now is a dusty, disheveled, abandoned black lump in tattered clothes full of holes, like a tramp. Imagine, as soon as he opened his mouth, he asked to eat. He told me they'd put him in solitary confinement after the last court hearing he attended, and they'd done the same with two detainees who spoke out against Sheikh Abdel-Gabbar in his lecture. They only get an hour of exercise a day. They have to go out alone, or, if two of them do go out together, they send an informer along too. He complained about the food, saying animals would turn up their noses at it: dirty plates, insects in vegetables that are impossible to identify, and such meager quantities that a small child wouldn't be satisfied. He said he and his fellow inmates ate orange peel and if the guards noticed, they would confiscate the peel from them or give them oranges that had already been peeled. Those brutes are starving the prisoners, Aida. They're going to kill them, not just by torturing them or with the injuries they have all over their bodies, but by starvation. Does anyone in this country starve to death these days? His eyes are the only things that seem to be still alive, though they do stick out. They sparkled when he picked up the pastry I gave him and began to gobble it down. When he'd finished it, he asked for more. But the only other thing I had was some candy I'd bought for Adam on the way there. I gave it to him because I would have been embarrassed to keep it. I'll have to be better prepared when I go to visit him next.

"I almost forgot that he asked me to tell you about something that cropped up in the last few weeks. Word for word, he said, 'If you speak to the widow of Dr. Murad Fathi, tell her to keep a close eye on her son. I'm hearing from friends that they're abducting children from schools now. Not any children of course, but the children of people who were in the Space, members of the movement and other groups.' In their cell, Aida, there's a kid in the third year of middle school and his family know nothing about him. He's called Amin Khidr, and Dr. Ibrahim asked me to tell anyone familiar with the name that the boy is well. But the prison denies he's there. No one will be able to visit him, but at least he's alive and he's there among the detainees. When I assured him I'd try to find his relatives, he pursed his lips doubtfully and his face looked more exhausted and despondent. Looking down, he said, 'They gave him electric shocks and they hung him on the bars on the door until his hand was paralyzed and almost had to be amputated.'"

Fayza reached Aida's house on time dressed in black and carrying a bag containing fruit and aromatic herbs. Aida looked through the peephole, opened the door, shook her hand warmly and invited her in. She led her into the sitting room, sat her down, and said she would go to make something to drink. Fayza insisted on helping her, so they headed to the kitchen together, chatting as they went. They had been visiting each other since meeting at the memorials for Murad and Shakir. They were brought together by a shared feeling of loss and by the same grief, although they disagreed over who was responsible for it. How often they saw each other depended on how busy they were, but they met often when something came up that needed to be discussed. They exchanged news about the people they knew, discussed the state of the movement and the changes it had been through. Whenever they had a rambling conversation, Aida couldn't ignore the role that the movement leaders had played in what had happened. She thought back to her conversations with Murad, but Fayza disagreed and claimed that the System had planned the massacre from the start, regardless of the details. At the end of every session they agreed that nothing justified the bloodshed, and they looked to an uncertain future with anxiety.

They were busy talking when Aida's cellphone rang. Steam was rising from their cups of cinnamon and ginger infusions.

The phone didn't recognize the number, so Aida hesitated till it stopped ringing. Who might be calling her at the beginning of the day when it was her day off school? Nour didn't call her before the afternoon. The phone began ringing again and Fayza advised her to ignore it. But Aida was worried Adam's school might need her, so she took the call. It was a woman's voice she couldn't identify, though it sounded vaguely familiar. The woman soon put an end to her uncertainty.

"I'm Zeinab," she said.

"Zeinab?"

"Zeinab, your friend from college days. We met by chance recently and we agreed that our families would get together."

The conversation with Zeinab lasted only two minutes. She sounded extremely agitated but she didn't want to say why unless they met face to face, so she and Aida arranged to meet. Worried by the unexpected call, Aida went back to Fayza. She didn't know what was going on with Zeinab but she was sure there was something wrong. She suggested they have coffee next, while Fayza started filling her in on the latest news about Adel al-Sabbagh in the Gulf.

"I don't think he's planning to come back. His business is booming there, I hear. He got out at the right time," she said.

Aida took a sip of her drink and sighed. "Many of the Brothers and people who took part in the protest have settled abroad," she said.

"I don't blame people who are worried their lives are in danger under these circumstances, or whose families or property might be harmed, but I don't think Sabbagh is in real danger," said Fayza.

Aida waved her hand, indifferent to Adel. "His daughter plays an important role. I'm sure she won't leave, even if she has the chance. She'd prefer to stay here and fight. May God not thwart her efforts. You can't imagine what she's doing. For weeks she's been visiting the detainees regularly and she's trying to help them out and she's looking for disappeared people in prisons and detention camps and hospitals. She's constantly in touch with people trying to help. She never tires and she's undaunted by the obstacles she faces. In fact, she works like a whole organization all on her own."

At the mention of detainees and prisons, Fayza said she had heard that a new prison was being built, financed by the Our Country Survives fund.

"I'm sure you remember the fund. The general was collecting donations for it a while back, Aida. They had ads on TV and the radio day and night," she said.

Aida let out a scornful laugh for the first time since her bereavement. She laced her hands together on top of her head as she thought back to when she first heard about the fund. She assumed that Qadri Abdel-Hakim had a role in building the prison, similar to his role in the Heart of the World project. The conversation moved on to Ibrahim and the sufferings of thousands of young men in similar situations. Aida stopped laughing and the lump in her throat returned when she said what she knew and explained the role Sheikh Abdel-Gabbar had played in the ideological tests, based on the information Nour had given her.

Fayza had a coughing fit and then exclaimed excitedly, "I heard from some of the Brothers that the sheikh told the security forces they could perform the 'fear prayer,' you know, the communal prayer you can do when you're in danger. He issued a fatwa in case the Raised Banner committed acts of violence in response to the massacre in the Space. He mentioned the movement by name, Aida, although he knows that most of the Brothers, great and small, are in jail, and those of them who are still free have fled the country, or have gone into hiding and assumed false identities. The fear prayer is right for us, not for them. They're raiding houses and taking people off without warning. Imagine, after all this, he says the security forces are still acting with kid gloves and not doing their job properly."

Aida frowned indignantly, while Fayza continued, fighting her worsening cough. "Two days ago, I had a visit from a friend. Her husband and her sons have been in detention for a month. She brought me a copy of the *Whole Picture* magazine with a long article about this fear prayer. None of the sheikhs in the big mosque dare to oppose Abdel-Gabbar, and those who do oppose him have done their best to keep their views under wraps. Sheikhs from outside his institution said in response that the fear prayer could only be performed in cases of necessity, and there was no need for some of the people praying to act as guards for those prostrating. Some of them made fun of him, saying the war hadn't started yet. When he found out they opposed his fatwa, he put out a statement saying people must not listen to anything associated with religion that hasn't been approved by the official state institutions. In other words, people should listen only to him and his fatwas!"

Aida scowled and felt even angrier. She raised her voice, "That doesn't make sense. But it's no surprise from Abdel-Gabbar and the people around him. They've all followed in the generals' footsteps and they've turned it into a fight and a witch hunt. People can only see one part of the picture. The state poses as the meek sheep and gives us the role of the wolf. They hold us responsible for acts we haven't committed, and carefully conceal their own crimes. Now people want to wipe us out as soon as possible."

"That's exactly why I came to see you today. Some of the Sisters have suggested we be active on social media. They want to set up Facebook pages to present the facts ignored by the System's media. There's scope to develop the idea. It would become a specialist website or a channel on YouTube. I don't know as much about these things as young people, but we have women who have internet skills, and we also have donations. I wanted to put it to you in case you want to take part. We need people to help in various ways—gathering information and news, authenticating it, formulating it, and organizing it, and then things to do with uploading it to the internet and trying to generate a larger audience, especially among ordinary people. As you can see, we're still at the preparatory stage, and it's all fluid. Or maybe you have another suggestion that would help us and support the idea."

Fayza said goodbye and left, still coughing her lungs out. From Aida she had a promise to think about it and put it to Nour and her acquaintances. Aida moved to the balcony, turning the conversation over in her head and weighing the consequences of getting involved in an organized activity of this kind. Political games in ordinary times were troubling, and she didn't have much skill or experience in the field. So what would it be like now that the situation was so complicated? Everyone was blowing their own trumpet and getting carried away. The Raised Banner was more and more a lost cause. It was on its knees, trying to save itself from collapse, but its attempts just made things worse. Its initiatives seemed pointless, while the System had shown how tough it could be and was eager to take revenge with unprecedented brutality. Sheikh Abdel-Gabbar was swaggering around, along with other such people. Should she take the risk of providing help and having contact with the resistance, or should she turn the suggestion down, let them be and cut her losses? She went inside to make lunch in time for when Adam came back from school, then went back to the balcony to wait for him.

She sighed, looked out at the rush hour crowds in the streets and muttered, "May God have mercy on you, Murad," she said. "You were right all along when I tried to think up excuses for opportunists."

Rabie resumed life in the camp. He went back to training, had three meals a day and listened to the lectures, which were rather less frequent. But he didn't join the other boys when they sat in the dining hall and he didn't watch television or take an interest in what they said. On the only occasion when he did watch television with them, it wasn't because he really wanted to, but because he was unable to leave the seat. He felt a heaviness in his chest that spread to his whole body and even his mind, so he stayed seated where he was and left his food on the plate until it went cold. He started playing with his spoon absentmindedly. Suddenly he saw Youssef. It wasn't a dream or his imagination, or a sign he had lost his mind. He really did see Youssef—on the TV screen at the start of the news. The picture was clear and unmistakable. The woman on the news was reading out the names of the officers and men who had died clearing out the Space, and when Youssef's picture appeared, she said, "Martyred officer Abed Wagdi." She repeated the name twice. Rabie had another good look at the face and rubbed his eyes in disbelief.

Rabie couldn't understand how Youssef's name could have changed in this way. He wanted to tell the woman so that she could correct it. This name should never change, whether dead or alive. For a moment he felt furious, but his anger soon abated and he just felt numb.

"They should remove his picture, like they removed his name," he mumbled to himself.

There were days when Adam, unusually for him, seemed very reluctant to go to school in the morning. He tried to avoid it as much as possible and invented excuses for staying at home. He would go and come back in distress, gloomy and scowling. Aida tried to draw him out, and she managed to establish that the conflict between adults had spread to children, and the System's battle with the Raised Banner movement had found its way into the classroom and the school playground. The school's PA system, which had been silent for ages, had come back to life, awoken from its slumber. In the morning it had started broadcasting slogans and rousing songs to the children, praising the ruler and his forces and cursing the movement. If anyone wasn't overtly hostile to the movement, the school threw accusations of terrorism at them and denounced them as traitors to the country. Adam wasn't stupid. He was well aware that he was seen as one of the outcasts and was not among those in favor. The people around him understood this too and abused him because of it. The staff spread rumors that the movement was trying to control the schools, so the boys went out of their way to ostracize Adam and others like him. The teachers were unusually strict with them. There was no one sensible around to curb the malice or argue that the solution didn't lie in inciting more hostility. None of them could see that if a boy of Adam's age had seen his father killed he was bound to feel bitter, or that when adults took pleasure in his misfortune, and even called for the extermination of the remaining members of his family and acquaintances and the whole movement, all they were doing was creating deep hatred.

Aida understood that the battle continued to rage. The conflict wouldn't end overnight, even if they built more prisons and walls in the desert, because the idea would survive till the Day of Judgment. The stupid System didn't understand that its violent attempt to wipe the idea out just made some people more attached to it. This is a recurrent story: the tyrant's turn will come.

Zeinab rushed up the stairs to Aida's apartment, as if in a race against time. She had an instinctive feeling that meeting Aida was key to her salvation. She came with a burden of misfortune, but also with plenty of gratitude: in the midst of all the other tragedies taking place Aida hadn't forgotten her or the appointment they had made. She had even suggested they meet in her house so that they could speak without inhibition. As soon as the door opened, she swept in, as if running away from serious danger. Aida didn't even have time to shake her hand. She could see tears welling in the corners of Zeinab's eyes—signs of terrible pain against which medication would be useless. Aida was alarmed and closed the door. She helped her to a chair, but Zeinab sat on the edge of the seat, reluctant to lean back and braced to stand up at any moment.

She said straight off that her blind son had gone missing. He had wandered off on the evening before the attack on the Space. In anguish she had walked around the Space looking for him. She went to the podium after people advised her to leave her contact details there. The minutes turned into hours without him turning up, and when she ran out of ideas and it was the middle of the night, she had to go back home, since on that inauspicious day she had left his brothers at home to do some school work. She had taken only her blind son, and the other two couldn't spent the night alone.

"Their father died some years ago, you know," she said.

Before she left the protest, the security committee people told her he was sure to be safe. Children didn't get lost in the Space. One of the protesters must have found him, taken pity on him and taken him to their tent. They said they would definitely find him early in the morning, or maybe earlier, but in the morning he didn't turn up. It was hell for Zeinab. Aida looked at her as she ended her story. She had lost half her body weight and her cheek bones were sticking out. Ever since the attack on the protest, she had been going around hospitals, looking in the morgues and begging at prison gates.

"It's torture. The other two boys are so stressed out they've given up going to school, and the principal has asked me to apply for a leave of absence without pay because one of my colleagues wrote a memo saying I had been at the protest. I heard from some Sisters about the good work you've been doing with Nour al-Sabbagh and I thought I'd knock on your door in case you could offer me some hope. I remembered us running into each other in the Space, and I felt in my heart it was the workings of fate. Nothing is left to chance. God arranges everything. They may be cunning, but He is more than a match for them."

Aida found the story deeply disturbing and depressing. She immediately thought back to when she lost Adam and it frightened her that Zeinab should have the same feelings, not just for hours but for days and weeks and months.

"I'll arrange for you to meet Nour," she said, in a voice that was decisive if trembling. "She now has lists of names of missing people and she has experience in how to look for them. All you have to do is pass on the available details and a photo of your son. Let's meet her in person in exactly two days, because it's unwise to talk about these things on the phone."

The website idea that Shakir's widow had suggested became a reality and soon attracted attention. It gathered thousands of conflicting comments and responses. There were some acrimonious exchanges, with vulgar and abusive remarks that went way beyond the bounds of decency. People seemed to have diametrically opposite views on every subject. They were divided between those who blindly supported the new ruler, defended the System and the general, and wanted to wage relentless war on the Raised Banner movement, and the opposite group of equally blind partisans, who said that the abducted ruler would soon be back.

Aida made up her mind and joined the team. If Murad had been there, he would have criticized the mistakes the movement had made, but then he would have given them what they wanted. One of her basic duties was to monitor the news every day. She passed on anything important to the woman in charge of the website, and Nour started providing her with information about missing people. The first thing the website published was about Zeinab's son, with a picture of him and his brothers and a short notice on his visual disability. They hoped that someone who had been present at the massacre might recognize him, or someone who had been out looking for relatives of their own. Zeinab waited for the result without giving up hope and as the days passed she became a regular visitor to the website. She found it consoling to read stories that were similar to her own, and her own hopes were revived when someone else found their son, their father or their wife, whether dead or alive. Aida thought her contribution was modest but it wasn't modest at all. It's true that the effort was well within what she could handle. She kept up her usual habits—reading, monitoring websites, and networking, but the outcome turned out to be disturbing. The amount and intensity of the exchanges increased, and people set up new web pages, adding to the level of contention.

Her days passed in an orderly manner, if tensely. She got over the frustrations resignedly and monitored closely a series of violent security campaigns against some of the people she knew, many people she had heard of, and hundreds of people with whom she shared only memories of the protest. Nothing troubled her as much as Adam's precarious situation at school, though she did everything possible to contain it. Patiently and with understanding, she gave him most of her attention to get him through his crisis, and her crisis too. She continued to work on the web page and did well—so well that after a while Nour suggested they work together preparing authenticated witness accounts by survivors of the massacre, so that their testimony wouldn't be lost but would become a resource for people who wanted to listen. Her suggestion sounded useful, though not for the foreseeable future. They agreed to sit down together to discuss the details, but the idea fell through before it began. Things took a truly alarming turn when the security forces raided the home of the woman in charge of the website and detained her. The next day Fayza was detained.

At school Adam hit a boy who kept throwing a ball at him in the playground and shouting, "Hey terrorist, hey Banner guy, looks like your banner isn't flying so high!" Adam threw a stone at him, then picked up a stick and hit his back with it until it was swollen and covered in welts. The principal asked to meet Aida, and the incident had other repercussions. Adam didn't write anything on his exam paper in the mid-year exams, not even the date. He sank into a permanent moody silence in his bedroom. He wouldn't answer his mother when she called him and then he would shout at her angrily if she called again. He went back to wetting his bed at night like an infant and then denied he had done it. She could hear him shouting in his sleep and calling for Halim or his father. She would get up in alarm to give him a hug and find that he had his arms raised in the air to protect his face from some invisible danger. As the situation deteriorated and Aida came under increasing strain, she had to take him to a mental health specialist. She chose a former colleague of Murad that she knew worked mostly with children. She booked an appointment by calling the clinic in the usual way, without mentioning her late husband. It wasn't a time for favors, now that Murad was dead. The days when she expected to be welcomed hospitably at the door to the doctor's clinic were over. She didn't want any deferential treatment because of Murad's status. She only wanted to restore Adam to the way he had been.

When Aida went into the room, the doctor looked surprised. Then he turned pale and seemed displeased to see her and Adam. In the blink of an eye his previously cheerful face suggested a range of negative emotions. The signs that he was annoyed were so obvious she couldn't miss them. For his part, he didn't try to put on a show and conceal or even tone down his displeasure. She was annoyed in return, but her annoyance was tinged with the pain of need and humiliation. Driven by her anxiety about Adam, she decided to overlook the fact that he was pretending not to have known her from before and ignoring the friendship between him and Murad. Instead she went straight to the reason she had come to see him.

"The problem, doctor, is that Adam has become very aggressive, impatient, and unmotivated," she said. "When he faces a problem, he doesn't know how to solve it other than by hitting out and going on the attack. Although he's small, he doesn't lack strength. He has a ferocity and a quick temper that I haven't seen in him before. He's also learned to be apathetic. He's killing me with his behavior. It's like he doesn't care about anything in the world. I get endless complaints from school and his grades are poor. If he goes on like this, he'll have to repeat the year for sure. I'm telling you this in front of him because I'm his mother. I love him and he means more to me than the whole world. I'm worried that my hopes for him, and his late father's hopes for him, will be disappointed."

As soon as she opened her mouth, the doctor avoided looking at her. He started fiddling with the papers and pens that littered his desk. When she had finished he raised his eyebrows and looked her in the face.

"Why did you come to me, Madame Aida?" he asked. "I don't treat cases of this kind. You and your late husband and your son were in the Space. There are plenty of doctors who were with you at the protest and you can go and ask them. Don't you understand that you're responsible for all your troubles—taking a child to such a place, when you, like all the protesters, were well aware of the risks and understood that people didn't support what you were doing and didn't want you and your man in power? Madame Aida, do the right thing. I don't have any cure for your son. Take him to someone else. Goodbye."

Aida was speechless all the way home. Her head was pounding. Adam tried to keep up with her rapid, nervous steps, his face even more somber than hers. He hadn't liked the idea of going to the doctor's with her. He had been prepared to defend himself against her in the doctor's clinic if necessary, but he hadn't taken into account the possibility that he and his mother might both be humiliated and would end up in the same boat. How could he rebel against her now? How could he reject her advice and her concern and her attempts to win him over when they were each equally outcast?

Aida grew increasingly distressed, especially as many of her relatives and acquaintances chose to restrict their contact with her as much as possible. As the detentions and the raids increased, some of them decided to ostracize her. She had to deal with Adam's successive crises alone. No one shared her concerns or helped to relieve her suffering. After the website was closed down and Fayza's detention was extended week after week, and then month after month, Aida built an extra wall of isolation around herself for fear she might come to harm. Fayza was sentenced to five years in prison in the court of first instance. On top of all that, the school principal openly threatened to have Aida dismissed from her teaching job. She gave up all activity associated with the movement, however distantly, and only maintained her friendship with Nour. Their meetings continued. They deplored the state of affairs and found some consolation in each other's company.

When there was no improvement in Adam's disturbed behavior, Aida thought of consulting another doctor that she didn't know. She would conceal her identity and ignore any reference to what had happened, whether good or bad. All that mattered now was Adam and his future, but she didn't know if the damage could be undone simply by ignoring the cause. The doctor would have to start from scratch and question Adam, and if Adam said the wrong thing it probably wouldn't end well. Everyone was digging into partisan positions, driven by hatred for their opponents. It was ordinary people on one side, and on the other side Raised Banner members and sympathizers, and even those suspected of knowing a member of the movement. The second group had been thrown together into a single basket, and the basket was constantly shrinking, crushing those inside. If one side of the basket was hit, the impact could be felt on the other side. When one of the eggs in the basket broke, it had repercussions for all the others. If Aida approached another doctor, he might refuse to help Adam, just as Murad's colleague had done, and ask them to leave, out of fear or anger or to punish her, or maybe a mixture of all these motives. There was a worse possibility: the doctor might report her to the authorities and she might end up in prison. Then Adam would be an orphan twice over. She might join Fayza in her cell, where they would meet their demise. The ban on visits to Fayza continued despite her declining health. Her lungs were congested, her cough had grown worse, and she was spitting up blood. In detention there was no medical care, and the dampness and the meager food didn't help her get better, or even stop her deterioration.

Aida ran out of options one after another until eventually it occurred to her to get in touch with someone who had contacts that might enable them to escape their predicament. Maybe Nour could talk to her father or one of his acquaintances or business partners about finding her a job in the Gulf. Many teachers of Arabic, chemistry, and biology had managed to find well-paid jobs abroad. Nour would never refuse her request when she knew what Aida had been going through. But should she run away from the fate God had assigned her? Wouldn't leaving the country now mean refusing to face her share of suffering?

She came back from school at midday one day, determined to seek God's guidance by praying, in the hope she could reach a decision. Adam watched her from afar. He bobbed up and down, never settling down. She kept one eye on him as she sat cross-legged on the prayer rug.

Her attention was caught by chance by something he was watching on television, so she watched it too for a while, then she bowed her head, trying to keep calm and muttering in a low voice: "O God, my trust in you tells me that victory comes after patience and relief after pain, and that with hardship comes ease. What consoles me is that this is Your choice for us and that everything You decree is for the best. Forgive us, generous God, but things are complicated and help is hard to find. The newspapers and television programs are like cogs in a grinding machine that never stops. The wise are losing their good sense one after another. Those with balanced views are reconsidering them and following the mainstream with enthusiasm. They are turning into a cross between the general and Sheikh Abdel-Gabbar. They are laying the foundations for hatred and they are eager to incite war. Some of them appear on television calling on people to mobilize against the Raised Banner movement and some write articles advocating that the movement be annihilated. Others sing delirious songs, goading their audiences to resist the movement like the plague. Even the smartest of the smart have lost their reason. Everyone has made mistakes, including without doubt the movement, but the punishment that the System has inflicted on the movement is out of all proportion with its error. It has gone miles beyond it. People are stumbling in confusion, they can no longer see clearly, and the plague has spread everywhere. O God, the only way we can get out of this hole is through You. He spoke truly and did not exaggerate who said: '*Death was the only way out and ruin was the fate of those who remained on the face of the earth.*' I cling to You for help, O Lord, and seek refuge with You. Do not abandon me and my child."

With the passage of time I've lost what was left of my soul. My only wish is to graduate from this rehabilitation program with an identity card. I don't even want the salary they've promised us. Recently I've become obsessed with the idea of leaving the camp, even if it means I go to hell. Hell is my certain fate but I know I won't see Youssef there. I'll be on my own there, too. Emad hardly talks to me now. I avoid listening to him and he doesn't like me looking at him. Maybe I look at him disapprovingly, whether deliberately or not. That's all I can do under the circumstances. Saad's wounds have healed and he's back to training with me. He's often tried to make me speak to him and laugh with him as usual, but it hasn't worked. I can't relate to his jokes, even the ones that remind me of my naivety.

We haven't been out on assignments since we came back and the training is less strenuous. Maybe they're giving us a rest after what we did for them in the Space, or maybe they're using bodies from other camps. I haven't been interested to know the reason, though I feel comfortable with the situation. I don't want to go out on any new assignments, or maybe I would go out and try to escape and my fate would be worse than the situation I'm in now.

In the evening Channel One broadcast news that General Ismail had been promoted. He only needed to take one more step and he would hold the highest position in the country. The boys felt proud and strong, as if his promotion meant they had been promoted too. Why not? After all, they were part of him, as he said repeatedly.

"If the general moves up in the world, we move up," one of them said. "If he rules the world, we'll rule it too and we can trample on other people. Aren't you happy, Rabie?"

The boy nodded his head in my direction and leaned over to Emad.

"That friend of yours is stupid," he said, without even bothering to hide what he was saying. "How did you come to be friends with him in the first place? He's just a useless body, too useless to ever be a master, too weak to ever hold power and reap the benefits. In fact, he's not really a body at all. He's a coward, too cowardly to have the same aspirations as us, or the same success. There's no way he can keep up with us. Power is life, man, our life, and your friend couldn't take the stress and strain, even if he wanted to, deep inside."

I stayed where I was, close to Emad and his friend's table in the dining hall. I heard them chatting and making snide remarks, and throwing gibes and jokes in my direction, but I chose to keep mum and pretend I couldn't hear anything. After the news about the general, there was a mood of elation and bravado among the boys in the hall. They all imagined themselves ruling in the general's name, carrying out his orders and obeying whenever he lifted a finger. The TV channel started showing a black-and-white film and none of them paid any attention, but I got into it and felt like one of the romantic heroes, in love with the heroine, saving her and weeping with her. I felt detached from the hall and the people inside it.

We went back to the dormitory early because there was a power cut and the whole camp was in pitch blackness. The two heads weren't around to tell anyone to fix the fault. The power cut ruined the end of the film for me and cut short my fantasy as the hero, so I decided to continue it in my dreams. I've forgotten where dreams come from but I'll do everything possible to make sure I dream today. In bed I stared at the ceiling but I couldn't see anything. While the others slept I listened, but all I could hear was a faint rumble and a droning like that of planes in the distance. I closed my eyes and just imagined things.

Channel One interrupted the Arabic movie that Aida was watching to broadcast some breaking news. The general had announced that the intelligence agencies had discovered a camp where members of the Raised Banner movement were training to carry out acts of violence against government and civilian targets. An official statement said the security forces had attacked and destroyed the camp using F-16 warplanes, wiping out those hiding there. They had seized large quantities of automatic weapons and tonnes of explosives that the group was planning to use against government facilities.

Aida watched the general's address to the nation, in which he urged people to unite with their leaders. He said that attacking the security establishment was much more serious than a few routine excesses committed against groups working against the country. She didn't understand the last phrase. Who were these people working against the country now and what were they doing? What exactly did he mean by "routine excesses"? Was he talking about torture? Starving people to death? The detentions? Detention that could last days, months, years, without charges or trial. Or did he mean bullets that ended up in the heads of people who showed no sign of resisting? It didn't matter what he meant by his words, which were as vague as usual, as one expects from those in power. What mattered now was the crimes being committed in the real world.

The general emphasized the need for national solidarity against the forces of evil. Then the broadcast moved on to live scenes of crowds chanting his name, with commentary by Nanice al-Nahhas, who unusually appeared in a small box in the corner of the screen. She said that people had reacted to the general's speech with relief and confidence, and that in a number of demonstrations they said they rejected the violence of the Raised Banner movement and stood behind the security forces.

A sequence of shots appeared on television screens soon after, undisturbed by any commentary or any other noise. It was as if all the sounds in the world had been silenced. The local channel, along with most of the satellite channels, broadcast pictures of the sky with a scattering of stars, obscured by smoke. Thick clouds slowly filled the sky, floating upwards. They came from tongues of flame that lit up everything around. When the camera looked down, a gray compound could be seen on a flat expanse of desert, marked out by walls topped by coils of barbed wire. The remains of low buildings lay here and there, flattened by the bombing. The clouds lifted after a while and the camera zoomed out to show two towers at a gap in the wall of the compound, with a metal gate between them.

Selected Hoopoe Titles

My First and Only Love
by Sahar Khalifeh, translated by Aida Bamia

The Lady of Zamalek
by Ashraf El-Ashmawi, translated by Peter Daniel

The Critical Case of a Man Called K
by Aziz Mohammed, translated by Humphrey Davies

*

hoopoe is an imprint for engaged, open-minded readers hungry for outstanding fiction that challenges headlines, re-imagines histories, and celebrates original storytelling. Through elegant paperback and digital editions, **hoopoe** champions bold, contemporary writers from across the Middle East alongside some of the finest, groundbreaking authors of earlier generations.

At hoopoefiction.com, curious and adventurous readers from around the world will find new writing, interviews, and criticism from our authors, translators, and editors.

www.ingramcontent.com/pod-product-compliance
Lightning Source LLC
Chambersburg PA
CBHW020338310726
48979CB00015B/2414/J

* 9 7 8 1 6 1 7 9 7 0 9 3 1 *